PENGUIN BOOKS

THE GOOD CATHOLIC

Julia Hamilton is also the author of *The Idle Hill* and *A Pillar of Society*, which is available in Penguin. Michael Joseph will shortly be publishing her new novel *After Flora*, and she is currently writing a biography of Mary Queen of Scots. She lives in London with her two daughters and a black Labrador.

The Good Catholic

JULIA HAMILTON

PENGUIN BOOKS

PENGUIN BOOKS

Published by the Penguin Group
Penguin Books Ltd, 27 Wrights Lane, London W8 5TZ, England
Penguin Books USA Inc., 375 Hudson Street, New York, New York 10014, USA
Penguin Books Australia Ltd, Ringwood, Victoria, Australia
Penguin Books Canada Ltd, 10 Alcorn Avenue, Toronto, Ontario, Canada M4V 3B2
Penguin Books (NZ) Ltd, 182–190 Wairau Road, Auckland 10, New Zealand

Penguin Books Ltd, Registered Offices: Harmondsworth, Middlesex, England

First published by Michael Joseph 1996
Published in Penguin Books 1997
1 3 5 7 9 10 8 6 4 2

Printed in England by Clays Ltd, St Ives plc

For my daughters, Sophie and Mouse

Come, see real
flowers
of this painful world.

On Love and Barley, Haiku of Basho, translated by Lucien Stryk, published by Penguin Books

PART ONE

PROLOGUE I

1955

Even now he can remember all the details of that day quite clearly. When he closes his eyes he sees himself in shorts and a crewneck navy blue jersey, bare legs, socks fallen down, feet in those brown leather Startrite sandals that his mother buys him in Barbour's of Dumfries. (Putting his foot in the X-ray machine and seeing his own bones like a skeleton's.) They – he and his mother – have come down across the lawn from the house and out through the gate that leads past the water garden built by his grandfather towards the sea. The tide is coming in. The cattle have moved inland. He runs ahead up the grassy track past the rocks and the gorse bushes that lead over the hill and down again towards the beach. He is desperate to get to the water and to be in it. He is a passionate swimmer on this treacherous coast.

His mother calls out 'Edward, Edward, come back' in her fussing voice, but he does not heed her and only runs faster. He is thinking ahead to the feel of the smooth flat sand under his feet, the fingers of the sea crawling in over the rocks, flooding the rock pools. Under his shorts his school bathing trunks with the name-tape in the back: *Edward St J. Parry* in that funny italic script his mother chose.

'That's for pansies,' he said, 'sissies have that.'

'Rubbish,' said his mother, 'I like it. You're just being silly. Who's going to look at your nametapes anyway?'

'Everybody.'

'What nonsense.'

She has stopped calling him. Or is it that the thick crown of gorse has muffled her voice? She is probably going slowly up the grassy track on purpose because still he cannot see her. Good. He is angry with her for siding with his father at lunchtime and making him wait to swim. Only sissies get cramp and he is not a sissy. He is a big boy for his age, which is ten, and a good swimmer.

'Silly old cow,' he mutters under his breath, '*silly* old cow. I'll give her a stone for her birthday. Then she'll be sorry.' But still she does not come. For a moment he is torn. Should he go back to see where she is? He knows that it is a man's duty to protect a woman because his father has told him so many times. The sea wins the argument because he cannot resist it. When he looks out to sea he forgets everything but the desire to swim.

He throws off his clothes any old how and runs into the sea in his bathing trunks, white legs going like pistons. He wades out past the fishing nets and even then the water is only up to his waist. The tides are extreme here and the coast famous for its quick sands and freak currents. The water is darker in places where rocks lie submerged. He plunges and twists in the sandy depths forgetting his mother, forgetting everything. But when the sun goes in he is suddenly blue with cold, so cold that it hurts.

It is then that he realizes he has no towel. His mother has the towel but she has not appeared. He is even angrier with her then.

'Silly cow, where's the silly cow got to?'

He takes off his trunks and throws them on a rock, then he dresses in his shorts again, his Aertex, his crewneck jersey. Carrying his socks and shoes and forgetting his swimming trunks, he goes slowly back up the grass track.

The sun has not come out again. The sky is suddenly the colour of granite.

His mother is lying on her back under a rocky outcrop, her tweed skirt rucked up above her knees. He can see her stocking top. One shoe has fallen off. Her green cardigan with the gold buttons is half off her shoulder. She is still holding the towel with the pattern of swans on it. Although her eyes are open she does not see him. He shakes her and shakes her. He wants to hit her to make her stop this game.

'Wake up, please wake up!'

He is on his knees beside her. His tears fall on to her face. He will have to go for help. He can do nothing himself. She is dead but she cannot be dead. Dead is not something that happens to children. He runs faster than he has ever run in his life, shouting 'Help!' at the top of his voice. The cattle lift their heads and watch him as he goes past.

His father who is much older than the young, pretty mother of this boy is distraught. He cannot believe she is dead. She is thirty-five, twenty years younger than him. A gift, a late joy discovered on a cruise: dark and luscious, full-breasted, wide-hipped, with a good ankle, she had delighted him between the monogrammed linen sheets of the matrimonial bed. And now she is dead.

A thrombosis, the doctor says, having talked to the boy. Terrible thing to happen to a child. He could foresee problems especially for a sensitive, only child like this one, and a boy to boot. A bad business.

'He ran on ahead,' said the doctor, 'and only found her, poor little devil, when he came back. There would have been nothing he could have done in any case. You mustn't blame him.'

But the father does blame him. He has lost his rose of Sharon, his lily of the valleys. In the light summer night, long after the boy is in bed, the father gets drunk and bellows his rage and misery up at the stars and across the water garden built by his father.

Edward, lying in his narrow boy's bed, thinks: 'I killed her. I disobeyed her. I killed her with my thoughts. I am to blame.'

He is Catholic like his mother. His father is not a believer. He disapproves of popish claptrap, as he calls it, but he indulged her. He always let her do what she wanted. Edward and his mother worshipped in a tin hut in Kirkcudbright with the Irish tinkers and the local dentist and his family.

The priest, Father O'Reilly, talks to Edward.

'You're not to blame yourself,' he said, 'it was an accident, a terrible accident. God's will.'

But Edward knows he is wrong. He will be punished. He has already been punished for his disobedience. God is watching him from on high through binoculars, noting his every thought, his every movement. He must be good or someone else will die.

PROLOGUE II

1975

The hotel had been recommended to Parry by his partner Tom Wilberforce.

'It's a charming place,' he said, 'in Montmartre . . . called the Hotel des Martyrs. It's in the Place du Calvaire, next to that wonderful old church Saint-Pierre, you know the one I'm sure. It's the one with the Roman columns in . . .'

'Any other suggestions?' asked Parry, scratching his chin.

'That's my favourite,' said Tom in a slightly miffed voice. 'I thought you wanted my recommendation. You'll love it. It's completely untouched since before the war. Brown varnish, bidets on wheels, hilarious plumbing. It's the authentic thing, right up your street.'

Parry, registering Tom's displeasure, glanced at him and then away out of the window of their shop in Coptic Street. 'Parry & Wilberforce' it said outside in dull gold letters on a dark-green background, 'Antiquarian Booksellers.'

The hotel sounded delightful, he couldn't deny it. What bothered him – and it was absurd this really, when you thought about it rationally – was the name of the place. It made him uncomfortable, even now when he hadn't been to Confession in years, let alone Holy Communion, to be committing adultery in a hotel named after Saint-Denis and his friends. It had an ominous ring to it. He didn't want to be dragged back into all that mumbo jumbo now at the age of thirty. He'd given it all up years ago. God had moved on in search of other witnesses, other exponents of the faith. There was such a thing as free will after all.

'Montmartre is cheaper too,' said Tom. 'It costs an arm and a leg anywhere else. Or are you trying to impress whoever it is?'

'No, not really,' said Parry. Rosie wouldn't mind where they were as long as they could be together for a few days. Her husband was going on a business trip somewhere, but as the firm wouldn't pay for wives, Rosie couldn't go.

'Thank God,' she had said, 'I can't stand going on business trips with Peter. I'd much rather be with you. I'll wangle some time off work. I'm owed some days.'

'What will you say to him?' asked Parry, putting his hand on hers – they were having a drink in the Ritz of all places – longing to be able to take her upstairs to a room here and make love to her all night.

'I'll tell him', said Rosie smiling, 'that I'm going to see my mother. He can't stand Ma. He'll never ring me up there. I can ring him from Paris. He won't know where the hell I am. Look, darling, I'd better go,' she added, glancing at her watch. 'I've got to meet Peter in half an hour in Curzon Street and I don't want to be late.'

He had watched her go out past the other drinkers in her little black suit and her high heels. She was exactly the kind of woman he liked: voluptuous, feminine, big-breasted, wide-hipped, yet slender. She had dark curly unruly hair like a woman in a painting by Caravaggio, the kind of hair that needed pearls the size of pigeons' eggs woven through it.

'I'll give them a ring,' said Parry, so as not to offend old Tom, 'have you got the number on you?'

He had rung around quite a long list of places but there had been some trade show or other on in Paris and there was not an executive bed to be had anywhere. The only place that had a room was the Hotel des Martyrs.

Afterwards, when he thought about it, he realized that he should have known it was a trap.

'Darling, it's divine,' said Rosie, going ahead of him into the room and putting down her make-up case on the bed. 'I adore it.' She looked behind the curtain at the bidet, opened the wardrobe doors making the coat-hangers rattle, and eventually bounced on the bed. 'Comfy,' she said, lying back. 'Come and join me.'

Parry put down the cases and put the key in the lock, turning it until it clicked.

8

'Don't want anyone bursting in on us, do we?' he said, taking off his tweed jacket and then his trousers before joining Rosie on the bed.

After a minute, she sat up and took off her shirt.

'Let me,' he said, reaching around her to unhook her bra.

'What about your skirt?'

'I'll do that,' she said, getting up to unzip herself before whisking out of her knickers and tights.

'That's better,' he said, 'turn around.' As she turned her backside towards him he looked up and saw an oleograph of the Virgin and Child staring out at him in sickly piety.

'What is it?' she said, looking over her shoulder.

'Nothing. Come here.' He turned her on her back and began to kiss her breasts with their large brown nipples.

When they had finished, he stood up on the bed and took the picture off the wall.

'What on earth are you doing?' Rosie asked, opening her eyes.

'I don't want to be watched by the Mother Immaculate, thanks very much.'

'It's just a picture, for God's sake, but you're a Cattolico, aren't you, darling, I keep forgetting.'

'Lapsed,' he said, 'utterly lapsed. I never think about it.'

'But you were thinking about it just now,' she said, teasingly, 'weren't you?'

'Not really,' he lied. 'It's a bloody awful picture.'

'I liked it,' said Rosie. 'I like kitsch.'

She reached for his penis and began to stroke it. 'I like this too,' she said, as he grew stiff in her hand, 'don't you, darling?'

'Yes,' he said, 'yes, very much.'

But although he tried to forget it he knew he was being watched. They were back again with their notebooks, recording his words, watching him make love to another man's wife, training their binoculars on him, lining him up in their sights.

At five they got up and went out into the spring evening in Paris.

'Shall we look at the church?' she said, as they came into the Place du Tertre.

'Wouldn't you rather walk for now? We could choose a bar and have a drink.'

'Just a quick peep,' she said. 'Whatever is the matter with you? Do you think you'll be nabbed if you put your head around the door? I wanted to look at the famous columns.'

'You go,' he said, 'I'm going to have a drink.'

'No, no,' she took his arm and looked searchingly into his face. 'I'll come with you. We came here to be together remember?'

'Yes,' he said, 'I do remember.'

'Are you all right?'

'I'm fine.'

'Cheer up.'

'I told you. I'm fine.'

They chose a bar and sat down outside. Parry ordered two glasses of red wine. Under the trees an artist was packing up his things. This was what they had come for.

When he was fourteen or fifteen, he told Father O'Reilly he didn't want to come to the tin hut anymore.

'I've lost my faith,' he said, 'I don't believe in it all any longer.'

At Eton, chapel was compulsory but he dreamed his way through it. And in any case there were hundreds of other boys to deflect attention from him. Safety in numbers. Hundreds of other sinners, although he doubted any of them had killed their mothers.

'That's because you're angry with God,' said Father O'Reilly, 'it's quite normal. We make God in our own image. To you he's an angry father, a monster. He isn't like that and he won't let you go. He still loves you.'

'I don't want his love,' said Parry, flicking his fair hair out of his eyes. It was 1960. 'I'm not interested in God anymore.' *He won't let you go.* Was that a threat?

'Ah, you say that, but you don't mean it,' said the old priest. Some boys of this age were sure of their vocations, others, like this one, thought they no longer believed and could just give it up.

'I do mean it,' Parry retorted. 'What if I want God to let me go? What if I don't agree?'

'Are you thinking of your mother?' It was the old problem of suffering. We suffer and die without explanation. Modern people are too far gone now to understand that there is a meaning in it but that you have to wait – sometimes a lifetime – to understand what that meaning might be.

'I never think of my mother,' said Parry coldly, 'not any more.' Which was not true, of course. Every now and again he would dream of her. Always retreating from him along the grassy path towards the gorse bushes and the sea.

'How's your father?'

'He's all right,' said Parry, 'I must go now.' He got up and held out his hand. 'Thank you for seeing me, I thought I should tell you what the situation is.'

'All right, Edward, all right. God bless you now. Come and see me any time you're passing. See yourself out, there's a good boy, my knees are bad this week.'

'Goodbye,' said Parry, going down the rather steep narrow stairs of the presbytery. There was a smell of polish and boiled cabbage and the cigars that Father O'Reilly smoked.

He stepped out into a cobbled alleyway with an iron gate at the end that led out into the square. These were old houses, older than the Georgian ones further down by the castle. He looked up at the sky as he went through the gate, an empty heaven, no squads of angels, no chanting bands of saints, no magisterial figure looking rather like President Castro in fatigues with an Uzi on his knee, just sky, just clouds. If only he could believe it.

'Darling, you're distracted,' said Rosie, putting down her glass. 'What's wrong?'

'Nothing,' he said, 'nothing. Sorry.'

He took her hand in his and kissed it.

'I love it when you do that,' she said.

'Shall we have another drink?'

'Yes, why not? Then I should go back and ring Peter. Then we can go out to dinner.'

'Do you have to ring him?'

'I should . . . yes . . . just to stop him even having to think about me. Not that he does.' She put out her cigarette. Parry noticed the red marks of her lipstick on the tip like blood.

'I just don't want him interfering with our time together,' Parry said.

'Darling, I am his wife. Just let me ring him and then that'll be that.'

'All right,' he said ungraciously. 'I'll stay here and have another drink. You go and ring him.'

He looked at his watch. It was five to six. He went in to the bar and ordered more drinks, noticing as he did so a little icon of the Virgin and Child sitting amongst the jumble of bottles.

He sat down again and began to sip his pastis. The bell of the church of Saint Pierre began to toll for the Angelus. Damn and blast. Was one never to get away? Three Ave Marias with versicle and a collect as a memorial of the Incarnation. He sipped his drink slowly. Where the hell had Rosie got to? He looked at his watch again. Five past six. After five more minutes had passed, he got up, paid for the drinks and went out into the square.

The bell had stopped tolling now, but he was buggered if he was going to go in to the church. Where was Rosie? He began to feel, for some reason, afraid. A faintly perceptible darkening had spread through the spring evening, like wine dripped through water, or blood.

If he went back to the hotel now he might miss her. He was seized by the idea that she had gone into the church without his noticing. Against his will he found himself pushing through the baize side door.

The whole great ancient edifice seemed utterly dark, utterly silent. It smelled of incense and stone, the heart-stopping smell of eternity. Saints crowded the side altars, banners hung over the aisles; on the high altar a great gold cross glimmered dully.

Parry walked around slowly looking for Rosie, then he found himself kneeling in front of a side altar dedicated to the Mother of God. There was a painted statue of her with candles burning at her feet as if she were treading on stars. Parry gazed up into her stainless doll's face. He remembered some story he had heard about the bull and the matador and how the matador will pray before the *corrida* that God will be with him during *El Memento de Verdad* – that moment of truth when matador and bull face each other alone in the ring for the kill. I am the bull, Parry remembered thinking, poor confused bull, baffled by the feints, the cruel cunning of the matador.

Parry looked up above the head of the Virgin. A voice seemed to say to him 'Now! Now is the moment! God is! He exists. You must do his will.'

He fell down on his face on the steps as if he had been hit with the flat of a sword. For some uncounted moments he lay there experiencing the knowledge of the possession of Truth. He knew that all his life had been a preparation for this moment and that the rest of his life must spring from it, *but only if he wanted it to*.

There must be that proviso. And he didn't want it.

He wanted another drink. He wanted Rosie. He didn't want all these burdens of belief. He didn't want to change. He liked his life as it was.

Outside, he looked around wildly for Rosie. Where the hell was she? He went back to the café where they had had their drinks but she was not there. It was a quarter to seven. Perhaps she was still at the hotel trying to get through to Peter in Stockholm or wherever he was.

An ambulance swept across the Place du Tertre and into the Place du Calvaire, its siren cleaving the air. Parry broke into a run.

A little crowd had gathered by the Hotel des Martyrs around a figure on the ground.

The wife of the proprietor recognized him.

'Monsieur!' she cried, 'she looked the other way, she did not see the automobile until it was too late.'

He looked down at Rosie. There was a smear of blood on her cheek. One of her legs was buckled underneath her in a way that suggested it was broken.

The ambulance men came pushing past, falling on their green-suited knees to examine the body with the practised deftness of those used to handling the broken bodies of the sick and the maimed.

Rosie was eased on to a stretcher and inserted into the back of the ambulance.

'You're her husband?' one of the ambulance men enquired.

'Yes.'

'You have insurance?'

'Yes.'

'We are going to take her to Saint-Louis. You know it?'

The door was slammed shut and the ambulance lurched off, making its demented noise.

'Is she badly injured?'

'Yes.' The attendant looked down at Rosie. 'She looked the wrong way. Every year hundreds of English tourists are knocked down because of it.'

'Will she die?'

'I cannot say.'

What was it the wife of the proprietor said? *She looked the other way.* Do not let her die, please. It will be my fault if she dies. I will do whatever you want. Just don't let her die, please don't let her die.

They came swiftly to the stone and brick façades and steep pitched roofs of the hospital. The ambulance drove at speed into a courtyard, stopped and reversed with a squeal towards a set of double doors painted green which were flung open.

Parry watched as Rosie vanished into intensive care, passing through another set of swing doors out of sight, but when he tried to follow her a nurse said, 'This way, please. You are the husband?'

'Yes.'

'Do you have insurance?'

'Yes.'

Will it be counted against me if I lie? What am I to say?

'This way please. You must fill out some forms.'

She handed him a detailed form to fill out and took his Visa card from him.

'My name is different from hers,' he said. 'We are not married.'

She registered what he said without expression.

'Where is the husband?'

'On a business trip, abroad somewhere. Stockholm, maybe. I'm not sure.'

'So you are not next of kin?'

'No.'

'Just a minute,' she said. 'I'll have to check.' She took his Visa card and went through a door into a back office.

What did you want me to say? Parry asked. I have to be honest, I have to face up to things, however unpleasant, don't I? It's the lesson I could never learn. *Otherwise she'll die.*

The nurse came back with his card.

'For purposes of insurance,' she said, 'it does not matter whether you are next of kin or not.' She shrugged. 'She could have been alone. She might have had nobody.'

'But I should contact the husband?'

Whatever she said, he would do.

'Of course. If you can.'

Was he being let off? He didn't have the number. Rosie had that, but he had no idea where, unless it was in her bag or something. But where was her bag? He was sure it had not been put in the ambulance. Then he remembered the proprietor's wife. She would know.

'Is there a telephone?'

'Through the swing doors on your left.'

The proprietor's wife had the bag. She had rescued it from the street.

'People are so wicked,' she said, 'they steal from the injured, from the dead.'

The dead.

'I need a number,' he said, 'it's very urgent. His name is Peter Wild. I must contact him. It may be somewhere in the bag. She had gone to telephone him.'

'Wait a moment.'

She came back to the phone. 'No. There is nothing. I'm sorry.'

'All right,' he said, 'all right. Keep the bag in the office. I'll be back as soon as I have news.'

'Monsieur?'

'Yes?'

'The car . . . that car . . . the one that knocked her down. It came out of nowhere.' Nowhere.

'What do you mean?'

'I was looking out of the window of my office. I myself would not have seen it. She was very unlucky.'

'Yes.'

He went back to the desk.

'Any news?'

'It is too early for news. You could sit in the waiting room. As soon as there is news we will tell you.'

'But what if she dies? I should contact the husband, the mother.'

He waited for her to reassure him, but when she did not, he realized that nobody was going to help him. Nobody was going to tell him what to do. They were watching him, waiting to see what he would do, how he would react.

'Please see if there is any news. Is there a doctor I could speak to? I have people to contact, people who will need to know.'

'One moment.'

She squeaked away in her rubber shoes through the swing doors of the intensive care unit.

After a minute a doctor in an unbuttoned white coat came out to the desk where Parry was waiting. His coat had blood on it. He reminded Parry of a butcher with his big hands, his red wrists.

'I am Dr Hardy,' he said. 'Your friend has been very badly hurt. It is too soon to say how badly, I am afraid. You should go back to your hotel, get some rest. Telephone us in the morning.'

'What if she dies?'

'Leave us your number. We can reach you if necessary.'

'Can I see her?'

'It is not advisable at present.'

'I don't want to leave without seeing her.'

'I'm sorry. It is not possible at present.'

You must do as you are told. You always were a disobedient boy.

'Leave your number at the desk so we can call you.'

He found Peter's number and that of her mother in Sussex in Rosie's Filofax beside the bed. Peter Wild was not at his hotel in Stockholm.

'The delegates are all in conference,' said a robotic Scandawegian voice. 'Please leave a message.'

Parry telephoned the mother in Uckfield. It was half-past eight in France, seven thirty in England.

'I'm sorry to have to tell you this,' Parry said to the upper middle-class, slightly aloof voice that answered the telephone, 'but your daughter is gravely ill. She has had an accident in Paris.'

'In Paris did you say?'

'She was with me in Paris. My name is Parry. Edward Parry.'

There was a silence.

'Does Peter know?'

'I can't get hold of him – I have tried.'

'How badly hurt is she?' Parry could hear the voice beginning to panic.

'Very badly.'

'Is she going to die?'

'I don't know.'

'But why were you with her? She's married to Peter.'

'We . . .'

'I'm appalled,' said the voice, getting a grip, 'at both of you. They hadn't been married for very long.'

'I'm sorry, I . . .'

'It's a bit late for that, I should have thought.'

Parry went and lay down on the bed. I need a priest. I should have asked at the hospital. But they were so unhelpful. But what can I do? What good would a priest be now? It's too late for that. Rosie's not a church-goer, I don't go any more. Why us? I must be allowed to refuse. Surely I can refuse? It was an accident, just an accident, a random thing. Then he remembered the voice of the proprietor's wife: *The car . . . it came out of nowhere.*

He fell asleep and was woken by the sound of the telephone.

'Monsieur, I think you should come.' It was Dr Hardy. 'She has come out of her coma . . .'

'Oh good.' Had he known she was in a coma? He couldn't

remember. He was still half in his dream. He had been on the beach waiting for his mother. He knew she would appear at any moment. He was full of hope and excitement.

'. . . but she is still extremely ill,' said Dr Hardy. 'It is still in the balance.'

Ah. They had given themselves away.

'I'll come,' he said. 'Is there a priest at the hospital?'

'Yes. I'll have him located for you.'

The same nurse was still on duty. 'Wait one moment,' she said. After five minutes Dr Hardy came out of the swing doors.

'The Priest, Father Ferrer, is with her now.'

'Priest?'

'You said you wanted a priest. I assumed it was for your friend.'

'She's not religious,' he said, 'let alone a Catholic.'

Dr Hardy sighed. 'Come this way,' he said.

She lay in a high bed in a high white room. There was a tube in her left nostril and another in her arm attached to a drip. Her hair was plastered damply over her pale forehead and her closed eyelids were the colour of violets.

'She has a broken leg, a fractured skull, and much internal damage,' said the doctor in a low voice.

With a sense of shock Parry noticed the priest in the corner of the room. He was wearing a black dickey, and a clerical suit. He looked young and strained.

'I've given her the last rites,' he said.

Parry was filled with an enormous rage. 'She's not a Catholic,' he said. 'I'm the Catholic. I'm the one who asked for you.'

'Compose yourself,' said Dr Hardy. 'There has been a mistake, that is all.' He shrugged.

'God will not care if she is a Catholic or not. Not now.'

'What do you mean?'

'She is very ill, Monsieur.'

Parry went to the bed and looked at Rosie.

'Don't die,' he said, 'please don't die.' He looked around for the priest.

'Can't you do something?'

'It is in God's hands now, Monsieur.'

'But what can I do?'

'Nothing. There is nothing you can do but pray.'

'Look,' said Parry, beside himself, 'you don't understand. How could you? You see, it's my fault. I'm to blame.'

The doctor and the priest exchanged looks.

'She was hit by a car,' said the doctor, 'how could you be to blame for that?'

'We were doing something wrong,' said Parry. 'We . . . we're not married . . .'

'You have guilty feelings,' said the priest. 'Are you a Roman Catholic, Monsieur?'

'Yes,' said Parry furiously. 'I should have thought that was obvious.'

'Calm yourself, Monsieur,' said the priest. 'Forgive me. You are English, I know, in spite of your excellent French, I assumed English people were not Roman Catholics.'

'Well, you assumed wrong,' said Parry. He felt defeated. They had won. They were waiting for him to confess, to spew out all the filth of the last Christ-knows how many years. They wanted him to vomit up his sins like a good boy so that he could be absolved. It was a conspiracy. He didn't stand a chance.

'I need to make my confession,' Parry said to the priest.

'Very well,' said the priest, unable to prevent himself from glancing at his watch.

They went into a bleak little waiting room which adjoined a glass-panelled room furnished with long, pale-blue velvet curtains. With a shock Parry realized this was the ante-room to the place where the dead bodies were laid out for the relatives to view them.

'Sit down,' said the priest. 'How long is it since you last made your confession?'

'I was fourteen, I think,' Parry said, trying to remember, 'or fifteen. I can't remember exactly.'

'So . . . a long time. Many sins.' The priest folded his white hands in his lap and waited.

'So many, I can't recall them all.'

'Never mind,' said the priest. 'But mainly you would say in the area of women?'

'Mainly. Yes.'

'Is your mother alive?'

'No.' Parry looked away.

'How old were you when she died?'

'Ten.'

'And you are not married?'

'No. But the woman I am with – Rosie –' he made a motion with his head, 'is. Her husband is on a business trip in Sweden.'

'How old are you, Monsieur?'

'Thirty.'

'Is it not time you were married?'

'Is that my penance then? To marry?'

The priest regarded him with tired eyes.

'Would it be a Penance?'

'It could be,' said Parry reluctantly. As a state it both attracted and repelled him. He found it difficult to imagine not being bored by one woman mentally if not sexually.

'You said earlier that it was your fault the woman was knocked down. Do you feel you are being punished, Monsieur? Is that why you wish to make your confession?'

'Do you think I'm being punished?'

'It is your own interpretation that matters. Do you feel that God is pursuing you?'

'Yes.'

'Why should God wish to punish you?'

'That's your province,' said Parry.

'He is a God of love,' said the priest, 'not a God of vengeance.'

They all say that, Parry thought, but he said nothing.

'He wants you to repent of your sinful ways and make a new beginning. Do you think you are ready to do that?'

'Yes,' he replied.

Was it his imagination or did something stir in the room like the beating of wings?

He remembered the force that had flung him on his face earlier in the church and wondered why he had ever thought he had a choice.

1995

Parry only remembered afterwards on the morning he left for Paris that he had forgotten to say his prayers. He remembered as he came downstairs and looked in the mirror in the hall to see if his bow tie was straight. It was. Not praying gave him a jolt. He looked at his Judas face: silver-white hair, ruddy complexion, yellow eyes. Everything normal, everything ticking over. Just another day.

He went to the front door and picked up the post off the mat. Several thick white important-looking envelopes addressed to his wife. Lloyd's. He knew the various typefaces by now. More demands for money they hadn't bloody well got. She had been a Name before she married him as a result of money left her by one of her innumerable maiden great-aunts. It had all seemed such a good thing at the time. Every year a new baby when they were first married and every year a fat cheque. Showers and showers of gold. They had traded up their old house around the corner for this one on the river. He had always wanted to live on Chiswick Mall with a view of the river and, finally, thanks to his wife, he had.

Parry opened an envelope addressed to him. It was from the Bursar of his eldest daughter's school.

'Dear Mr Parry,' he read, 'I am obliged to remind you that Mary's fees for this term have not yet been paid. If we do not receive the money within . . .'

Parry crumpled the letter and put it down. It never bloody well rained but it poured. From the basement kitchen came the sound of his children, all five of them, having breakfast. After the fourth Victoria had said stop. They measured their sex life these days with a thermometer. Safe period. Safe sex. The world was obsessed by sex, Parry thought, feeling the familiar rush of superiority. He lifted his chin in the glass and turned down the corners of his mouth. Victoria said there was a spot he always missed when he shaved, just under his lower lip. By Jove, she was right. The sound of five children having breakfast was enough to put you off sex for life. They ranged in age from fifteen to five: fifteen and fourteen were close (she was pregnant again when the first one, Mary, was only three months), then a gap, twelve and ten, and then Ben who had been conceived during one of Victoria's safe periods that had turned out not to be so safe after all; amazing the trouble a simple thermometer could land you in.

And of course there had been the one that died. That had been last year. Cot death. Quite ghastly. Tried not to think about it. Such a little corpse, such a tiny coffin.

On Sundays they shepherded their flock into the Oratory for the ten thirty. A good Catholic family. You could see everyone thinking that. Staring. Counting. Never giving a thought to how one was supposed to finance it all. Of course Lloyd's had done that but now they were supposed to finance Lloyd's even if it meant giving the shirts off their bloody backs.

Parry descended the basement stairs for breakfast with his family in a black mood. Victoria Parry had heard her husband come as far as the hall and stop. She knew what that meant. Bills. Cash calls. They had no cash. Try not to think about it. She looked in the cupboard under the sink for a large saucepan to make porridge in and noticed what looked like a yellowish stain at the back of the cupboard behind the sink where the pipe went through the wall. She touched it with her fingers and then sniffed. It couldn't be, she thought. It simply couldn't be. They had had dry rot before in the downstairs cloakroom, immediately above. But it had been dealt with in the days when they had had money to deal with the unforeseen. Now, of course . . . She shut the cupboard door with a bang. Best not to think about it. She would get after it herself, if need be, with a can of that appalling smelling chemical that killed off fungus. She had a vision of herself in overalls and a mask stripping back plaster to brick, sloshing chemicals, rebuilding walls, replastering. She had done a plumbing course last year at night school to save bills. Children threw everything down the loo from STs to silver paper to cigarette ends. It was Thomas who was too young to realize they didn't flush. It worried her that he was having one first thing, before breakfast. She would have to get Edward to have a word with him, she thought, but glancing at her husband's face shelved that idea for later. Later, another time, not now, don't talk about it. That was rather how they had come to lead their life these last couple of years.

'Who wants porridge?'

'Me,' answered five voices.

'Edward?'

'If there's enough, yes,' he said, looking in the coffee jar which was empty. Damn and blast. How the hell was he supposed to start the day without a decent cup of coffee?

'Oh sorry,' said Victoria, pouring a jug of water over the oats, 'we're out. I'll have to get some more today when I go to Sainsbury's.'

She had put off going an extra day to save money. It was one of her many economies. Her married but childless sister, Juliet, who lived in Notting Hill, was always telling her that it would be much cheaper for her to shop in Portobello on a Saturday, which was all very well for Juliet with just Giles, but you couldn't shop for five starving children and one husband in Portobello in any comfort. One needed giant packs of everything from washing powder to loo rolls, and a giant trolley to push it all in, all of which Sainsbury's provided with knobs on, plus a flunkey to go out to the car park with you.

'It'll have to be instant then,' said Parry glumly, putting on the kettle.

'What time is your flight?' asked Victoria, in order to distract him. Children and husbands were interchangeable, she thought bitterly, all needed babying and soothing over trivial things. Who mothered the mother? That was the question.

'Two,' said Parry. 'I have to be there at twelve.'

'I'll drive you then. I'm not working this morning.'

'I can take the Tube,' said Parry.

'No, I'll drive you,' she said. They had to make time to be

together otherwise they never saw one another except when surrounded by children. A car journey to Heathrow was a perfect opportunity.

'All right,' he said, 'thanks.'

'I wish I was going to Paris,' said Mary, the eldest, to her father. 'You are lucky.' She came and put her arms around him. She was tall and dark and thin with the same black curling hair her mother had.

'You've got to stay at school and work,' said Parry. Her hair smelled of coconuts. Once he had looked in the girls' bathroom upstairs and had counted twenty-five containers from something called The Body Shop (gruesome name), all of which seemed to consists of foodstuffs adapted to scent or cleanse.

'I hate school.'

Parry sighed with exasperation, remembering the letter upstairs, but said nothing.

'I'll make your coffee,' she said.

Mary. He watched her in her ugly uniform: grey short skirt, grey jersey, shoes with soles like tractor tyres; so pale, so young. He was immensely tender about Mary, his firstborn.

Thomas and Cyprian were arguing about something, sitting next to one another halfway down the table. Tom was like him – fair, hazel-eyed, pink-skinned. Cyprian was pure Digby, dark and swarthy like his ancestors on his mother's side (there was Spanish blood in there somewhere) with eyelashes, Mary said, like dustpan brushes.

'It is.'

'It isn't.'

'It bloody well is . . .'

'Cyprian,' said his mother, 'don't swear. Apologize to your brother.'

'Sorry,' said Cyprian sulkily, 'but he's so touchy.'

'No, I'm not,' said Tom.

'Yes, you are.'

'No, I'm . . .'

'Be quiet,' said Parry ferociously, 'otherwise you'll both leave the room without any breakfast.'

'I don't want any breakfast,' said Tom, pushing his chair back and rising. 'I'm late anyway.'

'Sit down,' said his mother, 'it's ready.'

'But I . . .'

'Tom,' she said warningly.

Tom sat.

Parry glanced at his wife. She was more patient than he was and in some ways more effective because of it. He tended to snap which frightened the girls and made the boys angry. God, how children showed up your failings. I'm so bloody weary of it all, he found himself thinking, so tired of being shown what an impatient old buffer I seem to have become, just like my own father. Family life wore one down to a ravelling. He remembered with a pang the Parry of twenty years ago, vigorous, good-looking, atheistical, sexually voracious, and contrasted it with himself now: careworn father of five living children and one dead, not allowed sex except for certain rare days of the month, dependent on his wife to tell him when this was, broke enough not to be able to pay the school fees for his daughter. I did as I was told, he thought, and look what happened. His confessor at the Oratory had told him that he must find a nice Catholic girl and marry her, otherwise sex would be his downfall. And where better to do that than in marriage with God smiling down from behind a cloud upon the lucky couple: Victoria in a white nightie done up to the neck and Parry in striped pyjamas thanking God she was too inexperienced to know quite how experienced her new husband was.

He had seen Victoria in the Oratory many times before he got to know her on a pilgrimage to Lourdes run by one of the Oratorian Brothers. In those days she had been a leggy girl with long, dark curling hair caught back loosely, displaying a long white neck. She had the curved brows, long nose and rosebud mouth of a Lelyesque beauty, but instead of satin dresses and lace cuffs she wore the dull uniform of her own century: a Loden coat, good, low sensible shoes, pleated skirts, silk shirts, Hermès scarves. It was easy, Parry thought, staring at her when he should have been concentrating on the homily, to see what she would

25

become when she was older: mother of many children, school governor, grower of astonishing roses.

He had made sure he had sat next to her on that trip. Got to know her a bit. Father Conroy who was leading the expedition was pleased, he could see that. She was such a suitable girl, it was written all over her. She was also an exceedingly nice girl: straightforward, gentle, intelligent, not sexually aware in any way, very naive; the product of a sheltered upbringing. Parry felt protective of her. The rest, he felt sure (he hoped, prayed) would follow. He was twelve years older than she was and it was clear to him from the word go that she looked up to him, believed in him, would take advice. She was not, in any sense of the word, a *tiresome* girl. Not headstrong, not like Rosie or any of those other mistresses that belonged to his former life: older women, usually married, and sexually experienced. Women who knew what they wanted and how to get it.

Their courtship had been swift and innocent and practically wordless, taking place amongst the crowds of Lourdes, heaving bodies, pushing wheelchairs, wiping bums, passing the bodies of the hopelessly disabled into the competent arms of the bath attendants, brisk, blonde girls of reassuring manner and impenetrable foreignness, but Catholic of course. Conducting a courtship in such a place seemed suitable and somehow flattering; there was glamour in the reflected gratitude of the patients, of being seen to be humble, of not minding how difficult or dirty a job was. Saintliness was definitely a self-perpetuating state, Parry thought; the more you did it the better you got.

Victoria had witnessed a miracle: a woman with terrible arthritis coming back up the steps with the wet sheet clinging to her lumpy body saying, in tones of amazement, 'I can walk!' And she could too. Her joints had been smoothed as if someone had got inside her with Three-in-One.

They had been married six weeks later in the family chapel of Victoria's family home at the Old Hall, Pontefract. The chapel had been lately rededicated to Saint Edmund Campion; a large cartouche had been commissioned and set into the wall on the right side of the altar showing the blessed martyr with his head on the block. Underneath was a plaque dedicated to the three fallen Digby sons of the Great War: Thomas, Edmund and Cyprian. The Digbys were descendants of some of the original recusants who had clung on through the centuries, refining their faith through persecutions and disfavour until the present time. John Digby, who had taken part in the Northern Rising, had been beheaded in 1570. There were seven children in the family, four girls and three boys, Victoria being the youngest. She too had been an accident with the thermometer.

In some sort of way, Parry thought, those early years of their marriage had been very blessed. He remembered reading in one of H.V. Morton's books that the early church had been possessed of a kind of holiness and sanctity, a magic that had gradually ebbed away. He sometimes wondered if there was not a parallel with this in life.

Parry had joined a tribe, the great tribe of Digbys, he was an honorary one now. He had married into the family; and to start with he had liked the feeling of belonging, having always been on his own.

'Oh, those Digbys,' someone had said to him, 'they all hunt in a pack.' Digbys had their own rituals. The girls rang their mother once a week, and went to stay every third weekend or so. With seven children, their husbands and wives and children, this meant the house was always full.

'Want a job?' John Digby would ask purely rhetorically, and assign whoever it was something to do. Refusal was unheard of. Parry became an expert at clipping yew trees and dealing with hornets' nests. He liked it. It was fun. To start with anyway. After dinner every Saturday they would all play bridge or, if there were elder children present, charades. Parry and Victoria had their own room on the nursery floor, a vast low-ceilinged room with four beds in it.

'That's for when we have children,' said Victoria meaningfully, two months after they were married when she was already four weeks pregnant.

'Ah,' said Parry, 'good.'

He was as much in love with his wife's family as he was with his wife. He felt he finally had found somewhere he belonged. Mary's birth the following June knocked him for six. A baby, his own baby. It made him wonder how his own father felt when he was born. Not like this, he would guarantee, remembering one tiny black and white photograph of his lugubrious and plainly rather unwilling parent holding a miniature swaddled bundle on his lap. He wasn't there for the birth – Victoria didn't believe in it (a Digby family tradition) – and when he went in to see her the baby looked straight up at him from her see-through cradle as if she already knew him. She was christened at the Old Hall by the family priest, Father Fraser, Mary after the BVM and Beatrice after Edward's mother.

Soon after Mary came Thomas, then, after a pause, Cyprian (whose birth coincided with the largest Lloyd's cheque they had ever received) then Agatha, then, after a further pause, Benjamin. When Cyprian was born they moved to Easter House, Chiswick Mall, a Georgian house, circa 1780, with a garden at the front as well as the rear, a wall in front of rose-coloured brick to match the house and high, old ornate gates. A dream house with a dream view of the river. In all seasons Parry would pause to admire that view; he was in love with the river in all its forms and the trees in all their seasons, with the rowers and the way the spring tides caused the river to overflow the road. The river had its own climate and its own moods and he knew them all and loved them all.

Then the baby, their last child, Teresa, died in her sleep on a cold grey spring morning in 1994.

He remembered standing at the window staring out at the so-familiar view. A sudden shaft of sunlight pierced the surface of the water and some words came into Parry's mind from somewhere or other . . . *for if you abandon us we sink and perish* . . . He suddenly recalled, at the same time, the day of his mother's death, and how he had stood at a window at Knockfern House looking out to sea, past the stone tips of the marker buoys in the bay with his heart as heavy as lead, knowing that nothing would ever be the same again. His mother who died that very afternoon was as dead and as remote to him now as Charlemagne or Diocletian.

She had gone forever, forever, forever. Forever. A terrible word, an unimaginable word.

At each death he had looked out towards the mysteries of the moving waters for comfort and not found it. Only the death of the tiny scrap, four-month-old Teresa, seemed to reawaken in him the long-suppressed terrors of that other death. He began to dream again of his mother in the landscape going along the grass path to the sea. In those dreams he saw her stocking tops and the darkness beyond. Sometimes, to his shame, she was naked. He had no idea what any of this meant and thought that he did not want to know. But what he did know was that he blamed God for it all. So much loss. He had always obeyed, hadn't he? Done as he was told.

He remembered with bitterness how his father had mocked him for returning to the church. 'Your mother,' he had said, 'had a weakness for the Roman church which I always found embarrassing, but I allowed her to have you baptized a Catholic because it meant so much to her. You're obviously taking after her in that respect.'

'I didn't know you found it embarrassing.'

'All those absurd rules and regulations, all that cant and hypocrisy. It beats me how you can take any of it seriously.'

'Do you believe in life after death, Father?'

'In the Resurrection, you mean? No. I believe in a darkness that covers us all forever. A silence. I look forward to it.'

'You don't believe in any other life?'

'There is no other life,' had come the contemptuous reply.

Parry remembered being filled with a terrible rage as he glanced at his father in his good, threadbare tweeds, his highly polished brogues bought twenty-five years before at Lobb, his bald pate with its sprinkling of liver spots, sitting in his chintz armchair with his glass of sherry on a little table by his side. He had wanted to smash something over that smug, shining egg of a head.

His father had believed in nothing. And I, Parry said to himself, I believe in a rewarding, loving God, or at least I did until the baby died. What had I done to deserve that? I hadn't felt this fear for a long time. I had been free of the tormentor, but now he was back again with his notebook and his binoculars, waiting, watching. Mother loved me, but mother died. I was to blame. I loved the baby but the baby died. Why? Mother loved me but she was taken away. Again, he saw her face on the pillow, the skin stretched so tight over those bones. Mother. Mother in a tight-fitting, waisted suit with platform shoes and sheer stockings at the races somewhere; a silly little hat like a pancake with a bit of net attached to it.

'Right, everybody,' said Victoria glancing at the clock over the door, 'time to go. Say good-bye to your father. He's going to Paris for a few days and I'm going to join him for the last bit of the time when half-term starts and you all go to Yorkshire Granny.'

'Do I have to go to Yorkshire?' asked Tom. 'Hector wants me to go and stay with his mother.'

'Hector Protector,' said Benjy.

'You do have to go, yes,' said Victoria. Hector's mother was an exceedingly unsuitable person in Victoria's view for any teenager to spend more than ten minutes with.

'Granny and Grandpa would be very sorry not to see you and you and Mary are going to have to help Granny with the younger ones.'

Tom looked mutinous but said nothing. Hector was growing cannabis plants in his bedroom with the help of a sun-lamp and acres of kitchen foil. His mother lived in a large run-down house in Portland Road and had love affairs. She was an earl's sister with money of her own who never did a hand's turn if she could help it, or at least so Heck said, and, as a consequence, Heck enjoyed a measure of freedom that seemed to Tom enviable, especially when he compared it to life in the barracks at Easter House with its regimented meal times, endless kids hanging around, parents bickering over money, a bedroom with a roof that leaked and nowhere but the bloody lavatory to smoke in. Heck smoked anywhere he felt like. He said his mother hadn't even noticed.

'What time will you be back?' asked Parry. 'I think we ought to go about eleven.'

'I'll be back about 9.30,' said Victoria, wondering, not for the first time, what her husband thought she did all day. 'I'm going to drop off Cyprian and Aggie – Benjy is being fetched by Camilla – so I should be back by then at the latest.'

'Why aren't you working this morning?'

'Because I told Jenny I wanted to take you to the airport.'

Victoria and her partner Jenny mended china in the summerhouse at the bottom of the garden. They had begun two years ago but the business was actually starting – finally – to make money.

'That was kind.'

'Was it?' She glanced at him. 'Why kind? You are my husband, you know.'

Parry did not reply to this. 'I must ring Tom,' he said, 'there are one or two details I need from him.'

Now it was Victoria's turn not to answer.

Since the death of the baby he had closed himself off to her. Quite a lot of the time he actually slept in the spare room because he was having trouble sleeping – or so he said – and didn't want to disturb her with reading in the middle of the night. She wondered – when she had time for such luxuries – what really lay behind his cutting himself off in this way. He had gone on going to Mass but he did not now always take the sacrament. How had it happened that she felt unable to ask her husband about something so important?

When everyone had gone, Parry went upstairs to the drawing room and rang Tom in the shop.

'It's me,' he said, when Tom picked up the phone in the shop in Coptic Street, 'I just want to check Gaby de Fonville's number and address with you.'

De Fonville was a contact of Tom's who had been buying things from them for years. Now, fallen on hard times, he wanted to sell.

'You go – you need a break.' Tom had said to him, 'I've got this other sale to deal with and, besides, I know him too well. He's fearfully charming, old Gaby, but beware. Be hard-hearted. He must have run through millions since I knew him. I don't know what he's burnt his fingers over this time, but it must be serious.'

'Not Lloyd's,' said Parry with feeling.

'No, old man, not Lloyd's.'

'Give me his address then, will you?'

When he had done that Tom said, 'Have a good time, won't you. Try and relax. Antonia was only saying to me last night how tired you look.'

'Thanks.'

'Listen, you arsehole, she meant it kindly. She's concerned about you. And Victoria. Her brother's a Name and he's being bled dry. She's seen it at first hand, knows what it's like.'

'Every week we get dunning letters asking for more money,' said Parry. 'Every bloody week. There were some in this morning. I can't pay Mary's school fees and I just sometimes bloody wonder what's going to . . .'

'Hold on, old man,' said Tom, 'hold on.'

He had never heard Edward, in all the many years he had known him, talk in quite this way with a genuine note of hysteria in his voice. Until now, Tom had thought it was only women who did that.

'I am holding on,' said Parry, taking a deep breath, 'sorry. I am tired, looking forward to getting away as a matter of fact.'

'Good,' said Tom soothingly, 'good, good. Victoria's going to join you, isn't she?'

'At the end of next week,' said Parry.

'Listen, old thing,' Tom broke in, 'why don't I pay Mary's fees out of the contingency fund. You can pay it back when you come back with a splendid haul from old Gaby.'

'I don't think that's a very good idea,' said Parry. 'I have five children. I may ask you to start paying your godson's fees next.'

'What's the school?'

Parry told him.

'Well then, why don't I do that? Stave off the evil moment for a little?'

'It's very kind,' said Parry, 'but I'll have to find a better way than that.'

'Don't be an ass,' said Tom. 'Why won't you let me help you? It's your money too, you know.'

'It's not the answer, Tom.'

There it was again, Tom thought.

'Well, think about it anyway,' said Tom, 'and ring me, won't you, from Paris and let me know what's what? You're staying with Sam, aren't you?'

'Sam's studio until Victoria comes,' said Parry, 'then a hotel. Oh, and Tom, thanks for everything.'

'De rien,' answered Tom, and rang off.

When Tom Wilberforce had finished talking to Parry he got up out of his chair and began to prowl around the shop for a minute or two straightening things, blowing a bit of dust here and there. The old green blinds were still rolled down and he pottered in the dim green light, rather like being at the bottom of a pond, he thought, enjoying the peace and quiet of an early morning. Even Jill, the secretary, hadn't arrived yet.

Antonia, Tom's wife, was worried about Parry and Victoria.

'Ever since that baby died,' she had said to Tom in bed last night, 'things haven't been right.'

'You'd have thought they had enough children,' said Tom, pushing his glasses up on to his forehead.

'They're not units, they're people with souls, each one different,' said Antonia. 'You can't replace one child with another because they're never the same.'

'Yes, you're right,' Tom said, 'but I'm glad we only had two. I couldn't have coped with any more. I sometimes wonder if Edward doesn't regret this great Catholic marriage of his. It was all right when they had enough money, I suspect, but now, what with Lloyd's and one thing and another . . .'

'I gather from Victoria that her parents have been badly hit too. There's talk of them having to sell the Old Hall.'

'Edward hasn't mentioned this to me,' said Tom in astonishment, 'are you sure?'

'That's what she said. Perhaps she hasn't told Edward.'

Tom gazed at his wife in consternation. 'She's going off to Paris with him at the end of next week and a good thing too. The children are going to Yorkshire, so Edward says, to the Old Hall, to those long-suffering grandparents.'

'Those so-called "long-suffering grandparents" simply adore having their tribe around them,' said Antonia. 'Both Edward and Victoria are exhausted. I hope they have a chance to catch up with one another in Paris. She works every bit as hard as he does without much help. You know that little set-up of hers in the summerhouse is just beginning to pay off.'

'At least she has willing parents.'

'Yes, but for how much longer. If the Digbys have to sell up the Old Hall, then what?'

'I don't know,' said Tom despondently. 'I hate the idea of people like John and Isobel having to sell up because some spiv in Lloyd's has been reckless with their cash. Perhaps the state will buy the house if they have to sell.'

'Fate worse than death, if you ask me. Better to let it go to someone who'll live in it.'

'It would kill old John Digby not to have that house any more.'

'Don't,' said Antonia, 'don't.'

Tom went and rolled up the blinds and looked out into the morning quiet of Coptic Street. It was funny without Edward here, bustling about, talking at the top of his voice, sticking his thumbs into the waistband of his trousers to heave them up. As he thought this, Tom had a sudden premonition that Edward would not return, that he had somehow gone from him.

'Don't be absurd,' he said to himself, 'get a grip. Perhaps I need a rest too.'

Business had been all right – just – but not brilliant, only it wasn't that he had been thinking of just now. His sense of lack and loss had been to do with dear old Parry whom he had spent most of his working life with since Oxford, with short stints for both of them with the grander auction houses. Parry was a most tremendously important part of his life. He could say with his hand on his heart that he loved Parry in the way that men in the trenches had loved the companions they had fought with in the same actions. He and Parry had been in a joint action for more than twenty years.

*

Parry came out of the drawing room and found Mary standing in the hall. She was crying.

'What on earth are you doing here?' he asked, going to her and putting his arm around her shoulders.

'I wanted to say goodbye to you,' she said, sniffing. 'I went upstairs to clean my teeth and when I came down you were on the phone.'

'You're going to be terribly late, darling,' he said.

'Is it true about my school fees?' she asked, wiping her nose on her sleeve.

'Yes, but nothing for you to worry about,' said Parry, trying not to sound exasperated. One tried to protect one's children from things but they found you out anyway, hanging about in halls, lurking in cupboards, listening on the extension, going through your desk when you were out. Perhaps it was best just to be honest.

'Will I have to leave?'

'No, my darling,' he said grimly, 'of course not.'

'But if you can't pay the fees then I'll have to.' She began to cry again.

'Look,' he said, 'I am having a temporary blip over the fees, but I certainly hope to have it all sorted out by the time I come back from Paris.'

'What are you going to do in Paris?'

'I'm going, primarily, to meet a contact of Tom's – someone he's done business with for years who has some important things to sell. If I can pay him less than I know I could get here in London by selling them on then I'm in line to make some money. Do you see?'

'Yes,' said Mary, 'I do see. I'm just frightened something's going to happen to you, that's all.'

'Why do you say that?' Parry held her away from him and looked at her. What did she know that he didn't? *Was this a message, a warning?*

'I don't know,' she said, 'it's just that . . .'

'What?'

'You're hurting me,' she said, trying to get out of his grasp.

35

'I'm sorry. I didn't mean to.'

'You don't know your own strength,' she said crossly.

'I'm sorry.'

'God, I suppose I'd better go,' said Mary. 'Can you take me?'

'Your mother's got the car.'

'Oh shit,' said Mary.

'Don't swear and don't say "God".'

'You sound just like Mum.'

'If your Yorkshire grandmother could hear you now she'd have a fit.'

'Will you bring me back something nice from Paris?' Mary asked, shrugging into a blue corduroy bomber jacket.

'What would you like?'

'I'd like a rose. Just like Beauty.'

She came and put her arms around his neck and kissed him on both cheeks. 'Have a lovely time,' she said, 'just don't forget me, that's all.'

She picked up her huge black bag that bulged with books and weighed a ton.

'Send us a card, Dad. See you.'

'See you.' He raised a hand. *Don't forget me.*

The door slammed. He could hear her running down the old brick path, and then the squeak of the gate as she pulled it back. He was filled with an urge to run after her and say 'Stay here, don't go. Never go'. But the thought passed through him like a painful spasm and was gone. He recognized it as one of those futile desires that parents suffer from: a longing to stop time, to turn the tide of years, so that one could keep one's children safe forever from the world, the flesh, the devil. Stay as you are now, my beautiful, precious, girl. Don't leave me, don't change, don't grow bitter and old like me.

He went upstairs to pack his things in a small brown suitcase made of pigskin that had once belonged to his mother. It had her initials on it: 'B. E. St J. P.' Beatrice Elizabeth St John Parry. RIP. She was buried in the Catholic cemetery outside Kirkcudbright, a cold, wooded, lonely spot. There was a plain headstone and her name and dates. Nothing else. No 'beloved this' or 'much missed that'. He had been there once and not returned. His daughter lay in the burial ground at the Old Hall. There was an inscription on her headstone which read 'A Lily of a Day'. Victoria had chosen it. They had buried her on a spring day in Yorkshire among the late daffodils and budding chestnuts. Spring was always later in the north. Even now, he could not really bear to think about it.

When he had finished putting in shirts and ties and underpants together with his bottle of Trumper's Essence of Lime he picked up the photograph of his mother in her sexy little suit and pancake hat and put it in his suitcase on top of everything else. He wondered what Jeremy Montagu would make of that.

Jeremy was his doctor and practised from a chic little roof-top apartment in Kensington Square. Parry had been to see him yesterday about not being able to sleep. He liked Jeremy but he hadn't particularly wanted to go and see him. He feared Jeremy's probing intelligence. He didn't want to be probed but he did want to sleep and he knew enough about the NHS to know that the hard-pressed woman Victoria went to with the children would give him short shrift and tell him he needed a holiday or some such nonsense. Even Tom subscribed to that view. He didn't need a holiday – he just wanted a pill that would stop him feeling anything ever again. At the back of his mind he knew there was only one cure for that particular yearning.

'So,' said Jeremy, 'what is it, Edward? You look tired, if you don't mind my saying so.'

'That's because I can't sleep,' said Parry, 'which is why I'm here as a matter of fact. I wondered if you might prescribe me some sleeping pills.'

Jeremy looked at Parry over the top of his glasses which had slipped a little.

'Are you anxious about something?'

'Yes, as a matter of fact. Lloyd's is rather getting to me, as Tom would say.' Lloyd's would do. If one mentioned Lloyd's then people, generally, looked no further. It was a splendid catch-all for the evils of the world.

'Is there anything else?'

Bugger, thought Parry.' 'Isn't that enough?' he asked plaintively.

'Are you feeling depressed?'

'Not noticeably.'

'What keeps you awake mainly?'

'Money, I suppose, or lack of it.'

'All the children are at private schools, aren't they?'

'Yes.'

'Could you move any of them, do you think? Catholic state schools tend to be better, I gather.'

'I don't want to move any of them,' said Parry, 'I just want to get some sleep so I can do a decent day's work and earn enough to keep them all.'

'What does Victoria think?'

'I haven't asked her.'

'How's your sex life?'

'Why?' Parry dropped his hands on to his thighs in exasperation.

'If you have five children who live at home then the only time you'll get to see your wife is in bed.'

'Well,' said Parry, '. . . we haven't been sleeping in the same room for some time – on and off, that is, for reasons already stated.'

'Do you feel like making love?'

'Oh, for God's sake,' said Parry crossly, 'I don't see why I should be given the third degree about my sex life. We've been married a long time. Everything's fine.'

'Apart from Lloyd's and no sleep, anything else?'

'No.'

'Edward, I'm just trying to get the full picture, that's all. Have you thought of anti-depressants?'

'Pills? No. Why? I'm not ill, I'm just a bit tired, that's all.'

'I don't want to give you sleeping pills because I'm afraid you might become addicted to them.'

'Might I?'

'People do, you know. And we generally take the view nowadays that if one can get to the bottom of what is causing the sleeplessness then that is a more desirable thing.'

'So what do you suggest?'

'How would you feel about going on Prozac?'

'I'm not a nut-case, you know.'

'I know you're not,' said Jeremy patiently, 'you don't have to be halfway to the loony bin to have Prozac prescribed. It will help you. It might make you less anxious and the less anxious you are the better you will sleep.'

'All right,' said Parry reluctantly, 'I'll give it a go.'

'Helen saw you in the Oratory last Sunday,' said Jeremy. Helen was his wife.

'Oh yes, that's right.'

'Are you still pally with Father Conroy?'

'Victoria is,' said Parry. 'I mean, I am too, we both are, she just sees more of him with the children than I do. Aggie is coming up for her first communion shortly. He's been taking her for confirmation classes.'

'Agatha is – how old now?' Jeremy rifled through some papers in front of him.

'Nine . . . or, no, ten, I think.'

Helen had mentioned that Edward had not gone up to take the sacrament which she had found odd in view of his reputation as an exceedingly pious and devout Christian.

'How is everything with the church?'

'Fine,' said Parry. 'Why do you ask?'

'I gather you don't always take the sacrament any more.'

Parry looked at him. *I gather*. They were watching him.

'I rather think that's between me and my confessor, if you don't mind.'

'I'm sorry,' said Jeremy, 'I know it was an impertinent thing to ask, but I am your doctor and if you have something on your conscience that you would rather be rid of . . .'

'There is nothing that I would rather be rid of, thank you,' said Parry coldly.

Jeremy glanced at Parry and opened his mouth to say something else then thought better of it. He wrote out a prescription for Edward St J. Parry.

'Come back and see me in a fortnight,' said Jeremy. 'And have a good time in Paris. Try and rest, Edward, put your feet up, don't kill yourself walking miles about town. These things will help but not immediately, give it a fortnight or so, all right?'

'Thanks,' said Parry, rising to his feet and holding out his hand.

Outside in the street he tore up the prescription and dropped it into one of those grand black and gold rubbish bins provided by the Royal Borough of Kensington and Chelsea.

When Parry had gone Jeremy Montagu wrote an extensive note about their interview. Parry, he wrote, seemed to be in pain but was also locked into a state of denial and was, as a result, defensive and paranoid. There were serious money problems and his marriage was in trouble – that much was quite clear. Looking through Parry's notes he saw that the mother had died when Parry was ten. A terribly difficult time for a boy to lose his mother. The seed of Parry's depression might lie there. Helen said he was pious – she was a convert so she was good at spotting other fanatics, she said, and he was exceedingly devout, until recently. There was obviously some huge upheaval going on in Parry's life, reflected in his unconscious and connected to his fear of sleeping, perhaps wrapped up with his religion and with the guilt and fear that seemed to attend Catholics everywhere. Religion could poison you as well as preserve you, Jeremy thought, if it was wrongly applied. It all boiled down, he supposed, to what one imagined God was, if one believed in him. And Christianity boiled down to Judgement. One died and then one was judged.

Anglicans (slackers, really), and Jeremy counted himself one, were awfully keen to insist on God as forgiving and loving, a friendly bloke, a kind of jolly social worker with a beard and a pair of Levis, sporting an Aids awareness ribbon, but there was plenty of evidence in the Old Testament and the New to suggest that this might be painting a rather optimistic and rosy picture of the Deity. Modern people couldn't bear to think of being judged for anything. If one believed, as he would bet Parry did, that God was a strict God, then one was dealing with another kind of reality altogether. God was thunderous and severe and Christ, his son, a tormented figure, a bloody cadaver, who died in agony.

There was nothing pretty about the cross, in fact there was nothing about the cross that was not unbearable.

He wondered suddenly, and with an unpleasant feeling of recognition at having stumbled upon something accurate about his patient and old friend, whether Parry were not just the right kind of rather highly strung perfectionist who might be unforgiving enough of himself and his own human weaknesses and frailties to commit suicide.

'Telephone in two weeks on return from abroad,' wrote Dr Montagu on a Post-it sticker and attached it to Parry's file. He would get his secretary to put a note in the diary. Or, perhaps, he would telephone Victoria Parry and have a word with her himself. Although she was not his patient except in absolute emergencies he reckoned he knew her well enough to interfere gently.

Mary's first lesson was geography, thank God, a subject which bored her and which she was shortly giving up as she had too many other subjects to sit for GCSEs, so that she was able to sit at the back and have a bit of a think about things. Amy, who was her best friend, was seated somewhere in the middle of the class, and had been unable to save Mary a place because she was so late. The receptionist had given her a rocket about that too.

'That's three times in ten days, Mary,' she had said. 'Once more and you'll have to see Miss Morrison.' Miss Morrison was the headmistress.

Luckily, she had managed to slip in and sit at the back without Mrs Langford, the geography mistress, apparently noticing.

As Mrs Langford droned on about demographic shift, Mary began to think about her father. She felt slightly embarrassed about her outburst in the hall at home. She couldn't really think why she had said that to him. Something had made her say it, she had felt it, and then it had gone, leaving her feeling a bit of a jerk. But there was a kind of atmosphere around her father these days, a kind of separateness. She felt it and she could see her mother did too. Her brothers and sisters were too busy arguing with one another to notice anything unusual, but being the eldest meant bearing the burden of noticing.

And she did notice and wonder why he was sleeping in the spare room. Her mother said it was because his snoring kept her awake, but Mary, going to the loo in the night, noticed his light was often on at funny times. Sometimes Mary went in to make his bed for him and although the spare room was pretty enough she always felt sorry for him in there on his own. There was a bleak look about the single dented pillow, the dusty piles of books, the bottle of Trumper's Lime on the basin. The toothbrush with bristles missing, his tube of Euthymol squeezed in the middle and encrusted at the end. She would fold his pyjamas, which smelt of him, and tidy up as much as she could. Occasionally, she would put some flowers in there for him, just to make it seem more like home. But seeing his bachelor state, like an island in the middle of the great ocean of family life, made Mary ache for him.

Of course the snoring was pretext for something else, she wasn't stupid, some problem between her parents. One accepted of course that they had a sex life although the thought was almost too disgusting to contemplate, but one did not wish to know exactly what was wrong, particularly if – as seemed likely – it was connected (as most things seemed to be in the grown-up world) to the said sex life. In her class, one half of the girls' parents were divorced. Amy's parents had been divorced for years and both parents had remarried and had more children. Amy lived with her mother and stepfather but Mary could see that she found it difficult now there was a new baby. New babies from second marriages displaced the children of the first marriage however carefully the parent in question handled it, there was no doubt of that. Amy loved her little brother but she hated the way he got all the attention, and the way she had to help at weekends.

'I have to help too,' Mary said, but Amy had replied, 'but you're used to it. They're your whole brothers and sisters. If I don't help Gordon gets cross with me.'

'But that would happen anyway,' said Mary.

'Yes, but he's not my father,' said Amy. 'Why should I help with his kid when he goes off to the pub?'

42

'Yes, pretty sure.' She passed a hand over her eyes. 'Unless the National Trust steps in that's all they can do.'

'But the Trust likes things to be well-endowed.'

'I know.'

'I'm so sorry.'

She turned her head and regarded him steadily for a moment.

'Edward,' she said.

'What?'

She held out her hands towards him then dropped them.

'I'm sorry,' he repeated without moving. It seemed that they had passed some critical point because they had lost the means of communicating with one another. They who had once been so close.

'What about Mary?' she said. She had stopped looking at him. As he waited for her to go on he saw a solitary tear rolling down her cheek. He wanted to help but he couldn't. Something prevented him from offering her comfort; it was as if his feelings towards her had completely closed down. He glanced at his watch.

'The bill, you mean?'

'What do you think I mean?'

'I'll pay it when I come back.'

Victoria went and stood in front of the fireplace as if she were looking for warmth from that source, but the grate was empty with old ashes of their last fire still in it. Parry gazed at the room he had arranged as if he were seeing it for the last time; the gilt mirror above the fireplace with the gilded eagle on top holding a ball in its claws. Mary had been fascinated by the eagle when she was little and had called it a 'seagull'.

Parry had chosen the material for the sofas, a dark raspberry pink brocade with a heavy fringe; he had found the bronzes that sat on the mantelpiece in a junk shop in Camden Town; he even bought and arranged the flowers each week. Everything in this room had been put in its place by him.

'What are you thinking?' she asked. He looked so bleak somehow, so chilled.

'I wasn't thinking of anything in particular.'

45

'I may be able to settle Mary's bill out of the business account,' Victoria said. 'I'll have a word with Jenny.'

'Don't. I said I'll deal with it when I come back.'

'It can't just be left, Edward, don't you understand?' Victoria heard a note of hysteria in her voice and was appalled.

'It can wait another few days.'

'What time do you want to go?' she asked, seeing that it was hopeless to pursue this subject with him at the moment. When he had gone she would sit down and think about how to deal with it.

'Have you packed?'

'Yes.'

'Can you leave me the number of the studio?'

'I thought it was in the book.'

'I don't think it is, but I'll phone Sam and Nancy for it if you like.'

'No, no. I'll give it to you now.'

'You will be careful, won't you?'

'What do you mean?' Why were they all saying this to him? Mary's voice: *I'm just frightened something's going to happen to you.*

'Just . . . be careful.' She shrugged. 'Do you mind my saying that to you?'

He looked so hopeless somehow, so vulnerable. She hated the way this made her feel angry. One of them had to be strong and it wasn't going to be Edward. When she most needed him he had failed her. It was as if their roles were reversed and she was now the guide and he the guided. It was not the way she had planned things at all. During the good years he had taken the lead – when it was easy – but now everything was so difficult it was she who had to find the strength.

'Why should I?'

'You look taken aback.'

'I don't mean to.' He shook his head. She had a look on her face that he particularly disliked, a bossy, probing, brisk sort of a look. 'If we could go in five minutes or so, would that be all right with you?'

He felt suddenly desperate to get away from this house and all its associated worries, the wife who knew too much about him and yet not enough.

'Yes, fine. I'll just go and clean my teeth. I didn't have time before.'

In the bathroom, Victoria glanced at her reflection in the mirror over the basin and thought that she looked harassed, which was hardly surprising. Since the baby had died Edward had become like another child; someone to be dealt with and soothed or placated depending on his mood, which was often irascible. He shouted at the children and was easily irritated by them and their noise, whereas before he had seemed to take it all in his stride.

He was also drinking far too much, which was one of the reasons they no longer shared a room very often, certainly not for a whole night. She didn't want to share a bed with someone who always had whisky on his breath and who snored and tossed and turned. He had nightmares and fought with the sheets and then would get in and out of bed all night long looking for aspirins and glasses of water and his reading glasses.

Since the baby died she could have counted the number of times they had made love on the fingers of two hands. He didn't seem to want sex any more. Perhaps he was frightened of fathering more children, although this was no longer likely as she had begun to use contraception, without telling him of course. She reckoned he was in too fragile a state to have that on his conscience. Although he wasn't a convert, his mother had been and his Catholicism was only one generation deep. He had all the pride of the convert; the longing to do everything by the book. It was a way of not taking responsibility for his actions and it infuriated her. The loss of the child had triggered something in him. He had definitely not been the same since, but it was up to him to do something about it. She too had suffered loss, she too had to carry on. She sighed, remembering that morning.

It had been Edward who found her, poor little pet, because her cot was in his dressing room. She herself had still been in bed as it was Saturday, having what she thought was an extra God-given hour's sleep. The baby usually woke at six or thereabouts but this

47

morning there had been a silence which Victoria (waking herself in anticipation and then going off again) took grateful advantage of.

'Victoria,' he had said, shaking her by the shoulder, not 'Tor' which was what he normally called her, but her full name, 'Victoria, wake up. There's something the matter with Teresa, I can't wake her.'

She had shot out of bed and had been at the cot in the other room in a split second. One glance had told her that the baby was dead. She was a terrible colour and not breathing.

'Please call the doctor,' she had said, picking up the little bundle. Her child. The baby's body was cold but her nappy was wet. She held the child to her, cradling her head and her body, feeling nothing but a kind of numbness. She was so lost in her grief-ridden thoughts that she did not notice Edward still standing behind her.

'The doctor,' she repeated, 'Edward, did you hear me?'

'It's too late,' he said. 'What's the point?'

'We have to do it. She has to be certified dead, don't you understand?'

'I understand all right.'

'Then do it.' She stared at him. She couldn't believe they could be having an argument now. At this particular moment. She shook her head in disbelief.

'Can I hold her?'

'Of course you can,' she replied, 'but please ring the doctor first. One of us should break it to the others.'

Again, no response.

'Edward, did you hear me? The others.'

She turned away from him and sat down in the big armchair in the window where she had spent so much time lately feeding this baby. When she looked up he had gone.

The doctor came quite quickly, Dr Patel, whose professional detachment had helped Victoria locate her own source of steeliness, of strength, but Edward had not come back again to do his grieving with her. He had left her to bear it alone, by herself. And so she had. But she had not forgiven him for it. When, eventually, she had gone downstairs to find the other children she had expected him to be with them but he had gone out somewhere, no one had a clue where. They were quiet, especially the elder two, Mary and Tom, and rather shaken. It had touched her to find them sitting in the kitchen on their own like a miniature parliament waiting for orders.

When Edward came back, very much later that night, he had been drunk, leglessly, hopelessly plastered. He had left her the whole day and most of the night to bear the pain of death alone. She could neither understand nor forgive him. Father Conroy had had nothing to say about his absence either except to counsel understanding. Understanding! Truly, it was a man's world still.

In order to try to recover after Teresa's funeral, Victoria had allowed everyday life to engulf her, grateful for the distractions of the children and her growing business. She was civil to Edward but a great deal of the time she managed to ignore him. She turned inwards towards her family, her children, always the source of her strength. When she thought about this she realized it was not enough. The elder children were growing up quickly. It was no longer the same. Nothing was the same anymore. She felt a sense of bitter disappointment, almost as if she had been cheated in her life. Everything seemed to be slipping from her grasp: her husband, her money, her children. It was not what she had expected. Not at all the picture she had had of herself at this point. She thought of her mother, seamlessly matriarchal, who made the transition from mother to grandmother without appearing to bat an eyelid. The best thing to do was not to think.

Victoria, having decided this, put on some lipstick and found a pair of reasonably decent black leather loafers in her wardrobe that she did not remember buying. She glanced at their bed on the way out of the room, their big marriage bed by Biedermeier that had come from the Old Hall, where she had slept mostly alone for so many months and wondered if Paris would or could possibly restore their marriage to what it had once been.

Edward put his things in the boot.

'You don't have very much,' she said.

'I don't need very much.'

'Looking forward to it?' Making polite conversation to your husband seemed ridiculous.

'Oh yes.' He nodded. 'I love Paris.'

She waited for him to break the ice as they drove towards Heathrow, but he was silent, gazing out of the window. When they reached the terminal and Edward had got his suitcase out of the back, she said, 'I'll see you in ten days, then?'

'Yes.'

As he kissed her she saw there were tears in his eyes.

'What is it?' She put her hand on his arm.

'Nothing.' He withdrew hastily from her touch. 'It's nothing. I'm tired. I need a rest.'

'But you're not going for a rest. You've got such a lot to do.'

'When you come it'll be a rest,' he said, picking up his case.

'Will it?'

Now it was her turn to have tears in her eyes.

'Of course it will,' he said. Then he added, 'I do love you, you know.'

'Yes.'

She watched him as he picked up his case and began to walk away. At the door of the terminal he turned around and waved. She waved back and then turned away. Several taxis had blocked the car in – an increasingly battered ancient Peugeot with two rows of seats in the back – and she had to wait until they disgorged their passengers and moved off. As she sat at the wheel of her car she was possessed by a tremendous sense of foreboding.

Parry did not care for airports. He checked in his suitcase and then went to the airport chapel to say his prayers. Horrible place it was too, more like a public lavatory than a place of God. By the chapel door a girl stood in full punk regalia. Her legs were joined by a chain at the back and her nose and her eyebrows were pierced with rings. Her face was painted chalk-white with huge black panda eyes.

'Not there,' she said, as Parry pulled open the door. 'E's fucked off.'

'I'm sorry.'

She smiled at him, her teeth yellow against the kabuki mask.

'God, darlin', that's who. Not there. Awol. Fucked off, like I said.'

Parry passed on into the chapel feeling slightly sick. He crossed himself and then genuflected before falling on his knees on to a red plastic hassock with a small, rather worn, gold cross in the middle.

In the middle of praying, he was afflicted by a sudden, terrible sense of bereavement, a sense of loss so great that he felt the tears come into his eyes. He remembered how, on the day his mother had died, he had stood on the edge of the big pool in the water garden and thought about throwing himself into its weedy depths. Then he had looked up to the sky beyond, a pale sky, lightly clouded, where the sun hung obscured like a piece of sea-glass, and he had known the meaning of eternity and death: a terrible heaviness, an endlessness never to be escaped from.

He got up and stumbled out. The punk girl had gone. She seemed to Parry like an emanation of some darkness, something horrible, a harbinger. He was being watched; it was a sign.

He thought he would get a newspaper and put himself through passport control so that he could linger with a strong drink on the other side. His heart was racing and the palms of his hands felt clammy.

In the bar there was a girl in a smart black suit with a briefcase by her side. She was drinking what looked like Coca-Cola. She had dark curly hair and equally dark eyes. She looked up as he came in and then down again at the page of notes in front of her. He wondered where she was going and what she was doing, but when he looked round from ordering himself a double whisky at the bar she had gone.

Victoria parked the car on the Mall and got out. She walked along a little way looking at the trees and the river. A blackbird sang in a willow above her head. The beauty of the view soothed her and she wanted it to make her feel less perturbed about Edward. Perhaps he was just tired, in need of a break, not only from all the children but from his normal surroundings. She wished she could feel confident of this but there had been something about him this morning that had scared her. Some finality in his way of looking at her, the way he had said 'I do love you, you know' as if that were a justification for some other course of action. But all he was planning to do in Paris was to see a few people, do some business and wait for her to join him. It was all quite simple.

Victoria went back to the car and got a packet of cigarettes out of the glove box on the front passenger side. She kept them there because the glove box was lockable and Tom couldn't get at them. Any other cigarettes she had in the house he somehow tracked down and purloined. There was nothing more infuriating than to go looking for a cigarette and not to find one. But she really would have to do something about Tom's smoking. Thinking this, Victoria lit a cigarette with the car lighter and sat on the driver's seat with the door open and her feet hanging out.

She had tried to give up smoking for years, but with five children something always prevented her although she felt guilty about it. Smoking was such a convenient way of protecting oneself from the endless demands and desires of small children. You could always say 'I'll do it when I've had a cigarette' and they would go away for a minute and leave you in peace.

When she had been pregnant with Teresa, her sixth child, people had given her funny looks and said things like 'Not another one' or 'Have you got room for another child?' The answer was yes. There was always room for another child – when there was enough money of course. Benjy had been a mistake – she hadn't really intended to have another child then – but that was eight years ago and Lloyd's hadn't started to bite. She had been thrilled to have another baby. But when she had conceived Teresa it had been another matter. She had known they shouldn't make love but they had anyway. It hadn't really been a mistake at all. If her temperature was up then the likelihood was she would get pregnant. And she had. Edward had been dismayed, then furious, and then, when the child was born, he had completely fallen in love with her. He had been with his last girl the same as he had been with his first. Besotted.

The fact of her death lay at the centre of their marriage trailing its cancerous tendrils, its jellyfish legs, across all their lives. SIDS. Sudden Infant Death Syndrome. Nobody really knew why. People talked about mattresses and smoking and this and that, they argued about which way up the baby should lie, but nobody knew why it went on happening.

She remembered how, one summer in Scotland, the children had seen a jellyfish the size of a small table. They had found a laundry basket and captured the horrible thing, dragging it out of the water and standing around it for hours afterwards with sticks, poking at its surprisingly tough hide; even the dogs had been scared of it, growling and backing off in alarm.

It had been in Scotland that Teresa had been conceived. Edward's father was still alive but he lived with a nurse in one wing of Knockfern. The rest of it was theirs for the summers. A fabulous place, the children adored it. It had been the evening – she remembered it so well – that they had walked out to the island; a long and unusually hot day had faded into the tranquillity of evening – a high, clear sky rose-pink at the edges. The tides were right that day too; low tide in the evening. They had gone, all seven of them, with Feather, their Labrador, in a crocodile across the narrow spit of sea-deserted sand, rippled by tides and full of the sand squiggles of sea creatures vanished beneath or carried out by the departing waters.

Benjamin had called, 'Look, Mummy, worms . . .!'

Feather had had her nose stung by a jellyfish and had gone round and round in circles trying to extinguish the sting, leaving deep rifts in the sand. The children had laughed and laughed, Benjy holding his sides like a clown.

They had climbed up over the rocks of the island. The four elder ones had run on but Benjy had been carried by Edward so tenderly. At the cairn, they had set the picnic out on tartan rugs: baps, hard-boiled eggs, salad, all the usual things, and those funny mutton pies from the baker in Kirkcudbright. The elder ones had gone to play some game the other side of the cairn on the slope overlooking the ocean. There was a rock there they could jump from into a pool. She and Edward had drunk wine and watched Benjy play some mysterious game of his own with stones from the base of the cairn.

They went home across the sands in the half-dark with a moon hanging in the sky like a glass fruit and stars spangled across the dimness.

When all the children had finally gone to bed she and Edward had drunk some more wine out of sheer exhaustion and exhilaration.

'This is the first summer I've ever felt happy here,' he had said.

'Why didn't you tell me?'

'I couldn't. Nobody ever believes you can hate somewhere so beautiful.'

It had seemed the most natural thing in the world that he should kiss her on the sofa, Edward who normally wouldn't touch her unless they were in their bedroom. In his kiss she tasted the land and the sea, the sound of gulls, the transcendental arch of sky deep pink at the edges like the colour of certain shells.

In the end he had carried her into their bedroom as if she were a bride again. He had undressed her slowly and laid her on the bed.

'You're so lovely,' he said. 'I'm so lucky.'

And that had been the night Teresa was conceived. Teresa, little flower. After that, everything had gone wrong. The pregnancy had been very difficult – she had been sick for fourteen weeks, her legs swelled up and she had to walk with a stick. Three of the five children chose those nine months to do something drastic: Mary had broken her leg riding; Tom had fallen off Hector's cousin's motorbike and cracked his skull; Benjy had started bed-wetting again. On top of it all, one of Edward's best clients died and the Lloyd's onslaught had begun in earnest. In the end, Teresa was born in Queen Charlotte's by Caesarean section, a beautiful dark baby with knowing eyes.

The evening after the day she died, Edward had said to her 'I don't know what I've done.' And she had replied, 'What do you mean? You haven't done anything. It's not your fault.'

He had turned away from her when she said that so she couldn't see his face.

'I'm responsible,' he said.

'Please,' she had said wearily, 'please don't.'

They had been in the drawing room having a drink, waiting for her parents to arrive.

'You don't understand.' He put down the decanter with a crash.

'What don't I understand?'

'It's me. I bring bad luck. I'm cursed.'

'Edward, what on earth is the matter with you?'

He turned to face her and with a sense of shock she saw that he was crying. This sense that he was to blame seemed to her utterly selfish, a way of saying that it was worse for him than for her, or for any of the rest of them. It also seemed theatrical and absurd. Briefly, she wondered if he were quite sane.

Victoria let herself into the house which was cool and quiet. It should be a relief to get home but somehow it wasn't today. Edward's departure had upset her more than she realized. For so long he had been at the centre of her life, with the children, of course. She loved having babies and by their very nature they were terribly absorbing. Had she been too absorbed in them, she wondered? Had she neglected her husband for them? These disquieting thoughts pursued her. Normally, when the children and Edward were out she loved the quiet of the house, except that she couldn't help but think there was one person who might have been here to meet her. By rights, there should have been a baby at home now with fat fists and legs like miniature tree trunks, just learning to talk. She heaved a great dry sob into the silence. My little girl, my Teresa.

Sometimes in the night she would wake and think of that child suffocating underground, cold in her little box, rotting away; her flesh frozen in winter, liquid in the summer. If she had been asked whether she believed in the Resurrection she would have said, without hesitation, that she did, but the thought of Teresa, the *fact* of her, seemed to suggest the very

55

opposite. Was this all there was? This and then that? The day they had buried her – it was about this time of year – the rooks had sat in the trees making their harsh sound like old men choking. She had raised her eyes from the pit and looked at those rooks and thought that they were alive and her child was not, and where was the justice in that? Father Conroy had said one could not talk of justice in terms of God, one could only talk of mercy. But what mercy? She had never questioned her faith before. It was one of a number of new and distressing questions which she could not answer. The old questions she had always slightly despised other people for going on about: Why suffering? Why the Holocaust? Why Lloyd's? Why me? She had been brought up in the faith by faithful parents in a seamlessly Catholic household, so in a sense it had always been easier for her than for other people. But it seemed that now there were no certainties any more, nothing that one could safely rely on. Three years ago, two years even, her life seemed to have unfolded in just the way she had expected it to: solid marriage, children, house, domestic contentments and concerns. The Church as a prop. How suddenly in retrospect things had changed.

Now there was nothing that one could safely rely on, other than bills. Bills, bills. Her eyes flew to the bursar's letter. The letters from Fenton and Stanwright. They made her want to scream. What justice, mercy and wisdom had taken away her child and threatened to take away her parents' house and her own? What had they ever done to deserve such a fate?

Victoria took the post which was lying on top of the walnut chest of drawers that Edward had bought at Lots Road for a song when they were first married. She went down the narrow basement stairs to the kitchen expecting to find the wreckage of breakfast but a good fairy in the shape of Jenny had clearly waved her wand here and the kitchen was immaculate. Jenny had even filled the kettle and left it on the slow ring of the Aga to boil. Victoria felt a sudden rush of gratitude for Jenny as she went out of the scullery door into the garden.

The workshop was a Victorian summerhouse that had been

falling to pieces when they bought the house. It had been the last thing they had spent money on in the days when they still had money. They had planned to make it a separate dwelling for the boys when they were older, a place where they could play their music and sleep over with friends, but it had been a godsend when Victoria had had to start up her own business and had needed premises.

She and Jenny had done the course together at City & Guilds, travelling in and out together and sharing childcare and school runs. Jenny lived around the corner in Eyot Gardens with her two children and a selection of Polish lodgers. Her husband, who was a vet, had run away some time ago with his secretary, and Jenny had the house but very little money. Her daughter, Henrietta, was at school with Mary, which was where Victoria had met her.

'You're an angel,' said Victoria, putting her head round the workshop door.

'Oh, you're back,' said Jenny, looking up. She was in the process of mending a Limoges vase and had been (as she found was more and more often the case) absolutely absorbed in her thoughts as she performed her painstakingly satisfactory task. She and Victoria talked about this sometimes and had decided that it was the Zen of china mending: the stillness and absorption required led one into a condition that was not quite a trance because one was very alert and very aware, but was probably something like 'perfect action'. Jenny had bought a book about Zen Buddhism and they would read bits of it to one another every now and again. Jenny was particularly fond of the lines: 'A tenth of an inch's difference, And heaven and earth are set apart' – which was very true of mending china and probably of most other things in life.

'Did he get off all right?' Jenny stood up, stretched and then took off her magnifying glasses.

'Yes. I got him there in good time.'

'Is everything all right?'

Victoria, who was tickling Feather behind her black silken ears, looked up.

'I don't know,' she said. 'Edward's in a funny mood. He hasn't been himself for ages.'

'Tell,' said Jenny. 'Let's go and have coffee, shall we? I put the kettle on.'

'I saw,' said Victoria, 'and you cleared away the remains of breakfast for me. You are a darling.'

'You've got too much to do,' said Jenny. 'I don't think it's fair on you. You need a char, a good old-fashioned char. The people whom we're supposed to call "helpers" these days.'

'Do they still exist?' said Victoria, opening the door. 'My mother has two in the country but you can't get 'em for love nor money in London.'

'What about a nice Pole?' asked Jenny. 'They're good sloggers. Why don't you give Iza a go? She's my new lodger from Cracow. You'd like her. Most of the time she makes sandwiches in a hairdresser's in Notting Hill. She's desperate for more work but you wouldn't have to pay her what you'd pay an English helper.'

'How much?' asked Victoria, getting the mugs down from the dresser.

'£3.00 an hour. Treasures, English ones at any rate, are more like a fiver an hour.'

'Let me think about it,' said Victoria, sloshing milk into mugs and sitting down opposite Jenny at the table.

'Have you got any fags?' she said, 'I've left mine in the car.'

'Here,' said Jenny, digging in the pocket of her cardigan. She pushed a packet of Benson & Hedges across the table.

'Are you going to have one?' asked Victoria, meeting Jenny's large brown eyes. Not for the first time she thought how pretty Jenny was with her pale hair and dark eyes, her generous mouth, and wondered why the vet, whose name was Richard, had left her.

'I certainly am,' said Jenny. 'You said Edward's in a funny mood. Do you want to talk about it?'

'I don't know whether I do or not,' said Victoria slowly. 'You know that thing "How do I know what I think until I see what I say"? Well, I feel like that about Edward. I don't know how I think and I'm not sure I want to either.'

'Oh Tor,' said Jenny. 'I am sorry.'

'Don't be,' said Victoria. 'I may just be tired and confusing things. You know how you do? Two horrible . . . no, three horrible things have already happened this morning: a letter from Fenton and Stanwright . . . underwriting agents,' she added when Jenny looked blank. She envied Jenny not knowing what an underwriting agent was. 'Mary's school fees haven't been paid and they're agitating and I think there's dry rot under the sink.'

'Show me,' said Jenny, putting her cigarette out.

'At the back,' said Victoria, kneeling on the floor. 'Just put your hand against the wall and tell me what you think.'

As she got up she overbalanced and Jenny caught her firmly with both hands. They both laughed. Jenny put her hand on Victoria's cheek for a moment.

'You're a very brave woman, do you know that?'

'No braver than you,' said Victoria, strangely moved by this demonstration of loyalty. It was so nice to be held by a grown-up, someone from whom one could draw strength. It made her sad to think how long it was since Edward had held her properly. Briefly, she laid her head on Jenny's shoulder.

'Have you got a torch?' said Jenny, going down on all fours.

'Yes, but the batteries need renewing. As usual. The children use it for some game and there are never any batteries.'

'Kids!' said Jenny from inside the cupboard. 'Torches and plasters, I find. They're irresistible. Oh shit, Tor, it is dry rot. I can't say how bad because one never knows until one takes the whole place to pieces. I should just ignore it if I were you.'

'But it'll get worse,' said Victoria, 'and we haven't a penny piece to fix it with.'

'Ventilation's the thing,' said Jenny practically. 'Find out where you think it's coming from and leave everything open you can. Leave the cupboard door open.'

'It really is all I need,' said Victoria, who was almost in tears.

'I know,' said Jenny. 'It's as if one's house has cancer. Don't think about it. Let's take Feather for a walk, then we'll go back to work and make lots of money. Have you told Edward about it?'

'What's the point?' said Victoria sniffing. 'He wouldn't know what to do.'

'Sometimes it seems as if it's always women who are left to deal with everything, don't you think?' said Jenny. 'No wonder we're the superior sex. Men just bugger off when they feel like it. I remember when Richard and I had a row he'd just go off and leave me at home. I could never do that because of the children.'

'I know,' said Victoria, 'Edward's the same. Except we don't even seem to have rows any more.'

'Come on,' said Jenny. 'Let's go and get some air. Come on angel,' she said to Feather, 'come and have a swim.'

'What did your mother say?' asked Hector of Tom at lunch-time as they lounged in the cloisters in the sunshine.

'I have to go to Yorkshire. She says.' Tom spat out a piece of grass with feeling, 'which means Mare and me will have to look after the others instead of having a life of our own.'

'Can't your grandparents do that?' asked Hector lazily. 'Isn't that what they're for? I wish you could come. Ma's going away.'

'Where to?'

'I don't know. India, I think. She's going to see the Dalai Lama, it's her latest craze. She bangs on about "His Holiness this" and "His Holiness that".'

'Isn't he the one Richard Gere hangs out with?'

'Yeah,' said Heck in an American accent, 'and Cindy, don't forget Cindy, and Koo Stark or whatever her name is – the one who nearly got shacked up with Prince Andrew.'

'Never heard of her,' said Tom.

'Come around later after school,' said Hector. 'You can ring your Mum from my place and tell her to come and get you later. Or, look, Tomo, maybe you could stay the night. Ask her. That would be great. Then,' he said, talking out of the side of his mouth, 'then we can try my new dope. It's as strong as hell, you'll love it.'

'OK,' said Tom, 'I will. Dad's gone away this morning so she'll have too much to do to take issue.'

'Where's he gone?'

'Paris. On business. Lucky thing.'

'How long for?'

'Ten days, two weeks, something like that. Mum's going out to join him at half-term, which is why we have to go to Yorkshire.'

'But you like it there, don't you?'

'I do like it,' said Tom, wiping his mouth on his sleeve, 'but it's so boring. There's nothing to do except play tennis.'

'Don't you know anyone up there, any girls?'

'Not really. I see people at Christmas parties and things, but there's nothing . . . you know . . . going on otherwise. Pony Club.'

'Shooting? Can't you go out and kill something?'

'Grandpa's a pacifist about animals. He came back from the war like that, so Mum says, so nobody's allowed to shoot apart from the uncles who're allowed to shoot pigeons.'

'Bor-ing,' said Heck with feeling.

Hector had lost his door key so he had to ring the bell of the tall white stucco house in Portland Road. After he had done this twice he said, 'Damn, she must be out somewhere.'

'I think someone's coming,' said Tom, peering through one of the glass panels.

A slender Indian woman with long, dark lustrous curling hair in a red and gold sari opened the door to them.

'Hi, Vaneeta,' said Heck. 'Where's Thalia?' Thalia was his mother.

'Sssh,' said Vaneeta, placing a finger on her lips, 'your mother is having a yoga lesson in the drawing room. It is necessary that there should be absolute quiet.'

'Yeah, well,' said Hector, 'that's fine. We'll go downstairs.'

'Thank you,' said Vaneeta, standing back against the door to let them pass through.

As they passed the drawing room, a large double room on the ground floor, Tom saw Thalia Egerton-Dawlish, Heck's mother, lying on the polished boards of the floor like a corpse at a Hindu funeral. Her eyes were closed and she did not open them as the boys trooped past in their heavy shoes.

'At least she didn't ask us to take our shoes off,' said Hector, once they were safely installed in the basement kitchen. 'That's what happened last time. That woman thinks she owns this place, she's always hanging about lighting joss sticks and banging on about Thalia's Achilles tendons.'

'Why's your mother so friendly with her?'

'She thinks it's cool,' said Hector in a pitying voice. 'I think all that New Age stuff stinks.'

'But you smoke dope,' said Tom.

'Everyone smokes dope,' said Hector, 'it doesn't signify.'

'My parents don't.'

'No, but your parents are different.'

'I wish they bloody weren't.'

'Someone's got to stay married,' said Heck, 'and it might as well be your parents.'

'They don't get on though. Dad sleeps on his own now, has done since . . .' Tom paused, remembering the reason, and rather wished he hadn't.

'Since when?' asked Hector, offering Tom a cigarette and lighting it for him.

'Since the baby died last year,' said Tom.

'Do you think about that?'

'Sometimes, yes.'

'How old was it?'

'She. It was a she. Four months.'

'When my grandfather died,' said Hector, 'they laid his body out in the dining room and we all had to go and look at him. I'd never seen a dead body before. It was rather fascinating.'

'Hmmm,' said Tom, blowing a smoke ring. 'I'd better ring Mum or she'll be wondering where I am.'

On the same morning as Victoria Parry received a letter from her underwriting agents, a similar letter was delivered to her parents' address, the Old Hall, Pontefract, W. Yorks.

In West Yorkshire, the post arrived at ten by van, delivered by one of the Digbys' tenant farmer's sons. Both Isobel and John Digby had got into the habit of lying in wait for the post van in order to spare the other the terrors of the post.

This particular morning, Isobel saw Jack Happold's van coming around under the copper beech that had been planted on Armistice Day, 1918, and whose dark radiance had delighted her every spring since she had come to live at the Old Hall. She was in what her mother-in-law had called the Boudoir but what Isobel herself simply called her sitting room on the first floor, watering plants and generally pottering about after breakfast. But, chiefly, she was waiting for the letters to come. It was as if, by reading things first, she could somehow spare John, her husband, some of the terrible shock. Like shielding a brother officer from a bullet, she felt that if the missile passed through her flesh first then it would be less terrible, less dangerous for her husband.

This house, the Old Hall, had been in the Digby family since 1470. It was a rambling ancient structure set around three sides of a courtyard, with a Georgian façade on the garden front. There was a great hall and a priest's hole, and a chapel where all the children since 1470 had been married. She had come to this house a bride of twenty and had not thought to leave it except in a coffin to be taken to the burial ground.

Jack's van was just coming to a halt when Isobel came down the staircase into the great hall with its sofas grouped around the fireplace and the grand piano in a corner under the mullioned window. Normally, Jack put the letters just inside the front door on the window seat that ran around the porch that was filled with boots and coats. Isobel was halfway across the hall when she saw John come round the corner of the house. He was wearing his usual gardening outfit of a vet's khaki coat, unbuttoned over a pair of ancient cords bought from Pontefract Farmers years ago. In his friendly way he stopped for a chat with Jack, giving no indication that he was worried about anything at all.

It had not been like this, Isobel thought, since the war when everyone was waiting for news, but it had been better then because it was something in common. In those days, tension had bound one to one's neighbours, but this Lloyd's thing was much worse than that because people who didn't know you or who knew you slightly felt that you deserved your ill-fortune. The idea of the filthy rich being strapped for a bit of cash generally delighted people, not the old indigenous population, but the new ones like the people who had bought General Curtis's old house when he had died last year. Micklethwaite, she thought they were called, whose fortune had been made out of the successful marketing of the inside of loo rolls, those cardboard things. Ghastly vulgarians who had installed jacuzzis in the bathrooms and gold taps and had pictures of ships in full sail on their drawing-room walls. Mrs Micklethwaite had stopped her in the village shop and had said, 'I'm so sorry to hear of your troubles'. How dare she! Then she had added, 'Of course, we were asked to join Lloyd's, but my husband said "Unlimited liability means just that, Wendy. You can't take chances with your cash."' Horrid woman, covered in gold, just like her bathrooms!

John took the post, several large white envelopes, and began to walk away round the side of the house with it. He had a tendency these days to go somewhere well away from the house to deal with it, presumably so that he could take in what had been said in the correspondence, compose himself, and then return to her.

This morning, unable to restrain herself, she caught up with him on the west front.

'John,' she said, slightly out of breath from hurrying, 'is there anything for me?'

'Nothing specifically for you,' he said, looking down at the letters in his hands, 'some things addressed to both of us. I thought I would open them.'

'Let me help you,' she said.

'It's perfectly all right, my dear.' She watched him square his shoulders.

'I want to know what's going on. It's much worse not knowing. Then one simply embroiders.'

'Very well. Indoors or out?'

'Let's go and sit on the bench in the arbour, shall we?'

'Good idea.'

Together they sat side by side.

'Fenton and Stanwright,' she said with a sigh, opening an envelope.

'John,' she said, after a minute, 'they want £350,000. Now.'

'Don't forget the man's coming from Christie's in York today,' he replied, 'to value the Veronese. If we sell that, we should be able to hang on a little longer.'

'Yes, I suppose so. I shall be so sad to say goodbye to that.'

The Veronese, bought by a Digby in the late seventeenth century when the religious persecutions had settled down a little and the family was able to concentrate on other things, was a portrayal of the raising of Lazarus. In it, Lazarus, his flesh the colour of putty, is raised from out of the pit by Christ dressed in a simple robe of white and gold. The Saviour is surrounded by a crowd of people, men and women, dressed in the rich brocades of sixteenth-century Venice, some of whom are raising their hands to their mouths in astonishment. The background is of a city set upon a river spanned by a bridge against a background of wooded hills. The sky is suffused with a brilliant flush of cloud as day moves towards dusk.

Isobel had looked at this painting every day of her life since she first came to the Old Hall. It hung behind the altar in the chapel and had always been a source of tremendous inspiration. Now it was going to have to be assessed and labelled by a man in a smart suit from an auction house. Then it would be crated and taken away to London and another piece of the past would exist only in the collective memory of the family. If the house went, then, in a sense, the family would cease to exist, so perhaps it was better to let the picture go, that picture with its prefiguring of the message of salvation.

'It'll look very odd without it,' he said. 'It's hung in the chapel since it was bought. Sometimes, Iso,' he said, 'I can't bear to think I'm the last.' He hung his head slightly so that she might not see his expression.

Instead, Isobel took his hand. 'I know.'

'I wake up in the night,' he went on, 'and I find I can't believe it. I can't believe these things have happened and that the estate that I thought I had done so well with is slipping from me. What is a family without its house? Nothing. Nothing.' He dashed away his tears with the back of his hand like a schoolboy.

'Wait until the young man has been to see the picture. It may be worth more than we thought.'

'Even if it is,' he said, 'it won't make any difference.'

'We must pray that it is. We must pray that it will make a difference.'

'You're right,' he said, 'I'm sorry. It's not like me to give way.'

'Everyone gives way sometimes. No one is super-human.'

Nevertheless it appalled her to see him like this. He had always been so strong. The family had survived persecutions, wars, even Labour governments, but it seemed as if they might not survive Lloyd's.

'I am going to see about luncheon,' said Isobel, rising. 'If he's young, he'll be hungry. The least we can do is feed him properly. Then I'm going to ring Tor and find out when her lot are arriving next week.'

'Tor and Edward have been hit by this too,' said John, also rising.

'I know they have. Chin up, my darling.'

'I'm going over to Runyons Farm to have a word with Martin about the tree planting scheme,' he said. 'I'll be back in time for Mr Charles Kindersley.'

He raised his hand then marched off across the lawn around the back of the house to the stables where his old Land Rover lived. There was nobody in the yard. The girl, Megan, who ran the stables as a livery, taking in horses and looking after them for other people, was nowhere to be seen. An old collie belonging to Megan lay in the sunlight on the cobbles. Somewhere a horse stamped and snorted.

He looked up towards the clock in the belvedere, noticing that the wind was coming from the west; it came to him then, staring at the old stable clock, that he would rather die than leave this place. It would kill him to have to sell up. Of course he knew this was the devil whispering in his ear, but sometimes the devil was so persuasive. He put the thought from him at once.

But it would not leave him. He had been born here and spent his boyhood running about the estate. He knew every dyke, every rocky outcrop, he knew where all the particularly treacherous bits of sinking bog were, he knew all the people in all the houses. He went away to school and then to war, but he always knew he would come back here and farm the estate as his father had done before him. His father had been the fifth son of Thomas Digby who had lost three sons in the Great War. The fourth son, Ivo, had been killed in a car crash in 1920. This last death had hastened the end of his grandfather who was said to have turned his face to the wall when he heard of Ivo's accident, rather like James V of Scotland. When old John had died, Christian Digby, John's father had inherited. Christian once said that he never felt the place was really his, that he was always haunted by the spectres of his brothers. How could anyone else live here? He couldn't answer that question.

Charles Kindersley arrived promptly at twelve o'clock, driving an estate car with a brown and white springer spaniel in the back.

'Do you want to let him out?' asked Isobel, going out to greet the new arrival.

'That would be kind,' said Charles Kindersley, a thin, dark, rather anxious-looking young man. 'I'm sorry to bring him but my wife's away at the moment and I can't leave him at home all day.'

'Of course not,' said Isobel. 'Take him around the garden, then we'll have a drink, and then you can go and have a look at the picture.'

'I've looked up the history of this place,' said Charles Kindersley, 'I must say it's quite fantastic how long the Digbys have been here.'

'Since 1470,' said Isobel, 'it is a long time.' Without meaning to, she sighed.

'I'm sorry,' he said, 'I hope I'm not blundering.'

'No, no, not at all.' Changing the subject she said, 'Did you live in Italy studying painting?'

'I was at the Courtauld and then I went to work in Florence, for Sotheby's as a matter of fact.'

'And now you've changed foot?'

'Yes. My father farms near York and I wanted to come back up here. As one does.'

Isobel smiled and he thought how handsome she was with her iron-grey curls, her good tweeds, those very blue rather large eyes.

After they had walked on a little further, he said, 'The painting is actually in the chapel, is that right?'

'Yes. Installed there when it was brought back by Henry Digby in 1690. Of course you know it's of the raising of Lazarus.'

'Yes,' he nodded.

'This part of the house was added by Henry's son, John, in 1750.' They were now walking along a terrace looking up at the house with its stucco Palladian façade and Doric columns.

'It's a curious house because it's such a hodge-podge of different styles.'

'Like Topsy,' he said, whistling for his dog.

'My husband said he would meet us in the chapel. Shall we go now? Your dog can stay in the porch although we wouldn't mind a bit if he came in. We've always had dogs at our services here.'

When they went into the chapel John was kneeling under a statue of the BVM at a side altar. Isobel cleared her throat and he looked around. He got up quickly and came forward to shake hands.

'Would you rather be left alone?' John asked, 'won't we be in the way?'

'Of course not,' said Charles Kindersley, who was extremely well brought up, 'it's entirely up to you. May I go and have a look?'

'Please do,' said John. 'I think we'll leave you here for half an hour and then come back.'

When they went to fetch him together Charles Kindersley looked worried.

'Look' he said, 'I'm awfully sorry to have to tell you this, but I think your Veronese is a copy, a very good copy, but a copy all the same.'

'What would that make it worth?' asked Isobel after a horrifying second had passed in which John had said nothing.

'Well,' he said, 'I'd have to get someone else in to have a look. I'd like to do that anyway, if you don't mind. Of course, I may be wrong. I won't stay to luncheon, if you don't mind,' he said. 'I ought to get back to the office and talk to someone about this, probably someone in London. I am sorry.'

'Don't be,' said Isobel, 'please. It's not your fault. Would you like the documentation that goes with the picture. I think you should see it anyway. John, don't you?'

'Yes,' John said, but he seemed dazed, as if he couldn't quite take on board what had been said.

Parry had met Sam at Oxford where Sam, a good Southern boy, had been on a Rhodes scholarship. Sam's mother, like Parry's, was dead. He too had a distant father, a retired general who lived in the mountains of North Carolina. Parry took Sam home to Knockfern where they spent days roving the coastline and the endless hills. Sam longed to be an artist but his father wanted him to go into the army. When he came home from Vietnam he insisted on being an artist and living in France. He realized the importance, he had told Parry, of doing what he had always wanted to do. It was a promise he had made to himself, he said, during his time in Vietnam. The retired general had not liked it but that, said Sam, was tough shit.

Sam, bless him, had left the key with the woman whose house abutted the studio. Parry buzzed the entry-phone at the gate and she came out of her door to see who it was; a good-looking, well-dressed young Parisienne in a smart suit, just home from the office herself by the looks of it.

'One second,' she said, 'I fetch the key. Come in.'

Parry obeyed, admiring her shapely calves and high heels. She looked like a woman should: sexy but dignified, a little provocative, but not tarty. He didn't like tarty women.

The studio was in the corner of a quiet square near the Place Pigalle, reached by walking up the rue des Martyrs. The area was full of brothels and bawdy houses but the square was solidly and aloofly middle class and could only be reached by passing through ornate but solid iron gates that were locked at night.

While Parry waited he looked along the flagged path towards the entrance to the studio which was lined with burgeoning, flowering shrubs. There was a strong smell of lilac. Sam's vast portrait studio had once been occupied by John Singer Sargent, and Parry liked to think of him standing at his easel in a suit and spats, smoking an expensive cigar. Girls in white dresses had rustled along this path, all parasols and bustles, their hair piled high under little, elaborate hats set at a tilt over their smooth young foreheads. How Sargent had loved those details of feminine attire: the corsage, the stomacher, the lace sleeve. He thought of the little satin foot of Carmen Cita, the singer, whose full-length portrait was now in the Quai d'Orsay; that foot had always fascinated him, the outline clear and yet, when you looked, it almost seemed to move in front of the canvas, receding in front of your very eyes.

'Voila, Monsieur!' The woman came back, brandishing the key. 'Sam says the door is a little stiff. You will have to give it a shove.' This, last, she said in English. She placed the key in the palm of his hand.

'Thanks very much,' said Parry, picking up his bag, 'that's awfully kind.'

As he went away down the path he thought gratefully that it was just as he remembered it when he last stayed here, a long time ago now: the short flight of steps leading to the gothic door, the overhanging lilac and laburnum.

It was so private here, so singular, so peaceful. As Parry put the key in the lock and turned it this way and that he had a sudden sense of himself as alive. He paused to listen to the distant blare and hoot of the traffic, the woman next door calling to her cat. Beyond this hidden corner of Montmartre lay the square with its shuttered buildings and cobbles and, further still, through a tall gate hedged in by equally tall spiked railings, the district of Pigalle: the strange little cinema with its mad lights designed by Cocteau, the tarts in doorways, the cinemas showing breathless, seedy films, the steep slope of the rue des Martyrs where he would go in the morning to buy food from the market, whose stalls lined either side of the street, marvelling as he always did at such greedy plenty, such piles of innards and entrails, such cheeses, so many vegetables. Day after day the miraculous renewal and resurrection of all this plenty. This is happiness he thought suddenly and was shocked: I am happy. He had forgotten what it felt like.

The stairs had the same abandoned, derelict look as ever. Again, Parry thought of Carmen Cita coming up here to see her lover, Sargent, veiled and in furs, standing boldly in the middle of the studio for her portrait and then, afterwards, undressing, shedding one lace-trimmed layer after another until she was naked. His view of Paris was still – he was amused to note – irretrievably *fin de siècle*: carmine lips, veiling, lace, toes of satin slippers peeping out from under petticoats.

The kitchen was at the top of the stairs before one went into the vast space of the studio. It was furnished with a few old cupboards that looked as if they almost might have been there in Sargent's time, and an ancient refrigerator that made a loud droning sound.

A note, next to the elderly gas cooker, said 'See you later. I'm painting an old hag in Saint-Germain, but will be back at the apartment at about half seven. Give Nance a ring when you arrive. Help yourself to anything you want. PS. There's a girl staying in the turret room called Caroline. She deals in antiquities and sometimes stays here. Tell her to come to supper too if she's back in time. Sam. Oh, and help yourself to anything you want.'

Parry put his bag down and looked in the fridge. Sam, true to his generous nature, had stocked up with what he considered to be the necessities of life: several bottles of white wine, two huge smoked sausages, wrapped in greaseproof paper, a large jar of olives, and a Pont-l'Évêque in its flimsy box. He took out a bottle of white Bordeaux and opened it with a corkscrew that was lying next to the note. Sam always knew what one would want first, bless him. Parry poured himself a glass of wine and then noticed the little bronze that an unseen hand had placed by the bread bin, for some reason. He picked it up and examined it. It was only a few inches high, maybe five or six, and was a representation of Mars, complete with cuirass and helmet, holding the symbolic shield closely associated with his cult. It was a beautiful and somehow a slightly sinister object. Parry, having examined it, put it back exactly where he had found it. He imagined that it must belong to the dealer in antiquities who was staying in the turret room, but why leave it here?

Mars, as Parry well knew, had been a fertility god, long before he had been adopted as the Roman god of war, and the father of Romulus and Remus. There was a legend that the *Mons Martyrum*, the Martyrs' Hill, was not named in honour of Saint-Denis and his companions but was really the *Mons Martis*, after a shrine to Mars.

He went down the narrow passageway that led to the studio. The big black-out blinds were at half-mast on the tall, north-facing windows and what remained of the daylight fell on the canvases stacked against the wall, the vast sofa covered in ancient kelims, where Parry would sleep, and Sam's enormous portrait painter's easel which had an unfinished canvas on it of a woman Parry recognized as Nancy; a naked, pregnant Nancy with her hands folded coyly over her pubic hair. To his chagrin he found himself aroused by the sight of Nancy's naked body, the beautiful curve of the stomach, the large breasts with their pinkish brown nipples. Nancy was slightly younger than Victoria and had had her first child, Franklin, only six months ago, when she and Sam had completely given up on ever having a child. Parry was godfather to this infant and one of the functions of his time in Paris was to attend his christening with Victoria next week.

Behind Parry was a huge stone sink full of brushes soaking and others neatly wrapped up in pieces of torn newspaper like curlers. Sam had always been the kind of painter who believed in clearing up after himself. No sixties chaos of old tubes of paint and filthy brushes prevailed in this studio. On the shelves above the stone sink was a vast range of glass jars containing pigment, pure, intense colours of the kind used by Italian painters in the early fourteenth century, colours which those painters had believed contained in themselves some of the essence of heaven. There was a pile of empty tubes waiting to be filled by Sam who ground all his own colours on a marble slab with a large glass pestle.

Holding his glass, Perry began to turn around some of the canvases that were facing the wall to see what Sam was up to. The third or fourth canvas he examined was of a lovely girl, a three-quarters-length portrait of her standing with one arm raised holding an apple and the other holding a mirror in which she was admiring herself. The lower half of her body was swathed in Fortuny-like draperies but the upper half was naked. She had lovely firm breasts with large nipples and a slender little rib-cage tapering into generous hips. Her pale hair was bobbed like a twenties flapper and her curiously light eyes stared out of the canvas as if aware of Parry's gaze. He turned the portrait back to face the wall feeling as if he had seen something he shouldn't have done. Extraordinary to have all those naked bodies exposed to you all the time like that. Lucky old devil.

The bath was one of those enamel boxes with a seat and a place for your feet. Parry turned on both taps which belched water hot. When he put his razor on the shelf over the basin, he noticed a pot of expensive-looking face cream sitting next to a silver toothbrush with a handle in the shape of a woman's body. He picked it up and looked at it, then put it back again, vaguely disconcerted by this evidence of femininity. Victoria was a soap and water girl. Pots like this did not abound in their bathroom at Easter House. In fact, he probably spent more on eau de cologne and badger bristle shaving brushes than Victoria ever spent on her face.

When he took off his clothes he realized as he looked at his stomach that he had lost weight lately. One had to go away to realize certain things about oneself, it seemed, and it was so quiet here, so unutterably peaceful. Easter House resembled a circus at this time of day with all the children supposedly doing their homework which meant asking endless questions of Victoria instead of getting on and looking things up for themselves, lazy brutes. TV was banned, but Tom and Cyprian would have some ghastly pop music blaring away in their bedroom while they attempted to work, although how anyone could work against a

73

background of such sound was quite beyond Parry. Victoria would be cooking supper and unpacking the shopping at the same time, as well as shouting at Feather who was always underfoot whenever there was food in the offing. Parry realized guiltily that he had no desire whatever to telephone home. He would do it later, he said to himself, when things had calmed down a bit and Victoria would be able to concentrate.

After his bath, Parry shaved and dressed, putting on green cords, a blue shirt and a green tweed jacket that he was fond of. He telephoned Nancy but got the engaged signal; no doubt she was blathering away to someone. These Americans regarded the telephone as an indispensable extension of their psyches. He remembered the key, found his hat, made sure he had enough money and let himself out. No sign of the other inhabitant of the studio, the mysterious girl, as he now found himself thinking of her. In the house by the gate there was music coming from the sitting room, Brahms, which Parry recognized, going on his way whistling slightly. He pulled the gate to behind him, hearing the oiled lock click satisfactorily into place.

The Parisian dusk filled him with a sense of expectancy. The cobbled square was quiet, the shuttered façades of the houses mysterious. He felt his spirits lift even further. For a moment he wondered whether he would have time to visit the church of Saint-Pierre where the most important event of his life had happened all those years ago, but then decided that he would wait until tomorrow. Then he would visit not only the church but also the cemetery where Father Charpentier, the priest he had sought out at Saint-Pierre, was buried amongst the urns and angels in the graveyard at Place Clichy.

He passed the clinic where Nancy had had Franklin, a large house, set back behind railings, the windows of the upper part all lit up. By the time Victoria had had the last child, she had begun to have her babies very fast indeed. Ben had been born in the ambulance on the way to Queen Charlotte's and for the last birth they had brought her in early which was just as well as the baby had turned out to be a Caesarian section. Parry could hear the sound of a baby crying coming from one of the upper floors of the clinic and hurried on. He hated that mewling urgent sound. He had had enough of all that to last him a lifetime.

He strolled more slowly up the rue des Martyrs before turning into the Place Pigalle. At night huge anatomical blow-ups of women hung suspended in the air above the square advertising the pleasures of the district. He passed several cinemas on his way, cramped little joints, squeezed between the grey façades of houses, glancing guiltily at the huge photographs in their windows before looking quickly away. He had forgotten the seedy sleazy atmosphere of the Pigalle. It stank of sex. Against his will he found himself excited by the furtive atmosphere, the glimpses of breast and pelt, the women in dark doorways reaching out to him as he passed.

At the same time he was aware that he felt more alive than he had done for years. Paris was a very mineral city; the great grey buildings pleased him, some of them built on sites so ancient they beggared belief, Roman and pre-Roman. In the nineteenth century he knew that this part of Paris had been mined for plaster of Paris and now, beneath the streets, lay a honeycomb of old mine workings, making new building impossible. He wondered if there were not some parallel in his own life with this image of the city with its intricate but fragile foundation that might crumble altogether if too much stress were placed on it, but dismissed this as fanciful.

Paris pleased him. Of all cities it was most alive: it crawled and seethed with life; the bodies of couples making love, the shining entrails of fish and beasts in the market in the rue Lepic, the fact that the bars stayed open all night. Even if you weren't there, someone else was, leaning on the bar, drinking, being alive, alive-o. It was a city that gushed life like a fountain, or like a wound, pouring blood. Parry stopped for a second in the middle of the pavement, astonished at himself. It was as if he were thinking the thoughts of another Parry, a different, much younger man.

He stopped in a bar where Sam often drank wondering if he might be there, but the place was full and it was difficult to see into corners through the smoke and the press of bodies. A game of mini-foot was in full swing in one corner. Parry ordered himself a large pastis – which he only ever drank in Paris – and stood at the bar trying not to drink too fast.

As he was about to go, Sam came through the door with a girl, the girl Parry had seen in the painting holding an apple and a looking glass. Parry stared at her. She was very pretty, much prettier in the flesh than even in Sam's exquisite painting. Because he had had a stolen glimpse of her, Parry felt familiar with her. She seemed to be somebody he already knew.

'Edward!' Sam clasped Parry to him in the continental fashion which Parry secretly disliked. Rather like the 'peace' in church it seemed to him showy and insincere. The girl stood back, watching them with a look of suppressed amusement on her face.

Sam, as large and as bearded as ever, with very blue eyes and huge wrists like pink hams, was wearing his familiar uniform of antique tweed jacket worn old and smooth by the passage of aeons, a cream-coloured shirt missing a button with frayed collar and cuffs of similar antiquity to the jacket and a pair of linen trousers held up by a piece of rope, trousers that might once have been dark-blue but which had been blanched to this no-colour by a thousand Parisian laundries. On his feet Sam wore the customary pair of size twelve brogues that had once belonged to his father. In the pocket of the jacket his trademark Montblanc pen.

'Edward, I want you to meet Caroline de Belleroche,' he pronounced her Christian name in the French fashion, 'who is also staying at the studio. Did you get my note?'

'Enchanté,' said Parry, shaking hands and trying to conceal his surprise. For some reason he had thought Caroline must be English, a Carrie or a Caro.

'Are you a descendant of Henri de Belleroche?' he asked in French.

'The artist, you mean?' she replied, in English.

'The one who was friendly with Brangwen.'

'Yes,' she said, 'as a matter of fact I am.'

Again, he was struck by the lightness of her eyes and the way she appraised him without giving anything of herself away.

'Caroline has an English mother and a French father,' said Sam, 'but she was educated in both places.'

'And do your parents live somewhere near Orange?' asked Parry.

'Quite near,' she said, 'but the other side of Rhône. Orange, as you probably know, has been totally devastated by traffic. I don't know why they allow it.'

'I haven't been there for such a long time,' said Parry. 'I remember the Roman arch and the amphitheatre, of course. I remember it as being quite lovely.'

She smiled politely at this.

'Can I buy you a drink?' asked Parry.

'No, no,' said Sam, 'this is my shout.' He turned to the bar to order.

'How's Victoria?' he asked, over his shoulder, 'and the kids? Edward here has more kids than anyone else I know,' he added, for Caroline's benefit.

'How many do you have?' she asked.

'Five,' said Parry, feeling embarrassed.

'That is a lot of children,' she said, and again Parry noticed the colourlessness of her eyes. They were like pools of clear water, but at the same time there was an opacity about her that made it difficult to read her expression. She was guarded, watchful.

'Is that your bronze in the kitchen?' Parry asked.

'Yes. Did you like it?'

'Of course,' said Parry. Whether he liked it or not seemed irrelevant. 'It's Roman, isn't it?'

'Yes.'

'What are you going to do with it?'

'Sell it.'

'Where did you find it?'

'In Arles.'

'Ah.' Parry looked away. He could not go on staring at this girl whom he felt he knew but whom he did not know. The breasts, the eyes, the high cheekbones, the mouth; it was as if he had already made love to her in his dreams. He could not remember when he had been so attracted to a girl, which of course in his position he had absolutely no business to be. He had a sudden sensation of losing his footing, of being swept away beyond his control. Of course her pose in that oil had been a copy of the famous Roman bronze, the Venus of Arles.

'Edward here is as familiar with the Roman landscape, the Roman world, should I say, as the Romans themselves were,' said Sam.

'Oh,' said Caroline, 'why is that?'

'I've always had a passion for it, since I was a boy,' said Parry. 'Don't ask me where it came from.' He hauled his trousers up as he spoke, a bad habit he had. 'you must be pretty familiar with it yourself, aren't you, doing what you do?'

'Yes, I am, I suppose. But there is always more to learn, don't you think?'

'That goes without saying.' Under the light conversation he could sense a steeliness in her. Somehow she was managing to communicate to him that she was not particularly impressed by anything she had so far heard about him.

'When I was much younger,' said Parry, 'long before I was married, I used to spend summers down in that part of the world, Nîmes, Arles, Orange, just walking, sketching, looking.'

'So you got to know the lie of the land pretty well?'

Again, the sense of being humoured, mocked, by someone twenty, *thirty*?, years younger than he. How old was she? It was impossible to tell, but possibly twenty-two or twenty-three. Nubile, beautiful. She wore a waisted tweed jacket held together by a safety pin and a short red tweed skirt; long slim legs in black stockings, high-heeled lace-up shoes, very sexy. He felt like a schoolboy with his tongue hanging out. Pathetic, ridiculous.

He took the glass Sam pushed towards him and drank. Slow down, he said to himself, slow down, get a grip of yourself. Ignoring Caroline, he said to Sam, 'Who's the client in Saint-Germain, "the old hag"?'

'Some rich old biddy,' said Sam, 'American of course. Pure Wharton. Came to Paris before the war in search of excitement – found it of course during the Occupation – stayed ever since. Limitless cash – you name it, she's got it. There's a Rubens by the front door, a butler, a cook, little dogs. She sits for me in ice-pink chiffon and diamonds. I feel sick every time I look at her, but there you are. It's cash.'

'Does she want to sleep with you?' asked Caroline.

'I should think it's healed over,' said Sam, 'sorry, that's vulgar, but she's had so many lifts and tucks that her sexual organs must be located somewhere towards her ears.'

Parry guffawed but Caroline said, 'Poor old thing. She sounds a pathetic specimen. I think you should introduce me. I might be able to sell her something.'

'She's tight,' said Sam, 'like all the rich. I had hell's own job getting the deposit out of her.'

'Let me try,' she said, 'please darling.' She put her hand on his wrist, a slightly sunburnt hand, brown against the ruddy pink of Sam's skin. Parry felt his heart lurch. Were they lovers? None of his business of course. Sam always used to sleep with his models, but perhaps Nancy had put a stop to all that, although, as Parry well knew, some women went off sex rather after childbirth and Caroline was so gorgeous. Stop it, he said to himself once more, draining his glass. Just stop it.

'I'll think about it,' Sam said, putting his arm around her and pulling her to him. 'OK?'

'OK,' she smiled up at him from within his grasp.

Parry looked away.

'One more,' said Sam, 'and then home.'

'Let me,' said Edward.

'Not for me,' said Caroline, 'I've got some things to do before the shops shut.'

'You are coming to supper?' said Sam, 'aren't you?'

Parry was suddenly sure she would say that she had to go and meet someone.

'Is that all right?' she asked, 'you really don't have to.'

'We'll go out,' said Sam. 'Nancy's organized a sitter in honour of my very old friend Edward here.'

'That would be lovely,' she said. 'Shall I come to the apartment or shall I meet you somewhere?'

'Nine thirty,' said Sam, 'in that little Moroccan joint in rue Lepic. Nancy's crazy about it. Said she'd book a table.'

'See you there,' said Caroline, picking up her bag which lay on the floor at her feet. She did not look at Edward.

'Great girl that,' said Sam, when she had gone, 'but dangerous,' he added, as if in answer to something Parry had said.

'What do you mean?'

'I'll tell you. I met Caroline when I painted her mother. Beautiful woman, Caroline's really like her, but both of them made a play for me.'

'I don't believe you,' said Parry enviously 'you're making it up.'

'I swear it's true. Caroline likes older men, she told me so.'

'And . . . did you?'

'Of course not,' said Sam. 'I was tempted, but I'm not that stupid. I know a siren when I see one, mother or daughter.'

'Very out of character,' Parry said sourly.

'Hey!' said Sam, touching Parry lightly on the shoulder, 'hey, that's enough of that. How are you, old friend? You seem a little down. How are things in merrie England? You never told me how Victoria's getting on and all those kids of yours. We have to talk.'

'We're being nobbled by Lloyd's,' said Parry, 'so any money we have goes straight out again. It's so bloody depressing and worrying.'

'That's awful,' said Sam. He always forgot how incredibly English Edward was, like a character out of Wodehouse. 'How's Victoria taking it?'

'All right,' said Parry, 'better than me really. It's because of her we're in this jam.'

'But hey!' said Sam, 'if I remember right you made a lot of money in the first few years, didn't you? Don't blame Victoria, she's a great girl, is Victoria. She puts up with you which must be something.'

'Quite,' said Parry, hauling up his trousers.

'Are you blaming her?'

'Of course not,' said Parry, swigging his pastis as if it were going out of fashion. He didn't want one of these American heart-to-hearts, honest Joe sessions that Americans indulged themselves in. He wasn't a 'new man' and never would be.

'Well, I sure hope you aren't,' said Sam. 'It's going to be great to see her next week. When's she coming?'

'Today week,' said Parry. 'I have things to do here. There's a client of Tom's I have to see who has got a great many items to dispose of, plus two or three people of my own. Tom has high hopes of this particular man, de Fonville, his name is.'

'Not old Gaby de Fonville?'

'That's the one.'

'Well, I don't know him but I know *of* him, as you English would say. He lives in a fantastic apartment near the Invalides full of incredible pictures and books and *objets d'art*.'

'Has he much money?'

'How can you tell?' said Sam, draining his glass. 'Even if he hadn't you wouldn't know. There's a pretty girl, my God, gorgeous.'

'Where?'

'By the door.'

'You never give up, do you?' said Parry. 'How's Nancy?'

'Nancy's just great,' said Sam, 'a little plump still after the baby, but just great.'

Parry glanced at his old friend whom he had known through so many amorous adventures. Sam had always liked his women thin, whereas he, Parry, had always liked plumpness. How ironic that he should end up with a wife who was as thin as a rail. It wasn't as if she didn't eat either, she just didn't seem to put on weight.

'She'll soon lose that,' said Parry.

'Oh sure. It's just that . . .'

'What?'

'Well, she isn't so keen on it all these days.'

'That's babies for you,' said Parry, 'I should know.' And he did. How the six weeks after the birth stretched to twelve or, after Teresa, eighteen, twenty, he couldn't remember. How, just at the moment you turned to your wife in bed, the baby cried. The smell of milk, the faint farmyard stench in his dressing room from the nappies, the way children took over your life and made you number two or three or four on your wife's list for attention.

'Having a baby is the best contraceptive there is.'

'Right,' said Sam with feeling, giving Parry a look, 'OK. How long will it take?'

'Depends.'

'There's no one else if that's what you mean,' said Sam, 'and even if there were it wouldn't be Caroline. I'm just not that dumb.'

'I don't know why you keep referring to her,' said Parry.

'Oh come on, Edward, I saw the way you looked at her!'

'Nonsense,' blustered Parry, 'don't be ridiculous, I have a wife and five children.'

'Since when did that ever stop a man?'

'How long is she staying in Paris for?'

'A few more days, I guess, then she's going south again. She does business in Nîmes a lot and likes to use the house in Le Pin.' This was Sam's house in a little village near Uzes. 'She's a good tenant, but I haven't a clue what she gets up to when she's down there. I hear things, but I don't ask too many questions.'

'What exactly is the nature of her business?' Parry asked cautiously.

'She's a dealer and a restorer,' said Sam, 'and she goes poking about that part of the world finding things here and there.'

'Is it legal? Doesn't sound it.'

Sam shrugged. 'Those are the questions I don't ask,' he said. 'Life's too short.'

Outside, it was growing dark. Parry was struck by the strange glimmer in the air; spring running in the veins of the city. Mars had once been a god of the spring, a god of fertility. On this hill bulls and goats had been sacrificed to him. If one listened in the quiet of the dawn one would probably still hear the faint echoes of the death shrieks of those dying beasts; the blood running in the gutters.

They went up a flight of steps towards Sam's apartment in the rue Caulaincourt and stopped to look back over the city. All the great buildings were lit from below: the long roofline of the Louvre, the Eiffel Tower, the Pantheon, the churches: Sacré-Cœur very close, Saint-Sulpice very much further.

'I envy you,' Parry heard himself saying, 'living here.'

'You do? I thought you loved your own river view at Chiswick.'

'I do,' said Parry, 'I'm very fond of it . . .'

'But you're stale,' said Sam. 'I know the feeling. If you live anywhere long enough you stop seeing it.'

He's right, Parry thought. When did I last look at the river without a feeling of lead in my heart? It seemed that there had been too much sorrow for him to look straight at things from the staircase window of Easter House any longer. One had to go away to see straight or to see, as once he had seen from his own home, a view tinged with elation.

Sam and Nancy lived in a flat on the top floor of a high old building with no lift. The small hallway of the apartment was crammed with a baby buggy, two carrier bags full of empty bottles, an artist's palette standing on its side, and an empty picture frame.

'Come through,' Nancy called from the sitting room, 'I'm here with Franklin.'

Parry followed Sam down the narrow little passage to the sitting room at the end, wondering how on earth they managed a baby in such cramped surroundings. He was used to broad hallways, wide staircases, a garden. The windows of the sitting room looked out high over the rue Caulaincourt to the trees belonging to the old gardens of the villas on the other side of the road.

Nancy was seated on a low chair of the kind that had been in Parry's night nursery when he was a boy. She wore a pair of wide-legged black trousers made out of some silken material and a black T-shirt pushed up on one side to reveal part of a large white breast and the back of the baby's bald head covered with a few wisps of blond hair.

Victoria had never breast-fed any of the children in public and Parry was slightly shocked to find that he was aroused by the sight of Nancy sitting there so casually. Of course, she was an American.

'Hi, Edward,' she said, 'I'm a little immobilized at the moment as you can see. How are you? Good journey?'

'Yes, very good, thank you,' Parry replied, clearing his throat. 'How's the baby?'

'Big and hungry,' said Nancy. 'He bites my nipple sometimes really hard. I don't know how to stop him. What did Victoria do?'

'I haven't a clue,' said Parry uneasily. 'Smacked him or her, I should think.'

'You can't smack a baby,' said Nancy in horrified tones. 'Surely not!'

'I'm afraid I can't really remember,' said Parry. 'It all seems rather a long time ago.'

'But . . .' began Nancy and then stopped. She had been about to mention the unmentionable, but one glance at Edward's face made her realize that she was stumbling in a minefield.

'How is Victoria?' she asked instead.

'Oh fine, very well,' said Parry.

'And the kids?'

'Oh, they're all splendid, quite splendid, thanks.'

'Still in that lovely house?'

'Yes, absolutely.'

'Sit down, Edward,' said Nancy. 'Sam will get you a drink. I'll just finish feeding and then I'll get him to bed. It all takes such an age.'

She smiled at Parry over the baby's head and he thought she looked much the same in spite of dealing with a baby rather late, only tired around the eyes and mouth. She had the brown eyes and freckled skin of a typical redhead, although it was hard to see if she had put on weight or not from the clothes she was wearing. He rather felt that Sam shouldn't be disloyal to his wife over such a small matter, but then Sam had always been obsessed by appearances in a way Parry considered immature. Nancy had been a typical girlfriend of Sam's in appearance before she became his wife: lean, tall, outdoorsy, the kind of woman who wore T-shirts and jogging pants around the house and who tied her cloud of thick wiry hair back with one of those wooden hairslides. Not the kind of girl who wore make-up or nail varnish but rather the American model of beauty, athletic and scrubbed with a wide, white expensive smile. There was nothing about her to remind one of Aphrodite whatsoever; she was more of an Amazonian type or an Athena.

'He's a fine fellow, isn't he?' asked Sam, coming in with a bottle and some glasses.

'He is indeed,' said Parry. 'Does he keep you up at nights?'

'Not really,' said Nancy. 'If he cries we just get him in bed with us.'

'But can you sleep?'

'Sure,' said Nancy. 'We like it and he likes it. Don't we, sweetie?' she said to Sam.

'Oh yeah, sure,' said Sam, taking the cork out of the bottle.

The baby was making gasping, sucking noises.

'I think he's had enough,' said Sam.

'Have you, sweetie?' asked Nancy, sitting him up. 'See your godson,' she said to Parry, turning the baby around on her knee.

Parry waggled his fingers feebly at the baby who reminded him of nothing so much as a bald-headed eagle.

'Have a cuddle with him,' said Nancy, putting her hands under Franklin's arms.

'Oh well, I . . .'

'See!' exclaimed Nancy, 'he's holding his arms out to you, aren't you, treasure?'

She planted a kiss on the baby's head.

Parry took the baby and held him on his shoulder. He was bigger now than Teresa had been when she died, but of course he was reminded of the vanilla smell of her, the wriggling limbs, the smooth, smooth cheek. He handed the baby back abruptly to Nancy. Franklin, disturbed by the commotion and the swift exchange of arms, began to cry.

'All right then, all right then,' said Nancy, cradling the baby in her arms. 'Maybe it's your bedtime, sweetheart.'

'How the hell did you cope with five of them?' asked Sam when Nancy had gone out of the room.

'I didn't really,' said Parry, 'Victoria did most of it. And we had nannies. We had money in those days for such things.'

'Of course,' Sam said, 'you Brits always have nannies. I'd forgotten that. Where the hell would we put a nanny in this place?'

'You don't need a nanny with one,' said Parry. 'One's a doddle, believe me.'

'Not financially it's not. With Nancy not working we're really pushed for cash. That's why Caroline's renting the turret room. She insists.'

'Does she pay rent for Le Pin as well?'

'She insists on that too. I feel embarrassed about it, but she's such a great tenant – takes care of the place as if it were her own – that I can't turn her down.'

'There's nothing wrong with not having any money, is there?'

'C'mon Edward, don't be so British. Having no money is emasculating, admit it! Money is freedom, freedom to do what you want when you want.'

Parry did not answer this, but Sam's words burst in his mind with all the force and glamour of a Catherine wheel. Freedom. To do what you liked when you liked. He had been shackled for so long to the ideals of family and faith that he had forgotten what freedom felt like.

'So,' said Sam, 'what are your plans? We might go to the Louvre together in the morning. I haven't got a sitter tomorrow.'

'Good idea,' said Parry. 'I must telephone de Fonville first thing and arrange to see him, but that's the only pressing thing I have to do. I'm supposed to be resting up a little.'

'Why?'

'Been overdoing things slightly.'

'Ah,' said Sam, gazing ruminatively at his old friend. It was impossible to detect from what Edward said how he was feeling; instead, one had to indulge in detective work, disinterring and reexamining every remark from several different angles. 'Overdoing things' in Parry-speak could mean anything from mild stress to terminal illness. Edward seemed not so much tired to Sam as on edge.

'They've cleaned the Veronese of the *Marriage Feast at Cana*,' said Sam, 'you'll love it. It looks incredible.'

'I hope they haven't overdone it.'

'No, no. It's truly wonderful, magical. Just wait.'

'What else?'

'They've rehung the Marie de Medici series. Again, fantastic. Quite amazing.'

The buzzer went.

'That'll be Carmen, the baby-sitter,' said Sam. 'I'll let her in. Have some more wine, Edward.'

When Sam had gone out of the room, Parry got up and went to the window. There was a little balcony of ironwork reached by a French window which was already slightly open. Parry stepped out and leaned his elbows on the balcony. Far beneath he watched a couple embrace and then pull apart. Both the man and the woman had short, dark hair. She wore a tiny, belted mini-raincoat. She began to walk away. He said something that made her turn back and kiss him again, not on the cheek either, but full on the mouth. This was, after all, Paris, the capital of love, Parry thought sourly. He wondered how those lovers would react if he were to hurl himself like a cannonball from this height and land at their feet in an explosion of blood and shattered bone. Would that particular couple ever afterwards look up before they kissed?

The restaurant consisted of old-fashioned panelled booths painted dark brown with etched glass panels above. A huge fan turned slowly in the ceiling although it was not particularly warm. There was a long, mirrored bar with a comfortingly enormous range of bottles, and Moroccan waiters in ankle-length aprons.

'I just adore this place,' said Nancy, when they were seated, 'it's pure Tangiers, don't you think, rather Paul Bowles.'

'Marvellous,' said Parry distractedly, gazing around him at the fashionably bohemian crowd who occupied the other tables.

'Caroline's late, as usual,' said Sam. 'I shouldn't have let her go, I knew it. Once you leave go of Caroline she vanishes. She has her own sense of time.'

'Here she is now,' said Nancy, waving vigorously. 'Not so late, after all. You must have impressed her, Edward.'

'I think that's rather unlikely,' murmured Parry, knowing he had not, but flattered nevertheless.

'Sorry,' said Caroline, sitting down opposite Parry in the booth. She pushed her pale hair out of her eyes, accepted a drink, then lit a cigarette, offering one to Parry as well.

'Thanks,' he said.

'I didn't think you smoked, Edward,' said Nancy reprovingly.

'I don't,' said Parry, 'except very occasionally, and always op's.'

'What's "op's"?' said Nancy.

'Other people's,' Caroline answered for him, catching his eye and laughing. Now he was in favour it seemed. Nancy was right. He wondered what her game was. Blow hot, blow cold. Well, damn her, he thought, he wasn't going to be blown hither and yon by the whims of some girl scarcely older than his daughter Mary.

'Edward is going to see Gaby de Fonville,' Sam said to Caroline. 'Caroline knows him too.'

'Everyone knows Gaby, don't they?' she replied coolly.

'I don't,' said Nancy, who was feeling excluded from the conversation by undercurrents she couldn't quite follow.

'Come on, Caroline,' said Sam, 'own up.'

'To what?'

'Oh well,' Sam shrugged and summoned the waiter. 'Do you want drinks first or shall we go straight to the wine?'

'Wine,' said Parry, 'I've got to work tomorrow.' He glanced at Caroline, wondering what her connection with de Fonville was and why she did not wish to divulge it.

'You know him well?' he asked, avoiding Sam's gaze.

'He's a friend of my father's,' said Caroline. 'And, yes, I do know him well. Is he trying to sell you something?'

'That's the general idea. He's really an old friend of my partner's, but Tom wanted me to come instead. He told me de Fonville is very charming and rather slippery.'

'He's very charming,' she said, 'but he's not a crook.'

'I didn't mean to imply that he was.'

'He has the most amazing apartment,' said Sam, seeing Parry

bristle, 'I told you about it, stuffed with *objets de vertu*. He's always buying and selling, so I believe.'

'Trading, swapping, exchanging's in his blood,' said Caroline, 'he's part-Lebanese. French father, Lebanese mother. I'll take you to meet him,' she said to Parry, 'if you would like.'

'Well,' he said reluctantly, not wanting to be ruder than he could help, 'the thing is, I already have . . .'

'I can assure you,' she said, 'that things would go very much better if I were to introduce you.'

'Why?' asked Nancy.

'He likes girls,' said Caroline simply, 'much more than men.'

'Look,' said Parry impatiently, 'it's complicated, I'll explain to you later.'

He was suddenly tired of her and her games, and just tired generally. It was one of those days that seemed to have lasted the length of three normal ones.

'The cous-cous is wonderful,' said Nancy, 'and the mutton stew.'

'I'll have that then,' said Parry, suddenly too exhausted to care. He drank some wine and glanced at his watch. It was ten o'clock, nine in England.

'I ought to ring Victoria,' he said, 'she'll be wondering if I got here safely.'

'There's a phone in the basement,' said Nancy, 'by the toilets. Have you change?'

'Yes, yes,' Parry replied, getting up. He felt anxious and rather rattled. Just tired, that's all. Long day. He remembered Mary's school fees as he went down the stairs and the letter from Fenton and Stanwright. Suddenly, phoning home seemed not such a good idea. He didn't want to have an argument with Victoria when he was tired and she was tired at the end of a long day. Better do it in the morning. He went into the gents and peed half-heartedly into the stained urinal. He washed his hands carefully and held them under the blower to dry until every drop of water had gone, by which time he reckoned enough minutes would have elapsed to provide evidence for a civilized nuptial phone call.

'All well?' enquired Nancy.

'Fine, thanks.'

'Is she looking forward to coming to Paris?'

'No,' said Parry, without thinking, 'I mean yes, of course. It'll be a marvellous break for her.'

'What about the children?' asked Nancy.

'Going to Yorkshire to their grandparents who have plenty of room, thank God.'

'My mother hasn't even seen Franklin,' said Nancy wistfully. 'Sam won't let me ask her over.'

'Where would we put her?' said Sam, rolling his eyes in mock-horror. 'She can't sleep on the sofa in the studio, unlike Edward here, and we haven't room.'

'You could put her in the turret room,' said Caroline.

'No, no,' Sam shook his head. 'She's American. She can't stand discomfort. The bathroom would be enough to make her call for the health inspector straight away.'

'See what I'm up against,' said Nancy, shaking her head.

'Nancy's mother thinks Paris is a den of iniquity,' said Sam. 'She has a vision of it as Hemingway mixed with Anaïs Nin with a dash of opium thrown in.'

'Sounds rather tame to me,' said Caroline, and everyone laughed, including Parry.

With another of those sharp shifts of mood with which the day had been punctuated, he began, suddenly, to enjoy himself again.

They talked of the south, of Le Pin, where Sam's house was and where Caroline lived most of the time; that sleepy village dominated by the church and the hot, silent Place, the bead curtain of the only café clattering as one person after another passed in or out, the dogs that came out of the vineyards in the evening to lie on the warm tarmac.

Parry had known those villages of southern Provence long before he was married, and to talk of them again gave him both pain and pleasure. He had taken Victoria there on a walking tour (Parry despised the word 'holiday' which seemed to him to be something people in tour buses did) not long after Tom's birth –

(the babies had been left in Yorkshire with a nanny) but she had been exhausted after the births and not strong enough to keep up with him which had made him impatient with her. He had so much wanted to show her the glories of Caesar's 'province': the cypress trees, the apricot dusks, the Guigou skies, the baked tile roofs that echoed the furrowed fields, those avenues of plane trees that one saw behind one's eyes when half asleep in bed, but she had been just too tired to enjoy it all; too tired and too hot with a brain gone soft with hormones, he remembered thinking. The whole thing had been rather a disaster and had ended with them taking the train to Paris on non-speaks.

Outside, Sam said, 'Who's for a night-cap?'

'I guess I'd better get back,' said Nancy, 'I don't want to leave him too long.' She put her hand to her breast without realizing it.

'Just a quickie,' said Sam, 'come on, Nance, otherwise we never get to see one another without the kid in tow.'

'I can't,' she said. 'I can't. Sam,' she said, pleadingly, 'please try to understand.'

'OK,' said Sam, 'I understand. We'd better go back,' he said, sounding fed up. 'Edward, I'll meet you at the studio in the morning around ten and we can go off to the Louvre, OK?'

'That's fine by me,' said Parry. 'You go.' He put his hand on his friend's arm. 'She needs you,' he said, 'we'll go out tomorrow night and have some fun.'

'Sure,' said Sam, grinning. 'Sleep well. *A demain*,' he said to Caroline, and kissed her on both cheeks.

'Be a good girl,' he added, 'and go and get your beauty sleep.'

'What else do you think I'm going to do?' she asked.

'Edward will see you home,' Sam said, 'you can depend on Edward.'

'I'm perfectly capable of seeing myself home, thank you,' she said, in French.

'You understand, Edward, don't you?' Nancy whispered, kissing him. 'I'm sure Victoria was the same. You just have to get home to the baby.'

'She was,' he said, kissing her freckled cheek, 'she still is.'

When they had gone, Parry said to Caroline, 'We should have

91

a nightcap. My first night in Paris, I can't just fold it up and put it away. I haven't been here for so long.'

'OK,' she said, 'I know a good bar, near the studio, open late, you'll like it.'

'Where?'

'In the Place du Calvaire. Do you know it?'

'Yes.'

'Come with me then,' she took his hand and began to run with him up the rue Lepic.

They were both laughing like school children as people got out of their way or looked after them in astonishment.

'It is not dignified to run,' she said in French, as they slowed up to turn into the rue des Abbesses, 'not sexy.'

'Who cares about that,' he said, 'it's fun. I haven't run for too long. Race you to the end,' he said, but she was quicker than he, long-legged and swift.

'You won't have a heart attack, will you?' she said, waiting for him panting. 'You're just the right age, I'm sure.'

'Don't be so insulting. I'm extremely fit for my age.'

'Which is?'

'Fifty.'

'Ah, then you are the same age as Gaby.'

'The famous Gaby.' They were still talking French.

'Not so famous as all that,' she said. 'Where did you learn your French?'

'At school.'

'You must have been well taught.'

'I was.'

'Where was school?'

'Eton. And you?'

'The Lycée, Cheltenham Ladies' College, then the Courtauld. You were Cambridge, I suppose?'

'Oxford.'

'Same difference.'

'Certainly not!'

He began to chase her again and they ended up in the next street along, red-faced and sweating.

'Nancy's gone very broody,' she said. 'I think Sam's incredibly bored by all that baby stuff.'

'Men are.'

'You were?'

'Of course. But my wife is very capable, very good with the children.'

'So you didn't have to do so much then?'

'I did my bit.'

'What's she like – your wife?'

'Why?'

He didn't want to talk about Victoria now, least of all now. Talking about her made him feel guilty and he did not want to feel guilty because, out of long habit, guilt would make him stop and analyse why he was feeling guilty and he did not want to do that. Not now. He wanted the headlong momentum of the night to continue without check. He did not any longer wish to think about the past, about endings or beginnings.

'I'm just curious about people,' she said, slowing her pace.

'There's nothing to tell,' he said.

'Oh, go on. Spoilsport.'

'There's nothing to say,' he heard himself sounding quite savage.

'Sorry. I'm sorry.'

'It's all right.' Her face was very close to his.

'What about de Fonville?'

'What about him?' Now it was her turn to sound offended.

'You were very cagey about him.'

'No.'

'Yes, you were.'

'What's it to you?'

'Nothing.' He made a gesture with his hands. *Rien de tout.*

'Here's the bar. Café du Calvaire. I always like that. This continental business of eating and drinking and practising usury around the stations of the cross. The Banco di Santo Spirito – how unEnglish that is,' she said, in English, and laughed at his face.

'You look so shocked,' she said.

93

'Are you a Catholic?'

'Yes. Are you?'

'Yes.'

'Practising?'

'Yes. You?'

'No. But it never leaves you. What will you have to drink?'

'Wine, I think. Better not to go back to Pernod now.'

'How cautiously dull. I'm going to have brandy. Or Armagnac. Better still. Wouldn't you rather have a delicious Armagnac with me?'

'Yes,' he said, 'yes, all right.'

Was he, he wondered, 'cautiously dull?' Was that what he had become?

'After all,' she said, as if reading his thoughts, 'we've got all night. No wife waiting for you to return.'

Was it not possible that for one evening one could have no past? Parry looked away into the corner of the bar where a man and a woman sat very close together. They were kissing. Every couple in this wretched city seemed to be engaged in a love drama of one kind or another. It was in the air. Paris. Capital of Love.

When they were in bed, and Franklin was settled in his wooden rocking crib by their side, Sam wanted to make love but Nancy didn't. She was too tired and her mind was too full of pictures of their evening to be able to concentrate on Sam. Her breasts hurt and her back ached from all that leaning over the crib, hauling her heavy baby up and down. She wanted to talk for a little and then sleep.

'I hope it's safe to leave Edward and Caroline alone together,' she said in a low voice. 'You know her reputation. Ramsay still asks me about her.'

Ramsay was Nancy's brother who had had to be packed off back to his wife in North Carolina pronto after too much exposure to Caroline's sex appeal. Sam had chosen not to mention this to Parry because he had felt it made him appear to be a hick like old Ramsay, sort of by association. The old world devouring the new and spitting out the pieces it didn't want. That was Caroline at her worst.

'He's a big boy now,' said Sam, 'he can take care of himself, I guess. Anyway, he's still got his religion to protect him. In the old days he was as much of a predator as Caroline is. No woman was safe with Edward in the old days.'

'What changed him?'

'I dunno exactly,' said Sam, rolling over towards his wife and putting his hand on her stomach under the little lawn shift she wore in bed. 'But he got God bad twenty years ago.' He began to stroke the inside of her thigh.

'Or God got him, you mean,' said Nancy, catching her breath in spite of being resolved to sleep.

'What's the difference?'

'I always think . . . these priests are adding notches to their score,' said Nancy, 'collecting . . . souls like scalps.'

'For Edward it was real,' said Sam, 'as real as this. He had a genuine conversion experience, like you're about to have, he told me once and . . .'

'You shouldn't say things like . . .'

As Sam began to kiss her neck, the baby let out a small cry.

'Shhhh,' said Nancy, pushing him away, 'Sam! Don't wake him,' she whispered.

'I'm not waking him,' Sam murmured, 'I'm making love to you. Maybe he's jealous.'

As the baby began to cry in earnest, drawing loud, shuddering breaths, each increasing in volume, Sam remembered what Edward had said about babies being the best contraceptive there is.

'Let him cry,' said Sam, as he felt Nancy sit up, 'can't he sleep in the other room?'

'I can't,' said Nancy, sitting up, pushing her nightie down. She was upset by these conflicting demands, these males wanting different things from her.

'Jesus,' said Sam angrily, 'I don't know how Edward went through this five times.'

'Six,' said Nancy. 'In case you forgot, the last baby died.'

95

'Six, then.'

'I'll tell you how,' said Nancy, coming back to bed with the baby, pushing her nightie down so that he could feed, 'money, that's how. Money is space, money is nannies. They live in that enormous house, they can afford to.'

'Not any more,' said Sam, gazing at the back of his son's head pressed to his wife's white breast and thinking with the part of his brain that was not frustrated and irritated that he should do a madonna and child of Nancy and Franklin. 'Victoria's a member of Lloyd's. She's having to pay out now instead of receiving. Huge amounts. Edward told me.'

'Will that change their life?'

'Of course it will. Money is space and freedom. You just said so yourself.'

'But their Catholic principles will hold them together surely? It's more than just money, isn't it?'

'Sure it's *more* than just money, but a lot of it began with money. Where did the Digbys – Victoria's family – get their land from in the beginning? The crown, or the church, one or the other. Land becomes money and money, as we both agree, is power. The thing about *old* money is that it is civilized, philanthropic money, money as it ought to be, probably given that it exists at all, but when old families lose their money they've usually forgotten how to fight or how to cope without it.'

'But there's such a thing as dignity,' said Nancy, shifting the baby from one breast to another, 'Victoria is resilient and digni-fied. I think she's great.'

'Sure, I agree. But, so far, she's been able to live her life in a dignified continuation of the old order of things. There are no certainties any longer for those families. It's the survival of the fittest.'

'Victoria will survive,' said Nancy, yawning, 'I'd lay money on it. Edward is another matter.'

'What do you mean?'

'He seems very strung up, very edgy, I don't know, anxious.'

'Just tired, I guess.'

Nancy did not reply to this. Edward made her nervous however she contemplated him.

Victoria thought she would go to bed early – about half past nine – and watch television, but the trouble with children of so many different ages was that as soon as Ben and Agatha were settled in bed, the elder ones wanted attention. One of the things about older children was that it was impossible to get them into bed in good time.

Mary wandered in to her mother's bedroom wanting to lounge about and chat about her day. She was taking part in a debate the next day on blood sports at the school, defending hunting and shooting and wanted advice and ideas. Victoria felt too tired to have any ideas; all she could remember was a scene she had once witnessed at home as a girl when the hunt had gone through the village. There had been a woman standing by the post office holding a dog of some kind on a piece of rope and the hounds had simply swarmed over this dog like ants, as if it had been a fence post or some other inanimate object, bred to the chase and to ignore everything that stood in their way, rather as she herself had been bred for marriage and motherhood with no mention made of the barbed wire of life that tore one's flesh.

Victoria looked at Mary sprawled on her bed with her shoes still on (of course) and was suddenly glad that Edward was not here, although she was slightly surprised that he had not telephoned her to say that he had arrived.

'Has Dad arrived safely?' asked Mary without looking up, as if her mother had spoken.

'I don't know.'

'Hasn't he phoned?'

'He must have forgotten.'

'I hope he's all right,' said Mary, sitting up suddenly.

'Why shouldn't he be?'

'I don't know. I just had this feeling this morning that he . . .'

'That he what?'

'Nothing,' said Mary.

'I'll try him later. He's probably out with Sam and Nancy.'

'Can I try him?'

'If you want to,' said Victoria. 'I'll give you the number.'

She found the number and gave it to Mary, then went along the corridor and up a half flight to where Tom's and Cyprian's room was. She wanted a word with Tom without his brother being present but they were playing *vingt-et-un* on Tom's bed and didn't look particularly pleased to see her.

'This room looks as if it's been hit by a bomb,' she said, hating herself for being so predictable.

'What sort of bomb?' asked Tom cheekily.

'A neutron bomb – the one that destroys fixtures and fittings but leaves people intact.'

'How do you know we're intact?' said Cyprian, holding his cards against his chest. 'How do you know we aren't burnt to bits inside like the victims of Hiroshima?'

'Just guessing,' said Victoria. 'But, seriously boys, couldn't you just scrape off the top layer, pick up the clothes and the books. And I want your washing before you go to Yorkshire on Saturday, OK?'

'Mum,' said Tom wheedlingly, 'Hector's really keen that I should go and spend half-term with him. Please can I?'

'I thought we'd already discussed that,' said Victoria. But as she spoke, she thought how tired her mother had seemed on the phone this morning and how sad she was about the picture having to go. She herself had been raised looking at that picture; she wondered what on earth they would put in its place.

'Please,' said Tom. 'Come on,' he said to his brother, 'let's clean up a bit, shall we?'

'What's got into you?' asked Cyprian in a fed-up voice. 'He wants something,' he said to his mother, 'he isn't changing for the better or anything. He wants to spend half-term with Hector because Hector has got . . .'

'If you say anything else I'll garotte you,' said his brother, grabbing him by the sleeve.

'Stop that!' said Victoria peremptorily, 'or I'll beat you both. Tidy this room up and then, Tom, come and see me. Cyprian, clean your teeth and then get into bed. I'll come and see you later when I've dealt with your brother.'

'It's not fair,' said Cyprian predictably, 'he always gets his own way.'

'He hasn't got it yet,' said his mother, 'and don't whine. You're quite good at getting your own way yourself.'

Cyprian glowered at her.

'Come on,' said Tom, 'get cracking. I'll be along in a minute, Mum, OK? Where'll you be?'

'In my room,' said Victoria, going out and leaving the door ajar. She sometimes felt like a United Nations peace-keeper in this household. Conflicts were always breaking out and the boys were getting so strong now that someone had to intervene; and that someone was almost invariably Victoria. Edward snarled at them but mostly left discipline to her. Typical, she thought, bloody typical, and was startled by her vehemence. She hadn't known she was so irritated with him.

Mary was lying on the bed holding the telephone to her ear.

'He's not there,' she said.

'Well, put it down then. I told you he was probably out.'

'I rang Sam and Nancy. They were asleep.'

'What on earth is the time?'

'Half ten here, half eleven there.'

'I wish you hadn't disturbed them,' said Victoria. 'She's got a young baby. You probably woke him too.'

'Thanks a lot,' said Mary, 'I was only trying to help locate *your* husband.' She sniffed and then slammed the receiver down on the phone quite hard.

'What on earth is the matter?'

'Nothing.' Mary got up, gathered her books up, and flounced out of the room, banging the door behind her.

'Someone's got PMT,' said Tom, coming in a minute later. 'What's up with her ladyship?'

'Adolescence,' said his mother, 'a common disease. Come in and shut the door, will you, there's something I want to talk to you about.'

'What? Is it Dad?'

99

'No,' said Victoria, raising her eyebrows, 'why on earth do you ask that?'

'No reason,' said Tom, trying to look nonchalant and reassuring, 'nothing at all.'

'Why, Tomo?'

'Nothing,' said Tom, shaking his head so that his hair flung about. It was much too long, that hair.

'I want to talk to you about smoking,' said Victoria. 'Sit down.'

Tom sat down on the dressing stool her mother had given her as a present when she was first married; in those days it had been newly covered in ice-blue damask, now faded after all these years to a comfortable silvery grey.

'What?' he said yobbishly.

'Are you aware that cigarette ends do not flush down the lavatory but bob about on the surface of the water?'

Tom waited.

'Well, are you?'

'No.'

'Why are you smoking so much, Tomo? It seems excessive to have one before breakfast.'

'You do.'

'That's different.' In fact, she was longing for a cigarette now.

'Why?'

'Because I'm in charge of this household and I'm an adult. You have to accept that there is a hierarchy which has earned its privileges. You haven't yet. You're much too young to be smoking so much. You still haven't told me why.'

'Habit, I suppose,' said Tom sulkily, pushing his fair hair out of his eyes.

'Well, then, it's a habit you must break. You're not doing it at school, are you?'

'No,' said Tom unconvincingly.

'Tom!'

'Only like everyone else.'

'You're not everyone else. You'll get yourself expelled and then where will you be with your exams coming up next year? If that happens you won't get to go to another school like St Paul's.

We're running out of money fast thanks to Lloyd's. Next time it'll be a state school.'

'I wouldn't mind. All you lot go on as if a state education is a fate worse than death but ordinary people do it and get to university.'

'Oh, Tom,' said Victoria, 'listen to me, please. It's important.'

She went and put her arms around him holding his head against her breast. Because they were alone he let her.

'If I stop,' he said, after a minute, 'can I go to Hector's at half-term?'

'I'm not entirely stupid,' she said, 'that's the worst place you could go. He'll only encourage you. I know those Egerton-Dawlish's – they're all drug addicts of one kind or another. Thalia's no different. I knew her when we were debs.'

'Please Mum. I'm not a baby now, please.'

'I'll have to speak to your father first,' she said, softening her tone slightly, 'and you'll have to make a real effort, Tomo, not just a half-hearted go, but a real one.'

'I promise,' he said, 'I absolutely promise.'

When Tom had gone and she had seen Mary and Cyprian to say good-night, Victoria went downstairs to let Feather out and then to lock up. She opened the front door and let the black shape bound down the path in front of her, slipping round the gate which was not quite shut and across to the other side of the road where the grasses and weeds grew, encouraged by the regular flooding of the river.

Standing by her gate waiting for the dog, Victoria noticed that there were lights on in Ascension House, the twin building to Easter House, built by two brothers, Augustus and Samuel Cobb in 1787.

Since old Mrs Croft had died, the house had been unoccupied but not, apparently, for sale. There was a son, a doctor, according to gossip up and down the Mall, but he worked abroad somewhere. Now he must have come back, Victoria thought, unless it was burglars, but burglars didn't pass and re-pass the ground-floor windows in that leisurely way, nor did burglars play late-nineteenth-century French piano music. She thought she recognized the strains of Chabrier wafting out through an open window or door.

As she went up her brick path, a male voice said, 'Mrs Parry?'

'Yes?' She looked around but couldn't see where it was coming from.

'Here.'

He was looking over the wall that divided their two houses.

'Hugh Croft,' he said, 'returned from foreign parts.'

'How do you do,' said Victoria, smiling. She was amused by his way of introducing himself.

'Are you the mother of all those children?' he asked.

'I am.'

'Well, you don't look old enough,' he said. 'My mother used to write to me about you before she died.'

He was wearing a white collarless shirt open at the neck and was, from what she could see in the light from his sitting room and her own front door, rather sunburnt.

'I'm sorry about your mother,' she said, 'she was very kind to us. Your father must have died before we came here.'

'Yes, he did. But my mother was determined to stay on. She loved this house. She inherited it from her mother who was a Cobb, a descendant of the builder.'

'I don't think I knew that,' said Victoria. 'You're a doctor, aren't you? Haven't you been working somewhere in Africa, or was it India? Your mother was always terribly vague about your whereabouts.'

'She knew perfectly well where I was,' said Hugh, 'it just annoyed her, that's all. She wanted me to stay at home and become a consultant at Barts or somewhere like it.'

'Just as well you didn't then, wasn't it, in view of what that frightful woman has done.'

'With the blessing of the Conservative Party. They seem to have forgotten what the verb "to conserve" means.'

'Don't,' said Victoria, 'don't.' She sighed.

'Sorry,' he said. 'Being away for so long makes you hungry for talk about everything. Perhaps you and your husband – whose name I'm sorry to say I've forgotten – would like to come and have supper with me sometime this week.'

'That's very kind,' said Victoria, 'but he's away this week.'

'Well, why don't you come? I can cook – it's all right, I had to learn – and I promise you something delicious. The shops here, particularly the supermarkets, stun me. I go in and then I can't remember what I'm supposed to be doing there.'

'That happens to me too,' said Victoria smiling.

'What night would suit?'

'Tomorrow, Wednesday? You can see how busy I am.'

'Yes, I can,' he said smiling. 'Anyone with five children and a job must be run off their feet.'

'How did you know I had a job?'

'Gossip,' he said, smiling again. 'Come tomorrow, about eight thirty. Do you need babysitters and all that?'

'Not any more,' she said, 'the elder ones look after the younger ones, or at least that's the theory.' She sighed as she thought of Tom and his smoking.

'See you then,' he said, 'goodnight.'

'Goodnight.'

When she went upstairs she thought she would try the studio number once more. It rang and rang. Perhaps Edward had gone to see someone – de Fonville perhaps – and was having a late night.

It already seemed a long time since he had left.

On Wednesday morning Victoria had a dream just before she woke, one of those vivid pre-waking dreams which stay in the mind and do not dissolve. In the dream Edward had forgotten to lock the front door of Easter House and Victoria knew they were going to be robbed of their valuables. She tried to ring Edward in Paris on an old black Bakelite telephone with a dial instead of buttons to tell him of her fears about the house but the number took ages to register and then she found she had the wrong code. She tried again but when she got through he had gone. That was the point at which she woke up and could not sleep again. The tiny silver clock on her bedside table said half-past six. She began to think about the bills, Mary's school bill which she must deal with today, and Fenton and Stanwright which she was coming to the conclusion that she would have to tough out. She knew there were organizations set up by other Names which planned to fight the hierarchy at Lloyd's. Today she would make enquiries about joining one. She began to plan a letter in her head and, as she did so, she thought she would not tell Edward. He was so hopelessly honest, but then it occurred to her that it was not so much honesty as fatalism. And fatalism was laziness in a way: laying one's head on the block for lack of any better idea.

In a state of anxiety she got up, put on her dressing gown and went downstairs. She paused at the landing window to admire the view of the river – and in the early light everything looked strangely new and fresh as if it had all just sprung into being the moment before she paused to look – and then went on down to the kitchen to find the number of Sam's studio which was pinned to the cork noticeboard by the telephone. She filled the kettle and put it on the swift ring of the Aga, thinking as she lifted the iron lid with its twisted metal handle of that friend of her mother's who had lifted a lid on her Aga and fallen down dead at exactly that moment. Death by Aga. What a way to go. Rather a good way in fact, provided one had done one's stuff by the children and they were old enough to get on without you, although, as her mother had said once, 'That moment never comes as a parent. You keep thinking it will when they reach eighteen, then twenty-one, then they're thirty and suddenly they need you more than ever.' She would never be free to be herself, whatever that self was. The whole course of her life had been shaped and would continue to be shaped by the fact that she was the mother of all those children. How odd that she should never have thought of this before. The responsibility only ended in death.

She dialled Edward's number.

'Edward?'

'Yes.' He sounded terribly sleepy.

'It's me, Tor, did I wake you?'

'Yes.' He didn't sound especially pleased to hear her. 'Is anything the matter?'

'I was worried about you.'

'Worried? Why? We spoke yesterday, for goodness sake, there's nothing to be worried about, is there?'

'I had a dream, you know . . .'

He made no reply to this and seemed to be waiting for her to terminate the conversation.

'I had supper last night with our new neighbour.'

'Good,' he said, sounding bored.

'The children are well. Give my love to Sam and Nancy.'

'Yes, yes.' He sounded eager to be gone.

When she had put the telephone down and was sitting at the kitchen table she felt suddenly bereft. Did Edward not know that he was the centre of her life? Edward and the children, her house. She had dedicated her life to the goddess of the hearth. And now all her security was slipping from her. It made her want to cry out in fear, in terror. What was to become of them all? Stay calm, she said to herself, lighting the first cigarette of the day, and getting up to let Feather out, but Feather didn't want to get out of bed.

'Come on,' said Victoria, prodding the dog with her foot, 'don't you want to go out?' But Feather just looked at her in that injured Labrador way.

'All right then.' Victoria went out into the garden herself with her cigarette, wondering if Hugh was still asleep next door. Perhaps he was, lucky Hugh, not tormented by money worries, with his house all his, and a lovely nest egg in the bank. Old Mrs Croft had, apparently, been exceedingly well off, but, like so many of her generation, had lived frugally. Workhouse Syndrome, Hugh had called it last night, which made her smile now as she thought about it.

'I'm going out,' she had said to Mary and Tom the night before, 'so keep an eye on things for me, will you?'

'Where are you going?' The question that never changed however old your children were. What they meant of course is where are you going without *me*, the unspoken assumption of all children being that you were their property.

'Just out to supper.'

'But where?' said Mary. 'I must have a phone number.'

'Next door,' said Victoria teasingly, 'miles away.'

'Who lives there now?' asked Tom.

'Dr Croft, old Mrs Croft's son, returned from Africa.'

'Mum's got a date,' said Tom.

'Don't be silly,' said Mary. 'Don't listen to him, Mum, he's just infantile.'

'Still got PMT?' asked Tom.

'Oh, shut up,' said Mary. 'Given up smoking yet?'

'Stop it,' said Victoria wearily, 'just stop it. I'm going to see what Benie and Aggie are doing in the bath. Cyprian will be back in a minute with Rollo's mother. Let him in, will you?'

'Yup,' said Tom, saluting.

'You're such a little cunt,' he said to his sister when his mother was safely out of the room, 'but it's no good trying to blackmail me over smoking because Mum already knows. We've discussed it, so just piss off, OK?'

'Does she know you're still doing it?' she said, giving him a sour look.

'I'm not.'

'Yes, you are. I can smell it in our lav. It stinks of smoke. You should get some room spray or something.'

'I'll spray you,' he said belligerently.

'Door!' said Mary. 'You go, Mr Responsible.'

'Certainly,' said Tom, 'I don't mind taking my duties seriously.'

Mary hissed at him as he went out of the room. Brothers! Who needed them? Everyone always said 'Lucky Mary to have a brother close in age', but it wasn't lucky, it was a complete pain. All Tom did was to criticize her or makes jokes about her appearance or undermine her with their mother. Sometimes, quite often, she felt she hated her brother. Cyprian was younger, she could deal with him, but Tom was too close to her in age for comfort; he was also getting much taller now which made him more difficult to fight.

'Mare,' said Tom from the doorway in a different voice.

'What?' She didn't look up, just to annoy him.

'Mare, it's Iza. Jenny sent her. To clean.'

'We haven't got a cleaner,' said Mary. 'What are you talking about?'

'Come in,' said Tom, standing back to let a very pretty girl with fair curly hair into the kitchen.

'Jenny sent you?' said Mary in her best Lady of the Manor voice.

'Yes,' said the girl, struggling for words as if her mouth were full of stones.

Mary, feeling sorry for her, suddenly twigged.

'You're one of Jenny's Poles,' she said, 'I see. Sit down.' She indicated a chair.

'Get Mum, will you' she said to Tom.

At that moment Victoria came into the room.

'Mum,' said Mary, 'this is Iza. Jenny sent her. She's come to help clean.'

'I'd completely forgotten,' said Victoria. 'Hello.' She went and shook hands with Iza who smiled in a baffled way.

'Jenny sent me,' she said, 'I sorry no telephone.'

'Doesn't matter. You're very welcome. Have a cup of coffee? Where are you from?'

'Cracow,' said the girl, 'where the Pope he come from.'

'The Polish Pope,' said Tom, as if he had discovered something he didn't know.

'You're quick,' said his sister.

'I'll write a list,' said Victoria. 'Mary, make the coffee. Tom, go and do your homework.'

'I've done most of it,' said Tom, smoothing his floppy fair hair out of his eyes. He lounged against a cupboard admiring Iza's long legs. She wore a white shirt and a black skirt and black patent leather T-bar shoes that in spite of their astonishing hideousness she managed to make look quite sexy.

'What are you waiting for?' asked Victoria, looking up. It occurred to her, looking at her son's silly expression, that he was going to be a nuisance about girls, but at least, as Jenny said, he wasn't a poof. 'Either way it's sex, darling,' said Jenny, 'whether it's girls or boys, and Tom's much too good-looking to be wasted on men.'

'Nothing,' said Tom nonchalantly. 'Can I help, can I do anything?'

'He must be ill,' said Mary. 'Shall I call an ambulance?'

'No, no. Let him do the coffee, darling, and you go and get on with your work, OK?'

'Fine by me,' said Mary, rolling her eyes.

'Sugar?' asked Tom, getting a mug down from the dresser, 'milk?'

'No sugar,' said Iza, putting her hands on her slender waist. 'I get fat.'

Victoria lit a cigarette, but did not offer one to Iza.

'Start in here,' she said, 'then do the drawing room and Edward's study. Tom will show you where to go and where the hoover is, the dusters, and anything else you need, won't you, Tom?'

'Certainly,' said Tom, 'what time are you going out?'

'Now,' said Victoria, looking up at the kitchen clock. 'When can you come back?'

'Tomorrow,' said Iza, 'after work, is OK?'

'What do you do?' asked Tom slowly.

'I work in hairdressers in Notting Hill making sandwiches. Very hard work, all day. "Iza – coffee, Iza – sandwiches, Iza – tea for the lady . . ." all day. Is very hard.'

'Life's a bitch,' said Tom, pushing her coffee over the table to her and catching his mother's eye as he did so.

'Keep a note of your hours,' Victoria said, 'and I will pay you on Friday. Is that OK?'

'Yes. Is OK.'

The telephone rang. Tom answered it. 'For you,' he said to his mother.

It was Rollo's mother saying the traffic was terrible and that she would keep Cyprian for the night.

'How kind, thanks so much,' said Victoria, who had completely forgotten about him.

Victoria looked at herself in the hall mirror as she went out.

She wore some black linen trousers that Juliet, her sister, had bought in a sale and then found she was too fat for and a white T-shirt belonging to Mary. She had put on make-up, mascara, lipstick, even blusher, and hoped she looked all right. She had brushed her abundant dark hair and let it hang loose to her shoulders. She wondered if she would be the only guest and hoped not for reasons she preferred not to examine too closely. When you went somewhere always with the same person for years and years and years it was an odd experience to be by yourself. Odd and rather pleasant, she thought, pausing to glance towards the river through the drooping fronds of the willow tree.

Hugh Croft's front door was slightly open when Victoria went up the brick path that mirrored her own.

'Hello,' she called tentatively, 'it's Victoria.'

'Come in,' he replied from the room on the right which she took to be his drawing room, 'I'm up a ladder.'

She put her head around the door and found that he was indeed where he said he was, fiddling with a chandelier.

'I'm so sorry,' he said, 'this is so rude, but I took a piece of this thing apart – Mrs Betts tells me it needs a wash – and now I can't get seem to get it back into place, but now you're here I'm just going to leave it. We'll go and sit in the garden and have a drink.'

He came down his ladder and smiled at her. 'You look nice,' he said. 'I'm a bit scruffy, I hope you don't mind.' He looked down at his dark green cords rather worn around the knee and an old blue shirt with the sleeves rolled up.

'In Africa you forget what it means to dress up,' he said apologetically, 'you develop a kind of blindness about looking at people, women and men alike, because everyone wears the same old thing, day in, day out. What would you like to drink?' he asked, going to a half-moon-shaped table in the corner with a large silver tray on it covered in decanters and bottles.

'There's everything: gin, whisky, sherry.' He picked up a bottle and looked at the label, 'Bols, Grand Marnier, God knows what else my mother kept.'

'Could I have a glass of white wine?' asked Victoria. 'I don't drink gin anymore, I used to, but it makes me feel terribly hung over.'

'Of course you can,' he said, 'there's some in the fridge. Let's forget all this stuff. I forget that hardly anybody drinks anything but wine these days in England.'

'What were you drinking in Africa?'

'Anything we could lay our hands on,' he said smiling. 'Come on down, I'll lead the way. This must be a familiar layout to you. They are identical, aren't they, these two houses?'

'More or less,' she said, 'but this is a pretty room. I love the colour of the walls.'

'Do you know,' he said, standing in the doorway with her, 'I remember this room being painted when I was a child. It was a much more vivid blue then.'

'Don't change it,' she said, 'or are you going to?'

'I don't see the point. I like things better when they get old.'

'People too?' she asked without meaning to.

'I like people of all ages,' he said, leading the way down the stairs to the basement, 'young and old. You must know much more about the young than I do with your brood.'

'Too much, I sometimes think,' she answered and then laughed, remembering he was a doctor and might take her seriously.

The kitchen was done in the style of the late fifties with lots and lots of wooden, cream-coloured cupboards and a linoleum floor. There was a table in the middle of the room covered in faded red Formica and work surfaces to match.

'I am going to change this,' said Hugh, looking over his shoulder, 'it's hard to imagine anything coming out of a kitchen like this other than shape or spotted dick.'

'Or dead man's leg,' said Victoria, 'we had something at school called that. Meat in a pastry case that resembled armour-plating. But she had a cook, didn't she, your mother. She didn't venture down here much, I suppose?'

'She did indeed have a cook,' said Hugh, 'the redoubtable Lizzie, now in the nursing home at the convent.'

He poured her a glass of white wine in a beautiful old wine

glass and they went outside and sat down on an antiquated wooden bench under a canopy of roses.

'There are two other people coming,' Hugh said, 'old friends of mine, one's a journalist and one's a sculptor.'

'A husband and wife?'

'No, no,' he said, 'quite separate. Patrick is a journalist and Sarah a sculptor. You'll like them,' he said, 'or at least I hope you will. One should never say that of course as people invariably hate people when you say that.'

He thought she looked alarmed at the prospect and was curious. She was a nice woman and an attractive one, shy but warm, quite poised in her own way. He wondered what it was that had rattled her.

'I'm sure I shan't hate them,' she said, and took a sip of her wine. 'Am I the only boring married then?'

'Is it boring?' he asked lightly, then added, 'Patrick and Sarah have both been married, they're just not married at the moment.'

'Oh. Have you been married too?'

'Once,' he said, 'a long time ago.'

'Children?'

'No. I wanted them, she didn't. So we didn't have any.'

'So you let your wife choose?'

'Yes,' he nodded. 'It seems a bleak decision, I know, but in fact I think she was right. We were in Africa – she was a doctor too – and our marriage simply wasn't good enough.'

'Do you think if you'd had a child you'd still be married to her?'

'I hope so,' he said, 'but, realistically, no. Does this sort of thing offend you? I know you are a devout Catholic.'

'I know how the world works,' she said, 'how could it offend me?'

'You never know these days. People are so intolerant, so touchy, particularly the so-called liberal intelligentsia. I've worked in Africa for years, I know the form, and I know how corrupt African countries are, but try saying so here! Orthodoxy in this country is now liberal from top to bottom.'

'I do know what you're talking about. People are always

condemning the Pope at parties. They say things like "He's a silly old fool, or a silly old fart" but because he's not a liberal sacred cow so-to-speak it doesn't matter. It's all just another form of intolerance. You squash one sort and another pops up in its place.'

'Especially in North London.'

'I don't know North London very well, I'm afraid,' she said laughing.

'There's the knocker,' Hugh said, 'excuse me a minute.'

Left alone for a moment, Victoria felt herself to be utterly separate. It was a most unaccustomed feeling. The enveloping texture of family life rarely allowed her this sense of self. Without children, without husband, she was . . . herself: a woman of almost forty with much behind her and much ahead. She shivered suddenly as with a premonition. She wondered what Edward was doing now. They were apart so rarely. Was he thinking of her? She thought not.

'I hear you live next door,' Sarah said to Victoria when Hugh had gone indoors to do something to the dinner, 'and have five children.'

'They're my distinguishing mark,' said Victoria wryly.

'Did you do anything before you had children?'

'Not really. I just fiddled about, waiting to get married, I suppose. I'm rather like Lady Di, I went straight from my ancestral home to my own home with nothing much in between.'

'Do you mind that?'

'I don't know,' said Victoria, 'it's odd, but it's only just occurred to me. It just seemed how my life was. I never thought of changing any of it, but now I realize that it's changing anyway, whether I like it or not.'

'Change is hard to reconcile oneself to, I know,' said Sarah, 'but I suppose one has to accept there's nothing one can do about it other than accept it. We're not in control of any of the things that happen to us from birth to death.'

'It's just that we think we are,' said Victoria, 'and that is our error. Do you have children?' she asked.

'I had one,' said Sarah, 'a daughter. She was killed in a road accident.'

'I'm sorry. How terrible for you.'

'It was terrible,' said Sarah. 'It will never stop being terrible, but it made me realize that we live with death second by second, life and death. A continual process of becoming.'

Victoria waited.

'It's something to do,' Sarah said, 'with the perfecting of each instant, of not looking back and thinking "if only I were this or that, if only Tara were here, if only" . . . it's a kind of acceptance of the present. I'm not explaining very well.'

'I understand,' said Victoria, wanting the conversation to continue, but then Hugh came back with the man, Patrick, the journalist, in tow and the introductions banished her thoughts.

'Did you enjoy yourself?' asked Jenny the next morning, leaning her elbows on the work bench so that she could massage her temples with the palms of her hands.

'Yes, I did, very much,' said Victoria. 'I was nervous to start with but they were all so nice to me . . .'

'Why shouldn't they be nice to you?'

'Because . . . I'm not as interesting as they are.'

'Of course you are,' said Jenny. 'You're very interesting, very attractive. And very nice.'

'I don't feel it,' said Victoria. 'I'm completely unused to myself . . . I feel so submerged by family life, by dry rot and money problems, by Lloyd's.' She stopped talking and put her hand to her mouth.

'What is it?' asked Jenny, feeling her headache surge on her like a wave coming up the shingle. It was always in the same place. Sometimes it felt like a piece of jagged glass lying submerged among the skin and bone and brain.

'Nothing,' said Victoria, shaking her head. She avoided Jenny's gaze.

'Tell me.'

'Once I start,' said Victoria, 'I feel as if I'll never be able to stop.' If one's body was a map of emotions, then a great lake lay below her heart, an inland sea, that in moments of stress and tiredness or great feeling she felt move heavily against its containing walls.

'You should talk,' said Jenny. 'Don't keep things bottled up.'

'People are always saying that, but I have to keep things contained otherwise I'll fall apart.'

'You might for a bit,' said Jenny, 'so what. I'll catch the bits and glue them together again.'

Victoria looked at her gratefully, then she said, 'What's on the agenda for today?'

'Mrs Parker's Meissen – she's coming in at tea-time.'

'Right,' said Victoria, 'let's go to it then, shall we?'

She leaned back and put on the radio which sat on a shelf behind her. It was permanently tuned to Radio 3 – what Edward still called the third programme. It was a considered part of his studied old-fogeyism, together with talking about the wireless, and the home service and the League of Nations, not that one ever talked about that if one could avoid it. Once upon a time it had amused her; now she was not so sure. The world was not what Edward wanted it to be or hoped it was: a late fifties' dream sequence when the police drove Wolseys with running boards and little boys in grey shorts and school caps called middle-aged men 'sir' and people talked to one another on Bakelite telephones. She thought of her dream and then found she was thinking once more of Hugh Croft: his sunburned skin, the way he was going grey at the temples, the backs of his brown capable hands, the heavy signet ring he wore.

'How was Iza?' asked Jenny sometime later.

'She seemed fine,' Victoria looked up. 'She was thorough too, Tom told me. He followed her around, I think. She's very pretty.'

'Yes, she is, isn't she. Was Tom smitten?'

'Tom is smitten with everything at the moment. He's smoking like a chimney. I had to give him a talking to.'

'Henry went through that, too.' Henrietta was the same age as Mary. Jenny's other daughter, Maisie, was ten.

'Is she still?'

'I don't think so but obviously I don't know. She wouldn't tell me. But she doesn't smell of smoke like she used to.'

'Tom promised me he'll have a good go at stopping. He wants to spend half-term with Hector, so he's trying to please me, and

I'm dead against it, but I can feel him winning the argument by some kind of erosion. He just keeps on and on at me and eventually I know I'm going to cave in.'

'Cave in with dignity, darling,' said Jenny, 'that's the thing, believe me. Why can't he go to Hector's?'

'Because his mother is one of those hopeless, rich, failed debs who've taken up the New Age with a vengeance which means never noticing what your children – or in her case, child – is doing. Tom likes going there because there are no rules.'

'Oh, let him,' said Jenny, 'let him have a little fun and don't think about what he might be getting up to, otherwise he'll resent you like mad and that's much worse, darling, believe me.'

Victoria sighed. 'You're probably right,' she said.

'What does Edward think?'

'Edward doesn't think at the moment,' said Victoria tartly.

'Oh,' Jenny made a face. 'Are you looking forward to going to Paris?'

'I suppose so. When I've done everything else. Got the kids off, tidied up, sorted out Mary's school fees and so on and so forth.'

'Are you driving to Yorkshire?'

'Yes.'

'Why don't you go by train?'

'Too much stuff. I want to drive, it's easier. Five children and Feather are easier in a car.'

'You're mad,' said Jenny. 'You should just put them all on the train with Mary in charge and send them off to York on their own. It's not very far. Nothing will happen to them.'

'Something's more likely to happen to the other passengers, I agree,' said Victoria, 'but anyway, that's how I'm going to do it.'

'You're stubborn,' said Jenny, 'but you know that, of course.'

Victoria glanced at her. 'I know I am,' she said, 'but I'm always being told how to lead my life and I want to do it myself.'

'Fine, darling. Am I always telling you how to lead your life?'

'No, but Edward is.'

'Ah well, that's different then.'

'Jenny,' Victoria hesitated.

'What?'

'I need to ask you something delicate.'

'Go on then.'

'I hate to do this – but I need to borrow the money to pay Mary's fees from the business. I'll pay it back as soon as I can. I haven't told Edward but I've sent my pearls to Phillips to be flogged. That should do a couple of terms; the clasp is a really good one.'

'Of course you can borrow the money . . . if it's there . . . but must you sell your lovely pearls?'

'I reckon I'm lucky to have held on to them for so long,' Victoria said, putting a brave face on it. She loved her pearls. Who was it who said, 'All a girl needs is one good piece'? Well, her one really good piece was going and there was no point in mourning it. Except that one did of course.

'Thank you about the money,' she added. 'I do appreciate it. The bills are stacking up and Edward is no bloody use.'

'He knows about the fees?'

'Oh yes.'

'So what's he doing about them?'

'Leaving it to me.' Victoria made a gesture with her hands. 'He's not here. Something has to be done. I was hoping to keep the pearl money in reserve, hidden away somewhere from Lloyd's.'

Jenny looked at Victoria with sympathy. She knew about money worries, inside out and backwards. How one woke in the night worrying and couldn't get off to sleep again. How they just ate one up inside. When her husband had left she hadn't been able to pay any bills. The telephone had been cut off and the electricity. She reckoned she had aged a decade during that year when she was finding her feet.

'It's nothing,' said Jenny lightly, 'it's only money. Now it's my turn to ask a favour.'

'Anything,' said Victoria, 'ask away.'

'When you come back from Paris, I'm going to need a few days off.'

'Of course. What is it?'

'Nothing,' said Jenny, 'at least, I don't know. But you know I get these headaches and feel sick quite often, well, Dr Short says I need to go and have a head scan, have my brain photographed or something.'

'What are they looking for?'

'God knows, darling, but I'm going to have to go into the Charing Cross for a few days.'

'Oh, Jenny,' said Victoria in distress. 'Here I am going on about my problems and you've got all this to deal with. The girls must come here, of course. Why don't they go to Yorkshire with my lot for half-term. Ma wouldn't mind.'

'You'd never fit them in the car for one thing,' said Jenny, 'and for another, I want to spend the time with them. I don't want them to feel pushed out. We're going to go to the cinema, go shopping, I'm going to paint Henry's room with her, we're . . .'

'But I'll be away,' said Victoria, 'how will you manage?'

'Look, these girls don't get up until practically tea-time. It's early summer, the days are long. I'll work and then I'll go home and have fun.'

'Jenny, tell me true. What is the matter?'

'Truthfully, they don't know,' said Jenny, 'but they think it might be a brain tumour.'

'Oh Christ,' said Victoria uncharacteristically. 'Why you?'

'Why any of us?' said Jenny. 'Life has to go on. There are children to be seen to, food to be bought, jobs to be done, money to be earned. I try never to ask that question.'

'One shouldn't,' said Victoria, 'you're quite right, but, never-theless, one does.'

'Oh yes,' said Jenny, 'I know.'

Victoria went on with what she was doing but she thought to herself that one had to ask these things if one believed in God, because sometimes there was an answer or a clue to something important contained in illness or misfortune. If one believed in a higher power, that is. If one didn't then one blamed oneself instead for an illness, and the moral issues that the old kind of questions provoked became subsumed in the modern world into questions of guilt over 'lifestyle'. What one had eaten or not eaten, the exercise one had or had not taken.

'But,' she said, after a moment, 'I can't go to Paris and leave you to cope, I just can't.'

'You can,' said Jenny, 'and you will.'

'What? Lying around having a lovely time while you cope with two children, a brain tumour, and a business.'

'They don't know for certain what it is yet,' said Jenny gently, 'and, darling, as we've just been saying, life has to go on. You must go away, it's really important.'

The bar closed at 3 a.m. Parry and Caroline left just before. They were the last to go. They went out into the Place du Calvaire with its cobbles and the dark mass of the church looming over them. The city, at this hour, was silent. It was the lowest point in the whole diurnal round; the time of night people died or woke with their palms sweating, wondering what was going to become of them.

Their footsteps sounded loud to Parry whose whole comprehension was, he felt, enlarged and refined by the amount of Armagnac he had had to drink.

'We should go home,' he said, not wanting to look up at the accusing bulk of the church.

'Home?'

'The studio. Sam's studio.'

'I'd like to walk a bit first. I love it here at night.'

'Where to?'

'Down to the river.'

'All right.'

He glanced at her as they walked along the shuttered, sombre night streets, the odd cat scuttering in their path, a drunk weaving ahead of them and then vanishing into the shadows.

'How long will you be staying?' he asked.

'I'm not sure. It depends.'

'On what?' Suddenly he had to know how long he would be able to be with her, to look at her.

'On whether I can sell anything or not. Otherwise I'll go back south.'

'To Le Pin?'

'Yes.'

He waited for her to say something else. It occurred to him that she might have a lover there, someone to draw her back. This thought filled him with a sense of urgent disappointment, as if he had been on the brink of discovering something only to find the trail had gone cold. This encounter with her had illuminated his life sharply like a sudden flare of light in the darkness. He must make her stay.

They leant on the parapet of the Pont-Neuf, staring down into the oily darkness of the river.

'Will your wife stay in the studio?'

'No. We're booked into a hotel. It's more comfortable for her.'

'And for you.'

'I don't mind discomfort,' he said, as if she had insulted him.

'The sofa is large and squashy. You'll be all right there.'

'Yes,' he glanced at her. Waiting.

Somewhere in the gloom a tug hooted.

'We should go back,' she said, 'it's late.'

'Actually, it's early.'

'What is the time?' She came close to him.

'Four.'

'It's hardly worth it, is it?'

'Not for you, perhaps. I'm exhausted.'

'I forget,' she said, 'you oldies don't have the stamina.'

He made as if to smack her but she dodged off. He could hear the sound of her footsteps as she ran over the bridge. When he reached the road that ran parallel with the river she was waiting for him under the bronze dolphins that supported the street light. She looked tired. There were dark circles under her eyes accentuated by the light. For a moment he was aware of the skull beneath the skin, the sudden impulse, the quick flicker that is our life, a light, soon extinguished, the drop of water returned to the ocean.

He opened the gate to the square with his own key and they walked across towards the studio behind its further gate saying nothing. Again, he used his own key, allowing her to pass ahead of him along the overgrown path. The house by the gate was shuttered and quiet. No Brahms now.

In the studio, she put on the lights in the dark hallway, going ahead of him into the main room where she turned on an old standard lamp Sam had acquired from somewhere.

'I hope you have everything you need,' she said politely.

'Yes, thank you.'

'Well, goodnight then.'

'Goodnight.' He felt as if he had been turned to stone.

'Sleep well.'

He heard her footsteps going slowly up the stairs to the turret room. Under the lamp on the floor was a pile of sheets, a padded Indian bedspread, a towel, and two square continental pillows in linen covers edged with old lace. Sam had a passion for old linen and was always buying sheets and pillowcases in markets.

Parry made the bed carefully and then went to the bathroom. Caroline came barefoot down the stairs in a huge, white man's shirt. Her legs were bare. He noticed that she painted her toe-nails a dark pink.

'You go first,' he said, stopping at the door.

'After you.'

'No, no.'

'We'll be here all night,' she said, coming down a step.

'Please.' He looked down at the towel he was holding in his hands. 'Just go, will you.'

'Thanks,' she touched his bare forearm with her left hand and he jumped.

When he looked up she was smiling at him, her face pale, her hair brushed, like a little girl ready for bed.

He leaned towards her, and then drew back.

For a moment they looked at one another and then she went into the bathroom and closed the door.

Parry slept on his sofa and dreamed that he was with Victoria at Lourdes. They were about to go through the gates into the baths together. Victoria was pushing a wheelchair. Parry looked down and saw the body of his dead child wrapped in a shawl propped in the chair. He knew Victoria was going to immerse the child's dead body in the freezing holy waters in order to bring her back to life. He wanted to run away but Victoria said 'Lazarus was raised from the dead. My baby will be born again in the waters of death.'

He knew this was wrong, but the dream faded. He woke with tears on his cheeks. At first he could not remember where he was and turned on his back expecting to see in the half light from the window the luminous hands on his watch face, but the window was in the wrong place. Then he remembered where he was.

Parry slept restlessly until quarter to eight at which point he was awoken by the telephone. It was Victoria.

'You are there,' she said, 'we were wondering. Why didn't you phone last night to say you'd arrived? Mary was trying to get you too.'

'Was she? Why? I'm only in Paris.'

'She wanted to know if you were safe. She was worried about you.'

'There's no need for her to worry,' he said crossly.

'You sound hung over,' said Victoria, 'did you have a night on the tiles with Sam?'

It was only after she had asked the question that she realized she already knew the answer. Sam and Nancy had been in bed when Mary phoned. She had said so.

'Yes. We were rather late, actually.'

There was a silence.

'Are you there, Tor?' he said.

'Yes, I'm here.'

'What have you been doing?'

'Just the usual.'

He had lied to her. She felt as if she had been stabbed. I thought I knew this person, she said to herself, and yet I don't. Not at all. He is completely strange to me, a bundle of shadows, and evasions. *Why* is he lying to me? It's probably me, something I've said or done. Hounding him, that's what he thinks. He made it sound like that anyway.

'Yes,' he said, feeling the need to make things good with her, 'we had dinner in a Moroccan restaurant Nancy knows and then

Sam and I went off on a bit of a bender.' As he said it, he almost believed it. Nothing had happened. He was still a faithful husband, for God's sake.

'How nice for you.'

'Tor? What's the matter?'

'Nothing's the matter,' she said, and put the phone down quite gently so that he was astonished to hear the whine of the dial tone.

He tried to ring back but the number was engaged. Of course. She couldn't know anything. He hadn't done anything, for Christ's sake. I'm innocent, he thought, I haven't done a thing to be ashamed of. Damn her. Bloody women. I know I'm being watched, well, too bad. His old image of God with binoculars and a notebook came back to him powerfully reinforced.

Sam arrived earlier than he had said he would, which was most unlike him.

'Babies,' he said, going into the kitchen to make coffee. 'She won't sleep with me because it wakes the baby, then the baby wakes us at five or some similar hour and we can't sleep again. I tell her she should put Franklin to sleep in the living room. Then we'd get some peace and some semblance of a normal life. How're you, old buddy, this fine morning? You look a little tired.'

'Don't you start,' said Parry, 'I've just had my wife on the phone accusing me of God only knows what because I failed to ring her last night.'

'Now you mention it,' said Sam, spooning coffee into the pot, 'she rang us quite late. I said you were in the studio. I didn't tell her you were on the rampage with a pretty girl.'

'Some rampage,' said Parry defensively, thinking so that's how she knows. 'We just had a few brandies and went home.'

'That's what they all say,' said Sam teasingly.

'It's true,' said Parry, with all the outrage of someone who was telling a half-truth.

'Just joking,' said Sam, 'take a joke, boy.'

'I don't like being accused of things I haven't done,' said Parry sanctimoniously.

'Nobody's accusing you of anything,' said Sam. 'Have you had breakfast?'

'Yes, thanks.'

'More coffee?'

'That would be nice.'

'Have you telephoned de Fonville?'

'Yes, I have, I'm going to see him this evening.'

'On your own or with Caroline?'

'On my own. She's nothing to do with me.'

'But she seems to know him quite well.'

'Yes.'

'Sugar?'

'No, no thanks.'

'Caroline up yet?'

'I don't think so.'

'I'll go and give her a shout,' said Sam, striding off into the studio. Parry could hear his footsteps crossing to the door which led to the stairs and the bathroom. The door opened and Sam's footsteps vanished into the noise of a Paris morning and were lost among the other sounds of birdsong, wheels of a baby buggy on the cobbles beyond the gate, the sound of a child crying in the house belonging to the woman in the smart suit.

'She's coming,' said Sam returning, 'she's just getting dressed.'

She came down wearing jeans, and what looked like the same shirt she had worn in bed, and a pair of old boots with scuffed toes.

'I slept like a baby,' she said, 'Armagnac agrees with me. It sends me into a coma. But in my sleep,' she said, 'I heard telephones. Did your wife ring?'

'Yes, she did.'

'All well?'

'Yes, thanks.'

Parry exchanged a glance with Sam, who said, 'We're going to the Louvre. Do you want to come with us?'

'Would you mind?' She looked from one to the other. 'Edward looks tired,' she said.

'I hear you two had a late night.'

'Not really. Only three or so. Doesn't count.'

'She's got stamina, this girl,' said Sam, putting his arm around her shoulders.

'No sitters this morning?' Caroline lit a cigarette and offered Parry one, but he refused.

'No, thank God. I'm too tired to put brush to canvas. Our child kept us up in the night. It's all right for Nancy, she can get back to sleep again in the day, but some of us have to work.'

'Having a baby's work too,' said Caroline.

'Women always say that,' said Sam.

'Isn't it true – Edward?'

'It's not creative in the sense that Sam's is. Having a baby is about maintenance. The mother is the mechanic for the first years anyway. You can't work properly if you're tired.'

'You win,' she said, putting her cigarette out under the tap. 'I'm just going to go and put on some make-up and then I'll be ready. Is that OK?'

'Here's your bronze,' said Parry, handing her the figure of Mars. 'You shouldn't leave that lying around – it's too valuable.'

'It wasn't lying around, was it? This place is quite safe.' She put it back where it had been before.

'Is it OK with you, Edward, if she comes with us?' said Sam when Caroline had gone upstairs again.

'Fine by me. Why?'

'I don't know. You seem a little edgy with one another.'

'Nonsense,' said Parry, 'just a late night, that's all.'

'Oh, right.'

'We'll walk,' said Sam, when she came back, 'is that OK with you two?'

'I never thought we'd do anything else,' said Caroline. 'We walked down there last night in the dark, didn't we, Edward?'

'We did indeed,' said Parry, wishing to gloss over his activities of the night before in which he felt almost everyone was taking far too much interest. It was not as if he'd done anything wrong.

'Loathsome thing,' said Parry, gazing at the glass pyramid in the courtyard of the Louvre.

'I suppose it is,' said Caroline, 'but I quite like it all the same.'

'I don't know how you can.'

'Well, I do. Do you mind?'

'Why should I mind?'

Parry glanced at Caroline as he spoke and, as he did so, remembered how she'd looked in that crumpled shirt the night before with her bare legs and her dark pink toenails; her feet and legs were as smooth and sunburned as her arms and hands. He was overcome by a wave of desire so violent and immediate that he felt giddy and breathless.

'I just don't think', he said slowly, 'that that monstrosity is a perfect accompaniment to Bernini.'

'You probably have a point,' she said, turning round to admire Louis on his bronze horse. 'It is rather like going into an airport.'

'Those entrances were designed to lead one towards the exhibits,' said Parry. 'Winged Victory prepared one for something monumental.'

He wanted to touch her so much that he had to begin to walk towards the pyramid for fear that she might notice. He hadn't desired a woman so much for years, years and years, and it felt frighteningly exhilarating, like driving too fast, or touching something white-hot for an instant. It also made him wonder how he had forgotten this pleasure that drove out all sense of caution, all reason, all loyalty.

They went down the escalator, bought their day passes in the gleaming hangar-like entrance hall and entered the body of the museum. They passed through gallery after gallery: seventeenth-century French painting, seventeenth-century English painting, Agonies in the Garden, Crucifixions, Depositions, allegorical scenes. Parry's feeling of excitement did not diminish but expanded, fed by the astonishing imagination and range of what he was looking at: Caroline was behind his appreciation of every wood, every grove, every column, every classical city; slow butter-coloured cows grazed the edge of luminous seas, Europa ran to meet the bull, Circe played idly with her pearls. He knew that he should not confuse desire with love, he was too old for that, or he should be. That delusion was for the young, people in their twenties and thirties, except that there was a part of one that never aged, a part of one that went on remembering. And this was Paris, after all.

The enormous painting by Veronese of the *Marriage Feast at Cana* was surrounded by Japanese tourists taking flash photographs. They never appeared to look at the painting at all except through the lense of a camera; small groups of men and women in Crimplene trousers and washable shoes hung about with the expensive photographic equipment, consuming the painting without actually looking at it.

'Extraordinary,' Caroline whispered in Parry's ear. 'I wish they'd all leave, don't you? What on earth can it mean to them?'

Parry half-turned towards her so that he could see the hollows at the base of her neck, the colourless swing of her hair, he could smell her smell, but, as he did so, he caught the eye of the Christ figure in the painting which looked straight out of the canvas at him, a gaze consumed with self-discovery and a sense of destiny; joy to come and horror mingled.

Parry could not answer Caroline. He had hardly heard what she said. The face of the Christ seemed to be asking him some question; if he was only still a little longer he would hear what it was.

'Edward, look at the dog,' said Caroline, putting her hand on his arm. He felt her touch through the linen of his jacket as if he had been burned.

'The dog?'

'Up there, with its head between the balusters, looking down on the feast, knowing things will drop under that tablecloth, hoping for dinner.'

Parry gazed upwards and it was as if a string had been cut. He was no longer mesmerized, but free to look away. Gradually, the sounds of the gallery returned to his ears, the whirr of film winding on, the click of shutters, the strange, flat babble of the Japanese. The face of Christ receded into the canvas, became, merely, an amalgam of paint and brush strokes, a clever piece of design created to astonish and baffle, and which had succeeded. For a moment.

Parry turned away and followed Caroline and Sam across the gallery away from the crowds.

'Time for lunch, I think,' said Sam.

'Good idea,' said Parry, catching Caroline's eye. Was it his imagination or did she hold his gaze for a second longer than really was entirely proper?

'Where?' asked Caroline. 'Shall we stay here or go back to Montmartre?'

'Edward?'

'Why me? I'm happy whatever you decide.'

'Let's go back,' said Caroline, 'then we can have a good lunch and go to sleep afterwards.'

'Done,' said Parry.

'What time are you seeing de Fonville?' asked Sam.

'Not until this evening. Seven or so.'

'So you've spoken to him, have you?'

'This morning,' said Parry.

'You didn't tell me.'

'There hasn't been a chance.'

'I'm sure you'd rather go alone,' she said.

Parry said nothing. In the general confusion and upheaval of his feelings he wanted something to remain clear. He had come here to do business. He did not want that to get blurred as well. Too much hung on it all: his dignity, Mary's school fees, Tom's opinion of him, the whole tangled web of his home life, his own sense of failure, that above all. That which poisoned everything.

'Perhaps you'd have dinner with us afterwards,' said Parry.

'That's a good idea,' she said, in French, making him feel somehow as if he had done exactly the right thing. He liked talking French but couldn't with Victoria as hers wasn't up to scratch. He liked himself better as a Frenchman. It allowed him to indulge certain vanities he could no longer allow himself in English. In French there was still a little mastery left available to him which the remorseless glare of his home life had driven out in England. At Easter House he was either in combat with his wife or his children. Everyone seemed to regard him as fair game.

127

After lunch, Sam said, 'I'm going to go up the hill and see how Nancy is. Give me a ring later, Edward, and we'll fix something up, if not dinner than we can meet for a drink afterwards in a bar, or whatever.'

'Time for a sleep, I think,' said Caroline, taking his arm. 'How does that grab you?' she asked in an exaggeratedly English accent.

Going up the narrow studio stairs Caroline stumbled a little. The slippery sole of her boot meeting the equally slippery surface of old polished board; that and the wine. Parry automatically put out a hand to steady her, feeling the warm narrow flesh of her back under the voluminous shirt. At the top of the stairs she turned to him in the half dark – the kitchen door was shut – putting out a hand to him as if to push him away at the same time as she ensnared him. She put her cheek against his, as a daughter might, and all at once he found himself trembling like a girl. He put his hands on her upper arms and pulled her to him, kissing her half-open mouth, his self-control running out as rapidly as sand in an hourglass.

They went awkwardly through the door into the kitchen and stood facing one another for a moment in the bad light.

'Come on,' she said, taking his hand in hers and leading him into the studio. The blinds were down and Parry could see the afternoon sunlight falling slantwise across the building at the back of the studio, a seedy apartment block with ironwork balconies covered in pigeon droppings. The balcony immediately opposite contained a large dilapidated wire cage in which, side by side on a perch, sat two tattered, glum-looking pigeons with bedraggled tail feathers.

'Take off your shirt,' she said, sliding her fingers over his flesh between the buttons. She began to undo them one by one, running the flat of her hand over his nipples.

'Now these,' she said, indicating his trousers.

'You first,' he said. 'Your turn now. Take your shirt off.'

She slipped it over her head in a single gesture and flung it on to the floor in a heap. Her breasts were larger than he had expected, surprisingly voluptuous for such a slender body, and reminded him of the breasts of women in paintings by Delvaux: Venus dreaming of death. He began to kiss them but she stopped him saying 'Wait! Let's undress.'

She stood up, unbuttoned her jeans and stepped out of them neatly.

'No underwear,' he said. Her bush was the colour of straw.

'No,' she came towards him. 'Do you mind?'

Parry could not think of an answer to this. When he had taken off his own trousers and his underpants, they continued to embrace one another still standing up.

'I like it like this,' she whispered, 'it's so much more erotic, don't you think?'

He thought he would not forget this. The voluptuous girl with her narrow waist and large breasts, the soft wetness between her legs, the urgency of his own desire. It was as if he had never made love to anyone before.

Afterwards they fell asleep on the sofa lying face to face, Parry's arm draped protectively over the curve of Caroline's waist and this was where Sam discovered them at five.

He came into the studio whistling, making enough noise, so he thought, to wake the dead and found them there.

'Jesus,' he muttered angrily under his breath before backing out. He didn't wait to see if he had woken them, but went back down the stairs fast and across the square as quick as he damn well could to the nearest bar where he drank two pastis in quick succession.

Caroline woke as the door opened but lay quite still until Sam – for it must have been he – had gone again. Edward was still deeply asleep. She looked down at him for a moment noting the sunburned skin of his neck and the white, almost blue tinge of the hidden skin of shoulders and chest. One of her earliest memories was of her father's brown neck and the sunburned V where his shirt buttons had been left undone. The line where the brown skin stopped and the white started. It had been her earliest erotic experience. She thought of her father, knowing that at this moment he was probably also having a siesta, lying in his upstairs room with the shutters half-open and the sunlight falling on the marble floor of the room he still shared with her mother.

Parry shifted and stirred without opening his eyes. Caroline lay down beside him again under the sheet and began to stroke his penis which was half-stiff as if, even in sleep, he desired her. Older men made better lovers, there was no doubt about it. Parry opened his curious tawny eyes and began to kiss her. She thought she would not tell him about Sam. It would only upset him, spark off the guilt that was sooner or later bound to gush forth like blood from a wound about the wife, the children, that dreary life he was shackled to, like a hamster on a treadmill. Of course there was no reason why wifie should ever know. If Edward had any sense he would know to keep his mouth shut, except that Anglo-Saxon men so seldom had the sexual aplomb of their Gallic counterparts. Continental men had mistresses and never worried about it. Gaby, after all, had a wife – somewhere; but he had never really done more than mention her in passing.

At six thirty they got up. Parry was due to meet de Fonville at half-past seven. He thought he should wash and shave, make some division between one thing and another, try and shift his brain into gear, as Tom would say.

Caroline came into the bathroom when he was peeing and he looked around alarmed.

'I'm sorry,' she said, 'I didn't think you'd mind.'

'No, no,' he said unconvincingly, shaking his dick hastily and doing up his trousers. Tor would never do such a thing.

Watching Caroline in the mirror sitting on the edge of the bath naked under the baggy shirt, legs apart, quite unselfconscious, he thought with a sudden stab of uneasiness how peculiar it was to have a woman he scarcely knew in such intimate proximity. Twenty years of faithful marriage had made him decorous, prim almost, about the naked bodies of women; once he had not been like that. Once he had been as glad to walk around naked as the next man, but Tor had discouraged it. It was bad for the children, she said, don't. Even Agatha wouldn't now have him in the bathroom if she was having a bath and she was only ten, for God's sake. He turned to Caroline to tell her this and then remembered that Agatha's modesty was hardly a suitable topic of conversation in his present situation.

Caroline had lit a cigarette and was tapping the ash into the bath.

'Can I come with you?' she said, 'to see dear old Gaby?'

'It's business,' he said, 'not pleasure. He doesn't even know that we know one another.'

'So?'

'Well, I think it would look a little odd.'

'A little odd,' she repeated, mimicking him.

He made a lunge for her with one hand, keeping his razor in the other, but instead of running away, as he had expected, she pressed herself to him and began to try to kiss him, getting shaving foam everywhere.

'I say,' he said, aroused against his will, 'I say. Look, if you go on like this I'll be late.'

'I'll make you late,' she said, 'unless you agree to take me. Don't be such an old stick-in-the-mud,' she said, 'such an old fuddy-duddy. Where's your sense of fun?'

'Why are you so keen to come?' he asked, half-suspicious.

'I told you' she said, 'I know I can help. That's why. I know how his mind works.'

'How does it work? Tell me now.'

'No.' She leaned backwards and turned the tap on to drown her cigarette end.

'All right' he said, trying not to sound tetchy, 'all right. But you'd better hurry and get dressed. I can't be late.'

De Fonville's apartment was in one of the aristocratic mansions that line the rue de Varenne. The newly gilded dome of Les Invalides rose above the trees, gleaming in the evening light.

Parry walked along briskly carrying the old attaché case that had once belonged to his grandfather. He was wearing a grey suit of pheasant's eye cloth that he had made in the days when they were still rich. It fitted him properly and made him feel smart. Caroline had vanished for five minutes and had reappeared im-maculately turned out in a long black dress with cap sleeves cut on the bias so that the skirt swung when she moved. On her feet, black narrow shoes that looked as if they were made of string with a low heel. He couldn't help comparing her with Tor who would have looked neat but not like Caroline did without effort; not glamorous, not sexy.

Mahogany doors as tall as those in a church faced the street, but Caroline pushed on a section of one and stepped through followed by Parry. They were now in an inner courtyard paved with marble slabs where orange trees in great, swagged terracotta pots were placed at strategic intervals around the edges. A fountain in the shape of a nymph holding a shell dripped gently into a pool containing the glassy, swaying shapes of goldfish.

Crossing the courtyard they went through another set of double doors, this time of glass and mahogany, into an entrance hall of white marble. In a niche stood a statue of Aphrodite of Cyrene, freshly risen from the sea in the act of wringing out her hair. Parry paused to admire it but Caroline turned towards the stairs where a tall lean man in a charcoal grey suit was descending to meet them.

'What are you doing here?' he said to Caroline in French, 'when I am expecting Monsieur Parry. I had no idea you knew one another.'

He took Caroline's face in both hands and kissed her on the mouth.

'Monsieur Parry,' he said, holding out his hand, 'How do you do.'

'How do you do,' repeated Parry, glancing at Caroline; but she was smiling up at de Fonville who really was immensely tall. Six foot four or five, Parry estimated. He was six foot himself and he felt small in this man's presence. De Fonville had an expensive-looking suntan, the darkness of his skin contrasting dramatically with his grey/white corkscrews of hair. He looked with his aquiline nose more Jewish than anything, Parry thought, and the hair only served to deepen the impression of height.

'Let us go up,' said de Fonville, leading the way. He took Caroline's arm and they ascended together with Parry behind.

The apartment was a series of, as far as Parry could see, linked ante-chambers, several of them leading one from another, book-strewn, densely lined with pictures and magnificent pieces of furniture; looped curtains, heavy as sails, decorated tall windows; the whole place gave off a rich, tassled, carelessly faded, aristo-cratically cluttered sense of disordered luxury; pleasures of the mind and of the flesh all catered for. A hedonist's paradise, Parry thought, looking about him with envious admiration. This was the apartment of his dreams.

The room chosen for them to sit in was tall and pale, cream and gilt shutters blistered a little from the sun, eighteenth-century portraits of de Fonvilles in ice-blue satin and gauze, tottering cones of powdered hair sprinkled and looped with pearls; two sofas covered in ice-blue damask, gilt chairs; a silver tray the size of a small table contained bottles, glasses, decanters.

'Caroline, my dear, whisky?' De Fonville was already pouring as he spoke.

'Thanks,' said Caroline lightly. She lit a cigarette but avoided Parry's gaze, going instead to a window in what Parry thought of, in irritation, as a rather affected manner. But, like an accident victim, he kept having flashbacks of the sight of her breasts, her curiously colourless eyes gazing into his as they kissed.

'Monsieur Parry,' said de Fonville, turning round, 'to drink?'

'Oh,' said Parry – they were all speaking French – 'whisky as well, please.'

'I hear the Japanese are now making whisky,' said de Fonville, with a hint of amusement in his voice, 'but I somehow do not think they will be able to match these Islay malts.'

'Of course they won't,' said Parry, rather more crushingly than he had intended, thinking of the Japanese who had devoured the Veronese in the Louvre with their clicking shutters. Slit-eyes, Tom called them, blasted yellow peril.

'Well, you never know,' said de Fonville, 'they are so very very clever these Nippon. Such brilliant imitators.'

'A civilization made of paper,' said Parry, 'I wonder.'

'You do not admire the Japanese,' said de Fonville, 'do sit down. Caroline, come and sit down.'

'Not really. Do you?'

'Oh yes, I admire them all right. I just don't particularly like them. Paris is saturated with them as you've probably noticed. Now tell me, how is my dear old friend Tom?' Caroline sat next to de Fonville on one of the ice-blue damask sofas. After a minute she got up again to find an ashtray.

She seemed to know where everything was, Parry thought, watching her. He glanced at de Fonville, but he had the oriental ability not to display on his face what he was thinking. Parry wondered uncomfortably just how well they knew one another.

'Where are you staying?' asked de Fonville, lighting a cigarette.

'In Sam Hoskyns's studio. He's an old friend of mine,' Parry continued, 'but his wife has just had a baby and there's no room in their apartment for an extra any more, so I'm down in the studio.'

'Ah,' de Fonville raised his eyebrows and glanced at Caroline, who looked back at him impassively.

'Do you know him?'

'Yes, slightly. I quite like his work, as a matter of fact. I have commissioned him to paint a portrait . . .'

'Oh, don't bore Edward with all that,' interrupted Caroline, this time in English.

De Fonville, prevented from finishing his sentence, looked at her in astonishment. 'I didn't know I was being boring,' he said.

'It's a problem of old age,' she went on, 'you just don't realize.'

'Oh, I say,' interjected Parry. 'That's a bit stiff.'

Caroline smiled and shrugged.

'She is wild, this girl,' said de Fonville. 'Her father cannot control her. She does just as she chooses.'

'Why should he control me? I'm too old for all that.' She sounded bitter.

When they had gone next door into a small library lined with books on all four walls, from floor to ceiling, de Fonville turned to Parry.

'She is a lovely creature,' he said, 'but sad. I try to help. Her father is a business man, very busy, very successful, also in love with the mother like a young man might be, so Caroline is left out. She is very vulnerable.'

'Oh,' said Parry in what he hoped was a suitably unconcerned sort of a voice, then he added, 'she seems remarkably capable to me, doing what she does, living on her own.'

'Caroline reinvents herself every time she meets somebody new,' said de Fonville, smiling in an irritatingly knowing way.

'What . . . you mean she . . .?' Parry stopped. He must not appear to be too interested.

'She is young, she is beautiful. Vulnerability is very sexy, you know.'

'Quite,' said Parry briskly, 'absolutely.'

'Now,' said de Fonville, leading Parry to a round table in the middle of the room covered in calf-bound volumes, 'to business. These are the things I wish to sell. There is the list. Look through and tell me what you are interested in. I will leave you for a little while.'

He closed the door behind him. It was very silent in the room. Parry could not hear either the sounds of traffic or even the murmur of voices. He tip-toed across the room and opened the adjoining door. It was empty. He closed the door softly and went to the table and looked down at the books. Where were they, he wondered, his sense of unease growing. He imagined Caroline naked on a bed, locked in a passionate embrace with de Fonville, but no . . . it was as if he had a fever, Parry thought. He could only think of the girl when he should be concentrating on work, on making money, on the plight of his family, Mary's school fees, what did he think he was doing?

He picked up a book and began to examine it. They couldn't possibly be lovers or could they? De Fonville talked of her as a father might, but that might only be to put him off the scent. What had he said? 'Caroline reinvents herself every time she meets someone new.' What the hell was that supposed to mean?

Parry looked carefully at the book in his hands, then picked up a printed sheet laid in the middle of the table giving the valuer's suggestions. It couldn't be. He was over-wrought, seeing things that weren't there. The price given was 3000 francs. He put it down and began to go slowly through the other books. At the end, he picked up the original volume and looked at it again. He took it over to the window in order to examine it in the light and as he did so an idea began to form in his mind.

The other room was still empty when he opened the door. He cleared his throat and walked heavily around the room. Silence. He decided to pour himself another drink. He had his back to the door when de Fonville returned and to his shame jumped guiltily as if he had been caught stealing.

'Good,' said de Fonville, 'help yourself. Have you finished?'

'Yes.' Parry thought suddenly that it was a trick. A test. The volume placed there to persuade him into revealing himself.

'And?' De Fonville was waiting, gazing at him as if something amused him about Parry.

'Well . . . there are one or two things I think we would be interested in, yes. Most definitely.'

'Perhaps we should discuss it tomorrow,' said de Fonville, glancing at his watch. 'I'm afraid I have to go and have dinner with my mother now.'

Parry looked around the room and then back at de Fonville.

'You are wondering where Caroline is?'

'As a matter of fact, yes, vaguely.'

'She has had to go home. She was not feeling well.'

'Oh, I see. Well then,' Parry too looked at his watch. 'Let me think about it all overnight.' He was trying not to sound flustered: ill? What with? Worn out, no doubt. He put his glass down very carefully on the tray.

'We shall speak in the morning,' said de Fonville, guiding him to the door and then leading the way to the entrance, back through the series of marvellous rooms. This time, however, Parry scarcely did so much as glance at their contents. He felt quite sure she was still here somewhere, waiting for him to go.

In the rue de Varenne, he walked very quickly towards the Invalides. It was half-past eight and still light. On an impulse he turned into the Eglise du Dôme – there was something going on and the doors were open, the church lit – and found himself standing gazing at Napoleon's tomb. Inside that great mound of porphyry lay the shrivelled bones of the great man. He looked up at the inscriptions on the frieze around the gallery and read:

'Wherever the shadow of my rule has fallen, it has left lasting traces of its value.'

Grandiose nonsense, of course. Nothing lasted. This shadowy little life, so soon over. So soon we all come to this. There is so little time.

He went out quickly and walked away very fast from the glimmering, darkening gold of the great dome, past the enormous, important hotels, with their great imposing doors, all conceit, pomposity, all vanity. At the end of the street he saw a tall man in a charcoal grey suit accompanied by a woman that looked, from behind, like Caroline. He hurried after them, but when he reached the rue de Bellechasse the couple – had it been them – had vanished.

Parry walked back to Montmartre and went to the bar where he had met Sam and Caroline the night before. Sam was sitting at his usual table reading *Le Monde*.

'I thought you might be here,' said Parry, sitting down.

'Yeah?' said Sam, 'well, you were proved right. What've you done with Caroline?'

'What do you mean, "What have I done with her?"'

Sam smiled and took a sip of his drink. He rolled his eyes in a maddening way as if to say 'You tell me'.

'I haven't a clue where she is, if you really want to know.'

'She'll show up. You don't have to worry.'

'I'm not worried,' said Parry angrily.

'Let me get you a drink.'

'No, no. I'll do it.' Parry got up and went to the bar.

When he came back Sam said, 'You know your Jung. Well, she's an anima figure. Beware.'

'I don't know my Jung. I've no idea what you're talking about.'

'Come on, Edward. She's a temptress. You're being a fool. You're a married man.'

Parry stared at him. 'How did you know?' he asked.

'I saw you. Christ, Edward. If you must be unfaithful to your wife for God's sake find somewhere better to do it than in the middle of my studio.'

'It was a mistake,' muttered Parry, 'a silly mistake. It didn't mean anything.' He took a swig of his drink.

'Watch it,' said Sam, 'truly. She's a menace.'

'You didn't tell me that yesterday.'

'Why should I? There was no need. Yesterday. Maybe you should come up to the rue Caulaincourt and stay on the couch for a few days there, until Victoria comes.'

'No, no,' said Parry, 'totally unnecessary. I told you. She means nothing. It was just one of those things. Not entirely outside your experience either.'

'No,' said Sam, 'not entirely. But I'm not setting myself up as this great figure of sanctity, this great family man. It would be better if you left the studio.'

'I'll be the judge of that, if you don't mind,' said Parry pompously, his face darkening. He was not a child.

'Do you want to come up and have supper with me and Nancy?'

'No, no. I think I'll get an early night.'

'Sure?'

'Sure,' said Parry.

'Well, suit yourself,' said Sam. He drained his glass. 'How did it go with de Fonville?'

'Fine.'

'Did Caroline go with you?'

'Yes.'

'So what happened to her?'

'I told you, I don't know,' said Parry, but he could see Sam was waiting for further explanation.

'She vanished when I was looking through the books he wants to sell. By the way,' he added, struck by something in the conversation between Caroline and de Fonville, 'did he commission you to paint her portrait?'

'Why?'

'I just thought that he might have done.'

'No,' said Sam. 'I wish.'

'But you are painting her portrait. I saw it.'

'Yeah,' said Sam, calmly. 'She's a good model. I'm sure I told you that.'

'I don't think so.'

'I'd better be going,' said Sam rising. 'Sure you won't come? I know Nancy would like it.'

'Perhaps tomorrow,' said Parry, 'it's very kind, but I'm exhausted.'

'I'm sure you are,' said Sam, clapping him on the shoulder. 'Get some rest, old buddy. See you tomorrow, OK?'

'OK,' said Parry, raising his hand. He thought he would have another drink on his own, but found that he couldn't be bothered to push through the crush at the bar.

The studio was dark when he let himself in. Wherever Caroline was, she hadn't yet returned. He found that he was violently disappointed not to find her there. Whatever he had said to Sam about it not meaning anything was a lie. It meant something, but he was too alarmed to wonder exactly what.

He put on the light in the studio, and as he did so the telephone rang from its stool by the basin, making him jump.

It was Mary. He found that he was shocked to hear her voice here. It was as if she belonged to another world, a parallel universe, that should not be allowed to impinge on this one.

'Daddy?'

'Yes. What is it?' he heard himself saying in a voice different to the one he normally used to her.

'I just wanted to see how you were.'

'How kind,' he said formally, 'I'm very well, thank you.'

'You don't sound well.'

'Nonsense. I've just got in. I'm in the dark.'

'Are you cross about something?'

'No, not at all.' He made an effort. 'How are you, darling?'

'All right.'

'Is your mother there?'

'No, she's gone out to supper.'

'Who with?'

'Someone next door. A man called Hugh Croft.'

'Old Mrs Croft's son, in other words.'

'In other words, yes.'

She laughed tentatively and he realized that she was trying to establish some communication with him, some of their normal camaraderie. The trouble was he could not respond to her. He felt too far gone, too changed. It was as if he had gone back to how he had been before he had even known Victoria. Someone else, another skin. The slate wiped clean.

'That'll be nice for her,' he said, 'a bit of fun.'

'Mum needs to have some fun,' Mary said. 'I know she's looking forward to coming to Paris.'

'Jolly good,' said Parry wearily. 'Hadn't you better be going to bed now. It's late.'

'No, it isn't,' said Mary, sounding offended.

'Well, I'm going to bed,' he said. 'We're an hour ahead of you and I'm exhausted.'

'OK,' said Mary. 'Good-night, Dad.'

'Good-night.'

Parry went into the kitchen and poured himself some wine from the bottle that was already open. He drank it off quickly and then refilled his glass. It was then that he realized the little bronze had been removed.

He went back into the studio and sat on the edge of the sofa. He felt tired and restless at the same time, angry and anxious. Where was she? In the end, he got undressed, climbed into the stripy pyjamas that Victoria had packed for him and tried to sleep.

On Thursday morning Tom went off to school jubilant, having persuaded his mother to let him off going to Yorkshire, but instead of going to Hector's, Hector was to come to him at Easter House. The two boys could spend the time together under the watchful eye of Jenny.

'Hadn't they better sleep at my house?' she had said to Victoria. 'I don't think they should be left alone at night. They can doss down on the playroom floor.'

'That's just more work for you,' said Victoria sighing, 'I don't want to impose.'

'It's not imposing,' said Jenny, 'not in the least, and anyway the girls will like it, having a couple of chaps in the house.'

'All right,' said Victoria, 'if you're sure.'

Tom cornered Hector in the cloisters during the break. 'You come to me,' he said, 'it's all solved.'

'OK,' said Hector, 'brilliant. I can bring some weed.'

'Be careful,' said Tom, 'if Mum suspects she'll do her nut. I had enough trouble getting her to let me off Granny and Grandpa.'

'How did you do it?'

'A process of attrition, my dear Watson,' said Tom, 'based on the principle that if you go on about something for long enough, it's easier for parents to give in and feel magnanimous.'

'I doubt if Thalia knows the meaning of the word,' said Hector.

'Well, she doesn't have to know what it means,' said Tom, 'she just has to get the feel-good factor. How is Thalia anyway?'

'Getting ready for her holy pilgrimage, which means hairdresser, manicurist, heavy-duty shopping trips to Nicole Farhi . . . a trendy clothes shop,' he added when Tom looked blank, 'aromatherapy, you name it.' Dear old Tom was an innocent when it came to women. Dinny Hall, Nicole Farhi, Browns, Prada, Hector knew them all. 'Vaneeta hangs around the whole time now. She even sleeps there sometimes.'

'Is she going too?'

'Yes, thank Christ,' said Hector. 'Let's just hope she's so pleased to see her homeland she decides not to come back.'

'Unlikely,' said Tom in a worldly voice, 'she likes Notting Hill Gate too much.'

Hector rolled his eyes.

'There's only one proviso,' said Tom.

'What's that?'

'We have to stay at Jenny's at night. She's Mum's partner in the business.'

'Girls?' asked Hector.

'Two daughters, quite pretty, one's a bit nerdy but the other one, she's called Henrietta, who's Mary's age, fifteen, she's all right – and a very pretty lodger.'

'Ah,' said Hector in a heavy foreign accent, 'but is she sexy?'

'Very,' said Tom.

'Then this is an excellent arrangement, absolutely excellent. I'll tell Thalia that I'll be with you, that'll make her feel better.'

'Is she worried about you?'

'Thalia? Nah, not really. Thalia's only worried when she can't get the brand of massage oil she wants.'

'Must be an awful drag for the poor old Dalai Lama having all these people trailing about after him, isn't it?' said Tom.

'He must like it or he wouldn't do it.'

'I guess. Well,' said Tom, as a bell rang, 'see you later.'

'Can I come tonight?' said Hector, 'Thalia's having a farewell party. I won't get a wink of sleep.'

''Course you can. Farewell to what?'

'To herself, burk face, who else?'

Victoria saw the boys coming along the Mall as she came downstairs and went to open the front door to them. Hector, like Tom, was tall with long limbs that looked a little too large for him and fair hair that flopped over his face and got in his eyes; but when he brushed it out of his face it was possible to see that, also like Tom, he had an old-fashioned face with large blue eyes widely spaced, a Roman nose; the kind of sepia-tinted innocent face seen so often in those photographs of the First World War. The problem for modern boys of course was that they were in danger not of death from bullets or bombs but of living a life without any meaning.

As Victoria opened the door and came down the steps she saw the boys stop and talk to Hugh Croft who was brushing the top of his wall that overlooked the street. He looked round from his ladder as the boys came through the gate in the wall, saw Victoria and waved. She waved back.

'That's Mum's boyfriend,' said Tom to Hector.

Victoria laughed. 'Fat chance,' she said, 'what an amazing idea.'

When the boys had gone inside she glanced over her shoulder again and found that Hugh was watching her. He raised his arm and, after a second, Victoria did the same. Today the shirt he was wearing was of cornflower blue.

'Do you want tea, boys?'

'Oh yes.' Hector rubbed his hands together in a strangely old-fashioned gesture.

'Come on down, then,' said Victoria, 'everyone else is down there. Mary's got Amy with her and Henrietta, and Cyprian's got Rollo.'

'Hang on a moment,' said Tom, as Hector prepared to go down to the basement.

'Why? Get off!'

Tom dragged him by the arm to the door of the drawing room and pushed him inside.

'This is Iza,' said Tom, 'who I told you about.'

'Hello, hi,' said Hector flushing. He pushed his hair out of his eyes.

Iza, who was dusting the mantelpiece looked around.

'Hello,' she said. 'Tom is bad boy. He come always to interfere with the work.'

But she smiled as she said this, smoothing down her short skirt with one hand as she did so. Today, she was wearing a short flippy skirt of lime green printed with daisies, a pink cardigan over a tiny cropped T-shirt and pink spangled plastic shoes with high square heels.

'I can imagine,' murmured Hector, admiring Iza's legs.

'Come and have tea,' said Tom.

'No. I cannot. I do not eat and I have much work to do.'

'Never eats a thing,' said Tom to Hector.

'Silly boy,' said Iza, turning back to the mantelpiece, 'go now.'

Mary, hearing the boys coming down the basement stairs, turned to Amy and began to talk to her about homework. Secretly, she was a little in love with Hector although she would have died rather than admit this to her brother, or to anyone for that matter.

'Find somewhere to sit, boys,' said Victoria, who was buttering scones and reading the *Evening Standard* at the same time, 'tuck in. There's lots to eat. Cup of tea, Hector?'

The telephone rang.

'Mary, you do the tea for the boys,' said Victoria getting up, 'I'll answer that.'

'I was wondering what time you were coming on Saturday,' said her mother's voice.

'About tea time. Why? I mean, why in particular?'

'We've got a young man from Christie's coming and he's bringing someone else with him. Another of these wretched experts.'

'To look at what?'

'The Veronese.'

'Oh,' said Victoria, glancing over her shoulder. This was not the moment to discuss that with so many of the children in the room.

'Will tea time be all right? We can come earlier or later. Whatever suits.'

'They're coming in the morning,' her mother said, 'and they must be asked to stay to luncheon, so tea time will be fine, darling. Are you managing without Edward?'

'Yes, thank you,' said Victoria.

'How is he getting on?'

'Oh fine – as far as I know,' Victoria added, before she could stop herself.

'Is everything all right between you, darling?'

'Yes, it is. Sorry. I've got a roomful of children. We're all having tea. I'll see you on Saturday.'

'Children,' said Tom in disgust, 'we're not children.'

'Milk, Hector?' said Mary, brandishing the jug.

'Yes, please.'

'Mary's being mother,' said Tom.

'Shut up,' said Mary furiously, trying not to blush.

'You'd make a very good mother,' said Tom.

'You can do your own,' said Mary, pushing a cup at him.

'That's not very gracious,' said Victoria, coming back to the table.

Mary sat down and whispered something in Amy's ear.

'Whispering is rude,' said Aggie. 'Can I have another scone, please?'

'Of course you can, they're there in front of you,' said Victoria, trying to control her irritation. She supposed she might have guessed the Veronese would have to go but, all the same, it was a shock, like losing a limb. But if it meant the house could be saved then of course it would have to. I hate change, she thought, any change, especially, particularly, a painful one like this. I don't want things to change but they will whatever I do. The trouble is that all the changes in my life feel like threatening ones. Is there such a thing as a change for the better?

'Cheer up, Mum,' said Aggie. 'What's the matter?'

'Nothing,' said Victoria, shaking her head, 'nothing at all.'

'You should be looking forward to seeing Daddy,' said Aggie.

'I am, yes.'

But she thought that this was not completely true. She felt that she wanted to see Edward more because she was angry with him – she wanted the satisfaction of a row – rather than genuine delight at the idea of time on her own with him. The idea that this trip was to be a second honeymoon was a joke really; as soon as she realized that this was what she was thinking, she was shocked at herself and at the depth of the bitterness she was nurturing towards her husband.

But again, this was not a topic she could think about now with the children around, particularly Aggie who could read her state of mind with alarming ease.

'Mum, we're going to do our homework,' said Mary rising, together with Amy and Henrietta.

'We're going to play ping-pong,' said Tom, 'why don't you come too?'

'Do you want to?' Mary raised her eyebrows at the other two.

'OK,' said Amy, hooking her dark hair behind her ears.

'Hen?'

'Yeah, OK,' Hen shrugged an assent, but she hung back and let the others go on ahead to the old garage where the ping-pong table was.

'Has Mum said anything to you?' she asked Victoria when the younger ones had gone upstairs.

'About?' Victoria watched Hen carefully.

'How ill she is.'

'She's told me that she'll have to go for tests. I'm sure she's told you that too.'

'Yes,' said Hen, pressing the palms of her hands together, 'she has, but . . .' She looked at Victoria, 'I don't think she's telling me the truth. She says there's nothing the matter with her, but if that's the case why tests? I know she's lying.'

'She's not lying to hurt you,' said Victoria, thinking how like her mother Hen was with her pretty pale hair and eyes, the same wide mouth and generous expression, 'she doesn't want to frighten you. She doesn't want to frighten herself either and I think that's what's important here. If you're scared, she'll be scared for you as well as for herself. Try and think of it like that, Hen.'

Hen looked down at the tiled floor. Two large tears ran down the sides of her face. 'I'll try,' she said.

'Your mother has great courage,' said Victoria, 'you know that, don't you?'

'Yes.' Hen looked up and smiled through her tears. 'That's what she says about you.'

Victoria was so touched by this that tears came into her eyes. 'Don't start me off too,' she said, 'or where will we be.'

At eight o'clock Juliet, Victoria's favourite sister, and her husband Giles arrived for supper. Cyprian opened the front door to them, Aggie brought glasses and a bottle of white wine into the drawing room, then Ben came up with crisps in a bowl and some olives.

'A real little labour force you've got here,' said Juliet when Victoria came into the room, having shooed the youngest children upstairs to bed. The boys and Mary and Hen were still playing table tennis.

'Do they ever go to bed?' asked Giles, lighting a cigarette. 'That's the bit I'm not sure I could hack.'

'Oh, don't be ridiculous,' said Juliet, 'you wouldn't have to be there. I wouldn't expect it. Edward isn't a "new man," is he, Tor?'

'He's rather an old man,' said Victoria, 'but no, he's not. I never really expected him to be. He's like all men, he does a bit and then buggers off. I don't mind, I'm used to it.'

A lie, of course. She did mind but she was used to it, as she said.

'How is Edward?' asked Juliet.

'Fine, I think.'

'Hasn't he rung?' asked Giles, 'the old so-and-so.'

'Oh yes, he has,' said Victoria.

'When are you going, Tor?'

'Next Wednesday. I'm leaving the children with Mum and Dad.'

'You don't think that's a bit much for them at the moment,' said Juliet, also lighting a cigarette. The quacks in the fertility place had told her not to smoke as it might affect her chances, but one had to have some pleasures in life, especially now that their sex life had become dominated by temperature charts and test tubes and sniffing hormones every morning.

'Why? Do you think so? Mum seems as keen as ever to have them and they have got the space, you know.'

'For how much longer?'

'Christie's have been asked to value the Veronese,' said Giles, who worked at Sotheby's and was rather cross about the whole thing, but Christie's was the family firm and the Digbys did things their way, the same way they had been doing them for three hundred, or was it four hundred years. Pity they hadn't adopted the same principle of cautiousness towards Lloyd's, but dear old John Digby had gone for Lloyd's lock, stock and barrel, got poor old Tor and Edward embroiled in it too. Of course they would never have been able to afford this glorious house if it hadn't been for Lloyd's, and the school fees for the enormous tribe of children, certainly not on Edward's salary, which couldn't be more than fifty grand a year, if he was lucky. Of course if he worked for Sotheby's he would be paid even less, thought Giles gloomily.

'I knew that,' said Victoria quickly, 'Mum told me.'

'Of course, one of the problems with that picture is that it's not by Veronese,' said Giles.

'Don't be ridiculous, Giles,' said Juliet sharply, 'of course it's by Veronese, everyone knows that. It's always been by Veronese. If you thought it wasn't by him why didn't you say so before?'

'Because what the hell did it matter?' said Giles. 'I knew I'd get it in the neck if I attacked one of your family's sacred cows, so I just kept my mouth shut. Very sensible in view of your reaction.'

'It's not a sacred cow,' said Juliet, 'how dare you!'

'Jules,' said Victoria in a low voice, 'that's enough . . .'

Giles rolled his eyes. 'All of us poor buggers married to you Digby girls know a sacred cow when we see one – we've lived with them: the house, the chapel, the land, . . . since the 1470s blah, blah, blah . . .'

'Giles,' said Juliet rising, 'I think you'd better leave.'

Giles got to his feet and looked at Victoria.

'I'm so sorry,' he said, 'if I have offended you by stating a simple fact that the picture you all go on about is not a Veronese. I do not know what it is – it is a very good copy – but it is not by Veronese. Now I will go.'

'You haven't offended me,' said Victoria, 'but perhaps it would be better if you two were apart for a little while so that you can calm down.'

She sat down again and looked at her sister, then she lit a cigarette for Juliet and one for herself. The front door slammed. Giles's footsteps could be heard going down the path and through the gate which squeaked because it badly needed some oil and nobody had done anything about it. As usual.

'Why does he have to tell us now?' said Juliet, taking a deep drag on her cigarette, 'why couldn't he just keep his little pedantic trap shut?'

'Don't be too hard on him,' said Victoria, 'if it's true it's true. There's nothing we can do about it.'

'He always has to score points,' said Juliet, not appearing to have heard a word her sister said. 'He's such a bloody little show-off.'

'Come on, Jules, have another drink. You are allowed to drink, aren't you?'

'Oh God, yes,' said Juliet, holding out her glass. 'It's all this wanking into test-tubes that's put him into such a foul mood.'

'Enough to put anyone in a foul mood, if you ask me.'

'They give him a test-tube and a dirty mag and off he goes. It is a loathsome process. What seems so unfair is that I'm the only one who can't manage children.'

'I know,' said Victoria soothingly, pouring her sister an extremely large gin, 'it does seem unfair. How many more times are you going to try?'

'Once more, maybe twice. It's so damned expensive,' said Juliet, reaching up for her glass. 'I sometimes think I'd rather just have a nice dog or a horse.'

'Well then, why don't you?'

'I can't very well keep a horse in Burton Court,' said Juliet.

'Why not? It could graze in the grounds of the Royal Hospital and cheer up the Chelsea Pensioners. They'd all think they were back at Waterloo or on the North West Frontier or whatever.'

Juliet hooted with laughter. 'Then if I have a baby I could keep a dear little pony there as well. Who was it who used to take ponies in railway carriages with them? Was it the Mitfords?'

'Probably,' said Victoria, laughing with her sister, relieved to have broken her sour mood.

'Actually, Tor,' said Juliet, 'I'm terribly worried about Ma and Pa. You know they keep getting these dreadful letters from their underwriting agents – well, you would wouldn't you – but the sums are horrendous. How are they going to find such amounts of money?'

'They're not,' said Victoria. 'They're talking of selling. Did Mum tell you?'

'She hinted at it. I don't think she wanted to upset me. I found Pa crying in his study. I went in without knocking and he couldn't disguise it. It gave me such a fright. He always seems so calm, so capable, so reassuring; and there he was blubbing like a girl. I hate it when things aren't what they seem, Dad crying and the Veronese being a fake.'

'Giles didn't say it was a fake, he said it wasn't by Veronese.'

'Same difference surely?'

'No. It'll still be worth something if it's by a contemporary. They could all paint in those days, not like now when nobody can.'

'Is Edward worried about Lloyd's?'

'Yes.'

'Are you?'

'I've almost gone beyond worry.' Victoria shrugged her shoulders slightly. 'What's the point?'

'Will you have to sell up?'

'Not if I have anything to do with it. The house is in Edward's name alone, at least we got that right, so I can't be nabbed for that. He says we'll have to sell, but I told him to stop being so stupid.'

'Men are stupid, I find,' said Juliet, gazing into her glass.

'I must just go and peer into the oven,' said Victoria, 'come down with me.'

'Who's that divine-looking man?' asked Juliet as they crossed the hall. Hugh Croft was just going out of his gate looking rather smart in a grey suit as if he were going to a dinner party.

'Oh,' said Victoria, 'that's Hugh. Old Mrs Croft's son.'

'Is he married?'

'No. Has been but isn't now.'

'God, he's dishy,' said Juliet, who was still holding her mostly empty glass of gin.

'He's very nice,' said Victoria firmly.

'Oh, don't be such an old prude. He's gorgeous. I should take my chance while Edward's away, if I were you.'

'I beg your pardon, I happen to be happily married. And I don't believe in having affairs.'

'I do,' said Juliet dreamily.

'You're tight,' said Victoria, 'come on down, for goodness sake.'

Hugh, she thought, nice name, Hugh. Hugh Croft. Mrs Hugh Croft. He was so kind, Hugh, and he listened, *really* listened when you talked to him, instead of doing what Edward did which was a sort of drifting off, a kind of blankness, either that or he began to talk, at the first opportunity, about himself. Pull yourself together, Victoria, she said firmly to herself, that is no way for a married woman and mother of six to be thinking.

Hector lay on the floor in Tom's room wrapped in a sleeping bag. Cyprian was in the other bed, having refused to move out, much to Tom's disgust.

'He just wants to be with you,' his mother had said, coming out of her bedroom upon hearing the row. Juliet had had to be sent home in a cab, Victoria first having made sure she had her keys and enough money. Would there ever be a moment when she could stop mothering the world?

'He is with me,' said Tom, 'all the bl . . . all the time. Why can't he just move into Ben's room for one night, or the spare room, for that matter, as Dad isn't here.'

'He wants to be with you,' repeated Victoria wearily, 'if you don't provoke him he'll soon drop off. Give him a chance, Tom, you are his older brother. Try and remember how you felt at his age.'

'All right,' said Tom sulkily, unwilling to challenge his mother at such a critical juncture. One false move and he would be packed off to Yorkshire with 'the children'.

'Have you done your homework?' she asked.

'It's revision,' said Tom swiftly. 'Exams after half-term.'

'Let Cyprian go to sleep and then go back up. Go and play some more ping-pong or something.'

'We've done that,' said Tom in a bored voice.

'Well, go and find something to do that doesn't include smoking,' said Victoria wearily. 'I've had it. I'm going to bed.'

Hector and Tom had watched something on television and then come upstairs again. As they reached the first-floor landing the telephone rang and was immediately picked up.

'That'll be Dad,' said Tom, 'waking Mum up as usual, selfish bastard.'

Tom paused outside his mother's door which was ajar, nodding to Hector to go on into their room. He wanted to know what was going on.

'But that's wonderful,' said his mother's voice, 'you must be terribly pleased. It's made it all worthwhile.'

Pause.

'You don't sound terribly pleased.'

Pause.

'Tired? Try being here. I'm the one who's tired. You're in Paris. I know you're working, I know it's been a tense time . . . well, now we can, can't we, I mean, isn't that what you're ringing me to say . . .?'

There was another pause, this time considerably longer than the others.

'. . . *not* go to Paris! But why the hell not? I haven't had a holiday for ages. I'm taking the children to Yorkshire on Saturday and then coming back on Monday especially so that I can join you in Paris and have some fun, relax a little. It was going to be our second honeymoon, remember?'

Tom shifted his feet silently outside his mother's door, trying to figure out what was going on between his parents. Whatever it was it sounded bad.

'I don't want you to come back, I don't care how much bloody money it would save.'

Long pause followed by a new tone of voice, brisk rather than loving. At least they weren't the goo-goo type, Tom thought. But his mother never swore. Something must be wrong.

'All right. Good. I know you've been worried. So have I. Will you confirm our booking at the hotel?'

Hector was reading one of Cyprian's Asterix books when Tom went into his room.

'Ça va?' he asked, turning over a page in an elaborately casual fashion.

'Think so,' said Tom non-commitally. 'Just parents, you know . . .'

'I don't actually,' said Hector.

'Mmmh,' muttered Tom, throwing off his clothes and scrabbling about for his pyjamas, not wanting to be outdone by Heck whose elaborately studied casualness about his lack of normal family life was sometimes bloody annoying.

'He doesn't want her to go to Paris,' he said suddenly. 'My God, what a bloody bastard he is.'

'Language,' said Heck. In the bed under the window Cyprian stirred and groaned, flinging out an arm.

Mary's room was up another short flight of steps from Tom's and was the largest of the children's bedrooms with a view of the river. When Tom had complained that it was unfair that she should have her own huge room and he had to share, his mother had said that she was the senior child and he, Tom, would get his own larger room when they had had the attics seen to. Due to Lloyd's, this had never happened.

'Mare, are you awake?' Tom put his head around the door. Her light was out, but it was a clear night with a large moon, so that he could see she was lying in her bed with her hands folded behind her head as if she had been waiting for him.

'What is it?' She sat up suddenly and put the light on.

'I want to talk for a minute.'

When the baby had died last year they had talked like this for weeks after it had happened, usually at night when everyone was in bed, experiencing an extraordinary change in their relationship which consisted, normally, of undiluted antagonism. But their father had been so peculiar and distant and their mother had needed them to help her. They had both known that and had turned to one another instead.

Mary leaned over and patted the space on the end of her bed which was her way of inviting him in. She handed him a pillow so that he could lean against the wall.

'What?' she asked.

'That was Dad on the phone just now. Did you hear it ringing?'

'Yes. Yes I did. What?'

'I listened. He told Mum he didn't want her to go to Paris and she was furious. What's going on between them, do you think?'

'I dunno,' said Mary, 'but it sure ain't good. I rang him the other night when Mum was out and he was all chilly, you know how he can be, acting as if he didn't know why I was ringing. I hate it when he's like that, I hate it.' She took Tom's hand and squeezed it. There were tears in her throat which she wanted to control but was not sure she would be able to.

'Do you think they're going to break up?' said Tom in a funny voice.

'Do you?'

'I don't see how they can go on as they are.'

'People do, though, don't they?'

'Catholics do. People like us do. We're supposed to be the perfect family, aren't we? Well, fuck that, I say. Fuck it all.'

He thought Mary would tell him not to swear but she didn't.

'I don't think I can stand it,' said Mary. '*Is* Mum going to Paris?'

'I think so. She was so fucking angry with him, I've never heard her like that. In the end he caved. She asked him to confirm the booking at the hotel, so it looks as if she will be going.'

'She's been looking forward to it. He knows that,' said Mary angrily. 'She needs a break. She's been working so hard since the baby died.'

'He wasn't much help to her then either, was he?'

'I think he was terribly upset, too,' said Mary.

'Don't make excuses for him,' said Tom.

'I wasn't really.'

They were silent for a moment.

'Where's Heck?' asked Mary, rearranging her hands behind her head again.

'In my room, on the floor.'

'Is he asleep?'

'Wasn't when I left.'

'Get him up here and we can play cards,' said Mary, pushing her abundant dark hair back behind her ears, 'I don't think I can sleep yet.'

'OK,' said Tom, 'good idea. Plus I'll go and get some stuff from the kitchen to eat. I'm starving.'

'Me too.'

Tom went back downstairs to the kitchen. When he came back with some bread and cheese and a packet of Gypsy Creams in a carrier bag, he put his head around his mother's door. She was sitting up in bed reading.

'Night, Mum,' he said, waving at her.

'Oh Tom! Why're you still up? It's terribly late.'

'Can't sleep,' said Tom.

'At least you can get your own glass of water now,' Victoria said.

Tom grinned at her. That had been his great ploy for years in order to prevent her from leaving him at bed-time. A glass of water.

'Everything all right?' he asked carelessly.

'Yes, thank you, fine. Everything's fine. Why?'

He shrugged. 'Just checking.'

'Dad rang.'

'Oh yeah?'

'He's made a fantastic find, so that's good news, but don't tell anyone.'

'No, OK.' Tom hovered.

'He was tired, but he's looking forward to me going over.'

'Really?' said Tom. It began to dawn on him that most of the things one's parents told one were lies, as this was. The whole of one's childhood underpinned by falsehoods, fibs and evasions. It was babying and degrading. He remembered how she had talked to his grandmother of 'the children'.

'Look, Mum,' he said, '. . . look, you don't have to, you don't have . . .'

When it came to it, however, he did not want to suggest to his mother, whom he loved, that she was lying. It was more complicated than that, as he was beginning to realize.

'What are you trying to say?' his mother asked, somewhat sharply.

'I'm trying to say you don't have to protect me,' said Tom in a rush. 'Me and Mare, we want to help. We know what it's like for you.'

Victoria looked at her son. 'You overheard my conversation just now, didn't you?'

'Bits of it.'

'Which particular bits?'

'That Dad doesn't want you to go to Paris.'

'And what else?' Victoria enquired.

'I dunno,' said Tom. 'Can't remember.'

'He wanted to come back because he thought it would save money. He meant it kindly.'

Tom looked at his mother warily. 'Well, that's all right then,' he said. It had suddenly occurred to him that his mother was fantastically hurt and that she was trying to hide it from him as a matter of urgency; it also occurred to him that she must be allowed to do so. It wasn't lying after all, but a question of survival. This insight made him feel astonishingly, astoundingly adult, as if he were the parent and she the child.

'Gotta go,' he said, slouching round the edge of the door, returning with some relief into his adolescence. 'Fuck the perfect family,' he said under his breath, climbing the stairs with his carrier bag, 'fuck them. Fuck, fuck, fuck.'

After a few seconds he began to feel more like his normal self. Hector was sitting on Mary's bed which annoyed Tom although he was no longer prepared to ask himself why this should be the case. Introspection was exhausting and uncomfortable, usually yielding results one would rather not have known. Tom got some cards out of the top drawer of the chest of drawers.

'Budge up,' he said to Heck, and began to shuffle the cards.

Victoria turned the light off. If anyone wanted her now it was too bad. She was officially asleep. She had heard Hector thump upstairs followed by Tom. It was a schoolday tomorrow but that was too bad. They were young and healthy, well able to go without sleep. If Tom was there Heck and Mary wouldn't be able to get up to anything they shouldn't even supposing they wanted to, although Mary's furious blushes at the tea table had made her wonder.

The tears, when they came, ran down behind her ears and on to the pillow. He hadn't wanted her to come and that was so wounding that she still felt slightly breathless with the shock of it. She couldn't work out why. It was more than a commendable desire to save money, much more. But what? What could have happened to him in such a short time?

Victoria must have dozed off for she awoke with a start to hear a bedroom door closing. Must be the boys. But once awake she couldn't sleep again. She got up and went slowly down the stairs, pausing on the landing to look at the sleeping river.

Hugh Croft was just going through his gate. She glanced at her watch: it was one in the morning. When she looked out of the window again he was walking slowly up the path looking in her direction. She glanced down at her white nightie and then back again. He waved. And, after a minute, she waved back.

At a critical moment on Saturday morning, Hugh Croft appeared again. Victoria was assembling luggage in preparation for the desperate business of packing the car when he appeared at her elbow. She hadn't even noticed him coming out of his house, but there he was all of sudden, radiating calm and technical expertise.

'Let me do this bit,' he said, 'is this everything?'

'I hope so,' she said, biting her lip, 'but you don't want to get involved with this rabble.'

'You go and chase them up and I'll pack what there is. I'd like to help,' he said, 'if you don't mind.'

Mind, she thought, going up the path. *Mind!* No one with as many children as she had had time to be a feminist. Seize help with both hands was her motto. It was all she could do to prevent herself from embracing him.

In the hall Victoria met Agatha humping a huge bag downstairs.

'What's in there? You better hurry if you want that lot to go in the boot.'

'I don't. This is my bag for the journey.'

'I see. Sensible girl.' She kissed her younger daughter, suddenly relieved that she now had time to go downstairs and write a list for Jenny.

'Aggie,' she said, 'when you've put that lot on the back seat, run upstairs and find Tom for me, will you?'

157

'He's still asleep.'

'Well, go and get him up. He should be here helping me.'

'All right,' said Aggie reluctantly.

'And, while you're up there, tell Mary to hurry up.'

Aggie rolled her eyes in reply.

'Go *on*,' said Victoria, feeling the panic rising again. So much to do she couldn't think how she was going to remember it all. It would be a relief to be on the road. This was always the worst bit. Bless Hugh for doing the car. She tried not to think about Edward, that would be for later when she was in her very own old bedroom at home.

Feather, locked in the kitchen, looked up at Victoria with anxious Labrador eyes. She was staying in London with the boys as she took up too much room in the car.

'Go and lie down,' said Victoria, after she had fallen over her twice on her way round the kitchen looking for her pen. The usual story: it had been 'borrowed' and not returned. With children everything moved around the house all the time; scarcely an object was to be found in its original resting place.

Jenny came in wearing an Indian pleated skirt and a cyclamen-coloured T-shirt.

'How's it going?' she asked.

'Saintly Hugh is packing the car for me,' said Victoria, opening a drawer in the table. 'I've sent a messenger to get Tom out of bed. Are you sure you don't mind having them?'

'Quite sure,' said Jenny. 'It's only a few nights, after all, not for ever.'

'How are you feeling?'

'Fine,' said Jenny dismissively, 'absolutely fine. Hugh is packing the car, did you say? That's kind.' She looked amused. 'He's rather turning into your knight on a white charger.'

'All help gratefully received,' said Victoria, pretending to be distracted.

'Of course.' Jenny sat down. 'Is there anything special I should know?'

'Make sure the boys feed Feather,' said Victoria. 'Open the post for horrors. If Edward rings tell him I've left.'

'Doesn't he know that?' Jenny gave Victoria a puzzled look. 'When did you last speak to him?'

'Of course he knows,' said Victoria, avoiding Jenny's gaze, 'it's just he might ring to see if we've gone.'

'Oh right.'

'I'm coming back on Monday.'

'Awfully quick for you,' said Jenny, lighting a cigarette.

'As long as I have time to see Mum and Dad,' said Victoria, 'that's all I mind about.'

'When were you last up, I can't remember?'

'A couple of months ago. There's been so much on here.'

Tom came stumbling in, still in pyjamas, rubbing his eyes.

'There you are,' said his mother. 'Help Jenny, won't you?'

'Yes, Mum,' said Tom in a bored voice.

'And don't forget the poor benighted dog.'

'Ye-es,' Tom glanced longingly in the direction of Jenny's cigarette smoke.

'And don't get up to wicked things with Hector.'

'I'll make sure he doesn't,' said Jenny, winking at Tom.

'Yeah, Mum, sure,' said Tom, 'why don't you just go?'

'I'm doing my best.'

Outside, the four children had organized themselves in the car, and Hugh was just shutting the immaculately packed boot.

'Goodness,' said Victoria, 'I can actually see out of the back window! How did you do it?'

'Long practice,' he said, handing her what looked like a small torch in a case.

'What's this?'

'A mobile telephone,' he said.

'But I haven't a clue how to use it,' she said, flustered. 'Is it yours?'

'Yes, it's a spare. I always have to be on call, you see. But I want you take it for the journey. I don't think you should drive four children north without a phone.'

'But I've done it hundreds of times.'

'Don't you usually have your husband with you?'

'Not always.'

'It's just a precaution,' he said. 'Otherwise I'll worry about you. All you do is this.' He showed her how to use it. 'Just stow it away in your bag,' he said, 'and use it if you need to.'

'I've always disapproved of these things,' said Victoria.

'Stop being such an ostrich, Mum,' said Tom, who had come out to the car in his bare feet and still in his pyjamas, 'it's jolly useful. I'll have it if you don't want it.'

Hugh grinned at him, and then at Jenny who had followed him with Feather on her lead to stop her trying to get into the car.

'Feather,' said Aggie in a voice rich with unshed tears, 'Feather.'

'Shut up,' said Cyprian, 'you're not going away for long.'

Victoria got in and slammed her door.

'Thanks,' she said to Hugh, 'that's so thoughtful of you.'

'It's nothing.' He shook his head slightly, adding in a lower voice, 'I'll keep an eye on those boys for you, too.'

'Would you?'

'No problem. I've got one or two things I need a hand with too which I'm prepared to pay for.'

'Brilliant,' said Victoria gratefully, 'thank you.' She put the car into gear.

'Drive carefully,' said Hugh, stepping back.

'Ring me when you get there,' said Jenny.

Tom waved and yawned.

In the driving mirror Victoria saw Hugh say something to Jenny and watched as they turned together and went up his pathway into Ascension House, leaving Tom and Feather to return into Easter House on their own. As she waited for the lights at the Hogarth Roundabout she realized she felt that Hugh was her find, her property, and that Jenny had no business going into his house like that with him. She knew, of course, that this was absolute nonsense but the feeling of injured propriety persisted.

John Digby woke just before five a.m. It was already light and the birds were singing fit to bust. The room in which he slept these days had been the room in which he was born, the Blue Room, on 27th January, 1927. His mother, Teresa, was nineteen when he was born and had not seen a doctor during the entire duration of her pregnancy, other than at the very beginning to confirm it. He, John, had been her first child, the first of five, a lusty, noisy baby who thrived from the moment he was born, a gifted, precious child who walked and talked early and was generally held up by his doting mother to exemplify all that was good in baby and boyhood. She had been a good mother, Teresa, taking an equal and energetic interest in all her children, making up for the father's moodiness and his habit of favouring one child over another. She had died of cancer of the pancreas in her late sixties, a horrible illness which she had defied until the end without grumbling or complaining or, as far as John could see, any fear. She was an intelligent and energetic woman but she had also had the great gift of faith. She had always known that her sojourn here was something temporary, a half-way house, a spring-board to another world; and because of this she had died as gracefully and as humorously as she had lived. When told she was dying she had said, 'What a bloody nuisance'.

What would she say now, he wondered, if she knew what her son and heir had done with his inheritance? And the ghastly thing was he had done it all for what he thought was the best of reasons. And it had put on the roof and paid for weddings and regilded the chapel. But now, now what? Every day he faced this knowledge anew, the knowledge of his own ghastly, aching failure, the knowledge that he had ruined his inheritance. He knew Isobel knew what was going through his mind and he was even more ashamed of himself for showing what he regarded as weakness. Yesterday he had found himself in the gun room staring into the locked cabinet at the oiled, gleaming, lethal barrels. The key was in the secret drawer of his desk, hidden under the bottom drawer on the left-hand side. His sons shot things occasionally, pigeons, that kind of thing, the guns were really for them. He himself never shot, would never again, ever, put a bullet through the soft body of any undefended creature.

He looked at his watch: five thirty. He got out of bed, dressed in his usual uniform of cords, check shirt, brushed his hair and went downstairs. The chapel was reached by a passage lined with books and busts of cardinals that led past the library and was entered from this end of the house through a gothic doorway, all redone by a nineteenth-century Digby who had got hold of a disciple of Pugin and let rip. There was a family joke that the Palace of Westminster was just like home.

He knelt at the altar rail to say his prayers, raising his eyes to the great crucifix on the altar and then to the place beyond where the painting hung. At midday the young man from Christie's in York would return with another wretched expert. Together they would examine the picture and pronounce whether, in their view, it was a genuine Veronese or not. The chances were, Iso said, that it was not and if it was not then the house would have to be put on the market. The farms could not be sold, as they were tenanted, so it was either the picture or the house. And if the house goes, he said to himself, I go too. There were some things, it seemed, in which one's faith could not sustain one. He turned his back on the altar without genuflecting and marched out.

Isobel Digby was walking the dogs when she saw her husband come out of the west door of the chapel. He was walking fast and the expression on his face was one of shocked blankness. She broke into a half run herself upon seeing him, so urgently did he appear to be in need of solace, and then stopped in her tracks feeling that it would be better for him if he did not know that she had seen him in that condition. She was constantly having to exercise this tact in all her relations with her husband these days. She sometimes wondered if he knew what a strain it was for her to have to be so endlessly splendid. If they had to go from this place then she would make the best of it: a smaller house somewhere, a garden, the dogs, her charity work, her children and grandchildren; but she feared it would kill her husband.

Charles Kindersley and his colleague arrived on the dot of midday in Charles's car, but this time there was no springer spaniel in the back wanting to be let out. The colleague, Matthew Home, was from Christie's in London and was a world authority on Veronese. John was nowhere to be seen. Isobel apologized for this and offered them coffee which they refused. She then took them to the chapel and left them there. Fielding, the joiner, had taken the picture down that morning, unscrewing it from the wall with the help of his assistant. Charles Kindersley had said that naturally they would need to look at the back of it. To Isobel it felt uncomfortably like the first step of their ultimate removal had been taken. But men were such cowards. Where was John?

She said to nice Charles Kindersley, who looked pale and serious, that she would be in the library and that they were to come and find her as soon as they were done.

Isobel sat down on a window seat and tried to read the newspaper but her eye kept straying towards the clock on the mantelpiece over the fireplace. Its gentle ticking was driving her mad. She got up and, as she did so, the telephone rang which made her start.

'It's me, Granny,' said Mary, whose voice sounded as if she were inside a bucket.

'Where are you?'

'On the motorway. We're going to stop soon for lunch. Someone lent Mum a mobile phone and I thought it would be fun to ring you. Are you all right?'

'I'm very well,' said Isobel, 'just a little busy at the moment, darling. Give my love to Mummy. No, I don't want to talk to her, I don't think it's safe while you're driving.'

'Of course it's safe,' said Mary, 'everyone does it.'

'That does not mean it's safe,' said Isobel firmly. 'I'll expect you at tea-time.'

'Good-bye, Granny.'

Isobel put the receiver down. She had sixteen grandchildren and it was they who were the future, not bricks and mortar, not books, not broad acres, but it made her so sad to think that there would be no more Digbys in this house. One became so attached to one's material trappings. No wonder the rich found it harder to die. She went to the window and then back to her chair again. Come on! She took a cigarette out of a silver box on a small table, found a match and lit it. The smoke went through her head like a drug and made her feel dizzy and remote. She only smoked about two cigarettes a year these days, although once she had been a heavy smoker like Victoria.

'Mrs Digby?'

Charles Kindersley put his head around the door. She was sitting in an armchair smoking a cigarette. She wore a cornflower-blue tailored shirt that deepened the colour of her eyes and a black pleated skirt and black shoes with bows on them of a kind his mother wore but only for parties.

'Yes.' She rose.

'I've left Matthew in there. It's not a Veronese, I'm afraid, he's as certain as he can be. It's the work of a contemporary – a very good contemporary – but it means, of course, that the picture is not worth what it would be if it were the genuine article.'

'I see.' She bent over to put her cigarette out in a small silver ashtray. 'Well, it can't be helped. Would you like a drink?'

'Very much,' he said.

'So should I. What about Mr Home?'

'I'll go and get him,' said Charles.

They went into a sitting room with pale pink damask walls and an elaborate cornice picked out in gilt. There were comfortable sofas and a mahogany secretaire containing porcelain. Pictures in gilt frames lined the walls, oils, watercolours, miniatures, a serene room, apparently imperturbable, with everything designed to give the impression of an elegant permanence.

The Lloyd's bills must be very bad indeed, thought Charles, accepting a whisky. He glanced at Matthew who was looking politely incurious, but at that moment old John Digby came in looking pretty pale around the gills.

His wife returned from the small closet where she had been pouring drinks, holding a glass which she handed to her husband.

'Drink that,' she said, 'you're going to need it,' which was her way of warning him that the news was bad. He thought how like his mother she sounded in a crisis, the same brisk way of dealing with the end of the world.

John Digby took the glass from his wife but seemed unable to decide what to do with it. After a second he drank the contents and then put it down.

'I am afraid the picture is not by Veronese, sir,' said Matthew Home, glancing at Charles Kindersley.

'But what about the documentation,' said John, 'surely that's . . . surely that proves that you are wrong?'

'The documentation does indeed suggest that the picture is by Veronese, but our examination of it suggests that this is not in fact the case.'

'Who the bloody hell is it by, then?'

'John,' said Isobel warningly. There was a pulse beating in his forehead, always a bad sign.

'I mean, how the hell do you know it's not Veronese?'

'It's quite complicated,' said Matthew Home, 'to do with . . .'

'I'm not a complete idiot, you know.'

'No, sir, of course, what I was trying to say was that we can tell by the way the draperies of the figures are painted, the hues are not quite as rich as one would expect to find in a painting by Veronese himself and they lack . . .'

'I want another opinion,' said John, 'I simply don't believe we can all have had the wool pulled for so long.'

'We'd be perfectly happy to get someone else along to have a look if that's what you want, sir.'

'Well, I do want. I'm not going to take this lying down.'

'They are the experts, John,' said Isobel, 'they do know what they're talking about. I can't see any . . .'

'Absolute rubbish! Experts!' said John in disgust. 'Everyone's an expert these days and we all have to defer to their half-baked opinions about everything from exercising your dog to valuing a painting. I don't believe a word of it.'

'Excuse me a moment,' said Isobel, putting her glass down carefully on a glass-topped showcase containing some family medals. She took her husband by the arm and steered him out of the room and along the corridor, past the busts of the cardinals, and on through the gothic door into the chapel.

'This is hardly the moment for an outburst,' she said, still gripping his arm. 'It's not their fault the painting isn't what it's supposed to be.'

'They're wrong.'

'They know what they're doing,' said Isobel. 'Be sensible.'

'You don't understand,' he said, turning on her, 'it means we have to go. Leave. We have to leave.'

Isobel gazed at her husband. He was a bad colour, the skin around the eyes and mouth had gone the colour of putty as if the blood had deserted from shock or outrage.

'You must calm down, John,' she said, 'you must. Take deep breaths.'

'Don't tell me what to do!' He wrenched his arm out of her grasp and began to tear at his hair with both hands as if he wanted to pull it out.

'I am going back now to look after our guests and then to take them into luncheon,' she said.

When he did not reply, she left him there and went out, hoping the atmosphere would soothe him and bring him to his senses.

'It is not the end of the world,' she said to herself as she returned to the drawing room. The polite young men were standing by the fireplace, talking in low voices, but stopped when she came in.

'My husband is overwrought,' she said, 'please try and understand.'

'I am sorry,' said Charles Kindersley who looked worried, 'I am so sorry. I know what a shock it is when something one has always imagined to be one thing turns out to be another.'

'It wouldn't matter if it weren't for Lloyd's,' said Isobel. 'If it weren't for that we would never consider selling the painting in any case.'

'It must be dreadful for you. I am so sorry.'

'It all seemed such a good thing at the time, you see. Getting a double return on your share portfolio. I suppose one should have known, but we didn't. We thought Lloyd's was run by honest men, but it seems we were mistaken.'

The young men exchanged grave looks.

'And not only you,' said Matthew Home.

*

166

When Victoria arrived at half-past three with the children Isobel came out to greet her, followed by Minnie, her black pug.

'I'm so glad you're here safely,' she said.

'Me too. Out you all get,' she said to the three children in the back. Mary was already hugging her grandmother.

'Darling,' said Isobel, 'it is so lovely to see you.'

'And it's lovely to see you too,' said Mary.

When the others had said hello to their grandmother, Victoria sent them all off.

'Go and find something to do,' she said, 'what time's tea, Mum?'

'In forty-five minutes,' said Isobel. 'You're all in the usual rooms.'

'Can I take Minnie?' asked Agatha.

'Of course you can, but just be careful when you pick her up with her back legs. She's feeling arthritic, aren't you, Minnie?'

The pug, delighted to be the centre of attention, gambolled and pranced, showing off to a delighted audience.

'Can we have a pug?' asked Agatha, picking Minnie up and squeezing her in exactly the way her grandmother had asked her not to.

'No,' said Victoria. 'Feather would hate it.'

'She'd soon adjust.'

'No, she wouldn't,' said Cyprian, 'you've spoilt her. Feather wants to be top dog. She hates Minnie.'

'She doesn't.'

'She does, stupid.'

'Go away,' said Victoria, 'I want to talk to Granny. Go on, shove off.'

'We're going,' said Mary in an offended voice, 'all right?'

'She's so tall,' said Isobel, watching her grand-daughter walk into the house.

'I know. It makes me feel old.'

'How old are you, darling? Thirty-seven, thirty-eight?'

'Thirty-something we're supposed to say. Isn't the modern world hideous? I'm thirty-nine.'

'And you feel old,' said her mother in an amused voice. 'I seem to remember I felt rather the same at your age.'

'And what do you feel now?'

'I never think about it any more.'

'But you must? Doesn't everyone?'

'You get out of the habit. I think more of Minnie's life expectancy than my own. Let's walk on, shall we? There's something I need to talk to you about.'

Instead of going in to the house they took a path that led off to the left, a grassy walk made dark by the height of twin yew hedges on either side which led, eventually, to a walled garden.

'Your father is very upset about the picture which turns out not to be a Veronese after all.'

'Does that mean you won't sell it?'

'We may have to. We may also have to sell this house.'

'I knew it was on the cards. I've known it for some time. How could I not what with Lloyd's? Ju knows too. Do all the others?'

'They must have guessed, I suppose.'

'How is Dad taking it? Ju said that he . . .' she hesitated, changing her mind about what she wanted to say, not wanting to tell her mother how Juliet had found their father crying, '. . . was taking it all badly.'

'He is. Very badly. I'm terribly worried about him. Before lunch . . .' Isobel broke off to blow her nose on a handkerchief she had taken out of her shirt pocket. She was still wearing the same clothes but she had changed into an old pair of shoes after the young men from Christie's had left.

'Mum, are you all right?' Victoria put her hand on her mother's shoulder.

'Yes. I think so. Give me a minute, will you? I'm sorry, darling, but it's all been such a strain.'

'What happened at lunch? Was Dad being awful? I know he can be.'

'It's because he's so upset,' said her mother, 'he finds it hard to come to terms with what's happening. I think it will kill him if we have to leave this house.'

Victoria gazed at her mother. 'What's to be done?'

Isobel shook her head. 'You know as well as I do. Nothing. We live from day to day, like you do, from one ghastly letter to the next. And they write in such a peremptory manner as well, as if we're criminals. *We've* done nothing to be ashamed of. We may have been stupid but we haven't been dishonest.'

'Tell me about lunch.'

'They told him the picture wasn't a Veronese. He lost his temper and then he stalked off. I haven't seen him since.'

'That's ridiculous,' said Victoria, 'can't he do any better than that?'

Her mother did not reply as they had reached the door of the walled garden, that old, ferrous red door, the paint blistered by years of sun, that was so familiar to Victoria. Since she could remember she had stolen up here in pursuit of illicit fruit or vegetables or just for the sheer pleasure of wandering the sunlit pathways in this settled and peaceful place. Not to be able to come here when she felt like it seemed suddenly unimaginable.

'Take my arm, darling,' said Isobel, as they began to walk along the gravelled pathways.

'Enough of me. Tell me about you. You've left Tom in London with Hector.'

'Under the eye of Jenny and staying at her house at night.'

'That was wise.'

'Essential. I'm still worried about him.'

'You have to let them have their heads.'

'I suppose so. But I don't remember anything going wrong with the boys.' She meant her brothers.

'That's just because you're the youngest. Simon had some friends round once to play tennis, fourteen-and-fifteen-year-olds, just the same as Tom is now, and they got at the gin and your father's cigars.'

'What happened?'

'They were all as sick as dogs of course. Served them right. See my rocket, I'm so pleased with it. It's the first year I've tried. Grows like a weed.'

'I adore rocket,' said Victoria.

'How is Edward?'

'He's in Paris.'

'I know that, darling.' Isobel glanced at her daughter's face. 'How's it all going?'

'Well, I think. He's made some tremendous discovery, he says, but he didn't go into detail, so that's good. We need the money.

'Oh dear. I sometimes think it would have been better if Muriel hadn't left you that money, then you would never have managed to become a Name.'

'We can't go over all that again now,' said Victoria, 'it's too late. This is the deluge, now, and no amount of worrying about what might have been will stop it.'

'I'm going to go in shortly and look for your father.'

'You're sure you don't mind having the children while I'm away? Ju said it might be too much.'

'Juliet is not used to children as I am,' said Isobel, 'as you are. She's become selfish, as people do, without them. They're all old enough to help me now. It's not as if we don't have the room, although . . .'

'I know what you're going to say,' said Victoria, 'it's all right.'

'Sufficent unto the day is my motto,' said her mother.

'Hello, Grandpa,' said Mary, putting her head around his study door, 'I wondered where you'd got to.'

'Did you indeed,' said John, getting up from his old, red-leather chair with the brass studs, where he had been snoozing with his feet on the Delft tiles of the grate which depicted the pilgrim's journey from the dawn of life – the snatched glimpse of heaven over the shoulder of the newborn – to the gate of death where the view beyond is laid out like a great plain bathed in everlasting light.

'What are all these?' asked Mary, looking at her grandfather's desk which was littered with enormous, old red morocco albums, all stamped with the family crest, a heron holding a crucifix in its beak, and the family motto in Latin, 'Honour is all'.

'Photograph albums,' said her grandfather, 'some of them going back into the last century. Got pictures of everyone in there.'

'Even the ones who were killed in the First World War?' asked Mary who had been studying that war at school.

'Oh yes, they're all there. I'll show you.'

'They all look alike,' said Mary, when he had found the place. She looked up at her grandfather. 'You look like them too. It's not just the moustache.'

'There's a strong family likeness in our family,' he said, 'always has been.' He coughed and blew his nose.

'What's the matter, Grandpa? You seem so sad?'

'Nonsense. Just a touch of hayfever.'

'Everyone seems sad at the moment,' said Mary, thinking of her father. 'Is it Lloyd's?'

'What do you know about that?' asked her grandfather.

'Enough. I see their faces when the post comes. That's bad enough.'

'Well,' said her grandfather, 'well . . .'

Mary noticed that he was gripping the edge of his desk so hard that his knuckles were white.

'Children know,' said Mary, 'we always know. Why is it that grown-ups think we don't?'

'You're so sharp you'll cut yourself,' said her grandfather. 'Let me show you the ones of the Coronation.'

'Which Coronation?'

'George VI, of course.'

Victoria came along the top-floor corridor to Mary's room – no 26 – a fact announced by a little, white china disk on the door with the number on it in black – she had always had this room since she was old enough to sleep in a bed and was automatically put into it when she came to stay. There were some of Mary's books on the shelf as well as some of her old clothes in the cupboard. The walls were covered in faded, sprigged Victorian wallpaper; there was an old black fireplace with a paper fan in the grate, a chest of drawers and a tallboy which smelt strongly inside of camphor.

Victoria knocked.

'Yes?' said Mary's voice, 'who is it?'

'It's me.' Victoria put her head around the door. 'I wanted a word.'

'Oh?' Mary, who was sitting crosslegged on her bed, put down her book and tossed her hair over her shoulders.

'I want you lot to have supper on your own in the back sitting room. Would you mind?'

'No,' said Mary in a voice that suggested she did. 'Why?'

'I need to have a chance to talk to Mum and Dad on their own,' said Victoria.

'About what?'

'Lloyd's and all that.'

'Grandpa's unhappy,' said Mary. 'I found him in his study looking through those huge old family albums. He showed me all the Digby brothers who were killed in the trenches, then we looked at pictures of the Coronation of George VI. I felt he was going over things in order to try and hurt himself.'

'What do you mean?' Victoria sat down on a white painted chair under the window.

'Well, memories do hurt, don't they? All that might-have-been stuff,' she added, seeing her mother's enquiring look.

'Yes, I suppose they do. And photographs bring back the past so poignantly.'

'And he looks so like all those dead Digbys,' said Mary. 'What will happen to him if he has to sell this house? He'd be like a refugee, wouldn't he, no different from all those people who've had to leave their homes in this century. It's been a terrible century, hasn't it? They showed us films when we went to the Imperial War Museum of all those Jewish refugees shuffling along, waiting to get on trains. I couldn't bear to watch.'

'Did he say to you that he might have to sell?'

'No,' said Mary, 'but we *know*, Mum, that's what you lot don't seem to understand. We know. We know everything.'

Victoria sighed. 'I wish you didn't.'

'But we do. You have to accept that.'

'One always wants things to go on in the old way,' said Victoria, 'just as they always were, but I suppose our family came this way to this place through troubles and upheavals and

172

we've just got unused to it, that's all. Since they stopped hounding Catholics in this country we've gone soft.'

'But what will happen to Granny and Grandpa if they have to go?'

'They'll just have to buy a smaller house and live in it. Other people do. We're not the first old family to hit the rocks.'

'I don't like the rocks,' said Mary.

'Nobody does, darling, nobody does.' Victoria got up and came and kissed her daughter.

'I do love you, you know,' she said.

'I love you too.'

Having settled the children in front of the box with plates of shepherd's pie made by her mother earlier, Victoria went upstairs to have a bath and change. In Juliet's old room she found a taffeta skirt of black and white checks in a cupboard which she thought she would wear for supper with a black jersey she had remembered to bring. Her parents still changed for dinner and would expect her to do the same. She found them in the drawing room, sitting in a sort of frozen silence like two people in a second-rate play who had forgotten their lines. Her father was wearing a maroon velvet smoking jacket and the velvet slippers with his crest on that they had all given him when he was sixty. Her mother was in black, like a widow, without any jewellery, even her pearls, to relieve it.

'Ah,' said her father, getting to his feet when she came in, 'there you are.'

'I'm not late, am I?'

'Not in the least,' said her mother. 'Are the children all right?'

'They're as happy as Larry, thank you.'

'Gin and tonic?'

'No, thank you, Daddy, could I have a glass of wine?'

'Don't think we've got any wine.'

'Of course we've got wine,' said Isobel crossly. 'The cellar is full of it and there are two bottles of white in the fridge in the back pantry.'

'I'll get it,' said Victoria quickly.

'No, no, certainly not. I shall go,' insisted her father, not even glancing at his wife.

Victoria sat down and lit a cigarette.

'What's the matter with him?' she asked.

'He needs someone to blame,' said her mother, 'and he's decided that it shall be me.'

'But that's utterly childish,' said Victoria, 'as well as selfish.'

'When did you know men to be anything else?' asked Isobel. 'Can I have one of your cigarettes please, darling?'

'I thought you'd given up,' said Victoria.

'I have. This is my second today.'

'Oh Mum,' said Victoria, 'what an awful mess everything is in.'

Her father came back with a bottle of a particular cheap white wine he was enamoured of and bought in bulk in the local Co-op supermarket.

'Here you are,' he said, brandishing it at Victoria, 'it's only £2.19 a bottle if you buy a dozen at a time. Frightfully good value.'

'It tastes filthy,' said Isobel.

Victoria stubbed out her cigarette and lit another. When her father came back from the closet she said, 'I'm sorry about the picture, Dad, but you mustn't blame Mum. It's not her fault.'

'Of course it's not her fault,' he said. 'Nobody ever suggested it was. Anyhow, I don't believe those young turks. I don't think they know what they're talking about.'

'Of course they do,' said Isobel impatiently. 'You're being an ostrich, John.'

'I shall be getting another opinion,' he said, as if his wife hadn't uttered. 'Sotheby's are coming next week.'

'A complete and utter waste of time,' said Isobel.

'I want Edward to go through the library and see what there is. There may be something there that's worth a packet.'

'But he's already done that, surely?' said Victoria, sipping her wine, thinking it was the kind of drink that used to be served at student parties.

'You never know what might turn up.'

'I suppose so.' Victoria glanced at her mother. 'If nothing does turn up, Dad, what then? We're being bombarded by Fenton and Stanwright, so I hate to think what they're doing to you.'

'I don't think we should pay,' said Isobel. 'There's nothing they can do.'

'That is dishonest,' said John.

'The same thought had occurred to me,' said Victoria. 'I'm going to join one of those groups and fight back.'

'There's nothing to be done but to pay,' said John, 'those groups will achieve nothing.'

'Yes they will, Daddy. Don't be so defeatist.'

'It is dishonest,' insisted John Digby. He turned to his wife: 'You never mentioned such a thing to me before. What makes you do so now?'

'Because I can't bear to see everything that makes your life bearable slipping away from you. You must fight, John. Your ancestors fought for what they believed in. This is just another kind of persecution, that's all.'

'We knew what unlimited liability meant when we joined. You know we did. We had some wonderfully good years, now we have to pay.'

'We knew what unlimited liability meant, of course, but we did not know then what unlimited dishonesty meant. It's time to fight back.'

'Hear, hear,' said Victoria.

'I cannot agree with you,' said John Digby, 'a gentleman stands by his word and I shall stand by mine.'

'And bring everything down with you,' said Isobel bitterly.

After dinner Victoria asked her mother if she could make some telephone calls.

'Of course,' said Isobel, 'go and use my sitting room. It's private there, no one will hear you. Give my love to Edward,' she said.

'I will.'

She rang London and got Tom.

'All well?'

'Everything's fine. We're going off to Jenny's in a minute, don't worry, Feather's coming with us, of course – she likes the late-night walk along the river – oh, and yeah, Mum, Dad rang,' he added, as if he had just remembered – pure adolescence this attack of memory; sometimes it took days for telephone messages to be disinterred – 'and he says he's going south until Monday when he'll be back. He says you're to go from the airport to Sam and Nancy's place in the rue Coulaincourt and he'll be there. OK?' He changed the subject quickly, 'and Hugh is taking us on the river tomorrow in his boat, me and Heck and Henrietta and Jenny.'

'Jenny!' exclaimed Victoria, unable to conceal her dismay.

'Why not Jenny? She needs a break and it's a Sunday. Loosen up, Mum, you sound a bit tense.'

'I am a bit tense.'

'Why?'

'Things are a bit difficult here,' she said, 'I'll tell you when I see you.'

She said goodbye and put the phone down, leaning back on the sofa with her head on a little, hard white tasselled cushion. Edward had gone south. Why? What to do? Back on Monday. It didn't make sense. And he had chosen to tell his son rather than his wife. It was very odd. She felt breathless with the outrage of it. All week he had dealt her a series of muffled blows from Paris. Deliberate? She couldn't tell. And then she thought about what Tom had said about Hugh. She could just see them all having a lovely time on the river – she hadn't known Hugh had a boat – and here she was, as usual, on duty in Yorkshire. Much as she loved her parents it was duty rather than pleasure to be here with them at this particular moment ... and, oh God, her head ached ... the business of Edward.

She got her address book out of her handbag and dialled Sam and Nancy's number in Paris. Glancing at her watch she saw that it was only half-past nine which would make it ten thirty in Paris; not too late to ring, even people with a baby. Last feed was usually sometime around eleven in her own experience, although Nancy, being American, was probably into demand feeding.

A potted female voice answered the phone: the message was in

English first and then French, Nancy's light, rather tentative voice giving instructions, but the receiver was then picked up at the other end and Sam said 'Hello' in his slow, deep American voice.

'It's Victoria,' she said, finding, as always, her own voice reedy and absurd against Sam's deep, rounded vowel sounds.

'Oh Victoria,' he said, ridiculously Uncle Remus, 'how are you?'

'Fine, I'm fine. I'm in Yorkshire with my parents . . .' She wondered how quickly she could get to the anxious heart of her phone call. How baldly could one say to someone one didn't know frightfully well, 'Excuse me, but do you know where my husband is?'

'Oh yes, Yorkshire. Lovely place. How is the weather?'

'All right,' she said. Bugger the weather. 'Is Edward there? I can't get hold of him.'

All of a sudden this strategy had presented itself to her. If she pretended not to know anything then she might find out more.

'Er no,' said Sam, 'he's not as a matter of fact. Hasn't he called you?'

'No, he hasn't.'

'Oh.'

A silence ensued during which Victoria managed to prevent herself from talking. Well-brought-up Englishwomen were always taught to abhor silence and to fill it at any price, but not this time. Wait. Let him explain. Make it work for you, as Jenny would say.

'He's . . . er . . . he's gone south. For the weekend. The sun. I guess . . .'

'Sam, would you mind telling me what's going on?' It was time to go for the jugular.

'Nothing's going on. Edward's just gone for a relaxing weekend in Nîmes, I think he said it was. The bull-fight is on there this Sunday and you know how he enjoys a good *Feria*.'

'Is he staying in a hotel or with someone?'

'I wouldn't know, I'm afraid.'

Liar.

177

'He didn't leave a number? I like to know where he is in case the children are ill or something happens to one of them.'

'I understand what you're saying about the kids getting sick, but I'm afraid I don't have a number for him.'

'All right,' said Victoria, 'but if he phones could you say I was trying to get hold of him? And could you give him this number please?'

'Sure,' said Sam. When he had written it down he said 'We'll see you soon then. Look forward to it.'

'Has Edward confirmed our booking at the hotel, do you happen to know?'

'I'm sorry,' said Sam, 'but I don't. You know Edward. Do you want me to go around and see?'

'No, no, really . . . thanks,' said Victoria. It had been more a way of prolonging the conversation than a real worry. Those sort of worries about detail now, in a way, seemed to belong to another world. She felt as if she had entered another kind of landscape altogether where it was not a question of whether the roads were metalled but more a question of whether there were any roads at all.

It was what Iso had said that had made him think of it again. 'Bring everything down with you', she had said. Her voice had been so bitter. But by God she was right. He would let her know that in a note. She was right. He either had to pay up or die.

John Digby thought he had worked out how he would do it. It would have to be a gun of course. Any other way was cowardly. Hanging was grotesque. A gentleman would simply have to blow his brains out. If he did that, he thought, the estate would go to Ivo, his eldest son, a merchant banker, not (thank God) a Name, but a prosperous business man married to a wife with money. Ivo would be forced to try and save the estate and he was probably ingenious enough to be able to do so.

It would break his heart to live anywhere else, so it was easiest that he should bow out gracefully, thanking God for so many good years in this marvellous place. Isobel would manage. She was the managing kind and would probably be perfectly happy in the dower house or one of those pretty alms cottages in the village. She would probably be happier without him. This was how he reasoned with himself.

He would do it in an outhouse, one of the stables, probably, and try and be as tidy as he could. Leave a note. All that sort of thing. Explaining. Other Digbys down the years had gone to wars and sacrificed themselves for a principle and now it was his turn to do the same. He hoped that God would forgive him.

Other than Lloyd's, everything was in good order. The chapel especially. No rot there or in the main house. Roof good, guttering sound, windows painted recently. The wilderness had been planned and planted before they had begun to lose money. The lime avenue he had planted along the main road to the village would flourish and grow long after he was gone. He had made his mark, such as it was. Now it was time to go.

He tried not to think about how much it would hurt. He hadn't handled a gun for years, not since the war, but it would only be for a second, then he would be gone on his voyage towards the stars. He still thought of heaven as he had done when he was a boy as being like the ceiling of the chapel, a navy-blue dome studded with gilt stars: the place where God ruled, the pendant in the middle of the dome, the Pantocrator raising his holy hand in blessing and judgement.

Jenny, lying in bed upstairs, heard Henrietta let the boys and Feather into the house. Beds were made up for them in what had once been the playroom at the back of the house but which now was really Henrietta's room, a place where she did her homework, watched television and hung out with her friends. She heard Hen lock up – it was nice having Feather in the house as a guard-dog – and then the three of them went off into the kitchen for a cup of tea. She could vaguely hear voices, then she must have dozed off, only waking when the phone rang.

'Jenny?' A woman's voice, not immediately identifiable.

'It's Antonia Wilberforce here. I'm so sorry to ring you at this hour, but I wondered if you knew where Victoria was. I've rung the house and there's no reply. Is she in Yorkshire?'

'Yes, yes, she is.' Her head, when taken unawares like this, began to ache with small hammer blows.

'Is everything all right, do you know? It's just that we've had Edward on the phone from France, somewhere in the south, Nîmes or Arles, sounding most mysterious and, frankly, drunk, when, among other things, he's supposed to be in Paris working and waiting for V. to arrive.'

'I only know that Victoria has gone to Yorkshire with four of the children. Tom is here in fact with Hector, his friend, and she'll be back tomorrow night so that she can get ready to go to France. I know he hadn't rung her before she left, or at least he hadn't – let me think – this morning. It all seems such a long time ago now.'

'I see,' said Antonia. 'Oh dear. I won't ring the Old Hall now. I'm sure they keep early hours there. I'd better ring her first thing.'

'Do you think you should?' said Jenny, 'it'll only worry her.'

'But she must know her husband isn't where she thinks he is, surely? What if something happens to one of the children?'

Jenny sighed. 'All right. Ring her in the morning then. I suppose she should know. Poor Tor. What do you think is going on?'

'God knows,' said Antonia in her usual forthright manner, 'but Edward has been under tremendous pressure lately and sometimes something gives, if you know what I mean.'

'I'm sure it's nothing serious. He probably just wanted a bit of a break.'

'Absolutely. Well, keep your fingers crossed.'

To his great joy, Tom had found Iza in the kitchen when he went in there with Heck and Henrietta. She was making some horrible potion in a china mug, herb tea or something. Whatever it was it smelt vile, in absolute contrast to how she herself looked of course. Tonight, she was wearing a short white skirt, white shiny shoes and a white T-shirt with a large blue heart on the front over her breasts under which was written the word 'Love'.

'What is that?' asked Henrietta, staring into Iza's mug.

'Herbal tea for my . . .' she put a hand over her front, 'for my digestif. I am pharmacist, you see, and when I go back to Poland, I am going to specialize in herbal solutions . . .'

'Remedies, you mean,' said Hen.

'Ja, remedies. You like?' She held her mug aloft.

'No, thanks,' said Hen. 'I'll stick to PG Tips, thanks. Heck? Tom?'

'I'll try some of your tea,' said Tom to Iza.

'You're barking,' said Hen, 'it smells awful.'

'I'm not brave enough either,' said Hector. 'Is there any beer?'

'No,' said Henrietta, 'sorry. Mum doesn't keep it.'

'Anything else a little stronger?'

Henrietta shook her head. She looked uncomfortable.

'Tea will be fine for you,' said Tom. 'I've got some dope. Who wants to try some?'

'You'll have to wait 'til Mum's asleep,' said Hen, 'she's got a nose like a bloodhound.'

'We can do it in the back room with the French windows open. She sleeps at the front, doesn't she?'

'Yes, all right.'

'You have drugs?' said Iza, putting down her cup of tea. 'Is very bad for you.'

'It's just marijuana,' said Hector, 'it's not heroin or opium or anything.'

'I not try,' said Iza firmly, picking up her mug. 'I go to bed now. good-night.'

'Oh, come on,' said Tom, 'stay a little bit. We're going to watch the midnight movie on television.'

'I have to work in the morning very early. I cannot lie asleep like you.'

'Oh, come on,' said Tom, 'just for a little while.'

'OK,' she relented, 'just a little time. But no drug, OK?'

'OK,' said Tom, 'we won't. We'll just drink our tea, watch the film and go to bed.'

He caught Hector's eye and looked away.

They sat on cushions on the floor, leaning against the sofa, French windows open to the night, which was clear and calm with a moon and a light dusting of stars. Hen sat next to Hector who had rolled a joint and was smoking it on his own. He offered some to Henrietta who refused and to Tom who also refused.

'What's happened to you?' said Hector, 'scared?'

'No,' said Tom, 'but I don't want any.'

'C'mon,' said Hector.

'No,' Tom shook his head. Beside him he could sense Iza glancing at Hector.

'It rot your brain,' she said, 'Hector is silly.'

'Nonsense,' said Hector, 'all my mother's friends have been smoking for years.'

'And look at them,' said Tom, 'what a shower.'

Hector ignored this remark in a lofty fashion.

They watched the film in silence for a little while longer, then Henrietta said, 'I'm going to bed, I'm knackered. Come on, Iza, you've got to work.'

'I coming,' said Iza, getting to her feet. 'See you tomorrow,' she whispered to Tom, 'is one of my days at your mother's house.'

'OK, great,' said Tom, feeling the beginnings of a flush and hoping Hector wouldn't notice.

'Go on,' said Hector when the girls had gone, 'have a puff.' He held the cigarette out to Tom across the expanse of cushions.

'Nup,' said Tom, shaking his head. 'Don't want any, thanks.'

'What's wrong, sweetie, you in love or something?'

'Fuck off,' said Tom, brandishing a cushion.

'Got a will of iron that Polish bint, I must say.'

'She's not a bint,' said Tom, whacking Hector over the head so that the joint flew out of his hand and landed on the tiled surround of the fireplace.

'Yes, she is,'

'No, she's not, you bugger.'

Suddenly the door flew open. It was Henrietta in her nightie.

'Be *quiet*,' she said, 'Mum's not well and she sleeps badly.'

'Sorry,' said Tom, picking up the joint and stubbing it out in the saucer Hector was using as an ashtray before he was tempted to give in, 'we're really sorry, aren't we Hector?'

'Yes. Really sorry,' said Hector, suppressing a giggle. The joint had been slightly stronger than he intended and he had smoked more than he meant to.

'OK,' said Henrietta dubiously, half-closing the door before opening it again. 'I'd better take that,' she said, indicating the saucer with the incriminating object on it, 'before Mum finds it.'

'What's wrong with your mother?' asked Tom, handing the saucer over at the door.

'I'm not sure,' said Hen, 'but she gets terrible headaches and the doctor wants her to go and have a brain scan.'

'How awful,' said Tom, 'I am sorry. Night Hen.' He pecked her on the cheek without quite knowing why.

Very early on the Wednesday morning following Caroline's vanishing act the night before, Parry awoke on his sofa from a dream that had seemed so real that to wake from it was heartbreaking. He dreamed that she had come back, she was in his arms, they were making love . . . he opened his eyes to look into her eyes – those colourless eyes that were like pools of clear water – but she was not there. He was alone. The sun had risen in a brilliant flush of pink and apricot cloud – a sky full of expectation and beauty – he remembered dawns like this in his childhood, those treasured days (so rare in Scotland) where the sun rose over the sea like a piece of burning glass – and yet there was no hope. She had not come back.

He climbed the stairs to the turret room. Her things were there, the bed was made, the curtains tied back in neat folds. The jeans and the shirt she had been wearing were lying on the bed. He picked up the shirt and held it to his face, smelling her faint scent smell. What was it, that smell? He looked at the table where her make-up was and saw a black bottle marked Joseph. He sprayed the smell on his hands and then wiped them on his pyjamas, so that he could keep her with him. She must come back, she must! It was as if he, Parry, had ceased to exist, the slate of the past wiped quite clean. He would give anything to see her, anything. He felt bereaved by the lack of her, tantalized by the sense of her presence, her essence, that her possessions suggested.

He went to the window and looked out over the city, the quiet cobbled square, the shuttered streets beyond just beginning to stir with the early morning life that replaced those creatures of the darkness whose desperate hands clawed at you from doorways and the entrances to alleys. He went back down the stairs, pausing to stare at the miserable pigeons in their cage at the back of the dingy apartment block behind, and lay down on his sofa again among the muddle of cushions and blankets. He had not even bothered the night before to make up the bed using sheets.

He must have slept again because he was awoken at seven thirty by the telephone. He stumbled up in a daze and grabbed at the machine which was still sitting on its stool by the great deep sink where Sam washed his brushes and sometimes himself.

When he heard Victoria's voice he was filled with apprehension and a sense of dread that he would be unable to prevent himself from betraying the fact that he did not wish to talk to her. The effort of wrenching himself back from his state of desolation seemed quite beyond him. He listened to the brightness draining from her voice and was relieved when the truncated conversation ended. He sat on the edge of the sofa with his head in his hands. Suddenly the telephone rang again, making him jump.

When he heard her voice, tears of relief sprang into his eyes.

'Edward,' she said in a low but urgent voice, 'it's me.'

'Where are you? What happened to you?'

'I can't talk now,' she said.

'But where are you?'

'I can't tell you, don't press me. I'm sorry. Meet me in the garden of the Musée Rodin by the statue of Balzac at eleven. I can tell you more then.'

'All right,' he said, 'all right, I'll be there.'

'I must go,' she said, and put the telephone down very suddenly as if someone had come into the room while she was talking to him.

Parry went into the kitchen and filled the kettle. He felt absurdly, madly happy. He found himself singing arias from Gilbert and Sullivan, from *Iolanthe* and *The Pirates of Penzance*, always a measure of happiness with him. His children knew that if he was whistling any of those old familiar tunes then he was likely to be in a good mood, easily approachable, not snappish. He looked at his watch. It was now just before eight: three hours and four minutes of knowing that he would see her. Suddenly hungry he cooked himself breakfast, bacon and eggs, made coffee and piles of buttered toast and ate the lot on his knees in the studio, relishing every mouthful. After that he bathed, shaved and then dressed himself in a white linen suit he was particularly fond of, slopped Essence of Limes down his front and under his collar at the back of his neck and then went back into the studio to sit and think about de Fonville and what he must do about him. Was it he that Caroline was with? He wished he knew; if it was, and if de Fonville was keeping her against her will, then he would hear about it from me he thought, clenching his fists. But his position was a difficult one if it were de Fonville Caroline was with, very difficult indeed.

Last night de Fonville had shown him the books he wished to sell with a list attached, saying roughly what he hoped to raise by each individual purchase. One of the books on the list was so rare that Parry had almost believed he was mistaken. From the evidence it seemed clear that de Fonville did not know what he was offering for sale. Certainly the book was worth an enormous sum of money, enough by itself to settle their Lloyd's problems, and school fees for some considerable time, but Parry was uneasy in his mind about de Fonville's intentions, his aims and motives. He felt instinctively that there was a trap somewhere which he must do his best to avoid. De Fonville was as wily and as cunning as Reynard himself. He would have to be very careful. At the same time as he knew all this, he also knew that he did not want to think about any of it; like a boy in love, he only wanted to think about the object of his desire. The rest of it, all the cares and worries and sorrows could go to hell.

At nine he went out, wishing to avoid Sam but ran slap into him outside the maternity clinic as he crossed the square. There was only one exit and therefore no way of politely dodging him.

'You're up early,' Sam called out, raising a hand in greeting, 'come and have a coffee, or are you in a hurry to meet someone?'

Parry was not sure whether this remark was intended to corner him or not, the 'someone' of course meant Caroline, but it effectively prevented him from refusing. It hurt his pride to be seen as guilty or furtive and he was used to Sam's estimate of him as an honourable fellow.

'Good idea,' said Parry, 'have you got the time to spare?'

'Oh sure,' said Sam, 'I'm painting the old lady in St Germain but not until later. She doesn't get up until lunchtime, so I'm in no hurry.' He glanced at Parry's suit: 'Fine little number you've got on there. Sure looks like a special day for you today.'

'Well, it isn't particularly,' said Parry crossly.

'Going to see de Fonville?'

'At some point, yes.'

'Oh.' Sam made a sharp left-hand turn into a dark café. 'Let's go in here,' he said, 'best croissants in Montmartre.'

'So, what's your plan?' said Sam. 'Me and Nancy sure hope to see you tonight for supper. We'll get a sitter and go out. There's this amazing Japanese place we want to try.'

'I didn't come to Paris to eat Japanese food,' said Parry. 'I want to eat French food.'

'OK,' said Sam, raising a large hand. Again Parry was struck by the pinkness and strength of his wrists. 'We'll go some French place, Nancy will know somewhere, she always does. One of her hobbies is finding new places to eat. Do you want to bring Caroline?' he added diffidently. 'I haven't mentioned a thing to Nancy, so you've no need to worry.'

'How very kind of you,' said Parry sarcastically.

'Come on,' said Sam, 'it's a joke.'

Parry did not reply to this. It was very dark inside the café which was in the rue des Martyrs just at the point where it joins the rue des Abbesses and his eyes had not quite adjusted to the dimness after the brilliance of the morning, but he thought he had seen her out of the corner of his eye on the other side of the street hurrying along. She was wearing a short white skirt and a little white shirt and dark glasses. Mules. She was running in mules, nearly running. Sunburned legs. His heart was suddenly beating very fast and before he knew it he had pushed back his chair sharply so that it squawked on the tiled floor and then fell over, but Parry did not care. He ran out of the café and turned left up the rue des Abbesses in pursuit of his Daphne; Apollo in a linen suit. Outside the church of Sainte-Joan l'Evangeliste he caught another glimpse of her now in the rue Yvonne-Le-Tac. He tried to cross but was prevented by the municipal rubbish track making its slow noisy progression down the street. He ran all the way to the Square Willette, so close to his old friend Saint-Pierre de Montmartre, but there was no sign of her. She had vanished.

It was now half-past nine. If it had been Caroline he would have to wait to see her until eleven. He turned back down the rue des Martyrs feeling a fool, walking slowly. There's no fool like an old fool, he said to himself. A middle-aged man, a bit plump round the middle, running after a girl like an old goat, his dick practically hanging out. What had happened to him?

In the café, Sam was drinking his *crème* and reading the *Herald Tribune*. 'I never thought to see you run like that again, Edward,' he said, glancing up from his paper with an amused look on his face that seemed to Parry to closely resemble a smirk. He found he would like to punch that smirk, wipe it off Sam's face like snow off a bough. He sat down and then got up again.

'Where're you goin' now?' said Sam in his lazy, insulting way.

'To get some cigarettes,' said Parry.

'I didn't know you smoked.'

'I don't.'

When he came back with a packet of unfiltered Gitanes he found Sam had ordered him a coffee.

'Did you see someone that you knew?' asked Sam, changing his grip on the newspaper.

'Yes. Someone I knew years ago,' lied Parry.

'Did you catch up with her?'

'It wasn't a her.'

'Oh. Did you find him then?'

'No.'

'Shame.' Sam folded his newspaper in half. 'Did Caroline come back last night?'

'I've no idea,' said Parry. 'She may be in her room.'

'Oh come on, Edward,' said Sam, 'you would have heard her come in, surely?'

'I told you. I have no idea.' To his annoyance he found that his hand was shaking, so that he was obliged to put his coffee down.

'She's not balanced up, that Caroline,' said Sam, 'she's incredibly wild in some ways.'

'Oh, do stop saying that,' said Parry. 'I don't know where she is, it's none of my business. She won't be the first young girl not to spend the night in the place where she's supposed to be.'

He tried to sound nonchalant, paternal almost, but was aware that he had miserably failed to convince Sam. Sam knew him too well to be put off the scent.

'I don't know what her relationship is with de Fonville,' he added, compounding the felony, 'but it seems a little convoluted.'

Sam put down his cup gently. 'Look,' he said, 'let's talk this through honestly. I don't know if Caroline is fucking de Fonville or not, but my guess is that she is. She's a lady who likes to play games. She's had a lot of lovers, she'll have a lot more. Want my advice? Lay off. You'll get burned. Besides, you have a wife of your own.'

Edward looked at him in silence. 'I know I do,' he said eventually.

'Then what's going on?' Sam caught the waiter's eye and ordered more coffees in sign language.

I'm in love with her, Parry wanted to say, that's what's going on. I'm like a boy starting afresh. I can't remember my real life; or I don't want to.

'I don't know,' Parry said eventually, when the voices had ceased their clamour in his head, 'I wish I did.'

'Anyone can lose their head temporarily,' said Sam, 'but you have too much at stake. Victoria, the kids. Just forget her. Put it behind you. Come and stay up at the apartment with me and Nancy.'

'There's no room,' said Parry, feebly. 'There's no need,' he added hastily, 'I hear you. I'm fine. It'll be all right. I quite like the solitude down here. After home, you know, so many people all the time. Children multiply themselves at school, double up – they all bring home friends.' He knew he was gabbling but found he was unable to stop.

'Edward,' said Sam, 'I have a very good doctor.'

'So do I,' said Parry, 'he's in London. You probably know him: Jeremy Montagu?'

'No, I don't.' Sam gazed at his old friend in perplexity. How to put this? 'I didn't mean that kind of a doctor, I meant a psychiatrist.'

'A shrink,' said Parry, 'is that what you think I need?'

'We take a different view of all that where I come from,' said Sam. 'If you're in trouble then you need help.'

'I'm not in trouble,' said Parry, 'I'm perfectly all right. And I don't want to go and see a shrink.'

He lit another cigarette and inhaled deeply, feeling the deliciously polluting smoke coil and snake its way through the chambers of his lungs.

'OK,' said Sam, 'OK, it was just a suggestion. What's your plan today?'

'Sort out of few things on the business front,' said Parry briskly, getting out the little sketchbook with a dark-green cover bought from Cornelissen's in Museum Street that he used as a notebook. He turned up a page and read *M. Rodin. By statue of Balzac*, the handwriting swift and oddly untidy, as if he was changing character.

'So things went well, did they, with de Fonville?'

'Oh yes, very.'

'So, a gallery perhaps when you've done that?'

'Yes, I thought the Musée Carnavalet. I always enjoy going down there.' He thought of Voltaire's niece who had also lived in the rue des Francs-Bourgeois to whom Voltaire had written, 'I kiss your cute little arse, and all the rest of you'.

'OK,' said Sam, picking up the chit, half-relieved at being deprived of having to deal with whatever had got inside Edward's head. He could say with a clear conscience that he had tried. If the guy was on a crash course for disaster, then so be it.

*

He had got to the museum early and gone inside after buying his ticket. He walked swiftly through the rooms with their long windows and creaking wooden floors, empty at this hour of people; there was a smell of sun and hot wood and polish. Lucky Rodin to have been allowed to live here in this grand but intimate atmosphere. Parry stood in front of *The Kiss*; so much passion locked up inside that cold unmoving stone; the willing angle at which the girl leaned into the embrace, the man's eager hand on her marble flank. He was filled with an absurd envy looking at this sculpture with all its promise of perpetual fulfilment. Anxiously he consulted his watch. It was ten to eleven. He walked on through more rooms, not looking carefully at things, but pacing to and fro as a way of dealing with his anxious desire to see her, to touch her, to put his hand on her slender thigh, to feel that jutting breast pressing against his chest.

At two minutes to eleven he went outside into the garden. He knew the statue of Balzac well but he did not go towards it at once, but loitered instead at the ornamental pond gazing at *Ugolini et fils* while the seconds peeled away towards the hour. Just after eleven he went towards the statue of Balzac but she was nowhere to be seen. He waited. Five minutes, then ten. It was now almost a quarter past eleven. Parry lit a cigarette. Five more minutes passed. He looked round. Other than a couple canoodling by the pond he was the only person in the garden. Perhaps he had misunderstood. He went back inside with his heart banging up and down in his chest like a fist. Again, he walked through the hot empty rooms so full of the stilled passionate masterpieces. He wanted to pound his fists against the walls, or scream or cry his anguish at not knowing where she was or when he would see her again. Other than that, nothing mattered to him. He could not find her anywhere. She was nowhere to be seen. At twenty-five minutes to twelve Parry left.

He walked very quickly down the rue de Varenne and, remembering the number, stepped through the mahogany panel of door into the great imposing courtyard with the orange trees in pots. No one stopped him or asked him what he was doing or where he was going.

He crossed the courtyard, passing through the glass and mahogany doors and began to ascend the white marble stairs, without so much as glancing at Aphrodite of Cyrene. The doors to the apartment itself were as tall and as imposing as the outer doors to the street. These quarters had been built for the slightly super-human, those Olympian beings, Napoleon's deputies perhaps, Sully or Nay, men who, like Alexander, were more god than man.

At the entrance to de Fonville's apartment, Parry began to feel more Lilliputian than ever, dwarfed by the crushing weight of anger and grief. As in a dream he could not see a bell or a knocker of any kind. He banged on the door with his two fists like one of his children in a tantrum.

At length the door was opened by a diminutive Filipino maid.

'Monsieur de Fonville?' enquired Parry. 'Is he at home?'

'No one home,' she said, shaking her head, 'all gone out.'

'Monsieur and Madame have gone out?'

'I not know when they back.' Her little monkey jaw was set, her eyes cold and unfeeling, like a criminal's or a reptile's.

'Madame is not at home?'

'All gone out.' She put her head on one side, avoiding his gaze, waiting for him to go. She wore a maid's outfit from a Coward play, black dress, crisp white headdress, black lace-up shoes. Parry gazed over her shoulder into the long line of interlocking rooms, the point of light narrowing towards the end like a tele-scope. It was then that he saw her, not in white at all, but in her black dress, moving against the light at the very far end of all those great rooms, the black like a stain against the glittering light, the gold and cream.

He pushed through, ignoring the cries of the Filipino maid: 'You come back!' in the sharp simian French of the Tagalog speaker.

Caroline was horrified to see him. 'What are you doing here? You must leave at once. Go now. Hurry.' She was almost in tears with anxiety.

'We had an arrangement. Where were you?'

'I . . . couldn't get away. It's difficult. You don't understand.

Look,' she said, shooing him out like an animal, 'I can come tomorrow – at the same time – to the studio. Don't ask questions now. Trust me.'

He tried to kiss her, but she evaded him.

'What's going on?'

'I can't tell you. Trust me,' she repeated, 'but go, now. Please!'

'What are you so frightened of?'

'Go on!'

The vast door clicked to behind him. He found himself again on the white marble staircase, and then in the courtyard where the nymph held her dripping shell in the midst of the fountain. The fish lay like ingots in the depths.

Parry hadn't visited the Eiffel Tower since he had first come to Paris aged eleven to stay with a French family who lived in an apartment in a tall old narrow house in the Latin quarter. Then he had been struck by the peculiar shapes of the pillows and the fact that salad was considered a course on its own. He had been on a boat on the Seine, one of those absurd pleasure cruisers covered in bunting and American tourists wearing a variety of sports clothes, and of course up the Eiffel Tower.

He wasn't even sure why he had decided to take the lift to the top. It cost him 53 francs, money that would have been better spent in a bar getting drunk, but perhaps that would come later. Aged eleven, he had brought back a miniature Eiffel Tower as a present for his father. Three inches high, the model sat for years on the mantelpiece of his father's study gathering dust under an oil painting of his grandfather's horse and dog, Nobby and Fly, those accoutrements of country gentlemanness that he had acquired together with his fortune.

As he went upwards Parry thought of his father and that room, that picture, that was synonymous with a sense in his childhood of depression and coldness, of being in some way or other excluded from things that other children took for granted, things like love, that pointed, exclusive affection he had known with his mother and lost. Because he had not obeyed her. Now, stepping out on to the platform, it was almost as if she were with him again as he had known her before her death, loving him, protecting him from his father, not assuming that because he was eleven he was too old to be kissed goodnight.

The height he was at, the view, gave him a sense of exhilaration. He had a sudden, powerful sense of God's love and compassion, that he was not alone, that his sufferings were noted. This was followed by an equally powerful desire to hurl himself off the edge into infinity.

The platform was protected by a guardrail and a high screen of wire. A woman holding a small girl by the hand looked at him curiously. She seemed to be about to say something. Parry wondered if he looked mad. One of those demented types that people turn from in the street. The child was wearing a flowered skirt with a frill around the bottom and a shirt with matching floral, frilly piping. In her left hand she held a raffia basket with a pattern of fruit and flowers woven into it. She was about the same age as Teresa would be now, if she were still alive.

'Monsieur, are you all right? Would you like to take my arm?'

She was kind and young, a well-heeled juvenile matron from, perhaps, St Germain; her clothes were good, her expression sympathetic. The child gazed at him with large dark eyes.

'No,' he said, 'it's nothing. I'm sorry. I'm no good at heights. I don't why I'm here really.'

'Many people feel like that up here, I think. That is why there is a barrier. To stop people from flinging themselves over the edge.'

'Did you think that that was what I was about to do?' He couldn't resist asking her that question.

'You had . . .' she hesitated, 'a strange look on your face, Monsieur. I must say that I thought it was possible.'

Unable to answer this, he turned away sharply, walking to the barrier of wire and staring through it without seeing anything until, looking round, he saw that she had gone.

The cinema was half of a small grey building with one window displaying its wares. The usual stuff. A naked girl in handcuffs knelt on what resembled a hospital trolley with her legs apart and her backside in the air. Behind her, a man in a leather mask but also otherwise naked brandished a large whip. The man had a huge erection. 'S&M' the caption went, 'all your fantasies catered for: dogs, girls together, men together, mix 'n' match, you choose'!

Parry paid at the little kiosk, 200 francs, and went down the rickety, gloomy stairs, lined with posters behind glass of men and women doing unimaginable things to one another and to animals. He ordered a bottle of champagne and paid for it with his credit card, vaguely noting that it cost as much as half a year's road tax, not that it mattered. Nothing mattered any more.

With the champagne came a blonde girl who said her name was Michelle. The roots of her hair were black even in the semi-dark. She wore a leopard-print dress made of nylon, very short and cut very low at the front so that her breasts were pushed up and out like globes; but her legs were long and pretty and she wore very high peep-toe, matching leopard-print sandals.

Parry drank quickly, partly because Michelle kept filling his glass. By the time the floorshow came on, 'Claudette et Gabrielle', he was quite drunk. He ordered another bottle of the champagne that cost the same as – what was it now? A trip to Sainsbury's or something – and watched the girls making love to one another in a state of considerable excitement.

The room was tiny and tawdry and also very hot. The lamp by the bed had a pink bulb in it that cast a dull rose hue over everything. Parry's linen suit almost resembled flesh in this light, flesh that had not seen the sun. He was reminded then of what he did not wish to think of: sunburned limbs, colourless hair with a heavy swing to it; of pain, of rejection, of being thrust out of de Fonville's apartment.

In the act of removing his jacket these thoughts struck at him like a knife, draining away his sexual desire as the hot sun might dry out a swamp, revealing the corpses of dead animals.

Michelle, however (if that was her name) knew nothing of this. She saw only that he had ceased to undress himself and that that might be bad for business. She was not interested in reasons. She came up behind him and slid his jacket off, letting it drop to the floor, moving against him like a lizard; with practised hands she massaged his groin which, after a moment, began to have its inevitable effect. He had had almost no sexual contact since the death of his daughter the previous year – other than the episode with Caroline – and the desire that he had thought damped down for ever now seemed to rage in him like an underground fire, consuming pain, consuming rage, devouring everything but the thought of present satisfaction.

Before he knew it he found himself on the bed lying beside this woman with the shining supple body of a reptile. She took off her knickers and threw them with practised ease across the room and then, spreading her legs, pulled him on top of her. He tried to kiss her mouth and then her breasts but she pushed him away as if he were preventing something else happening. After that he came quickly in a series of spasms that were almost painful, aware that she had not had an orgasm and almost sorry because of it. He rolled off her and put a hand on her breast rolling the nipple in his fingers and feeling it harden but she removed his hand gently and moved away from him slightly. He slept after that and awoke from a dreamless sleep, unable to measure how long he had been asleep. He felt tired but clear-headed, as if he had expelled something vile from himself during that act of passionless sex.

She had her leopard-print dress on again and was sitting at the kidney-shaped dressing table putting on fresh make-up. The tips of her hair were wet at the back and hung in little jagged fronds suggesting that she had washed during the time he had been asleep. His suit had been picked up and the jacket hung on the back of a chair, the trousers and his shirt and socks on the seat neatly folded. He was reminded absurdly (as perhaps all Englishmen in similar situations are reminded) of prep school, and how one would get good marks for tidiness. No more than four objects on your chest of drawers, drawers must be neat, clothes left out tidily folded.

Seeing him sit up she said, 'You are English?'

'Yes.' He did not want to know how she knew. His accent was impeccable. He hoped she had not been through his suit and

195

seen the photograph of Tor and the children. The French invariably took him for one of their own. He thought suddenly and uncomfortably that it might be something to do with the way he made love. What he remembered Rosie had called 'The Channel Ferry Effect'; ro-ro – roll-on, roll-off.

'Frenchmen never try to kiss you,' she said, 'only the English. Because they feel so guilty. They feel they must be nice boys, considerate.'

'How much?' he asked, getting off the bed and going to the chair. He did not want to have to listen to this women's magazine crap, this pop psychology, nor did he want to be lectured on guilt by this whore in her leopardskin dress. Her dirty little life, like a stain. What did she know of guilt?

She named a sum. 'You can pay by credit card,' she said, 'I take Carte Bleue, Amex, Diners.'

Parry was suddenly overcome by a great tidal wave of rage and resentment. All the things he had been trying to flee from suddenly threatened to overwhelm him: the guilt over the deaths he had been responsible for – his mother, his daughter – his sense that God had abandoned him in his hour of greatest need – the debts that piled up and up, the living children whom he could not serve, the wife whom he could no longer properly love, all these things combined forces in him in the form of this murderous rage.

He grabbed a handful of her hair, yanking her head back. Taken by surprise, she cried out and dropped her eyeliner. Fear made her ugly, vile, pitiful. He could so easily squeeze that fragile neck until her bones cracked and her eyes popped. He let go of her suddenly and she began to cry.

'Why are you so angry?' she said. 'You men. Always angry. What have we done that you want to hurt us so much?'

He could not tell her that she was simply a representative of the forces that hounded him, the Furies that pounded at his heels, how could he say such a thing? She was just a woman, a frightened rabbit, pitiful and powerless. This need to hurt someone or something had turned, for a moment, dangerously outwards. How easily he could have murdered her and left her here in her tawdry little bordello for the police to find, or her pimp.

He sat down on the bed again, still naked. 'I'm sorry,' he said. 'I didn't mean to frighten you.' A lie, of course.

'Pay now,' she said, naming the sum, 'and then go.' She was taking off her smudged eye make-up with lotion on a piece of cotton wool. Starting again.

'I'm sorry,' he said from the door, having paid and dressed.

'Just go,' she said, contemptuously, 'I don't want your sorry.'

Caroline was sitting on the bottom of the steps to the gothic door of the studio. She looked as if she had been crying.

'I forgot my key,' she said, looking up at him.

He was aware how very strong the smell of lilac had become as the weather had got warmer and wondered why he should suddenly be reminded of his mother.

'How did you get through the gate,' he asked, 'without your key?'

'Marie-Chantal's nanny let me in. She offered to let me sit in the house, but I said no, I'd rather wait here.'

'I see.'

'Aren't you pleased to see me?' she asked, like a child.

'Should I be?'

'I couldn't help it,' she said in a rush, 'Gaby, all that. I'll explain but you might not understand.' She got up as he pushed the key about in the lock this way and that.

'What might I not understand?'

'Please don't be angry with me. I know you are,' she sounded humble and rather scared.

'I'm not angry,' he said, shoving the door and then kicking it.

'Let's have some wine,' she said when they had gone into the studio and were standing there staring at one another. 'No Sam this afternoon?'

'He's at St Germain.' Parry turned away, took off his jacket, and lay down on the sofa which an unseen hand – probably Sam's – had tidied. He closed his eyes.

'I'll open a bottle,' she said. He could hear her footsteps going towards the kitchen.

'Not for me,' he said.

She did not answer, but he heard the fridge drone grow louder as the door was opened and then closed. Clink of glasses, sound of corkscrew. She came back holding a bottle and two glasses.

'I don't want any,' he said. 'Didn't you hear me?'

'Just one glass.'

She sat down beside him on the sofa and put her hand on his face, stroking his cheek.

'Edward,' she said, 'I'm sorry.'

He thought of Michelle and the look of fear on her face when she had thought he was going to beat her up and of how she had said 'I don't want your sorry' and his own subsequent feelings of disgust and remorse.

'Why did you do it?' he asked.

'It wasn't me, *I* didn't want to . . . you see, there's so much you don't understand.' She handed him a glass but when he didn't take it, she began to drink from it herself, her hair swinging forwards slightly.

'Well, you'd better explain,' he said abruptly. 'I'm not used to being treated like some . . . some lackey or other.'

'I know you're not,' she said soothingly, touching his hand briefly with hers. Contact with her was more electric than ever. He tried to conceal the urge to jump as if he had been stung.

'Well?'

'Do drink some wine.'

'No. I want to keep a clear head.' Besides, champagne must still be running in his veins. He pushed this thought away.

'You see, Gaby is a friend of my father's. And my father and I don't exactly see eye to eye. He and my mother . . .' She hesitated as if uncertain of her footing, 'they disapprove of my life, the things I do, the way I live. They want me to marry and have children, settle down, you know,' she shrugged slightly, as if to indicate what she thought of such a dreary bourgeois notion, 'so Gaby is like my father, he takes care of me, he keeps an eye on me, you know, like a father would.'

'Does he fuck you too? Like a father would?'

'How dare you!' She slapped him so hard in the face that he saw stars.

Without in any way thinking what he was doing, Parry grabbed her by the hair and slapped her back.

'Oh!' She put her hands up to hide her face, pretty suntanned hands.

Parry watched her. He was breathing heavily as if he had run a long race. Sweat started out on his brow. He could feel the imprint of her hand on his face like a burn.

He pulled her to him and began to kiss her; somewhat to his surprise she began to kiss him back urgently, making small sounds in the back of her throat. Like an animal, a whimpering animal who has been beaten for a misdemeanour.

'We can't do this here,' he said, holding her away from him strongly as if he had rescued her from drowning or some other heroic act.

'Why not?' She was tearing at her clothes, a tiny cotton cardigan with short sleeves and pearl buttons, tight trousers that ended above the ankle. Sandals the same pinkish colour as her cardigan with straps and buckles and thongs that wound around her legs like a Roman soldier.

'Because Sam might come in at any minute. He's already seen us once.'

'I know,' she said in an excited voice, pausing in the act of taking off the scrap of satin and lace that passed for a bra.

With difficulty Parry got up. 'We'll go to your room,' he said, holding her against him tightly like a rag doll.

They stumbled across the studio and up the turret-room stairs as if they were drunk. After a moment in her room Caroline went to the window which was slightly open. She stepped out on to the tiny balcony that sloped gently upwards following the line of the roof. She was naked.

'Let's do it here,' she said, turning to him. The mark of his hand was visible on her face like a stigmata.

From quite close by the bell of a church began to toll for the Angelus. The noise filled Parry once more with an urge to violate and despoil. In spite of all he had had to drink, in spite of all the rage and the fear, all the despair, the elation of this moment overtook everything that had happened to him. She leaned over the rail with her feet off the ground like a child, a taunting, teasing child. He could see the shape of her sex outlined between her buttocks. Like a child she looked around to see where he was and then turned back again to the view of rooftops, the wide pale sky.

With the sound of the bells beating in his ears Parry went towards her. He put his hands on her slender hips and pushed his penis between her buttocks. For a moment he could only find her anus but then, turning her head slightly, she slipped down on to all fours, holding the railings like a prisoner pleading for freedom. He entered her with one massive thrust, driving down on her. She began to make urgent sounds. She was saying something but he couldn't make out any longer the shape of words. There were just noises, jumbled, disconnected. And then, after that, there was only the sound of blood in his ears like the roaring of a crowd waiting excitedly for the bull to die, for the old sacrifice to be complete. Do not let it end, said a voice in his head, let this last for ever.

'Come inside,' she said, standing up. She took his hand and led him indoors. The bell had stopped tolling but Parry no longer noticed.

She pulled back the Indian coverlet on the bed revealing clean, smooth linen sheets with a deep border.

'Lie down,' she said, and knelt over him kissing his belly and his penis until he began – quickly – to stir again under that darting serpent's tongue, those proficient hands stroking his belly, touching his nipples. He pulled her towards him, trying to angle her sex so that he could enter her again, but she said 'no, wait!' and pulled away from him and began to massage her own breasts like a siren sitting there with her legs folded beneath her like an oriental goddess.

Parry sat up and moved towards her. She wrapped her legs around his waist so that he could enter her. As they kissed, tongues entwined, she took his hand and placed it on her sex, moving it gently up and down. He pushed her down on the bed and withdrew from her afraid that he would come too quickly. He kissed her breasts, feeling his penis throb against her flat belly, still stroking her down there. He looked into her face, into her open colourless eyes, as she began to come in a series of gasps and then he entered her and came himself in a series of slow spasms.

Then, for some uncounted time he slept; and in his sleep he dreamed that he was in Paris on a boat on the Seine with his mother who was dressed in the same clothes – green cardigan with gilt buttons, tweed skirt in pretty squares of green and blue vegetable dye – that she had worn on the day of her death.

'Isn't it funny,' she was saying, 'the way the French eat salad as a separate course.'

The boat was covered in bunting, tiny triangular-shaped flags, and there were chairs on the deck of striped canvas under an awning. And then his mother was gone, Parry looked for her wildly everywhere, tears streaming down his face, but she had gone and nobody had seen her or knew anything about her and he was alone with his grief. He woke, opening his eyes on to an unfamiliar ceiling, disoriented for a moment. Then he turned his head and looked into her eyes.

'You were crying,' she said, putting a hand on the hollow tender skin of his collarbone.

'I was dreaming of my mother,' he said and turned on to his back again, suddenly desperate to remember with aid of the cracks in the ceiling what exactly his dream had been about.

'Is she still alive?'

'No,' he said. Of all the remarks she could have made this was the one that illustrated most graphically how little she knew about him; the possibilities of that excited him. Perhaps if he said 'Yes, she's still alive' her belief in what he said would to some extent bring his mother back. And then he remembered the dream exactly; that he had been looking for her and had not found her. And he began to weep again.

She put her hand on his chest and then on his belly. 'What is it?' she said, 'why are you so sad?'

He turned to her and once more they began to kiss. He closed his eyes and was in his dream again, the atmosphere of it, searching for what his body told him was possible. Then he forgot the dream, forgot everything, except Caroline.

He felt her slide out of the bed and opened his eyes.

'Where are you going?' he asked, watching her bend over like something out of Degas. 'I'm afraid you'll vanish again.'

'Don't be afraid.'

'What time is it?' he asked to cover his fear. He knew that he must not show her that he was vulnerable. He could see that what she liked was to be hit or smacked, called to heel, and that that was the part of her, wayward, errant, that had to be controlled.

'It's getting on,' she said, glancing at her tiny gold watch, 'nearly seven.'

'Let's go out,' he said, lying back. 'Let's go out and get terribly drunk.'

She was doing up the zip at the back of her trousers as he spoke, a fluent, athletic gesture, something one might see in a magazine.

'All right,' she said.

'Do you have plans?' He had noticed the faint hesitation.

'No,' she said, 'not so far as I know.' She was spraying herself with that scent she used, whatever it was called, from a black bottle. His wife used . . . Victoria . . . used Jicky by Guerlain, an old-fashioned, good-girl's smell, not this husky, musky, powerful stuff.

Parry looked at her. She was lying of course.

'What about Sam?' she asked. 'Do you think he saw us fucking?'

'Yes.' He was not used to women using such terminology and found it exciting, which shocked him slightly.

'What were we doing?'

'Oh, just fucking,' he answered, throwing back the linen sheet and sliding his legs over the edge of the bed.

'Did he say something about it?' Her eyes were shining.

'Yes. Do you like the idea of being watched?' *Le tout* Paris might have had a view of them earlier on the roof.

'No, not really,' she said coolly, turning away. Then she said, 'Are you going to get in touch with Gaby?'

'About what?'

'Well,' she said, 'about whether you're interested in any of that stuff he showed you. I don't think you're the only dealer he's in touch with so I should hurry if I were you.'

'Are you sure?'

'Of course I'm sure.' She turned back to him with a look of innocent enquiry on her face.

'I'll ring him,' he said, doing up his fly buttons, 'I'll go down and do it now.'

'Oh, let's have a drink first,' she said, 'then you can call him from a bar somewhere.'

'It's a damn sight easier to do it here, as a matter of fact.'

'OK,' she shrugged. 'What was it of his that you wanted? I won't tell him,' she said, smiling.

'Just one or two things, nothing much.' *A strong imagination brings on the event*, Montaigne had written somewhere, and Parry remembered this now. He must try to keep control of himself. In four days he would see his wife. He was almost afraid that if he went on like this his physiognomy would be altered totally and that he would appear to her to be someone else; at the same time he could not imagine seeing her or communicating with her. He felt as if he had left his life, his old life, completely, and that he would never go back.

'Tell me,' she said, stroking his cheek, but avoiding his mouth when he tried to kiss her.

'No, truly,' he said smiling, 'if there were anything of huge interest I would tell you. Of course I would.'

He went downstairs and telephoned de Fonville, who answered the call himself. He was very affable and warm.

'Good,' he said when Parry expressed interest, 'come tomorrow here and we can do our bargaining, Monsieur Parry. The morning, about eleven, yes?'

'Yes, that will be fine,' said Parry, doing his best not to sound eager.

'Oh, and by the by, Monsieur Parry, have you seen our little friend, *notre petite amie*, Caroline?'

Parry hesitated. 'No,' he said.

'Oh well. It is of no account. *A demain*, Monsieur Parry.'

'Try this,' she said spooning some of her *champignons forestières* into his mouth, 'they're beyond delicious, they're heavenly, food of the gods. This must be what ambrosia is meant to be.'

'Ambrosia is generally taken to be the elixir of life.' Parry wiped his mouth with his table-napkin.

'That's a matter of opinion,' Caroline replied swiftly, suppressing a smile. 'Do you correct your wife when she says something you consider to be inaccurate?'

'I don't think so,' Parry said stiffly in order to disguise his anxiety at the mention of the word 'wife'. It was not guilt that made him react like this, he had gone beyond guilt, but fear; fear of loss. For the last few hours he had lived in the bliss of the present moment: there was no past, there is no future, there is only now. When he was an undergraduate he had become interested in the mental discipline of Buddhism, and with horrible clarity the first of the Three Basic Facts of Existence, the Three Signata, came back to him: *all conditioned things are impermanent, transient.* This precious present would soon depart from him.

'I was only teasing,' she said, putting her hand on his.

He looked down at her fingers and then up into her face. 'Don't leave me,' he said.

'What about your wife?' she asked gently, removing her hand.

'What about her?' Even to his own ears his voice sounded toneless, dead.

'She's your wife, Edward. I'm just a bit on the side.'

'Don't say that!' He clutched her wrist.

'You don't know me, you know nothing about me. I might be . . . anything . . .' she shrugged, 'a drug smuggler, a dope fiend, a criminal. I steal artefacts from archaeological sites. I might be arrested at any moment.'

'That's not true,' he said in a loud voice, causing people at neighbouring tables to turn and stare at the older man and the younger woman with the knowing incuriousness of Parisians used to intrigue and sexual double-dealing. A lovers' tiff, a little dinner-time spat between the *cinque à sept* and the real business of the night.

'But you don't know, *cherie*,' she said, touching his face very quickly with her hand. As a child he remembered that his mother had used to give him what she called 'butterfly kisses' with her eyelashes on his cheek. The recesses and depths of the mind were like a hidden city where, every now and again, recollection like a lantern illuminated forgotten doorways, pillars, porticos, vistas, the gold ornament abandoned on a ledge and left there a thousand years . . .

'I do know,' he said fiercely, blowing his nose so hard that the candle which sat on the side of the table by the wall guttered in the draft.

'I have to tell you that I'm going away tomorrow,' she said, 'I have to go Nîmes. I have some business to do there.'

'I'll come with you,' he said.

'But you can't. You have work to do here. Gaby . . .' She stopped suddenly.

'What is it?'

'I've just seen him,' she said. She was suddenly afraid.

'Who?'

'Gaby. He's coming this way.'

'My dear Caroline,' said de Fonville's voice behind Parry's shoulder, 'I have been looking for you all over Paris. Where can you have been?'

He came and leant against their table.

'Monsieur Parry, how charming that we should meet again. I've just been talking to your partner, my dear old friend Tom Wilberforce. He would like to speak to you. "Get Edward to give me a ring," he said. He is in his home now, as a matter of fact.'

'I'll get hold of him tomorrow,' said Parry, glancing at Caroline who was in the process of lighting a cigarette.

'I think he is expecting to hear from you immediately. He sounded anxious at not having spoken to you. There is a tel-ephone in the basement of this restaurant, I happen to know. You could speak to him from there.'

'Jolly kind,' said Parry, 'but I'm sure there's no rush.'

'I must disagree,' said de Fonville. 'He sounded most anxious. I think you should put him out of his misery.'

'It wouldn't take a minute,' said Caroline. 'If you hurry,' she spoke in English, 'you'll be back by the time they bring the next course.'

Parry got to his feet reluctantly. 'I don't seem to have much choice,' he said.

'Oh,' said de Fonville, 'just put the poor chap out of his agony, why don't you.' He sounded exactly like Bertie Wooster. Parry wondered uncomfortably if he was being mocked.

When he looked back from the top of the stairs to the basement, de Fonville was still leaning against the table and saying something to Caroline who glanced in his, Parry's, direction and then at de Fonville, as if the latter had said something about Parry that she had not guessed at.

Tom answered the telephone after many rings in his usual relaxed way.

'Jupiter 3452.'

'Tom?'

'Ah. Edward. *Comment ça va?*' he said in his execrable French.

'De Fonville said you wanted to speak to me. Said it was urgent.'

'Did he, the old fox. Can't think why. Is there a problem?'

'No,' Parry almost shouted. 'He told me to ring you.'

'Be calm, old fruit, be calm. I just wondered, in a casual kind of way, how things were going.'

'Things are going well. One or two interesting items which I'll buy off him.' It was a trap of course. Why hadn't he known? What a fool, what a damn, bloody fool he was.

'I have your approval?'

'Of course you do. Are you all right?' said Tom, emphasizing the last two words.

'Of course I'm all right.'

'Jolly good.'

'I'll speak to you tomorrow, I'm in the middle of dinner.'

'Then get back to your frogs legs, *mon ami*.'

'Bye,' said Parry and slammed the receiver down so that it

missed the bracket and swung wildly on its cord, but Parry was already half-way up the stairs.

De Fonville was seated at the table in Caroline's place.

'Where the fuck is she?' said Parry, 'where's she gone this time?'

'Monsieur Parry, compose yourself. She is in the little girl's room.' This time he sounded like Maurice Chevalier.

'I have taken the liberty of ordering myself some wine,' said de Fonville, 'I do hope you don't mind.'

'Of course not,' said Parry. 'Excuse me a second.'

He went back down the basement stairs, past the seething, boiling kitchens, past the telephone which an unseen hand had put to rights. There were four cubicles in the women's lavatory, one of which was shut. The other three were clearly empty. Parry said 'Caroline' and waited. There was no reply. He crouched down and peered at a pair of black shoes planted either side of the lavatory. They might belong to Caroline, and then again they might not. She had been wearing . . . what the hell had she been wearing? He found that he could not remember, simply could not. Not the black dress, not the jeans, not the tweed skirt (it had grown too hot for tweed) – he began to wonder if his brain was going; he felt so vague and strange and bewildered – not the . . . the cistern flushed, the door opened and a young woman of about Caroline's age emerged wearing a short black skirt, a white shirt, and, of course, those black shoes.

The girl had very short, very dyed white-blonde hair cut spikily and alarmingly vampish eye make-up. Parry loathed too much make-up. For a fleeting moment he wondered if she was the girl he had seen all those aeons ago in the airport chapel. Perhaps she was spying on him.

'Excuse me,' she said calmly, 'I think you are in the wrong place. Yours is next door.' She held the door open for him.

It occurred to Parry as he went slowly up the basement stairs that of course he would have seen her if she had come to the loo. He could not have failed to have done so. Why had he not thought of that? He wondered if he was going mad. Everything trivial or ordinary had become such an effort.

'The gentleman has had to leave,' said the waiter disapprovingly, 'but he has left some money with his card.'

'And the lady?' Parry managed to say, 'the young lady. Which way did she go?'

'I'm sorry, sir, but which lady do you mean?'

'The young one,' said Parry, 'the young, beautiful one.'

'Why, she is here, sir,' said the waiter, as the blonde crop appeared at the top of the stairs.

'Not that one,' said Parry, 'not that one.'

'The other lady,' said the waiter patiently, as if Parry were a half-wit, 'has gone with the gentleman who left the money.'

'I see,' said Parry, and his heart sank. It was quite clear to him, despairingly clear, that she was de Fonville's plaything and that she had gone home with him. What a bloody fool he was. What a bloody, bloody fool.

The priest was young and wore glasses and a crumpled, pale-grey clerical shirt. His trousers did not fit him properly and were slightly shiny over the knees. His shoes were scuffed but his eyes were kind, and although he looked tired and slightly slovenly, there was something about him that was brightly attentive even though it was so early in the morning.

Parry, who had not slept at all, but had simply sat all night long on his sofa trying to think, trying to pray, had come for help to the church of Saint-Pierre, which he had first entered reluctantly twenty years ago in search of Rosie, and in which he had been struck to the ground like St Paul, the scales ripped from his eyes by the cruel, but unseen hand of God. Being cruel to be kind. He had to be taught a lesson. Like a dog he returned for a whipping. It was his last chance.

'You wish to speak to me?' he enquired, stopping as Parry got up from where he had been kneeling and stepped out into the side aisle in front of him.

'I need to talk to someone,' said Parry, 'a priest, I mean.' He thought how absurdly muddled he sounded, how confused and inarticulate; and of how he had always despised people who could not express themselves properly.

'Do you wish me to hear your confession? The hours are listed at the back of the church on the noticeboard. I am afraid I have a Mass now.'

'I have to talk to someone,' Parry repeated.

'There is no problem,' replied the priest, glancing at Parry narrowly, 'if you do not mind waiting until the Mass is ended.'

'Thank you,' said Parry humbly, 'I'll wait.'

The congregation consisted of three old men and five old women. There was no choir as it was a Low Mass, only this priest in his green and gold robes. Parry sat at the back watching his fellow supplicants receive the sacrament, healing their innocent lives, restoring themselves to grace, beginning again. He felt utterly outside these familiar rhythms of everyday life: no amount of the old cure could salve him now. He felt battle-weary and exhausted.

The priest came out of the sacristy in his everyday clothes.

'Come this way,' he said, indicating that Parry should follow him. One of the old women, who was wearing Valderma coloured stockings as thick as bandages, attempted to detain the priest but he said something to her in a low voice and she stepped back, glancing curiously at Parry as he passed her, as if she had seen someone on the way to the scaffold, Parry thought.

They went through a door beyond the screen in the north aisle into a passage of polished wood which smelt of beeswax and, faintly, of cigar smoke. The walls were painted dove-grey with every now and again a framed photograph of one of the former incumbents of the presbytery, all now at peace in Christ, no doubt, Parry thought sourly.

The priest opened the door to a small room with bare walls, unadorned except for a large ebony crucifix upon which hung the beaten and tormented body of the Christ. Parry averted his eyes. *For now the axe put unto the root of the tree, so that every tree that bringeth not forth good fruit is hewn down, and cast into the fire.*

'Please sit down,' said the priest. There were two polished wooden chairs with arms, one under the crucifix and one by a small plain table. 'So, Monsieur,' he said, when Parry had taken the chair by the table, 'what is it that you wish to talk to me about?'

Parry opened his mouth and then closed it again. Again, he felt this sense of confusion and uncertainty as if he had an illness of the mind. He who had always prided himself on his clarity.

'Would it be easier if you were to speak in English? My English is quite good.'

'You tell me,' said Parry in English.

The priest regarded him without speaking for an instant. 'Sometimes,' he said, 'it is confusing to talk in a language that is not perhaps the language of one's heart. In another language we are not quite ourselves.' He said all this in English. 'Which would you prefer, Monsieur?'

'Which do you think is a better language in which to express guilt?' asked Parry.

'That depends,' said the priest patiently, folding his hands in his lap. 'What is it precisely that you feel guilty about?'

'Everything.'

'Everything?' The priest looked puzzled.

'I am in love with a woman who is not my wife,' said Parry abruptly, in English. 'Because of this I feel I cannot go back to my wife.'

The problem was that one could not say *I am responsible for my mother's death* or *I am the reason my child died* because, rationally, it was absurd to make such a claim. And yet the part of him that felt this so strongly was not placated by reason and thus remained, painfully and elusively out of reach. How could one say *I am fatally wounded* when one looked whole? Christ at least died visibly. Everyone knew. Parry's crucifixion was a hidden, inward torment, a kind of cancer of the soul.

'You have been married a long time?'

'Yes.'

'How long exactly, Monsieur?'

'About eighteen years.'

'And are there children?'

'Yes. Six. One died.'

A sob caught him in the chest as if someone had hit him very hard with a plank of wood.

The priest waited for him to compose himself. He said, very carefully, 'And do you think this has anything to do with your falling in love with someone else?'

'Why should it?'

'With things like the death of a child there may be the temptation to blame someone.'

'And do you think that is what I am doing?'

'I do not know, Monsieur. I am only making a suggestion.' After a pause he said, 'It is not uncommon, you know.'

'Death or adultery?' Parry fished in the pocket of his jacket for a handkerchief but found that he did not have one. Of course, providing clean handkerchiefs was one of the functions of a wife.

'Both. The temptation with sin, I think, is to assume that it is irretrievable, that one cannot go back. That is not true. One can always ask for forgiveness.'

'And retrace one's steps, you mean?'

'What is needed,' countered the priest, 'is a change of heart.'

'And what if I cannot find it in myself to manage this?'

The priest looked perplexed. 'You must pray,' he said, touching his collar with his hand.

'What if I can't pray?'

'Then I will pray for you.' After a pause he said, 'Is this woman in Paris with you?'

'Yes.'

'And where is your wife?'

'In London.'

'I see. And does your wife know of the situation?'

'No, she doesn't.'

'And you are here on business?'

'Yes.'

'Could you not just go home? Leave as soon as you are able?'

'And not tell her – my wife – you mean?'

'Would you like me to hear your confession now? I think it would strengthen you.' The priest looked sombre but he remained utterly still, his hands folded in his lap once more.

'When I was a boy,' said Parry, 'I thought God could see everything I did. I was always expecting to be punished.'

'Do you still think of him like that?'

'Yes.'

'He is infinitely merciful to those who repent,' said the priest.

'But what happens,' said Parry carefully, 'if I can't forgive God?' It was a question that was never canvassed. Forgiveness was supposed to be one way: God to man. But if we are equal, Parry thought, if we are loved, as we are told we are loved, then why such pain? And why so much of it? Why is it that our loving father in heaven wants us to suffer so blindly, so endlessly? There is no answer, he thought. And that is the trouble. These good men do not know what to say to the darkness that is in God.

'I am not sure I understand you.'

'So much suffering. So much beyond what could strictly be considered necessary for the good of our souls. Now, do you understand me?'

'I do understand,' said the priest. 'But we have to put our trust in God. That is what we are told. We do not know the ordinances of heaven.'

'But we pay the price.'

'That is true.'

'I am beyond help,' said Parry. 'I can no longer accept what you say.'

'Monsieur,' said the priest, 'forgive me, but you look very tired. You do not look as if you have slept.' He was still talking in English. 'Why don't you get some rest and come back later on.'

'There is no point,' said Parry tiredly. He shook his head slowly, then he got to his feet. 'Nobody can help me.'

'The loss, Monsieur, of your child . . .?'

'Yes?' Parry turned from the door.

'Suicide is not an unusual reaction . . . many of us consider it when we have . . .' He stopped.

'Thank you,' said Parry, 'you have been very kind.' He closed the door behind him.

When, hours later, he arrived at the studio it was about five or so, and he found Sam in residence.

'Edward!' said Sam, putting down his brush, 'where in God's name have you been all day? De Fonville rang to ask where you were, but I couldn't tell him. He sent his assistant around with a parcel for you. It's there on the couch.'

'Are you sure?' asked Parry. He had walked all day around the city scarcely knowing where he was or what he was doing, but he had made up his mind to return to London the next day – the world of everyday ordinary things: children, the leaking roof, the pleasant humdrum of his working life. Later he would ring Victoria and tell her he was coming home. He was not quite sure how he would persuade her out of her long-awaited holiday, but that seemed so trivial, such a mere unimportant detail in the face of everything else, that he supposed he would manage somehow.

He looked at the parcel by his feet, a stout package in brown paper tied up tightly with string, and thought that he should open it. It occurred to him that it was rather an odd thing for de Fonville to do – some of the items that he had looked at in the rue de Varennes had been extremely valuable – and that he ought to check with de Fonville about insurance and so forth.

'Have you a knife?' he asked Sam.

'Sure.' Sam looked in a drawer and found a Stanley knife which he brought across to Parry.

'You look shattered,' he said, looking down at Parry, 'are you sure you're OK?'

'I've been walking around all day,' Parry admitted, 'I am tired. I went to see a priest this morning in that church – you know – Saint-Pierre?'

'Oh yeah,' said Sam curiously, 'what for? To confess your sins?'

'Not exactly,' said Parry. 'I just needed . . . to talk. That's all.'

'You can talk to me,' said Sam carefully.

Parry put his head in his hands. 'You wouldn't understand,' he said, 'you're not a Catholic. You Protestants don't realize how lucky you are in some ways. You don't suffer from guilt like we do, or at least not in quite the same way.'

'Do you still believe?'

'I believe that I am beyond help now.'

'Oh come,' said Sam, 'surely you're being unnecessarily gloomy? Why should you be beyond help? We've all strayed off the straight and narrow from time to time. Just say you're sorry and get back with your wife.'

'You make it sound so simple.'

'It is simple, that's why.'

Parry shook his head. It was pointless to discuss the situation, as he had known it would be. He cut through the string and paper of his parcel with Sam's knife and pulled out the volume of Lucretius that had been Montaigne's own, and that he had recognized. There was a list of prices folded inside the top of the parcel. It was clear that de Fonville did not know what he had had in his possession, but Parry was still puzzled as to why it should be included when they had agreed nothing. Unless . . . there had been some muddle and this packet was not meant for him . . . but for Caroline. He put the volume back inside the parcel and pushed the whole package around the side of the sofa with his foot. The Lucretius would make about £300,000 at auction, he reckoned.

'Caroline came by to collect her things,' said Sam in a carefully neutral sort of voice. 'She's gone back to the south, to Le Pin, I'm glad to say. It's the *Feria* in Nîmes, as you probably know.'

'Ah.' Caroline. The sound of her name on Sam's lips was extraordinary. It was hard to realize that she had a reality, a prosaic everydayness, when, to him, she was so much a creature of his imagination, his siren-goddess.

'A good thing too, if you ask me,' said Sam, who was watching Parry carefully. 'She does cause a lot of trouble, that girl, the devil of a lot of trouble.'

Parry said nothing.

'I'm afraid she has you snared, Edward.'

'No, no,' said Parry, rubbing his hands together anxiously. 'I've been thinking I should go home. I'm not feeling quite the thing as a matter of fact.'

'Sensible idea,' said Sam. 'Have you called Victoria?'

'I will do, later on when she's got time to talk.'

'OK,' said Sam. 'You always were a fool over women,' he added. 'Let's go for a drink.'

Much later still, after he had rung Victoria and failed to persuade her out of coming to Paris, Parry went slowly up the stairs to the turret room. He opened the door, half-expecting to find her there, lying on the bed waiting for him, but the bed had been made and the crewel-work bedspread with its stylized pink and green flowers smoothed neatly over the bolster. Everything belonging to her seemed to have gone: the pots of ruinously expensive face cream, the black bottle of scent; there was no scrap of her, no faint lingering smell. The window was open and a light breeze lifted the muslin curtains against the shutter. Parry stepped out on to the sloping roof and leaned against the railings that Caroline had held on to with her knuckles white. Only yesterday. Gripping the railings, Parry felt the tears falling on the back of his hand. He looked up at the sky where the breeze had blown the cloud about, thinning it, so that a light cover like gauze veiled the stars.

On Sunday morning Victoria woke up very early, at about five, disturbed by a dream she had had in which she had been at a party with Edward but he had failed to recognize her. She had followed him around a set of rooms which looked vaguely like the shop only much bigger, all lined with books, imploring him to talk to her, but he had looked through her as if she were invisible. Then her father arrived, holding a morocco photograph album. He said, 'It's not a Veronese, it's much better than that, it's a Leonardo.'

And she had woken in a strange state of excitement and sadness, to find herself in the old room she had shared for so long with Edward, with its four beds and cold lino floor covered in old, tattered Turkish rugs that a Victorian Digby had brought back from somewhere or other. The picture was not what it was supposed to be and neither was her husband. Was this the message of the dream? She lay there, thinking of Edward and the long history they had shared, with a sense of abandonment and loss that she was quite unfamiliar with; she felt that Edward had in some way become her enemy without her noticing. He couldn't blame her for Lloyd's, or the baby's death, or could he? Was there a part of him she did not know at all? The dream suggested there was. She knew that he had had a good many girlfriends before he met and married her, Tom had told her that, and she knew that Edward had returned to the faith a couple of years before they met, but she had been too young when she met him and too inexperienced to know what questions to ask. Then the children had come so fast that she had not had time. There had been no time. She had never been alone. The idea was both frightening and, at the same time, alluring. She thought of Sarah, whom she had met with Hugh. Sarah was alone. She had managed. Would I manage, she asked herself? Then she thought that

217

she should not even be thinking of such a thing. She still had a husband, didn't she? She was still married. Nothing had happened yet. But these thoughts and fears were part of the unpleasant wind of change sweeping across her whole family. This sense of insecurity and uncertainty permeated everything, like an underground stream eating away at the foundations of a building. Everything was contaminated by it, debased, eroded. Was this how those early Digbys had felt when they were hounded and tormented over their religion? History gave back a different answer. History said that people with strong beliefs, religious or otherwise, were sustained by the force of those beliefs when the going grew rough. Would her faith sustain her now? Would Edward's faith sustain Edward during whatever ordeal he was undergoing without her. Of the two of them she had always thought of Edward as the good Catholic. Edward had returned to the fold and was a hundred times more welcome than she, the boring old plodder who had never even thought of straying. And she hadn't. The death of her child had, if anything, strengthened her faith. Pain had drawn her in closer. Her own pain and suffering echoed by the knowledge that it was shared.

She suddenly felt a strong urge to be alone, to return to London as soon as possible. Victoria went downstairs very quietly, carrying her shoes in her hand. In the passageway to the chapel the cardinals seemed extra aloof at this early hour. She went through the gothic doorway and knelt down in the back row of chairs on a kneeler embroidered by her grandmother. A dove flew crookedly in space, holding an olive branch. The joiner had not yet put the picture back – perhaps it would never go back now – and it sat untidily behind the altar. Victoria looked around her, her glance falling on the cartouche, the picture, the statues. Every generation had done something here, it had been part of a family tradition to lavish love and care on the chapel, but it occurred to her suddenly and rather uncomfortably that it had not been God her family had been worshipping all these years but themselves: Digby worship. And when one pulled away the gilded carapace of tradition and beauty and dignity what did one find? A little, worm-eaten, shrivelled husk that had once been the germ of faith, long dead.

She got up abruptly and went out into the corridor and swiftly from there into the hall where she sat down on the huge old sofa that faced the empty fireplace and lit a cigarette. These, then, she thought, were the central, the interesting questions: what was one if one was not a) a Digby? b) a wife c) well-off? Answer? One had to face loss on a grand scale to find out. Most of the little fictions and stories by which we sustain ourselves, she thought, are nonsense, rather poisonous nonsense. We are not what we think we are. Perhaps this was what Edward had run up against.

Victoria knew her mother was coming downstairs because she could hear Minnie the pug, centipede claws on glass, crossing the great wasteland of polished floorboards between the foot of the stairs and the sofa, which she considered her own.

'Tor?' said her mother's voice, 'you're up early.'

'Hello, Mum,' Victoria got up out of the sofa and threw her cigarette end into the fireplace.

'Are you feeling all right?' asked her mother who looked grave and tired herself; her skin had a parchment-like quality which Victoria had not noticed before, but her eyes were bright and clear.

'I couldn't sleep,' said Victoria, as Minnie hurled herself at the sofa, failed, and fell back. She stooped down, picked the little dog up and held her. She was the same weight as a nice solid baby. No wonder the Victorians had liked to dress them up in mobcaps and pop them in prams.

'Tonia tells me that is a sign of depression,' said Isobel. Tonia was the eldest Digby daughter, a GP, who lived with her husband and children outside Hartley Wintney.

'She's probably right,' said Victoria, sitting down with Minnie on her lap. Her mother came and perched on the arm of the sofa. She was wearing her gardening clothes, an old pair of cords and a cardigan which had once belonged to Juliet.

'Are you depressed?'

'A bit,' said Victoria.

'It's a good thing you're going to Paris alone with Edward.' She glanced at her daughter's face, 'or is there something I don't know about. Is everything all right with Edward?'

'No. I don't know,' Victoria added hastily upon seeing her mother's expression of concern. 'I don't want to burden you with my problems, Mum. You've got enough of your own.'

'But what is the matter?'

'Other than Lloyd's, dry rot, and skirmishes over the school fees – do you really want me to tell you?'

'I wouldn't have asked you if I hadn't. You do so much, so well, my daughter. I'm so proud of you. Is it Edward?'

'Yes. It's hard to explain, but since Teresa died there has been a distance between us. We don't talk, we don't really even share a room terribly often.'

Isobel nodded.

'It isn't how I thought things would turn out,' Victoria said. 'You know how you have this vision of your life when you're young, well . . . mine's been turned on its head.'

'But, darling,' said her mother, 'life very rarely turns out as we mean it to, surely you must have realized that. You've been married a long time now, you have a family. Everything changes. It's not the same as it was when you were first married. Those dreams shatter and are replaced by something else.'

'Yes.' Victoria looked down at her lap where the pug was snoring. 'Perhaps it's just taken me a long time to realize that.'

Isobel glanced at her daughter. 'It's always difficult,' she said, 'being the last, the tail-end Charlie. It takes longer to grow up being the last, and having a lot of children, as you have done, really quite fast, probably just reinforces one's own childhood. Being always with children can bring out the child in one.'

'It's meant to make you grow up,' said Victoria, 'surely? Or do you mean . . . do you mean that you think I haven't grown up?'

'I don't mean that. What I'm getting at is that your family life has been an extension of your childhood. You were young when you married, one thing ran quite quickly into another. It's when they start to grow up that the reckoning comes, the weighing things up. Have I done it well? Who am I now they're gone? Will my husband still love me? Will I still love my husband? Can I bear to be with him for the rest of my life?'

'Can he bear to be with me?'

'Is that what is worrying you?'

'Yes.' Victoria told her mother what Tom had told her last night on the telephone.

'I have the oddest feeling about it all,' she said. 'It's so unlike him not to tell me.'

'It does seem peculiar, I admit. But perhaps he's just gone down south for a little sun. Nîmes is a lovely place. I won't patronize you by saying that men need a breather from time to time. They do.'

'So do women,' said Victoria. 'Dad's not in a good way, is he?'

'No. He blames himself, which takes the form of blaming me, that's what it is.'

'You're so wise. Will I ever grow as wise as you?'

'Darling,' said Isobel fondly, putting her hand on her daughter's dark head. 'You are. I meant it when I said I was proud of you. I am. Look at the way you cope with the children and your business and your difficult husband. I'm full of admiration for you.'

'Mum,' said Victoria after a moment, 'I'm going back this morning.'

'Are you sure? I hoped to have you a little longer.'

'I think I have to,' said Victoria. 'I need to think.'

'I understand.'

'Let's go and have some coffee. Would you put Minnie out?'

'I don't think she wants to go awfully.'

'Idle, little fat thing. Put her outside the front door.'

Victoria put Minnie out and watched her stand motionless for a second as if she had been put down in a strange country she had never visited in her life, then she tried to go back inside.

'Not so fast,' said Victoria, picking her up and walking over to the grass. As she waited for Minnie she looked back at the house with a sudden sense of herself as one person in a long procession of figures stretching back into the past and forwards into the future, a link in the chain, a strong link, she hoped, like her mother, forged out of steel and able to endure.

*

Chiswick Mall had a Sunday aimless look about it when Victoria returned. People in shorts wandered up and down holding small, grizzling children by the hand. Joggers shoved past the family groups engaged in the Sunday pursuit of worshipping themselves. The river looked oily and uninviting. Even the trees looked tired. Victoria got out of the car and slammed the door which groaned in protest. The rows of seats were covered in crisp droppings and sweet wrappers. Agatha's doll, Elizabeth, lay under the front passenger seat with just her bare feet showing.

The house was empty when she went indoors and someone (Tom) had forgotten to put on the burglar alarm, but as she went down the basement stairs she heard voices, a girl and a boy, who turned out to be Tom and Iza. There were books spread out on the table, textbooks by the look of them, and Iza was cleaning the teaspoons. Several of them stood in a jar of Silver Dip waiting to be fished out and polished.

'Mum!' said Tom, clearly horrified to see her. 'I thought you weren't coming back until tomorrow.'

'I wasn't, but I changed my mind.'

'Why didn't you ring?'

'I just came,' she said, trying not to smile. 'Don't mind me.'

'He is giving me lessons,' said Iza, who appeared to be perfectly composed, 'because my English is very terrible.'

'It's not terrible at all,' said Tom swiftly, glancing at Iza in a way that made Victoria feel superfluous. He's in love, she thought, oh God, poor Tom.

'Where's Hector?' she asked, putting the kettle on.

'On the river with Jenny and Hugh.'

'Oh yes.' Victoria paused. She had quite forgotten that Hugh had taken Jenny out on his boat.

'Is Hen with them?'

'Er, yes. That's why he wanted to go, I think.'

'Ah.' She made her cup of coffee and took it away upstairs with her. As she came into the hall she saw Jenny and Hugh coming up the path. Behind them were Hector and Henrietta. They all looked disgustingly happy.

Later, when the boys were watching *Blade Runner* on the tele-

222

vision, Victoria slipped out and went next door to find Hugh. His front door was slightly ajar, so she went inside and called his name. Silence. Feeling that she might be intruding, Victoria turned to leave and, in doing so, heard Hugh coming downstairs. His hair was standing slightly on end and he was buttoning his shirt up suggesting that he had been asleep and had just got up. His skin had gone darker from a day on the river in the sun which made his eyes look bluer, his teeth whiter. To her slight disgust Victoria found she was thinking in magazine clichés like a girl of her daughter's age.

'I was asleep,' he said, 'have you been here long? I lay down on my bed for a moment and then went out like a light. It must be all that river air.'

'I'm sorry,' she said, 'I didn't mean to get you up.' She turned towards the door again. 'I'll come and find you tomorrow, if you're here.'

'Stay and have a drink,' he said.

'Are you sure you don't mind?'

'I couldn't be more pleased,' he said, taking her by the hand as he came past, as if they had known one another all their lives and it was the most natural thing in the world to do.

In the kitchen she said, 'I must give you back your telephone.'

'Keep it,' he said, getting down some glasses, 'I don't need it.'

'But . . . they're so expensive, and, besides, I don't really need one.'

'I would have said you did need one with all those children in different places.'

'But I'm not used to it. Really. Please take it back.'

'If you insist,' he said, smiling at her. 'Shall we go outside?' He was holding two glasses and a bottle.

They sat where they had sat before on the wooden seat under the roses.

'Tell me why you came back early,' he said, 'I didn't want to ask in front of the young.'

'Two reasons, really. I needed to get away from the bulk of my children and I needed to get away from my parents' problems.'

'Which are?'

'Lloyd's. My father's a Name, like me, I'm one too, for my sins. It looks like we're going to have to sell our house . . .'

'Which house?'

'Sorry. Yorkshire.' *Our* house. Perhaps her mother was right and she never really had left home.

'It's been in the family a long time, you see, since the fifteenth century, so it still seems like home, if you follow me.'

'What about this house?' he inclined his head towards next door.

'It's in Edward's name, thank God. Not mine. Edward says we'll have to sell to pay the bills, but why should we if it's in his name alone? We have to live somewhere. And it might as well be there.'

'Is that the only way you'll be able to pay?'

'Looks like it. *If* we pay. Edward says he's found something in Paris, some great find, but . . . I don't know . . .' She stopped talking to allow her feelings to subside. The subject of Edward felt like pressing a bruise.

'There's just been such a lot of worry,' she said hastily, blinking the tears away. 'In the end it gets to you. Every time I go upstairs to my bedroom I go past my desk in the alcove on the landing. That's where the bills are, and the letters from Fenton and Stanwright, my underwriting agents.'

'I do understand,' said Hugh gently, 'it's terrible not to have any money when you've been used to it, especially when there are children involved. Your poor parents too.'

'Mum will survive if they have to go, but Dad won't. I think it'll kill him. Mum will adapt, she's that sort of person.'

'Like you,' said Hugh. 'You're that sort of person, too.'

'How do you know?'

'I can tell.'

'It's so difficult to talk to people about losing money,' she went on, ignoring his remark but secretly pleased by it, 'because most people assume you were lucky to have any in the first place and they think, although they don't say so, that you probably deserve it.'

'In Africa, at least in the part where I was, nobody had anything very much more than the clothes they stood up in and not very many of those. It certainly made me think about money and possessions in a different way.'

'Not wanting them so much, do you mean?'

'Not exactly that, but it made me think about how people do dignify themselves with their possessions. The whole of western society works on the principle that if you have nothing you are nothing. People here become their possessions through a process of identification with them. Lévi-Strauss called it *participation mystique*. You see it in traffic: all those men thinking they are BMWs or Range Rovers.'

'We're not what we think we are, that's what you mean, isn't it? I was thinking the same thing myself only this morning. I was in the chapel, it was quite early, and I suddenly realized that . . .' She paused without meaning to, watching his hand with its heavy signet ring holding the glass.

'That what?' he said, 'don't stop. It's interesting.' He looked away deliberately, sensing her sudden shyness. Gently does it, he said to himself.

'I don't want to bore you,' she said. 'I think I'd better go.'

'Why? You've only just arrived.'

Victoria stood up in a hurry. 'I'm in a bit of state and I don't want to bore you with it. Everything I say seems to lead me towards it.'

'Towards what? Sit down and let's talk. Sometimes it's easier to say things to someone you don't know so well.'

'But it's so boring for you.'

'No, it's not.'

'I don't want to be disloyal to my husband.'

'Is it disloyal to talk to someone?'

'No, but . . .'

'He's in Paris and you're going to join him, right?'

'Right.' She bit her lip. 'Except that he's not. I don't know where he is. He's been very strange all week. I think he may be having a breakdown. We lost our last child about a year ago and almost everything has been wrong ever since.'

Hugh nodded. 'What did the baby die of?'

'Cot death.'

He looked at her gravely. 'That's terribly hard to deal with.'

'Edward thought somehow it was his fault.'

'Why should he think that?'

'I don't know. I've been married to him for eighteen years, but I don't know the answer to that.'

'Guilt is a funny thing,' said Hugh, 'often completely irrational. Has he seen anyone?'

'I don't think so. Sometimes he goes to see Jeremy Montagu, our doctor, but Jeremy's a GP, not a . . . not a . . . psychiatrist.'

'Does he still go to church?'

'Yes. But he no longer always takes the sacrament.'

'I see.' Hugh raised his eyebrows. 'I'm not a Catholic, but it sounds like something fairly serious is going on. Have you asked him what it might be?'

'Edward wouldn't tell me,' she said, 'he wouldn't want me to see his weakness. I'm quite a lot younger than he is, so he likes to feel . . .'

'Superior?'

'Yes.'

'Does he, forgive me, does he have a girlfriend or anything like that?'

'I hadn't thought of that,' she said, amazed by how hurt she felt at the suggestion.

'I don't mean to trespass.'

'You're not trespassing,' she said, 'I do need to talk about it. I don't know if he has a mistress or not. I suppose it's stupid of me really, it's just that it hadn't occurred to me.'

'Did he have lots of girlfriends before he met you?'

'I think so. But when he came back to the faith he stopped. Until he met me.'

'So you'll go and look for him, is that it? And bring him back?'

'Yes.'

'Don't cry,' he said, touching her cheek. 'It'll be all right. You're very brave.'

'Don't say that,' she said, blowing her nose, 'or you'll start me off again.'

Upstairs, in the hall, he kissed her chastely on the cheek. His neck, she noted, thinking again in schoolgirl clichés, smelt of something sharp and clean.

'Thank you, Hugh,' she said.

'Don't mention it. Come any time. If you need to be alone come over here and be peaceful. Help yourself. I'll give you a key if you like. You probably should have one anyway. It must be difficult for you to be on your own.'

'I hardly ever am for long. It's a very kind offer, I appreciate it.'

When she looked back from the gate he was still there watching her. He raised his hand slightly in a gesture of farewell, to which she responded with a feeling of gratitude.

Victoria closed the front door behind her, and leant against it for a moment. Feather, dark and solid as a dugong, lay stretched out in front of the hall table, her head on her paws, her tail thumping.

'Where've you been?' said Tom in an accusing voice, appearing in the drawing-room doorway suddenly. 'You've been gone for hours.'

'I was having a drink with Hugh, next door,' said Victoria, turning on the lamp on the table.

'I know who Hugh is,' said Tom crossly. 'I'm not stupid.'

'Come and sit down a minute,' said Victoria going into the drawing room where Tom, hilariously, appeared to have been sitting up for her. Rather than switching on the lamps, he had lit the candles in the brackets on either side of the fireplace. A Mozart piano concerto was playing very softly in the background. Poor Tom was obviously undergoing a violent attack of young love, with all its accompanying symptoms.

'You've been gone ages,' said Tom crossly, flopping into a sofa. 'Where's Hector?'

'He's gone back with Jenny and Hen. I wanted to see you, so I waited. And waited. Why were you so long?'

'I wanted to talk to him,' said Victoria. 'I'm sorry if you wondered where I was. You could always have come and found me.'

Tom glared at her. 'Everything's become so horrible,' he said, 'I wish Mare was here. I wish I'd gone to Yorkshire.'

Victoria went and knelt by the sofa and put her arms around

him. He struggled for a moment and then gave in. She could feel from the convulsions of his body that he was crying.

'Why's everything so horrible? What's wrong between you and Dad?'

'Darling, I wish I knew,' said Victoria, stroking her son's face as tenderly as hers had been stroked by Hugh half an hour before.

'Will it be all right when you go to Paris?'

'I hope so.' Victoria sighed.

'What is wrong? Where is Dad?'

'You know more than I do about that,' she said. 'He didn't speak to me about it.'

'I'll bash his face in,' said Tom.

'That won't do much good. Try not to worry too much. You've got your own life to lead. You will be careful, won't you?'

'Yeah, Mum, yeah,' said Tom, suddenly defensively bored.

'I'm going to go to bed now,' she said. 'I think you should too. Put Feather out, would you.'

'OK,' he said, rolling off the sofa. 'Mum?'

'What?'

'You will be careful, won't you?'

'Yes,' she said, 'I will.'

Sam's house in Le Pin was built out of the rough local stone and stood on the edge of the village surrounded by a wall of the same stone. The gates, made by the local blacksmith in the previous century, hung crookedly from their hinges and squawked awkwardly when opened. A wooden box attached to the wall had a sign on it in faint ink which read 'Hoskyns'.

The walled garden had run terribly to seed. The grass was waist-high, a bicycle lay in the long grasses with one wheel missing and an old baker's van belonging to Sam stood under the shelter of a barn. Before Sam had bought this house it had belonged to the Foreign Legion who had used it as a rest-house for troops returned from a tour of duty in French Guiana or the hostile desert wastelands of the Red Sea.

A flight of tiled steps led to the terrace with its rose-covered pergola. Two or three old basket chairs were lined up crookedly outside the kitchen door. Basil grew in flowerpots on the kitchen windowsill.

Parry in linen jacket and trousers (thank God he had remembered his hot-weather kit) put his head around the kitchen door which was open. A wiry-looking, middle-aged woman was washing the floor on all fours. She scrambled to her feet when she saw Parry.

'Monsieur?' she enquired.

'I am looking for Caroline,' he said, as calmly as he could.

'Caroline has gone to Nîmes. For the *Feria*,' she added, 'it is today.'

'And is Monsieur de Fonville here?'

'No, Monsieur, not at present.'

The woman looked at him. She had a hard black glance that suggested she was not amenable to being questioned. She waited.

'She did not tell you I was coming?'

'No, Monsieur.' She was clasping her floorcloth in her hand, Parry noticed. It was dripping all over the tiles.

'I am a friend of Monsieur Hoskyns. He has said that I can stay here. I have been staying with him in Paris.'

She clearly did not believe him.

'I'll ring him,' said Parry, 'if I may, and then you can speak to him and he can tell you that it is all right.' Sam would be surprised, he thought, although he would not offer difficulties.

She hesitated, then she said, 'Very well.'

Nancy answered the phone in the rue Caulaincourt.

'Edward,' she said, 'where are you? Sam went to the studio and called me to say you'd left a message about going south or somethin'. Is everything all right?'

'I'm in Le Pin,' said Parry, 'and your cleaning woman,' he was speaking English now, 'does not believe that I am who I say I am.'

'Put her on the line,' said Nancy, 'I'll talk to her. When are you comin' back?'

'Monday.'

'Oh, OK. Just a quick weekend in the sun, is it?'

'Yes,' said Parry, 'that's right. I'm going to the bull-fight at Nîmes.'

'I don't know how you can,' said Nancy. 'See you Monday. I'll tell Sam when he comes in. He may call you as there are some things he wants. Is Caroline there?'

'No,' lied Parry.

'Ah. She comes and goes that girl. You never know where she is.' She sounded like Sam, Parry thought.

'No, that's true.' He gestured to the cleaning woman and said, 'Nancy wants to speak to you.'

He left them talking and went outside into the blinding sunlight to his rented car which he had left by the gates. Nothing stirred in the landscape except for the buzz of tractors in the nearby vineyard. A dog lay in the middle of the road asleep. A woman called out from the next door house: 'Nathalie, come here at once!'

He thought briefly with a pang of his own children: Mary's affectionate sweetness, her long thin legs, those huge shoes; Tom's blond good-looks, so like his own at the same age, Agatha, Cyprian and little Ben, then he forgot about them. There was nothing to keep them in his mind here: an unseen woman's voice calling a child, that was all it was. He went back through the gates with his suitcase.

The cleaning woman showed him a room without further ado. It was Sam and Nancy's room, a huge, dark, tiled cavern of a place with an uneven floor, whitewashed walls, a vast carved bed where, later, he would lie naked with Caroline. There was an old bookcase of dark, stained oak, and a large framed oil painting of a naked woman lying on her side on a rumpled bed. An oak trunk at the end of the bed held linen, sheets as stiff as boards from drying in the southern sun, deep pillowcases fringed with nuptial lace, part of some long-forgotten dowry, some wedding night somewhere. Parry made the bed carefully, refusing help from the woman. He wanted to do this himself.

Caroline was sleeping in the smaller room that led off this one. It had a single bed, an old iron bedstead painted white, the same tiled, uneven floor, white walls. Her bed was neatly made. A glass of water sat on a chair by the bed together with a single candle-stick and a novel. He picked it up. She was reading *Villette*. As he put the book back a condom in its wrapper fell out. Parry picked it up and put it in his pocket. The pillow smelled of her scent and he picked it up and buried his face in it. A pair of high-heeled shoes stood by the wardrobe, one had fallen on its side, sug-gesting that they had been tried and rejected in favour of another pair.

The bathroom shelf reassured him. The expensive face cream was there, the silver toothbrush in the shape of a woman's body.

The girl sitting next to him was a slim little thing; a Spaniard by the looks of her, tawny hair, dark shining eyes, pretty, brown legs, one of which was pressed extremely close to Parry's own thigh. They were packed in like sardines. She was leaning forwards with great concentration as, he noticed, all the women were, and the crowd was making a noise that Parry had never heard before. The Romans would no doubt have recognized the half-sobbing, half-exhilarated timbre of that single mob voice shouting for death. Parry's mouth was dry and he was trembling slightly, as he noticed his attractive companion was too. He also had an erection. The band was playing something he half-recognized, something excitable, but with a sad undertow to it.

He raised his field glasses and scanned the faces on the other side of the arena.

'That is where the rich people sit,' said the girl next to him, in French, 'in the shade.'

At that moment he saw her, completely and perfectly in focus, that swinging colourless hair held back by a white velvet band with gold studs on it; she was wearing a white sleeveless shift, and laughing at something that the man next to her was saying. Parry did not recognize him. He looked further along the row and found de Fonville's aristocratic and sardonic face. He looked well.

At that moment, the audience gasped collectively. The great Iberian bull had dropped its head, worn out with the pain of the *banderillas* that made his shoulders bleed black rivulets, like men-strual blood, and the matador closing upon him, prepared to plunge his sword through the hinge of bone, opened by that drooping head with its crown of horns, deep into the heart. *El Memento de Verdad:* the gushing submission to the matador, to the crowd, to the god. He remembered his own moment of truth, so long ago now, in that ancient church in Paris; and it seemed to him that he had turned away from the God of the New Testament, who had demanded and obtained his obedience, and who now had lost it; his allegiance had slipped back the centuries before Christ to these older, darker, crueller gods, gods of blood and dust and death.

Parry watched Caroline's face. She too was leaning forwards now, her mouth open, her eyes bright. The air of intense sexual excitement was tangible. The bull staggered and fell, his vast pizzle scraping the dust.

The crowd gasped. The girl next to him cried out something in a language he did not understand. He watched Caroline. She had the same look on her face she had before orgasm: lips parted, eyes eager.

He looked away. They were closing on the beast now. It was over. The girl next to him was crying with excitement and relief.

'They cut off the ears,' she said, 'and the tail and, sometimes, the . . . sprout.'

She made a gesture with her hands that left Parry in no doubt as to what she meant.

Now the picadors would come and drag the bull out. He raised his glasses again. She was still there talking animatedly to the man next to her. De Fonville was on his feet. Soon they would go. He had to hurry.

The crush outside the amphitheatre was amazing. Policemen in kepis waved their arms about, but were useless against the enormous numbers of people pouring forth through the massive archways and iron gates of the arena.

She appeared sooner than he had expected, her white dress almost luminous in the ancient depth of the passageway into the arena. She was walking alongside the man he had seen her sitting next to in the amphitheatre. Behind her came de Fonville.

Parry stepped into her path as she came out into the light and put his hand on her bare brown arm.

'Edward!' An expression of intense alarm crossed her face which she attempted to conceal. 'What on earth are you doing here?'

'I want you to come with me,' he said, tightening his grip.

'I can't. Please go away. I can't explain now.'

As before, in Paris, he could see she was near tears, but tears of what? Of love? Of fear? He would never understand her. The deeper in he went the less able he felt to cope, the further from the shore he seemed. There were no longer any familiar landmarks.

'I want you to come with me,' he insisted. As she had taken a step backwards he now found that he was holding her hand which was trembling.

'What is he doing here?' asked de Fonville upon seeing Parry. 'I thought I had told you . . .'

'I don't know,' Caroline said distractedly to Fonville. Her hand, still in Parry's, squeezed his.

'Come here a moment,' she said, ignoring de Fonville and steering Parry under an arch whose iron gates were barred.

'Meet me later,' she said, turning her back to the crowd, 'don't ask now,' she added, to forestall his questions. 'I'll tell you later. Meet me at the Maison Carrée at ten . . .' she said, 'no . . .', thinking swiftly, 'not there. Meet me at the Taure Magna. You know where that is, don't you?'

'Of course I do.' The great lookout tower built by the Romans, and visible from miles outside the city.

'Where are you staying?' she asked.

'At Le Pin. Where the hell do you think? I'm not going to let you go,' he said. 'Why did you leave me in Paris like that? I didn't know where you'd gone. It was terrible. Don't you understand?'

'It's all right,' she said soothingly, 'all right. I do understand. I'll explain everything to you later. Trust me this once, darling. Give me the benefit of the doubt. I will be there, I promise.'

'What about de Fonville?'

'He's leaving this evening, I can't explain now. He's going to

Marseilles. I promise you, darling,' she said entreatingly, 'on my honour, on my life, I will be there. I promise. Alone. Do you have a car?'

'Yes. Why?'

'I told you,' she said, 'don't ask now. I'll see you later, ten, Taure Magna.' She put her fingers lightly on his lips and was gone, leaving a faint, tantalizing drift of scent.

Parry remained where he was for a moment. He felt a leaden sense of bereavement, of loss, that was as familiar to him now, he realized, as the sight of his face in the glass each morning. There were tears in his throat. He coughed and blew his nose. He felt on the verge of something perilous . . . shedding his old life like a skin . . . what the hell did he think he was doing . . . lost like a child . . . shoved and pulled about by the crowds . . . losing his reason. That Hopkins poem . . . what had it been? *We hear our hearts grate on themselves: it kills to bruise them dearer . . .*

The town was *en fête*. Groups of revellers moved through the streets, gypsies, tinkers, men on stilts. There were bands playing in all the little squares and everywhere beggars and beautiful girls, young men with their shirts open, the girls showing the tops of their breasts. The Romans would have been quite at home in all this, Parry thought, seized suddenly by a mad feeling of gaiety, after the spectacle was over, after the crowd had been sated on bulls' blood, their cruelty roused and then satisfied, the urge to despoil and violate would spill over into the sex instinct; then they would get drunk and make love.

He found a tiny square with a couple of bars in it, chairs and tables everywhere on the marble pavements, and a great church looming with the statutory beggars loitering outside. The double doors were wide open and he could see straight into the candle-lit dimness. He pushed his way in, past the sightseers, the trippers, the merely curious, drawn by the old power, the mesmerizing, magnetic force that drew one, one knew not why, into this place of wounds and darkness and death. He gazed at the great crucifix hanging suspended over the altar, which no longer had the power to heal him, and turned away into his own darkness, pulling it about him like a mantle.

He found a table where he could sit with his back to the church, and ordered a pastis in order to numb the anxiety about Caroline which bubbled up in him like a spring – where she was, what she was doing. He could think of nothing but the feel of her arm under his hand, her trembling hand in his, the smoothness of her skin. He began to smoke Gitanes, one after another, until his mouth hurt.

'Good God alive,' said a male voice after some time had elapsed, 'if it isn't Edward Parry. What're you doing here, Parry?'

The speaker was a London art dealer whom Parry knew and was fond of, a beefy, agreeable man called Dickie Chatterton, with small black eyes that always appeared to have just remembered another joke, and black curly hair like a helmet.

'Where's Victoria?' asked Dickie, sitting down without being asked and ordering more pastis. 'Or have you left her behind?'

'Who?'

'Your wife,' said Dickie, gazing at Parry curiously. 'Are you all right, old thing, or have you had a falling-out with her? Is that why you're here?'

'No, it's not.'

'But she's not here?'

'No.'

'Hmmm,' said Dickie, not knowing quite what to make of all this. Parry's uxoriousness was well-known amongst his friends and the subject of a certain mild amusement. He wondered what had gone wrong.

'I've left Angela behind too,' he volunteered. 'God, but it's a relief not to be on holiday with screaming kids always wanting another Orangina – which cost a bloody fortune, as I'm sure you know – or an ice-cream. Angela's taken them to her mother's for half-term, ghastly old hag, and I'm here on biz – had to come and see an artist, nudge, nudge, wink, wink. Got that done quick, then thought I'd do the *Feria*, bloody incredible all that stuff, what?'

'You saw it?'

'Christ, yes. Makes you randy, though, don't you think. Of

course I shouldn't say that to you, old holier-than-thou Parry. Cheers!'

'Cheers!' said Parry sourly. If only Dickie knew the truth. Having thought this, he was overcome by the sudden urge to confide in him, to bridge the gap between one world and another. In a part of his mind he knew it was an indiscreet and stupid thing to do but having once thought of it he couldn't stop himself.

'I've actually rather fallen off my pedestal,' he said.

'Sorry?' said Dickie, 'don't follow quite.'

'There's a girl,' said Parry indistinctly. 'I'm seeing a girl.'

'Are you really? Do I know her?' Dickie drained his glass and signalled to the waiter.

'I shouldn't think so.'

'What's her name?'

'Caroline,' he pronounced it in the French way.

'You always have to be different, don't you, Parry. *Caroleen*. Caroline what?'

'Doesn't matter,' said Parry. 'Let me get this lot.'

'You do the next round,' said Dickie, getting out a leather pouch and offering Parry a cigar, which he accepted. Out of the corner of his eye he saw one of the beggars lumbering towards them. Perhaps he wanted a cigar.

'Now look,' said Dickie, 'tell Uncle Dickie what's going on. You're in France with a girl. First question, where is she?'

'I'm meeting her later,' said Parry, trying to conceal his anxiety.

'Does she have a husband here somewhere? How very . . .' Dickie looked around at the beggar, who held out cupped hands with ridged yellow fingernails like a supplicant. 'Fuck off,' he said, and went on talking, '. . . very French of you. I must say you have gone up in my estimation, old boy.'

'He wants a cigar,' said Parry.

'Well, he can want. Go on,' said Dickie, 'bugger off.'

The man muttered something uncomplimentary, but at that point the waiter came up with the drinks and he was forced to move on.

'It was an accident,' said Parry, 'I didn't mean to.'

'Why worry?' said Dickie, 'but that's the trouble with you

Cattolicos, you're always guilty and tormented. Don't get enough oats early on, that's your problem, then you break out later.'

'Do you . . . have you . . .?' began Parry, unable to continue.

'I've *thought* about it,' said Dickie, 'every man thinks about it, but Angela's marvellous in the sack, very sexy woman, you know.'

'Quite,' said Parry, who had a prudish streak, 'absolutely. Very good legs,' he said, trying to keep in the spirit of the thing.

'Ah, so you've noticed!'

'Of course I've noticed,' said Parry crossly. 'I might be a Catholic but I'm not blind.'

'So what are you going to do?' asked Dickie, 'you're not going to be a fool and blurt it all out to Victoria, are you?'

'I don't know what I'm going to do,' said Parry, 'I'm in love with this girl, you see.'

'Don't give me that,' said Dickie, 'you've got a wife and kids to take care of. Have a bit on the side by all means, but don't start going in for "love" and all that rubbish. The grass is always greener, dear boy, on the other side. Just remember that. And you'll have to pay through the nose if you go for a divorce with all those kids, but, of course you can't divorce, can you, you're a Cattolico, stuck with it for life.'

'I've lost my faith,' said Parry, lighting another Gitane. He was conscious of the church behind him like a menacing presence.

'How very convenient for you,' said Dickie sceptically. 'You Catholics always did make up the rules as you went along. I suppose when this affair fails you'll get it back again.'

'I don't think so.'

'Look,' said Dickie, who, as a good Protestant Englishman, did not care much for religion as a topic of conversation (it was something one endured, like bank charges), 'let's go and cat somewhere. There's a lovely little jazz bar I know near the gardens. There's a bar and a restaurant inside and then this terribly pretty garden where we can sit under the stars.'

'All right,' said Parry, suddenly glad to get away from this place. He glanced over his shoulder. Now that he had denounced them he must get away somewhere and hide or lie low. They would be after him soon, hounding and pounding.

At half-past ten Parry glanced at his watch and jumped to his feet, knocking over his little gilt chair to the intense annoyance of the woman sitting behind him.

'What the hell's the matter?' said Dickie lazily. 'You look as if you've seen a ghost.'

'I'm late,' said Parry, 'I had an appointment, I have to go.'

'God, you make me laugh, Parry,' said Dickie, 'this is like something from *opéra bouffe*. Eduardo has an assignation.'

'I have to go,' said Parry, 'how much will be the bill be?'

'God alone knows,' said Dickie. 'Stop fussing and settle up with me in London. When are you due back?'

'Soon,' said Parry, waving. 'I'll ring you.'

The streets near the canal and the water gardens consisted mainly of large, solid houses and prosperous-looking apartment blocks. A grand hotel stood on the corner. According to Dickie this was where the matadors and their wives and girlfriends stayed. A yellow and white striped awning with a scalloped edge ran from the entrance to the hotel to the edge of the pavement where large glossy cars were coming and going, disgorging their glamorous passengers on to the strip of red carpet. Parry skirted this activity and made his way across the bridge over the canal towards the water gardens. In the dust on the other side of the bridge, a handful of old men were playing *boules*. Once, Parry had known that same quiet contentment, that satisfaction with his life, with his lot, but no longer. As he hurried along into the lantern-lit gloom of the ancient gardens that had been planned and planted by the Romans with their passion for civic order, the desire to tame and control and contain all aspects of nature, he felt a great sense of foreboding. His head ached from all the drink and his whole body was pouring sweat like a broken dam. Parry passed the ruins of the Temple of Diana and began his ascent up the long flights of steps linking the terraces. At the grotto he paused for a moment to look into the clear, tinkling, moon-struck waters. There was a smell of ferns and cold water and piss. A couple moved away ahead of him going down the opposite path. Two men holding hands.

Panting, Parry reached the top. Behind him the whole city lay spread out, with lights here and there. There was a huge moon. Snatches of music from the revelries drifted up on the night air like smoke.

Black pools of shadow clung to the base of the tower, which seemed to Parry, with his heightened awareness, sinister and threatening. His footsteps made a crunching sound as he began to circle the tower.

A voice said 'Edward?' A woman's voice, shivery with panic and tears.

'Yes.' Parry stopped. 'Where are you?' He found that he felt no surprise to find that she was still there, but he did not know why this should be so.

'Here.'

She came out of the shadows like a wraith in her white dress. 'I thought you weren't coming,' she said.

'I'm late.' He waited.

'I've been so frightened.' She came close to him. He noticed that she wore a creamy white chiffon scarf around her neck that he did not remember seeing earlier; for a brief instant he wondered why or what this signified, then he forgot about it.

'What's wrong?' he asked, peering at her. 'Why were you frightened? What have you got to be frightened about?'

He thought of everything that he had abandoned simply to be here, now, at this moment, only, it seemed, in order to listen to lies and evasions. The anger came swiftly and surprisingly like the flickering lick of the forest fire, the flame almost invisible in daylight.

'Tell me,' he shouted, and shook her very hard.

'Stop it,' she said, and he could tell from her voice that she was crying. 'Stop. I will tell you.'

He let go of her and lit another Gitane.

'Gaby is a dealer,' she said. 'He smuggles artefacts, bronzes, all those kind of things. When he met me he offered me a job. We were soon lovers,' she glanced at him in the gloom, 'and then he said we were partners. But we were not. It was a lie. He was using me, using my knowledge, my connections, my ... sexuality ...'

239

'You didn't have to sleep with him,' said Parry.

'Oh, please,' she sighed, 'don't be so English, so . . .'

'Go on.'

'At dinner I told him I didn't want any more, that I wanted to be as I was, on my own. A professional woman, working on my own, leading my own life. He laughed at me. He told me I was a *puta*, a tart, that I would never be any good on my own. We had a row. I got up to go. He said to me: "Parry is a weakling, a loser, a dupe" and I said, "but I . . ."'

'You're lying to me,' Parry said. 'You're making it up as you go along. You always lie to me.' Again, the anger. The ripple of flame along a branch.

'I'm not lying,' she said. 'You must believe me.'

He took her in his arms and kissed the tears away, tasting the salt and the make-up. 'I do believe you . . .' he hesitated, 'but where is de Fonville now?'

'Gone,' she said, with a hint of impatience, 'I told you.'

'To Marseilles?'

'To hell, for all I care.'

'So,' Parry said carefully, 'what you told me about stealing artefacts from archaeological sites, is that true?'

'A little. I have done it once or twice.'

He noticed that her syntax faltered in English when she was rattled, or perhaps even that was part of her act.

'Tell me.' He pulled her to him.

'I am no good for you,' she said. 'You are a good man, Edward, you should go back to your wife, go home to your children. They need you.'

'You don't understand,' he said, 'I can't go back. I've come too far now. I've left all that behind me.' Briefly, he felt sick with longing for that other prosaic world, then it left him. It was over.

'So quickly? It has all happened so quickly.'

'Yes.' Again, the feeling of isolation, of being beleaguered, engulfed him. 'We should go,' he said. 'Why did you want to meet me here?'

'So that we should not be seen. Don't you understand?'

'I suppose so.'

'Where is the car?' she asked, rubbing her arms. 'Is it far?

'Miles away. We ought to go. Come on.'

At the top of the grotto, just above the waterfall, Caroline missed her footing and fell.

He heard her cry of pain and ran towards her.

'Are you all right?' He took her foot in his, easing it out of the absurd gold sandal.

'You wear such silly shoes,' he said.

'I think I've wrenched the tendon,' she said, 'it feels terribly sore.'

'Can you walk?'

'I'll try.'

She hobbled down to the gates with him. 'I'll wait here for you,' she said, 'could you come and get me. I don't think I can walk much further.'

He was suddenly afraid again.

'You'll vanish,' he said.

'I won't. Believe me. I promise you. I will be here.' She kissed him on the mouth and he began to kiss her back. It seemed years since he had kissed her.

'Not now,' she said, pushing him off gently. 'Go now. Soon we shall be home.'

Home. She had used that word in connection with him. It would be all right. All those other homes he had known, Knockfern and all the rest, always taken from him.

Outside the amphitheatre, the police had stopped all the traffic. There were police cars and police vans, dogs, flashing lights. An ambulance stood with its doors open. Parry looked over to where a group of people were clustered around a prostrate form that had something familiar about it. He picked his way through the crowds until he was very close to the group of paramedics and uniformed officers. They were lifting the body into the ambulance but for an instant Parry was transfixed by the length of the body and the sight of a head of grey corkscrew curls before the doors were closed.

She was there when he came back with the car, hiding herself in the shadows. The old men who had been playing *boules* in the dust earlier on had long since packed up and gone home, but there were still one or two cars coming and going outside the grand hotel.

'You've been ages,' she said, hobbling to the car, 'is the traffic bad?'

'Terrible. There was something going on outside the amphitheatre, someone had been shot . . .'

'Oh,' she said, as she eased herself into the front seat, 'how awful.'

'The man looked like Gaby,' he said. 'I thought it was him.'

'Oh now, come on,' she said, 'that's enough of a joke for one night. I tell you, he left for Marseilles hours ago.'

'Are you sure?' He had only her word for it.

'Of course I am sure. Why do you question me? Am I a criminal? What is all this?' She made as if to get out of the car, but Parry stopped her by putting his hand on her arm.

'You lie to me all the time,' he said, 'come on, admit it.'

'I admit nothing. I am going. Do not try and stop me.'

'Don't! Please. Forgive me. I've had a shock. A lot of shocks. So much has happened, all so quickly . . .'

'I do not like to be accused of lying.'

'I'm sorry.'

He told himself, as he drove off, that he was overwrought and that to have her with him was enough. A great many people had height and grey curls, only it had seemed so odd, so much of a coincidence; but since his faith in everything else had slipped or gone, and since, in order to survive, one had to believe in something, then he had to believe in Caroline. He had no choice.

At the junction with the main road two policeman waited on motor bikes. They looked menacing and Parry's heart missed a beat when they gazed with interest at his white rented Citroën. He glanced at Caroline, but she was massaging her ankle and did not see them.

'Police,' he said, 'everywhere. They must be looking for someone. Whoever it was who was responsible for the wounding of the man I saw near the amphitheatre.'

'The man you saw was probably shot by the police. They are

completely trigger-happy. They'll shoot anything. There's always crime during the *Feria*, stabbings, shootings – what you saw – it's just normal. You're so English,' she said, lighting him a cigarette as they drove up the long hill, away from the city, 'so jolly correct. God's in his heaven and all's well with the world.'

'Right with the world,' said Parry automatically.

'So,' she said, when they were driving along the dark, precipitous piece of road that edged the gorge, 'now we are alone, Edward, are you glad?'

Relief made her want to play cat and mouse with him, to prod him and withdraw, to tantalize him. It was her nature to be like that, she couldn't help it. She knew she shouldn't play games with him – it was he after all who had rescued her – and she was fond of him, her English Edward, very fond, plus the fact he was an exciting lover – extraordinarily good for an Englishman – and she still needed him. The game was not quite complete, there were still some loose ends to tie up. Gaby had behaved like a fool, running away from the policeman when he should have walked, he deserved what he had got. He would be all right, they would look after him in hospital, make him better. It would be taken care of.

'Edward, darling,' she said, 'tell me something.'

'What?' The gorge was empty, Parry could see, in the moonlight. Just stones and dust. No water. Just a wasteland, where the bony spine of the landscape protruded.

'Did Gaby send you a parcel of books?'

'Why?'

'I just wondered. Nothing serious.'

'I don't think so,' said Parry, 'not that I am aware of.'

'Are you sure?' She put her hand on his thigh.

'Don't you believe me? I don't like to be accused of lying.'

'You silly darling. I know you would not lie to me. I just wanted to know, that is all.'

'*Nein*,' said Edward, '*nyet.*' What would happen if he were suddenly to wrench the wheel and drive this car straight off the road? Over and over they would go, making gigantic cartwheels in the air until, with a smash and a flourish, they would land among those rocks. A column of flame in the still night air.

'What are you doing?' Caroline said, her voice shrill as the car swerved violently, 'Stop it, Edward. Stop!'

'I was thinking,' he said, 'how easy it would be to kill us both. All I need to do is to drive off the road.'

Hugh drove Victoria to the airport. Like everything he did it was done unobtrusively, but competently and calmly. Tom had been given a job – much too well paid, his mother thought – washing down the walls of Hugh's drawing room with sugar soap. He seemed happy to concentrate on this. Later, Iza would come and help him. The hairdressing salon in Notting Hill Gate was shut on Mondays.

'She's older than he is,' said Victoria, 'why is she bothering with a chap who's younger than she is?'

'Perhaps she likes him,' suggested Hugh, who was wearing a nice, white linen shirt with the sleeves rolled up.

'In any case, we all have to start with an older woman. I like Iza because she has integrity which she uses to protect her innocence. That is so refreshing. She's a good person for Tom to start off with because of that. She won't corrupt him.'

'If anything, it'll be the other way round.'

'How's the smoking?'

'Hardly anything. At least he seems to have stopped throwing them down the loo.'

Hugh laughed. 'It's awful being young, don't you think, particularly the age Tom and Mary are, partly because they remind us of awful parts of ourselves that we've buried. Awkwardnesses and pains we've forgotten.'

'I suppose you're right.' Victoria looked out of the window at the Wang building as they went past on the flyover. She had a feeling that a part of her life had ended and another begun. Chiswick was behind her and Paris ahead. She glanced at Hugh's profile and thought it extraordinary how he should make her feel so secure and so calm. She could hardly bear to think about Edward so great was her sense of his betrayal of her and her own feelings of guilt towards him.

'Do you want me to wait with you?' Hugh asked, as they approached Heathrow.

'No, no. Don't.' She glanced at him. 'I need to prepare myself.'

'Fine,' he nodded. 'I understand.'

When he dropped her off, he got out of the car to get her bag out of the boot. He put it down on the pavement and put his arms around her.

'Courage,' he said, 'ring me if you need to talk.'

'Yes.' Victoria swallowed. Now was not the moment to give way to tears. 'Thanks,' she said, 'you've been so wonderful.'

'Have you got everything? Passport, money, something to read?'

'Yes.' She smiled. It was so unusual to have someone fussing over her for once. It was a very long time since she had been anywhere on her own and the sensation was strange but immensely gratifying. No one to organize, no one to pacify, just herself. She wondered if Edward would be at the rue Caulaincourt when she got there, but the worry of this made her breathless. She couldn't decide which would be worse, if he was or he wasn't.

In the cab from Charles de Gaulle to Montmartre she could feel her hands tingling, a sure sign of anxiety. She tried to take deep breaths and steady herself. The cab had a sign saying 'No Smoking', so she had to concentrate on her breathing.

She pressed the buzzer of the apartment building in the rue Caulaincourt and heard Nancy's American voice telling her to push on the door and come on up. Inside, the building was cool and dark. Oak stairs with a high polish snaked away upwards, coil upon coil, for this was a building with no lift. How the hell did Nancy manage with a pushchair and shopping, Victoria wondered, as she lugged her bag to the top floor. She could hear the baby crying from halfway up.

'Hi,' said Nancy, answering the door in black trousers and a baggy pink shirt, the baby on her hip. 'Great to see you, come on in.'

She looked, Victoria thought, harassed, slightly anxious, but

245

ascribed it to the baby. He was the first after all and she had left it late to start.

'Leave your bag in the hall,' called Nancy over her shoulder. 'Sam can help you with it later.'

Victoria glanced around the sitting room and then at the baby. 'He looks well,' she said, smiling, 'and I'd forgotten how lovely this room was. It's been such a long time since I was here.'

She looked at Nancy, trying to divine when she could ask the question that burned on her lips.

'What time are you expecting Edward?' she said, as lightly as possible.

'Oh,' said Nancy, 'wait a minute now. He called this morning and said he was really sorry but he couldn't get a flight until tomorrow.'

'I beg your pardon,' said Victoria, who was prone to turning a little *grande dame* when she was rattled.

'I know it sounds crazy,' said Nancy, bending over to put the baby in his bouncy chair, 'but that was what he said. He thought maybe you could stay here tonight.'

Victoria considered this for a second before she answered. 'Look,' she said, 'I know this isn't your fault and I don't know you very well, but would you mind telling me what exactly is going on?'

Nancy straightened up, rubbing the small of her back. 'Well,' she said, 'me and Sam have been wonderin' more or less the same thing. He – Edward – has been behaving very strangely ever since he arrived. He's not sick or anything, is he?'

'Mentally ill, do you mean?'

'I guess that is what I mean.'

'He's been unhappy for some time,' said Victoria thoughtfully, 'there have been signs that all wasn't well, but nothing that I thought . . .' she sighed. 'We've also had a lot of money worries, what with Lloyd's and so on.'

'That never helps,' said Nancy, 'I know all about money worries, believe me.' She sat down on a chair facing Victoria. 'He seemed so nervous when he arrived. He told me he'd taken up smoking again . . .'

'Heavens,' said Victoria, 'he's been lecturing me for years. Talking of smoking, would you mind if I did?'

'Well,' Nancy made a face, 'it's not very good for the baby.'

'OK,' Victoria nodded. Never mind the fact that she'd brought up five children with a cigarette constantly on the go.

'And then,' said Nancy, sounding hesitant, 'there was this girl, I don't know, did . . .?'

'Ah,' said Victoria. It was the first time anyone had mentioned a girl. 'What girl?'

'I don't want to be the one to have to tell you this,' said Nancy, 'because I don't know all the story. Maybe you could wait until Sam comes in. He'll be here shortly.'

'Who is she?' said Victoria, trembling. She pushed her shaking hands into her trouser pockets.

'Would you like a drink of somethin'? Tea, coffee, glass of wine?'

'Just tell me what you know.' Victoria put her feet together and sat up straight, hands still in pockets.

'OK,' said Nancy. 'I'll tell you all I know.' She ran her hands through her thick hair. The baby, thank God, had stopped crying and was playing with the rattle that was strung across his chair on a piece of elastic.

'Caroline de Belleroche – that's her name – is a friend of Sam's. Sometimes she models for him, but her real business is in antiquities. She finds things and then trades in them. Sam says she has a really good eye . . .'

'How old?'

'Early twenties.'

Victoria nodded. 'I see.'

'She's also a very attractive young lady, slim, good-looking, kind of sexy, I guess, a bit wild, you know, unpredictable . . . Anyhow, she was staying down in the studio because we're really short of space here, as you can see, and I guess that's where Edward met her. He seemed struck on her as soon as he'd seen her. I'm sorry, Victoria, but that's how it is. Maybe he'll get over it. We didn't want to say anything to you. I guess we felt that if we ignored it it would just go away.'

'But it hasn't?'

'She went back to Le Pin,' said Nancy, rocking the bouncy chair with a bare foot, 'and the next thing I knew Edward had followed her down there. He called from the house on Saturday morning to ask if he could stay there. I said "sure" and, until this morning, that was it.'

'I see,' said Victoria, 'so you think he's with her there. I'd better phone him, I think. Have you the number?' She got to her feet.

'What will you say?'

'I don't know yet.'

'You wouldn't think of waiting until Sam was here, would you? He might know more about it all than I do.'

'I'd like to do it now.'

The phone was in the cramped bedroom beside the bed. Nancy had written down the number and Victoria sat on the bed and dialled it.

It rang and rang, perhaps twenty or thirty rings, until suddenly it was picked up.

A female voice said 'Oui?'

'Is Edward there?' said Victoria, sounding, even to her own ears, very grand and distant.

The phone was instantly replaced.

Victoria dialled again, her heart banging in her chest.

This time it rang. And rang. And nobody picked it up.

'Did you get him?' Nancy said as Victoria went back into the sitting room.

'No. Someone answered. A woman. And put the phone down on me.'

'Oh shit,' said Nancy. 'Do you want me to try?'

'You might as well. I'm just going out for a smoke,' said Victoria.

'No, don't do that. Stay here. I'll take the baby in the other room. I'll get you an ashtray, hold on.'

'No reply,' said Nancy coming back some minutes later. 'I'm really sorry about this, Victoria.'

At that moment the telephone began to ring in the bedroom.

'Hold it,' said Nancy, 'I'll get it.'

She came back into the room. 'It's Edward for you,' she said.

'Hello,' said Victoria into the receiver, having closed the bedroom door.

'Hello,' said Parry stiffly. 'Did you ring?'

'Yes. Who answered the telephone?'

'Never mind that,' said Parry.

'Who was it, Edward?'

'A girl who's staying here.'

'When are you coming back?'

'Tomorrow. I told Sam. I tried to get a flight and I couldn't. I'm sorry.'

'I don't believe that.'

'Well, it's true.'

'Why don't you just tell me the truth?'

'I have told you,' said Parry indignantly. 'I couldn't get a flight. They're all booked up.'

'Have you got one for tomorrow?'

There was a silence, then he said, 'They're working on it now.'

'They?'

'The airline people.'

'I see. Why did that person – whoever she was – put the telephone down when I asked to speak to you?'

'I can't imagine,' said Parry. 'Very stupid of her. Silly girl.'

'What's her name?'

'Caroline,' said Parry.

'Why are you there with Caroline and not waiting for me in Paris, as arranged?'

'I told you,' he said. And put the phone down.

Instead of bothering to ring back, Victoria sat on the bed trying to think. The reality of confronting her husband seemed to have taken her beyond shock. She felt completely numb. It was almost as if he didn't know who she was, behaving in that cold way to her.

'Are you all right?' Nancy's anxious face peered round the door. 'I heard the phone click so I knew you'd finished talking. Come on,' she said, coming to sit next to Victoria on the bed, 'come on through now, dear, and have a drink. And a cigarette. Have as many as you like. This must be a terrible shock for you.'

'It is,' said Victoria. 'It's unreal. I can't believe it's happening. We've had six children together and he just walks out on us. I can't believe it.'

'Things can't have been too good for a long time.'

'They haven't. But I didn't think they were this bad. I'll have to go down there and talk to him. He hasn't even booked a flight. Which means he doesn't want to, which means he won't. I have no alternative.'

'I guess you don't,' said Nancy. 'Come on now,' she handed Victoria a piece of kitchen roll. 'It's OK. Have a good cry.'

She sat down next to her and waited patiently for her to finish, just putting her hand on Victoria's arm from time to time.

'I'm sorry.'

'That's OK. You should cry. This is a truly sad situation. Edward can't be the same person any longer. I never thought of him as someone who enjoyed inflicting pain.'

'It was as if he hardly knew me,' said Victoria, 'and his lies were so contrived as to be insulting. They were transparent.'

'And you feel you should go down and find him?'

'What else can I do?'

'Nothing,' said Nancy, shaking her head. 'Nothing at all.'

As Parry came out of the callbox below the church a cloud crossed the sun; there was a sudden sensation of darkness, of chill. A feeling of absolute terror struck him. He was a boy again and God was watching his every move through field glasses, rather like the ones Parry himself had used at the amphitheatre, good, strong ones with Zeiss lenses. He would be punished for this.

The great limestone wall of the church reared above his head triumphantly, solid, ancient, immensely rooted deep in this earth. What chance did he, Parry, have against the power and weight of the forces ranged against him? The sun had come out again. He felt blinded by the heat and the white searing light. He stumbled slightly like a blind man or a cripple. Narrowing his eyes, he saw the line of poplars on the horizon. In the foreground there were cypress trees like spears and the rows and rows of vines; all the way up to the walls of the houses, there were vines. *I am the vine, ye are the branches.* Going carefully, Parry walked slowly back to the edge of the village, keeping in the shade, hugging the walls of the houses, trying, as far as possible, to keep out of sight.

An old woman in black sitting on a bentwood chair watched him as he went by. On her lap lay a rosary. Parry avoided her eye. She was a spy, of course. One of them. He concentrated on putting one foot in front of the other, noting how the white dust clung to the surface of his polished leather brogues. There was a mark on the left leg of his trousers just below the knee. Victoria's voice. *Why are you there with Caroline and not waiting for me in Paris?* Try not to think of it. He fumbled for his handkerchief, passed the back of his hand across his eyes, then blew his nose. Whistled a tune. He tried to tell himself that it was not the end of the world. When he looked back the old woman had the rosary in her hands again. Her lips were moving.

Caroline glanced at him then down at her book again as he came up the steps. She was wearing dark glasses so it was impossible to divine her expression. He stood there waiting for her to bestow something upon him, some corrective that would turn his life back in another direction, something that would break the spell the sound of his wife's voice had cast upon him.

'I telephoned Victoria,' he said.

'Yes?' The blank black gaze turned upon him. She glanced down at the page noting the number. She was reading *Villette*. He had seen it by her bed yesterday. It was the book that the condom had fallen out of. The condom had little bumps in it to stimulate sensation.

'I told her . . .' he began and then felt unable to continue with this sentence. He had told her nothing really, or at least not very much. Nothing. No, nothing.

'I thought you said you weren't going to speak to her?'

'I had to let her know where I was, surely . . .'

'It's up to you,' she said, shrugging her slender shoulders, 'what you tell your wife. It's none of my business. I don't want to know about this. Go back to her in Paris, why don't you?'

'Caroline,' he said, 'please . . .' He sat down on a chair by her. Again, a feeling of chill as if a cloud had passed over the sun.

'I'm sorry, Edward. I told you. I'm hard-hearted.' She put out her hand to him, that smooth brown hand with its pretty pale fingernails. He took it in his and held it like a talisman.

Inside, the telephone began to ring.

'You get it,' she said after a bit, withdrawing her hand. 'I'm not here if it's for me.'

Edward answered the telephone that was in the bedroom on Caroline's side of the bed. It was sitting on top of a pile of books on a chair. It was Victoria.

'I'm going to come down there and see you if you won't come up to Paris,' she said. 'I think you must be ill, Edward. Nancy and Sam seem to think so.'

'I'm not ill,' he said.

'Don't you want to know how the children are?'

'How are they?' he asked tonelessly like an automaton. That little dead scrap with her blue face.

'Tom is in London,' she said with a ghastly effort at brightness, 'he's got Hector there with him to keep him company. The others are in Yorkshire. They all send their love.'

Edward was silent.

'Edward? Are you there? Did you hear me?'

'Yes, I am here.'

'Why don't you say anything? Why won't you speak to me?' Her voice broke slightly at the end.

'I wish you'd tell me what is happening,' she said, 'I don't understand what's going on. I knew things weren't brilliant between us, but why have you just retreated from me . . . from us? Can't we talk?'

'I don't think there's much point.'

'Why?'

'I just don't.'

'Don't you want to see me?'

'I don't think there's any point.'

Still keeping the phone pressed to his ear, Edward opened the book that lay on top of the pile of books. It was a copy of *Justine* by Durrell, a hardback copy, one of the early editions. Inside, there were two aeroplane tickets from Marseilles to Istanbul in the name of Monsieur et Madame de Fonville. Astounded, he glanced at them and then put them back inside the book.

Caroline appeared in the doorway still wearing her dark glasses. She looked, at that moment, peculiarly sinister.

'I can't accept that,' Victoria was saying. 'I'm going to come and see you instead.'

'You can't,' he said, 'there isn't any point. I keep telling you.'

'You can't stop me,' she said.

'No, look,' he said, 'all right.' He had to keep her out of this house. 'I will meet you.'

When he looked up he saw that Caroline had gone from the doorway. He didn't want her to hear what he was saying.

'Where then?'

'In Uzes, in the Place aux Herbes.'

'When?'

'Tomorrow? You can take the train to Avignon and then get a bus to Uzes from there. The stop's opposite the station.'

'All right,' she said, 'I should be able to be there by the afternoon if I catch an early train. I'll meet you there at four unless you hear from me. OK?'

'Yes,' said Parry.

He went outside again to look for Caroline. She was nowhere to be seen. He went down the steps into the garden to look for her, his heart beating faster at the thought she might have vanished. Although it was about six in the evening the heat was intense, almost unbearable. The sky arched away into an infinity of blue, clear and hard-edged like glass. Parry thought of himself as an ant crawling over the surface of this ragged garden with its high grasses and ruined outbuildings. At the very far end of the garden there was a long table built of bricks and faced with tiles which had been the Legion's banqueting table. Caroline sat on the far side with her back to him swinging her legs like a child. Agatha might do something like that, but he must not think of

Agatha now with her thick dark fringe and her very blue eyes like pieces of lapis.

Shade in this corner was provided by a row of plane trees. Caroline had on a little dress that Parry admired with tiny thin straps and a pattern of flowers on a black background.

He called her name but she did not look round. 'Caroline,' he repeated, coming closer, 'Caroline.'

'What is it?' She was smoking a cigarette in a violent sort of way which she threw into the grass as he approached her.

'Don't do that,' he said angrily, 'don't you know the whole place could catch fire if you do that. It's like tinder this grass.' He stamped on the cigarette and then picked up the end and put it in his trouser pocket.

'How very careful of you,' she said mockingly. 'So, how is your wife?' Instantly, she lit another cigarette.

'Why are you being like this?'

'Like what?'

'You know bloody well, like what.'

'Are you going to meet her then?'

'Yes. I must. I don't want her coming here.'

'And meeting your harlot, is that it?'

'Don't say that. You know I care for you.'

'Do you?'

'Of course I do.'

'But when you see her you will forget all that. You will forget how you feel about me.'

'No I won't, silly girl.' He came up and stood in front of her. 'I owe her an explanation, that's all. Then I'll be back here with you.'

'Do you promise?'

'I promise.'

She leaned forwards and kissed him, shrugging off the straps of her dress so that her breasts, those extraordinarily voluptuous breasts, were exposed. Parry put his hands on them then kissed her nipples, one and then the other, so that she moaned. Victoria's breasts had long since slipped from so much breast-feeding and she did not like them touched in the way that Caroline did.

254

She jumped down from the table and wriggled out of her dress. She was not wearing any knickers either. She was now naked but for her shoes, little silver mules.

'Come on,' she said, 'let's do it here on the table in honour of the Foreign Legion.'

'Oh . . . surely . . .' Parry began to protest, but she was unbuttoning his shirt and then his trousers so that all his clothes just fell off his body into the dust. Then she pulled down his boxer shorts and took his penis in her mouth. He was so excited by the sight and feel of her mouth, her naked crouching body, that he was about to come when she pulled away. She was still holding her cigarette in one hand.

'Come and get me,' she said, running away from him around the other side of the table.

'Come *on*,' she called, laughing.

Parry ran up one side, his dick bouncing in front of him.

'You look so funny,' she said, as he reached out for her, before darting away again like a wood nymph.

'Put me on the table,' she said, when she had allowed him to catch her.

Parry picked her up in his arms and put her down on the warm tiles then levered himself up.

She put her arms around his neck and began to kiss him, exploring his mouth with her tongue, all the time keeping her eyes open, but Parry did not respond. 'What? What is it?' She took her arms away and sat up.

He took a handful of her hair from the back and pulled it. 'You've been lying to me,' he said, 'admit it.' He gave a tug at her hair.

'What?' Her eyes were large, but whether with fear or excitement he could not tell.

'Those tickets, for Istanbul, in the name of de Fonville. I should like to know what all that is about?'

'Where? What tickets?'

'Come on,' he said, bending her neck further back so that he could see the long column of her throat, 'otherwise I will hurt you more.'

'All right,' she gasped, 'but let me go. Then I'll tell you. How did you find out?' she asked.

'I saw them just now in your book.'

'What were you doing looking in my things?'

Parry waited.

'OK,' she said. 'I am going, on business. The tickets are in those names because it was easier that way – to pretend that we were man and wife – but we are not. Gaby has a wife already.'

'What about your passport?'

'They don't have to be the same, not nowadays, with so many women travelling on business. The world has changed, Edward. Women can do so much more now than they used to be able to.'

'What business?'

'A little buying and selling.'

'Of what?'

'Artefacts. This and that.' She shrugged. 'I have been lent a house there, on the shores of the Bosporus. You should come with me, you would like it.'

By way of a reply, Parry began to kiss her.

'Tears?' she said, putting her hand to his face, 'why tears?'

He entered her and came in what seemed like one, long simultaneous thrust. A voice was calling out something; with a shock he realized it was his own.

Afterwards he lay beside her, emptied in mind and body, a man with no history. The slate wiped clean.

'You liked that, didn't you?'

Parry did not answer. After a moment had passed, he said, 'What has really happened to de Fonville?'

'I told you,' she said, 'he has gone to Marseilles.'

'I don't believe you. He's the man I saw being put into the ambulance. I know he is. I wish you would tell me the truth.'

'Darling,' she said, 'it is the truth. It must have been very difficult for your wife if you never believed her.'

'I don't wish to discuss her.'

He was a man with no past. There was no God. The dead were gone. There was no other life. His father had been right – there is only that darkness which covers us all. 'I look forward to it,' he had said. All that Catholic mumbo-jumbo about guilt and sin and death and resurrection and God watching him. Pure, utter, bloody nonsense. Parry covered his eyes.

It was about half-past three the next day when Parry saw Victoria crossing the Place aux Herbes in Uzes. Her hair was tied back in a ponytail. She wore black leggings, tennis shoes, a white T-shirt belonging, no doubt, to Tom.

It gave him a shock to see her, as if he had suddenly remembered the person he had been all those years: the responsible father, the provider of a regular income, the good Catholic. The man whose heart had broken the day his child died. The man whose wife this was with all her claims on him: the money worries, the children, Lloyd's . . . he almost began to wish, watching her, that he hadn't done the decent thing and come to this rendezvous.

Victoria, he thought, looked both thinner and taller than he remembered, which struck him as curious. How could one forget such vital things so quickly? He had known her twenty years, every detail of her appearance ought to be etched on his heart.

As he watched, knowing that she had not yet seen him, a motorcyclist shot across the square – some traffic was absurdly still allowed amongst all the trippers – and appeared to aim direct for Victoria who was looking the other way. With dreadful clarity Parry remembered the last time this had happened – Rosie's face in the ambulance, the so-slender chance by which her life had been saved (capitulation on his part to *le Bon Dieu*) – and leapt to his feet, once again knocking over his chair.

The bike missed Victoria by a whisker. She stopped, shocked, and simply stared as it roared on.

Parry was also transfixed. It was a warning. He ran towards her and grabbed her arm. 'Are you all right?'

'Edward! There you are!' She shook her head as if she had water in her ears and blinked several times. 'I simply didn't see him coming,' she said.

She held on to Edward's arm as they crossed the square and

he was horribly, guiltily aware of the fact that she was shaking with fright.

'Have a brandy. You must need one. I know I do.'

'All right.' She glanced at him. She had been so near death without any warning. It shocked her; the easiness of it.

Victoria got out her cigarettes and tried to light one, but her hands were trembling so much she couldn't make her lighter work.

'Let me,' he said. 'Could I have one?'

'Of course. Nancy said you'd taken up smoking.' While he lit her cigarette and his she took the opportunity to study him. His hair flopped untidily across his forehead. His skin looked browner as if he had spent considerable time in the sun and he was also thinner.

'That suit is filthy,' she said.

'What!' He gazed down at himself. 'Yes, of course. White is not a good colour.' He seemed embarrassed to see her and at a loss for words, which was not at all his normal style. Normally, Edward liked to collar every situation early on.

'Well?' she said.

'I've met a girl.' He said this looking down at his hands on his thighs.

'I gathered *that*,' she said sharply. 'So you're having a fling with someone.'

'It's more than a fling.' He looked up when he said that. Yellow eyes, white hair, Judas face.

'A girl you've known for a week! Don't be ridiculous, Edward.'

'I know it sounds ridiculous. But it isn't.'

'So, what do you plan to do?'

The waiter put their brandies in front of them. Edward fished in his pockets for change.

Victoria looked away across the square at the plane trees, the stalls selling lavender bags made out of Provençal prints, the families wandering about.

When the waiter had gone, she waited for him to answer the question. As she waited, the bell of the church tolled the hour. Four. She half-expected a cock to crow somewhere. Traitor. But a little part of her, a tiny little part sustained itself with a clear, photographically exact image of Hugh's profile, the way his hair greyed exactly on the temples, his slightly slanting eyes.

'So?' Their eyes met.

'I'm so sorry,' he said.

'When are you coming home?' she asked, deliberately misunderstanding him.

'I don't know quite.'

'You seem to have lost your reason,' she said. 'And what about your faith? Surely that should sustain you through a crisis?'

'I know I will be punished.'

'You are being punished,' she replied, 'now, this minute. You look terrible, ill almost. Don't you care about me, about the children?'

'Of course I care.'

'Then . . .' she shrugged, '*why* are you doing this?'

'I don't know.'

'I think you've gone stark staring mad,' she said, pushing back her chair. 'I don't know why I bothered to come all this way.'

'No, please!' Parry jumped to his feet. He had to be careful what he said. There was so much traffic around. The danger surrounding her was intense. He was surprised she didn't feel it. 'Where are you going?'

'Back to my hotel.'

'You took a room?'

'Yes,' She was walking quickly through the people. 'Don't come with me, Edward. I'd rather you didn't.'

'No, look,' he said, taking her arm, 'you don't understand.' They were passing a church now. The priest was standing in the doorway at the top of the steps. He gazed at Edward and Victoria as they hurried past. It was a warning.

'Look,' she said furiously on the corner, 'I understand enough. You've met a girl, you don't want to come back. What else is there to understand?'

'God will punish me through you,' he said, 'don't you see? That's what that motor bike was about. They're trying to get you.'

259

Victoria gazed at him for a moment, lost for words. 'So, you think God wants you and will do anything he can to make sure he doesn't lose you, including having me killed. Is that what you're saying?'

'Yes.'

'Haven't you heard of free will, Edward. You are free to choose. You can either decide to follow God or you can turn away from him. He won't stop you. That's not his way.' She spoke more gently now, aware that her husband was very precariously perched on the dividing line between sanity and insanity.

'He has tried to stop me.' There were tears in his eyes.

'No, no,' she said, 'that's not so. He's not a God of vengeance, not in the way you seem to suggest. You must be mistaken. I don't think you're well, Edward. Come with me to my room. Come and lie down a moment.'

'All right.' He had to see her safe inside. Then he would go. He tried to take her arm but the pavements were too narrow, so he followed slightly behind her in order to protect her from hazards. They walked slowly to the hotel, a pretty building of honey-coloured stone with faded green shutters.

Victoria's room looked out over a small square. The shutters were closed when they let themselves in but she went straight over and opened them and stepped out on to the balcony.

'Be careful,' he said, before he could stop himself, following her out. 'These railings don't look very safe to me,' he said, shaking one.

'They're fine,' she said in a soothing voice, the gentle kind of voice she might use to one of the children, 'come and lie down a moment. I've got some water in the fridge. I'll pour you a glass. Have a little sleep.'

'No,' he said, standing and looking at her – they had come back inside from that treacherous, death-inviting balcony – 'Look, I have to go, I . . .' If only, he said to himself, if only I could get out of here and around the corner, then it's not my fault if anything happens, then I'm free . . .

The telephone rang.

'Answer it,' he said. He had to escape.

'Hello, *oui, oui* . . .' She waited.

'Who is it?'

'Mum!' exclaimed Victoria, 'what's happened?' She glanced up at Parry, her eyes wide with shock.

'Oh no. No. Oh no . . . I'll come at once. Today. Now. I'll be there as soon as I can. Are the children all right?'

'I'll be there as soon as I can,' she repeated. 'It may be tomorrow. You know I'm in Uzes? Yes. That's right.' Her eyes flew to Edward.

She put the receiver back.

'What is it?' he asked, fearing what she was going to say so much that his heart was jumping up and down in his chest like a fist.

'It's Dad. He's had a heart-attack . . . Mum's coping . . . you know she's got the children there too . . . I told you that . . .' She was crying sheets of tears which kept getting into her mouth. 'So look,' she said, '. . . could you drive me to a station or an airport. I'll have to get back to Paris and then get up north somehow . . .'

She put a hand out to him which he took and held briefly. He felt completely trapped.

'This is my fault,' he said.

'Oh, shut up! It has nothing to do with you. Stop trying to grab the headlines, Edward. All I want you to do is to see a doctor as soon as possible. I think you need help.'

She began to put the few things she had with her back in her bag. Of course it would make it so much easier if he was ill, if his sin could be medicalized and therefore rendered neutral, and not his fault.

'If you feel so strongly,' she said, getting the key and going ahead of him to the door, having closed the shutters, 'then come with me in case my plane crashes.'

'I can't do that,' he said solemnly.

'Why not?' It was like dealing with a large, helpless baby in a white linen suit and a panama hat.

'I would have to get my things.'

'I can get them for you. I'll have to go via Paris.'

'My things at Le Pin.'

'I think you should come with me now. You need help badly, Edward. Just come. I need you,' she said pleadingly.

He did not answer this but in the car he said, 'Let me sort myself out here today and then I'll come tomorrow.'

'I don't believe you.'

'I said I'll come.' His hands gripped the steering wheel tightly. 'I'm going to Avignon,' he said, in order to deflect her, 'you can get the train back to Paris again. Probably you'll get a flight tonight to London.'

Victoria glanced at him. There were moments when he seemed quite all right, quite sane.

'And you'll come tomorrow?'

'I said I would. I wish you'd trust me,' he added in his normal irascible tone of voice, his breadwinning, superior sort of voice. The voice of authority.

How can I trust you? she wanted to say, but kept silent.

'You see,' said Edward, in exactly the same tone, 'he'll die if I don't come. I'm the cause of it all.'

'You mustn't blame yourself,' she said, carefully. It seemed better to play his game, to humour him. It might be the only way – mad though it was – to get him to come home again.

Victoria saw Hugh at once, in spite of the crowd, as soon as she came round the corner with her trolley. She raised a hand and waved. He waved back and began to move along behind the line of people. His grave look made her fear what he had to tell her. When she had rung him from Paris and told him about her father, he had at once said that he would telephone the hospital and pull rank to find out exactly what was going on.

'How was Edward?' he had asked.

'I think he's having a breakdown. There is a girl. But he's been so odd with me. I'll tell you when I see you. He's promised to come tomorrow.'

'Will he, do you think?' Hugh could divine from her tone of voice that she thought it unlikely.

'I don't know,' Victoria replied, 'but my instinct says he won't.' She sighed deeply. 'I can't comprehend it, Hugh. It's too enormous for me, too quick. My whole world has broken up in a week. I keep thinking it can't be true.'

But when she had said it she had thought that, like an earthquake or a landslide of some kind, the earth had been moving imperceptibly for a long time, possibly years; that slight slippage, a loose stone here and there, were the indicators of massive forces at work. The surface of the earth, after all, was only as thick in proportion to its contents as the skin of an apple. Her marriage had been a skin – healthy-looking, rosy as an apple, but now rotting.

Hugh took her in his arms and held her. He did not kiss her but hugged her tight as people eddied around them. For a second Victoria allowed herself to relax into his quiet strength, his calm. It was so peaceful for this moment to be here with him, like floating in warm water.

Still holding her, he said: 'He's very ill. They don't think he'll make it. It's best you should know. I spoke to your mother, introduced myself as your neighbour and friend and a doctor. I told her I would meet you at the airport. She said, "Where's Edward?" I told her that you'd gone to find him.'

'What did she say then?' Victoria pulled away and looked into Hugh's face.

'She said, "I always thought he was unreliable." '

'Oh.'

'Come on, let's go.' Hugh began to push the trolley.

'How long has Dad got?'

'They won't say exactly. But you must get there quickly. I've booked you and Tom seats on the train to York tomorrow morning, the quick one. Your mother will meet you.'

'Oh, Hugh,' she said, trying not to cry, 'that is so kind.' Then she asked, 'Does Tom know?'

'I told him his grandfather had had a heart attack and was very ill.'

'How did he take it?'

'He was devastated, poor boy. I told him you were coming back tonight.'

'Did he ask about Edward?'

'No, he didn't. And I thought it better not to say anything.'

'Of course. Thank you, Hugh.'

'What a lot of things you seem to have,' he said, opening the boot of his car.

'Some of them belong to Edward. I collected them from Sam's studio in Paris. Some of them are books,' she said, indicating the box that de Fonville had had sent round to the studio in Pigalle the previous week. 'I must somehow get them to Tom pronto. I think some of them are valuable. Edward said so.'

'I can do that for you,' Hugh said, 'you need to concentrate on all this.'

'Is Heck still there? I'd forgotten all about him.'

'Yes, he is. Actually, he's been splendid for Tom, kept his mind off everything by jollying him along. I fed them quite a lot of beers earlier to keep up their spirits. I should think Tom will be asleep when you get back. Have you spoken to Mary and the others?'

'I spoke to Mary. Mum's been quite wonderful because she's calm, you see. She told Mary much the same as you told Tom. Thank God it wasn't the children who found him.'

'Who did?'

'Mum did.'

Hugh glanced at her quickly.

'And Feather?'

'Feather's fine. I've fed her and Jenny's going to keep her while you're away. She seems to love her. Nice girl, Jenny.'

'Yes, she is. Wonderful. The best. You know she's not well?'

'She said something about having a brain scan.'

'She thinks she's got a tumour.'

'It's hard to say until she's been looked at. It may not be as serious as she thinks.'

'That's the first piece of good news I've heard all day.'

Hugh took one hand off the steering wheel and patted her shoulder. 'Poor Toria.'

'That's what my family always called me. Tor or Toria.'

'I know. Your mother said it to me.'

When Hugh had taken her things into the house he said, 'I'm

going to leave you now. I think you need to be alone. I'll take you both to the station in the morning. The train goes at nine thirty so I'll be here at ten to nine or so. All right?'

He looked down at her so kindly that she wanted to cling to him and say 'Don't go', but she knew he was right. This was a night where she had to be by herself.

Tom was asleep on the sofa in the drawing room, a can of beer by his side. Victoria kissed him and he stirred but did not wake up. She found a rug in the hall cupboard and covered him, then, removing the beer can and substituting a glass of water, she turned out the lights and went upstairs.

She took half a sleeping pill and dreamed that the telephone by her bedside was ringing. When she picked up the receiver she heard Edward's voice a long way away saying 'Tor . . .'. Then the receiver was replaced and all she could hear were the hissing spaces of the airwaves. When she woke this dream was still so vividly in her mind that she wanted to weep. His voice had had a desperate quality to it, as if he were drowning. She wondered whether she had dreamed it or whether it was true. Perhaps it was both.

'There you are,' said Isobel Digby. She kissed her daughter and grandson. 'I must say, darling, I didn't expect to find you travelling first. Not your normal style.'

'Hugh arranged it,' said Victoria, 'you know, Hugh Croft.'

'Oh yes.' Isobel glanced at her daughter. Later, when they were alone, she would discuss this with her. But not now. Not with darling Tom present.

'I left the others behind at home,' she said. 'Tonia has come and Simon and Tilly and Juliet. The others are on their way. I want you and Tom to come with me now to the hospital.'

'How is he?' asked Tom, taking his mother's bag from her.

'He's very ill, darling, but it would do him good to see you.'

'I'm so sorry, Granny,' said Tom. He suddenly put the bags down and hugged her.

'Thank you, darling,' said Isobel, 'it means so much to me to have you here.' She sniffed faintly.

On the way to the hospital from the station, Isobel said to Victoria, 'The men from Sotheby's are coming this afternoon, I haven't put them off. It seems better to get it over with.'

John Digby was in a room by himself. A tube ran out of his nose attached to a drip. His skin was a terrible colour and his eyes were closed. The sound of his laboured breathing dominated the room.

'He's had the last rites,' said Isobel, gazing down at her husband. 'I want all the children to come back later on to say goodbye, but I thought you'd like a moment. They don't think he'll go at once, but of course they can't be sure.'

Victoria stroked her father's cheek and then his forehead. His skin felt paper-dry and strangely warm, as if a last surge of life had flushed through his body.

'Say hello, darling,' she murmured to Tom, 'kiss him.'

Tom looked down at his grandfather. 'Hello, Grandpa,' he said, and then he kissed him. Then he ran out of the room, leaving the door open. They could hear his footsteps receding down the passage.

'Leave him be,' said Isobel.

Victoria held her father's hand for a moment. Then she too kissed him. 'Shall I leave you?' she asked.

'If you would.'

'I'll be outside,' said Victoria.

Tom was standing by the car when she came out. His eyes were red and he kept wiping his nose with the back of his hand in the way that he had done when he was a little boy.

'Where's Dad?' he asked.

'He's still in France.'

'Why isn't he here? Now. When he's needed.'

'I don't know.'

'Fucking bastard,' said Tom.

'Tom!'

'He should be here with us. Why isn't he?'

'He said he would come.'

'I don't want him to come,' said Tom, 'not now. It's too late.'

Victoria gazed at her son. 'Is it?'

'Why aren't you more angry? Poor Grandpa!' said Tom and burst into tears. When Victoria tried to put her arms around him he pushed her away.

'Leave me alone,' he said, putting his fists in his eyes. 'I'll be all right. Sorry Mum.'

Victoria lit a cigarette and handed it to him in silence.

'Thanks,' he said, dragging on it gratefully.

Hugh parked his car in Museum Street on a meter. He had rung Tom Wilberforce and agreed to bring in the box of books at midday. He found the shop 'Parry & Wilberforce' halfway down Coptic Street, very smart-looking with its dark-green woodwork and handsome gilt lettering. He rang the bell and waited.

'This is very good of you indeed,' said Tom Wilberforce, opening the door. 'Come on in.'

Wilberforce was a striking-looking man in his early fifties with iron-grey hair and dark eyes and the kind of skin that is permanently an outdoor colour. He was wearing cords and a check shirt and a pair of suede brogues.

'Tor rang me,' Tom said, 'I am sorry about her father. He's a tremendous fellow. Is it all up, do you think?'

'It's hard to tell,' said Hugh, 'they weren't terribly optimistic when I spoke to them, but you never know. He may pull through.'

'Tor said something to me about Edward that I couldn't quite follow. Where the bloody hell *is* Edward anyway? I've been worried about him for some time, as a matter of fact, that's why I sent him off. I felt he needed a break.'

'What was worrying you?'

'I forgot. You're a doctor, aren't you?' Tom nodded. 'I dunno.' He shrugged. 'Memory lapses . . . he was crosser than usual about silly things, just a feeling that all was not well. Mind you, he's had every reason not to be feeling brilliant about life. An awful lot of rather horrible things have happened to him lately.'

'Yes, I know,' said Hugh.

Tom began to open the parcel with a knife. He could see that it had already been opened and then sealed again, but by whom he did not know.

'Well, well,' he said, 'goodness gracious me.' He pulled out the volume, bound in vellum, that had so interested Parry. 'I think there may be some rather tremendous things in here. I wonder how Edward managed to persuade de Fonville to relinquish this.'

'What is it?'

'Edward babbled on about it when he rang me, among other things. It's a volume of Lucretius, annotated by Montaigne. Edward recognized his writing, clever old boy. I thought he was joking, as a matter of fact, he certainly sounded plastered.'

'Who is this de Fonville?' asked Hugh.

'Oh, an old acquaintance of mine. I've done business with him for years. He's a slippery beast, Gaby, but always interesting to talk to. Lives in Paris, has a wife somewhere else, so I believe, rather an old reprobate when it comes to women. I've been trying to contact him but I can't get him, most odd. I can't get hold of Edward either.'

'He's somewhere in the south,' said Hugh.

'South! But he's supposed to be with his wife in Paris, that is, if she hadn't had to come back. What is he playing at?'

'This is what nobody seems to know.'

'But Tor's seen him, hasn't she?' Tom stopped going through the box and looked at Hugh. 'Why didn't he come back with her?'

'Victoria thinks he's having a nervous breakdown.'

'Well, what does that mean? I never know what to say when people tell me things like that. Is he potty or what?'

'It sounds as if he may be heading that way,' said Hugh cautiously.

'Mid-life crisis eh? I never really believed in all that. You can have a crisis at any point, it seems to me.'

'You can, of course,' said Hugh, 'but it depends on the person. I don't know Edward, you see. I've been away for so long. They moved in after I'd left. I've only just come back because of my mother dying.'

'He's a sensitive soul, Parry,' said Tom, 'a bit highly strung, tends to go off at tangents, can miss the point. I don't think he's awfully good at women, although he's been fantastically lucky in his marriage. Tor is a tremendous person, very supportive, even with all those children. Of course, Edward's been like another child in some ways. She's had to mother the lot of them and cope with everything else. It's typical of their set-up that it's Edward who's feeling the strain. Poor Tor.'

Tom sighed and shook his head. 'Well, I hope he comes back soon,' he said, 'so that I can congratulate him on his find.'

'Would it be worth a lot?'

'Oh yes, a very great deal.'

'I know she has problems at the moment with money, as do her parents.'

'Poor old dears might have to sell,' said Tom, 'such a disaster. I still don't know how Parry managed to get hold of this and I do need to know. Perhaps de Fonville didn't know what he had. Most unlike him, but of course anything is possible.'

'What will you do with it if you can't get hold of him?'

'Sit on it,' said Tom. 'I wonder if he made a mistake and gave Edward the wrong box or something. I wish to God I knew what was going on. It's like some sort of ruddy thriller: Parry's vanished, de Fonville's off the map, Tor's none the wiser. Anyway, let's have a drink and forget the whole damn business for a moment or two. What do you say to that?'

'Amen,' said Hugh. 'I suppose there quite often must be mysteries in your business, questions of provenance and so forth.'

'All the time,' said Tom, getting a bottle of whisky out of the filing cabinet that stood behind his desk. 'Things get sent in Jiffy bags with no accompanying letter, nothing. And of course there are forgeries, left, right and centre.'

'Could that be a forgery?'

'Could be, I suppose, I'd have to have a much more careful look at it to tell. It's not de Fonville's line as a rule. He may have smuggled it from somewhere and needs to get rid of it. I have no idea. Water? Ice?'

'He sounds a fairly dodgy character,' said Hugh.

'Oh, he is, he is. I probably shouldn't have sent Edward to see him. He's so impressionable, Edward, you see. It's just as well he's had his faith. It's stopped him going off the rails, I would say, made him behave himself. God alone knows what would happen to him if he lost it.' Tom looked around at Hugh. 'Perhaps he has lost it, perhaps that's what's gone wrong. He always seemed to me to have a rather peculiar attitude to God, like a little boy having to placate a parent. If I don't do this, that will happen, rather as if God were more like Zeus or Jupiter, and ready to chuck a thunderbolt at him if he didn't behave.'

After lunch on Thursday, Victoria waited behind for the two men to come from Sotheby's in London. The children had gone with her mother to the hospital to see their grandfather who was a little better.

'Won't it be a bit much for him,' Victoria had said, 'too many faces?'

'I think it'll do him good,' said Isobel, 'and, besides, I don't think I can bear to be at home when those vultures from Sotheby's come. Would you do that for me, darling?'

'Of course I'll do it.'

She was also glad to be on her own for a few minutes or half an hour without having to keep a stiff upper lip for the children. It was terribly difficult to be composed about Edward. She was still waiting for him, making excuses in her mind for him. Sam and Nancy had not heard from him and the telephone in Le Pin was not being answered. Hugh had offered to go and look for him but there was a limit, Victoria had decided; if Edward was going to come home then he must do it alone, but having thought this it now began to seem impossible that he would not come, part of some fearsome reality that she had been living in these last few days and which now had struck home. He must come. He would come.

The sound of the car sent her to the window. A new, shiny Mercedes estate car drew up, the colour of a holly berry, with two men inside. The vultures had arrived. Victoria watched them get out of the car and look around with their eagle eyes, costing and dating everything, roosting in the ruins of other people's lives. She went out to greet them and led them into the hall. One, a youngish man, with thinning brown hair and a wide, greedy mouth, did most of the talking. Gazing at his expression, Victoria felt he was like a blood-sucking ghost, the kind of man who would flatter you out of your possessions, even if you didn't have to sell, in order to survive.

He introduced himself and his deputy, and, accepting Victoria's offer of coffee, walked around eyeballing all the better pictures. When she came back with a tray, he was sitting on the sofa smoking and talking in a low voice to his companion, an older man in an expensive tweed suit and very good shoes.

'Giles Pitt is your brother-in-law, I gather,' said the younger of the two, whose name was Andrew Moore.

'Yes, that's right. You know him, I suppose.'

'Oh yes, I know Giles all right.' Andrew laughed and his companion smirked in unison.

'Giles says the picture is definitely not a Veronese,' Victoria said. 'I wish he'd told us before.'

'He may not have wanted to upset you,' said Andrew. 'Families have strong feelings about their pictures and don't like being told they're not what they're supposed to be.'

'That's right,' agreed tweed suit, also lighting a cigarette without offering Victoria one.

'I think we could have managed the disappointment,' Victoria said. 'I'm sure you would agree it's better to know these things.'

'Absolutely,' said Andrew smoothly, 'absolutely. And dear Giles is inclined to be a little hasty from time to time.'

'Heh, heh,' agreed tweed suit.

'Well, perhaps you'd like to have a look,' said Victoria. 'My mother sends her apologies. You know she's at the hospital seeing my father.'

'I am so sorry to hear about your poor father,' said Andrew Moore. 'Perhaps we shall have some good news for him later. That would be nice, wouldn't it?'

'But highly improbable,' said Victoria.

'Oh, don't be like that,' said Andrew Moore, 'you never know.'

The two men followed her along the cardinals' passage and into the chapel. Tweed suit genuflected but Andrew Moore marched straight up the aisle and walked around the back of the altar.

Victoria decided she couldn't bear to wait for them there. 'I'll be in the hall,' she said, 'when you've finished.'

'We won't be all that long,' said Andrew Moore, 'are you sure you won't come and join us?'

'Quite sure, thank you.' Victoria turned on her heel and marched out. She returned to the sofa and her cigarettes but then decided she couldn't sit down. She went outside and walked down to the copper beech and back again. It was a lovely, clear, warm summer's day, the sort of day that normally would have made her feel grateful to be alive, but not today. Today, everything she looked at seemed melancholy, unbearable. She thought of Andrew Moore and his greedy, raking glance, and wondered what he would make of the *Raising of Lazarus* and whether it held any meaning for him other than the purely academic.

She went back inside and waited by the sofa, not sitting down, but smoking nervously and rocking up and down on her heels. Above her head, a portrait of Georgiana Digby by studio of Reynolds, not worth enough to sell, thank God.

She heard the voices coming back along the passage and the palms of her hands began to sweat.

'Well,' said Andrew Moore, 'well, well. As I said, you never know what you'll find.'

Victoria looked at him, exercising extraordinary self-control.

'It's a very good picture indeed, most exciting, possibly by Jacopo Bassano, not Veronese. I can't think how Veronese got into the frame, so to speak, although of course a great many country-house pictures were misattributed in the nineteenth century . . .'

'Very common,' said tweed suit.

'How much is it worth?'

'Difficult to say, bottom's rather fallen out of the market, as you probably know, too many people trying to flog stuff.'

'Approximately,' asked Victoria coolly.

'One million, two million, who knows.'

'You're supposed to know,' said tweed suit. 'That's why you're here.'

'What now?' Victoria lit a cigarette.

'Back to London, homework. Bring someone else up to verify, if that's all right with you.'

'You'll have to talk to my mother about that,' said Victoria. 'Perhaps you'd put what you've said to me in writing.'

'Of course, of course.'

'Thank you so much for coming.'

'Well, it's been a pleasure. You have some very good pictures here, particularly the Reynolds over the fireplace.'

'Studio of Reynolds.'

'No, it's the real thing,' said Andrew Moore. He smiled. 'Just thought you ought to know.'

When they had gone Victoria went to the hospital. She put her head around the door of her father's room and found just her mother by the bedside, holding his hand.

'Hello, darling,' said Isobel, 'I sent the gang outside to romp about and get some fresh air. There's a McDonald's just over the road and Tom said he would go and feed them all some rubbish. What a responsible fellow he seems to be becoming.'

'And Mary too, I hope,' said Victoria. She went round her father's bed and looked down at his face. His eyes were closed, but he was a better colour.

'They say he's improving,' said Isobel. 'Isn't that wonderful?'

'I have news,' said Victoria, putting out her hand and touching her father's face. 'The picture may be a Bassano. Very valuable. He wouldn't say exactly, but six figures plus. They want to come and have another look.'

'Did you hear that, John?' said Isobel. 'The painting may be by Bassano. It's very valuable.'

'My mother always said it was Bassano,' said John Digby, opening his eyes. 'But my father said it was Veronese. And my father was always right.'

'You never mentioned it before,' said Isobel.

'Didn't think it was important.' John Digby closed his eyes again.

'And,' said Victoria, winking at her mother, 'you know the portrait of Georgiana – the one over the fireplace in the hall – well, Andrew Moore says it's a Reynolds, the real thing.'

'Studio of Reynolds,' murmured her father.

'Come outside a moment,' said Isobel, 'I want to ask you something.'

'What?' said Victoria, as her mother closed the door of her father's room.

'I have to ask you now – where *is* Edward?'

'I don't know.'

Her mother considered this for a moment. 'But has he left you? I don't understand where he *is*? The children keep asking me and I don't know what to say to them. Has he gone mad, is he having a nervous breakdown or whatever they call it nowadays, a crisis?'

'When I saw him he seemed to veer between sanity and madness.'

'Will you go back and find him? I mean you can't *leave* him there, can you?'

'I've no intention of leaving him there. Of course I'm going back.'

She thought she would not tell her mother about the girl. If she was ever to rehabilitate Edward into the family then the girl would have to be omitted. She would be the last straw. Probably she already was.

'I do think it's very selfish of him to do this now. Life is a series of crises, that's how we learn things. One doesn't give way to them. That is the difference between good and evil.'

'I know,' said Victoria, 'I agree. But I think it's been a long time a-coming.'

'I don't see why that should excuse it. He's let you down very badly. What triggered it off?'

'Teresa. Lloyd's.'

'Of course.' Isobel put her hand on Victoria's arm. 'I think you've been so brave. What will you do about Fenton and Stanwright?'

'What you're doing. Soldier on.'

274

'Will you be able to manage?'

'Somehow, I expect. I've paid Mary's fees out of the business account. Jenny agreed to that. Edward said something to me about a terrific find in Paris – that is, before he went off the rails – so I'll have to contact Tom about that. I brought back a box of books from Paris, but I haven't a clue what's inside. That's Tom's forte.'

'Of course, darling, of course. Well, at least there's hope, that's something.'

'Yes . . . and I'm so happy about Dad. That matters more than anything.'

'Thank you, darling.' Isobel left a decent pause. 'Who is that nice young man, Hugh Croft, who rang me up?'

'Next-door neighbour. Very kind and helpful. Old Mrs Croft's son.'

'Croft, Croft, let me think. What were they – gin or sherry or something? Lots and lots of lolly there.'

'Mmm.' Victoria glanced at her mother. 'Stop match-making, Mum,' she said. 'I'm still married to Edward.'

'I know you are, darling, I can't help it. I just want you to be secure. Edward seems to have done everything he can to make you feel the opposite.'

'Yes,' said Victoria, 'well . . . I'll survive, I expect.'

'You young are extraordinary,' said Isobel, 'so much stronger than we were.'

'You had the war, for goodness sake!'

'But we all hung together in that. You're on your own.'

'I told you,' said Victoria, 'I'll manage somehow.'

Later on, she rang Hugh in London. 'Any sign of him?' she asked.

'None, I'm afraid.'

'I'm going to give him until tomorrow when I get back to London myself. Then I'll have to act. I don't quite know in what way.'

'If he hasn't committed a crime, then the police won't gener-ally help you to find him. They'll put him on the Missing Persons register.'

'How grim,' said Victoria.

'Horrible for you. The sense of betrayal must be . . .'

'Enormous,' said Victoria, finishing his sentence for him. 'It is.'

'Anything I can do,' said Hugh, 'you know where I am. And, Tor . . .'

'What?'

'I mean it.'

'I know you do,' she said, smiling into the receiver, thanking goodness that he couldn't see that she was crying.

EPILOGUE

Even this early it was hot. So hot. Parry was still wearing his linen suit and his panama hat, the suit filthy and stained and torn where the brambles clutched at his legs, the hat soaking inside with sweat. His beautiful brogues from Tricker's were scratched beyond recognition and his feet blistered. Flies buzzed in his eyes and ears. To get to the top, the very top of the Pont du Gard required this climb up the cliff face through the tearing undergrowth. Several times he had slipped and fallen back down the way he had come. The structure itself loomed above him, Agrippa's masterpiece, honey-coloured stone slotted together without mortar, each slab the size of a motor car. Once, the sweet water from the deep spring in the garrigues had flowed across here all the way to Nîmes, twenty-five miles away.

As he slipped and clawed and clutched his way upwards, panting and groaning, these facts occupied the part of Parry's mind that was not thinking about what had happened at the airport the day before. She had betrayed him with complete brilliance, as he had always somehow known she would; as Victoria had by deluging him with children he could not sustain, as, once, at some deep inexpressible level his mother had betrayed him by not coming over the brow of the hill, by remaining hidden behind the crown of gorse; the crown of thorns. By dying she had betrayed everything. The dead are not with us, the church was wrong about that, the dead are gone. Vanished. What a fool he had been! What a bloody fool.

There was no way back now, there was only this thorny forward path to the top of the aqueduct. He told himself that he wanted to see what the Roman engineers had seen as the sun rose.

Once he was up there he would decide. God would tell him what to do. He thought of Christ on the high mountain with the

277

devil at his shoulder, breathing his ticklish hot breath into the ear of the Lord. Christ had not jumped. He had been tempted to do so, but he had resisted, turning away instead towards the Cross, the long torment. So brave. It would have been easier to jump, Parry thought, to tread out into the air.

There had been some muddle about the tickets, something he didn't understand. At Marseilles, Caroline had gone to the desk with the tickets whilst he, Parry, had waited with the luggage. He had offered to go, but she had insisted on doing it herself.

When she came back she said, 'There's a problem. The bookings are all in a mess. We can only have one seat on this flight. One of us will have to take the next one. They've promised to put whoever it is in Club.'

She gave him a look, a Judas look. A part of him knew then that it was all up.

'I'll wait,' said Parry, the pleaser, right on cue. 'I don't mind. What will you do at Istanbul? Go to an hotel or what?'

'I'll wait,' she said, 'it's quite simple.'

'But what if my plane is late?'

'If it's late, it's late.' She smiled at him. 'Don't worry, I'll be there.'

He pulled her to him. She was wearing the baggy shirt and the jeans to travel in, the gold sandals.

'Goodbye, angel,' she said, wriggling out of his grasp, '*à bientôt.*'

He waved back, watching her as she vanished through customs and beyond. She did not look back.

When it came to the time for his own flight, he went to the desk with his ticket and the luggage, one suitcase of which was Caroline's. He had hardly anything much himself. The girl took his ticket and his passport, glanced at the documents, then at him.

'Excuse me a minute,' she said, and went away past the rows of computers to a red wall telephone. Parry watched her, wondering what she was doing and why there were complications.

From behind, a hand on his shoulder. A male voice: 'Monsieur de Fonville?'

Parry swung round. He said in English, 'My name is Parry. Edward Parry. Edward St John Parry.'

The man, an official in a cheap blue suit, a swarthy fellow with a shadow already appearing on his chin, said, 'I'm afraid I must ask you to come with me. Your ticket is in the name of de Fonville. Monsieur de Fonville died of a gunshot wound in hospital yesterday.'

'What?'

'An incident at the *Feria*. He was stopped by a policeman and he ran.'

'So he got shot?'

'It is quite normal. Monsieur de Fonville was already known to the police.'

'If he was known, then why do you want me?'

'Because your ticket is in his name.'

'But that doesn't mean a thing, you know perfectly well . . .'

'If you will come this way, sir.'

The room was painted white. A window with bars on it looked out to the airport car park. Parry's luggage, most of it belonging to Caroline, was laid out on a long table.

'If you will give us the keys, we can open your luggage.'

'Why don't you just shoot the locks off,' said Parry. 'In any case, this is not mine, it belongs to Miss de Belleroche.'

'Miss de Belleroche is also wanted by the police. Illegal trade in ancient artefacts.'

'Oh, don't be silly,' Parry blustered. The stupid bitch, the stupid beautiful bitch.

'The key, Monsieur, if you please.'

The case contained some clothes of Caroline's – some of which Parry recognized – and, wrapped in layers of silk at the bottom – the little bronze of Mars that Caroline had said came from Arles.

'This is yours?' The man held up the statue.

'No. I've never seen it in my life. I told you, this is not my suitcase. It belongs to Miss de Belleroche. I was taking it for her. She had too many things with her, she was overweight.'

'I see.' The official bent over and examined the label on the suitcase. On it was written 'Edward Parry'. He pulled the card out and put it carefully on the table. Underneath, another card said 'Caroline de Belleroche'.

'Very well, Monsieur, but I think you have been duped. You say she has gone, Mademoiselle de Belleroche?'

'She went ahead of me,' said Parry. 'She said there was some confusion about the tickets.'

'I see.'

'Can I go now, please?'

'I must ask you not to leave the country at present. I will need an address and a telephone number for you. You must report each day to the nearest police station.'

'But this is ridiculous! I haven't done anything.'

'I am afraid you must do as I ask, Monsieur, until this matter is cleared up.'

'Who gave you my description, may I ask?'

'I am not at liberty to tell you that, Monsieur.'

He had been drinking all night, apart from a short period when he slept in a coma of alcohol. When he woke he knew at once that he must go to the Pont du Gard. It was as if someone had said it to him, so clearly did he know that that was what he must do.

Outside the house, he glanced up into the fresh, early-morning blue. He could not see them but he knew they were there. Watching. Waiting. The day smelt of dew and the memory of warm stone; the first layer of heat lay on his skin like silk.

When he emerged at the top, Parry's suit was stained and torn. He straightened up and gazed at the view the Romans had known: the river snaking away into the distance in loops of silver. The sun was much hotter now and he was assailed by the glare, the sense of height, the unlimited sky arching away into infinity over his head; the sound of cicadas, like a distant drum roll, faint but definite.

Beneath him, as he leaned out from his limestone platform, the cruel grey rock and the scrub of the garrigues.

Once the water had flowed here but now it flowed no more. The goddess of the spring had vanished back under the hill with all her mysteries.

Parry stepped out into the light.

When he awoke, Victoria was there, holding his hand. He looked at her.

'What are you doing here?' he asked. He wanted to say, 'Am I dead?' but he supposed, given the nature of his surroundings – a hospital room somewhere – that he couldn't be, unless hell was, as he had sometimes suspected it might be, simply a dreary continuation of everyday life. But this couldn't be hell because Tor was in it. And Tor was a good person. Much too good for him.

'I'm sorry,' he said weakly. To his horror a tear ran out of the corner of his eye. 'I wanted to die,' he added. 'I thought I had.'

Victoria looked at him. 'You fell,' she said. 'You jumped off the wrong part into the scrub. A tourist found you later. A young German boy. He raised the alarm. Now you're in Nîmes,' she said, seeing that he wanted to ask but did not know how to.

'I must have lost my mind,' he said. 'Everything just seemed to . . . I don't . . .'

'Not now,' she silenced him by touching his cheek. 'Later. We've got time for all that later. Now I just want you to rest and get well. Then I'm going to take you home.'

'How are the children?'

'They're waiting for you,' she replied. 'We're all waiting for you.'